# Hunted

## The Hunter's Oath: Book One
## Nicole B. Fletes

Edited by AK Reads & Edits and Scott Editorial

ISBN 979-8-9940081-0-2 (Paperback)

ISBN 979-8-9940081-1-9 (Hardcover)

ISBN  979-8-9940081-2-6 (EPUB)

# Contents

# Prologue

*It took some time to comprehend and accept what I am now—what I was turned into. Every time I close my eyes I'm brought back to the before, when the sun warmed my skin, back when I was normal—human and to the monster who took it all away...*

"YOU CALLED FOR ME, Mr. Leon?" I ask, pen and notebook in hand, just in case I need to jot down notes, eager to please.

He looks up from the documents splayed across his desk and smiles. "Yes, Sarah. Please have a seat."

Caesar Leon appears ageless but if I had to guess, I would say mid-to-late thirties, give or take a decade. His facial features are all sharp and angular, almost like a statue, accentuated perfectly by his milky-white skin with a light dusting of gray throughout his dark hair.

I take a seat in one of the leather chairs across from his large, L-shaped desk, as instructed.

We sit, staring at one another in awkward silence for a moment, or maybe it's just awkward for me. The air is thick and tense, which is perplexing.

He leans forward, hands steepled together, resting both pointer fingers on his lips.

I have a feeling he is deciding something in this moment, but I have no idea what it would be.

*Is he about to fire me? News flash, buddy. I'm an excellent worker, organized, great social skills. Plus, I love taking notes.*

He seems to come to a decision, because he stands, fastening the button on his fancy tailored suit.

I quickly stand, mirroring his stance.

"Are you happy here? Do you like being at the penthouse?" he asks, walking around and eliminating the barrier his desk created between us.

I'm taken aback by the questions. I'll admit, it took some getting used to working from his penthouse instead of Leon Towers. I was told I had no choice if I wanted the position as his personal assistant.

"Yes," I tell him truthfully. "I'm very grateful you gave me this opportunity, Mr. Leon."

"Would you be willing to undergo a promotion of sorts?"

"Umm, sure," I say, not really knowing exactly what I'm agreeing to.

This conversation is starting to get a little weird, but I guess he has always been a little off. I'm not sure what it is about him that seems so... old. Like he has seen and lived lifetimes, and is constantly trying to decide how to use all his infinite knowledge.

At the moment, however, he studies me like he wants to devour me. As if I'm prey and he an apex predator. I want to bolt for the door, but the scrutiny in his eyes has my feet glued to the floor.

He smiles, showing all of his perfect teeth. "Excellent, and how do you feel about me? I hope I've become someone you admire."

"You're a great boss," I reply slowly. What is he getting at precisely? The energy he is emanating is making me uncomfortable, to say the least.

He's never spoken to me like this. I don't like it. My mind tries to conjure up those three self-defense classes I'd taken a year ago.

He takes the two steps needed to close the distance between us, although he stops just short of actually touching me. I want to take a step back, but I still feel frozen in place.

Talk about invading personal space.

He hums. "It helps when the person is keen on their creator in a non-platonic way. The higher the chance of mating."

*Mating? What the hell? What in the world is he talking about?* I swallow hard saying. "I just watched a company training video on sexual harassment. You are displaying what is called a quid pro quo. The offer of promotion or advancement in exchange for se-sexual favors," I stutter out, trying and failing to keep my heart from beating out of my chest. My tone is laced with a warning, even as my lips give an involuntary tremble. I splay my hands out in front of me to stop him from getting any closer.

My eyes dart around the room, searching for... what? A weapon maybe. Something I can use against him if he tries anything. The only things on his desk are papers and a computer.

Mr. Leon laughs before I can find anything of use. He leans in as he brushes one side of my hair off my shoulder. I can feel his cold breath on my neck. It smells of copper and salt.

"I think you will make an excellent addition to my team, my future queen," he whispers before striking, sinking his teeth into my flesh.

I cry out. The pain is barely noticeable over the fear his actions instill in me.

It's an odd sensation. Whatever it is that he is doing to me, it isn't terrible, but it is paralyzing.

My breathing grows rapid as my eyes sting with tears.

He makes a sort of hungry moan. The sucking noises and the pulling of my skin between his teeth kickstarts something inside me. Bile rises in my throat at the sounds coming from him.

My brain finally gives power back to my arms and legs as I struggle against him, pushing against his chest as I try to get away.

He pulls away the second I start to fight, grabbing a white cloth handkerchief from his breast pocket and wiping the blood dripping from his mouth. It's then that I see... fangs? *That can't be right.*

"Forgive me, you tasted so good, I got a little carried away," he tells me.

I can see his fangs clearly now when he speaks. A panicked scream tears from me as I run for the door in terror. Just as I reach the door handle, I feel him touch my shoulders.

"Shh, darling Sarah," he coos, as if trying to comfort a crying baby. "It will be okay. I'll take care of you. This next part will be uncomfortable, but I will make it quick. I promise."

He grabs my head between his hands and twists...

# Chapter 1
# Sarah

I CHECK MY PHONE for what seems like the umpteenth time in the last thirty minutes. Where is he?

Adam, my best friend/roommate/blood bag dealer, is late. Although this isn't an unusual occurrence, he usually texts me if he won't be home on time.

Now that I know there are supernatural monsters that go bump in the night, I've become a bit of a worrywart that my friend might run into one of these monsters... other than me, of course.

It's been two years since my boss killed me and turned me into a vampire. I try not to think about the two and a half weeks I spent with the coven and how I escaped.

Adam Patel and I met in college. We didn't move in together until after I had already become a vampire, but we had always kept in touch. He was my safe haven the weeks after I escaped. Fast forward five years since college, and he is now a surgical resident at Mary Birkin's Hospital, and I couldn't be more proud of him.

Adam rushes into the apartment, holding an insulated lunch bag I know contains my blood rations for the week. I can get away with only drinking one bag every few days as long as I don't get hurt or exhaust myself, then I would need to replenish sooner.

He's wearing his usual teal scrubs and sneakers. Adam is a total fashion mogul, but he's always at work, so more often than not, he's sporting teal scrubs. But because Adam is Adam, he has a fashionable scarf wrapped around his neck to spruce up the scrubs a bit.

He takes his shoes off by the door. "Sorry, I'm late. I got to scrub in on a donor transplant. It went longer than expected," Adam says, handing the bag over to me.

1

"And then my phone died. Let me go put this thing on the charger. My parents are scheduled to call bright and early tomorrow morning. You know how Indian mothers are if you miss their phone calls."

"I know how *your* Indian mother is," I correct.

"Exactly, persistent and intrusive," he says from the kitchen island where he plugs in his phone.

"How was the surgery?" I ask as I stab one of the four blood bags with a metal reusable straw.

"Successful," he says, coming over to the couch and slumping down on it. "It was a teenage girl. She was diagnosed with pulmonary fibrosis, but she got new lungs just in time."

I smile. "That's amazing. I'm glad she is going to be okay."

When Adam talks about his job, his whole face lights up like the Fourth of July if the surgery is successful. I know how much helping people means to him.

I drink the blood bag down quickly. I used to be skittish about drinking in front of Adam. I didn't want to gross him out, but as time went by, we both got used to my new normal.

Adam took the news surprisingly well when I first told him what I've become. He was less grossed out about me drinking blood than I was. When I was human, blood used to make me queasy.

I sometimes feel horrible allowing my best friend to steal blood bags from hospitals. I wish I could just drink animal blood like they do in all the books and TV shows, but I live in San Francisco. It's not like I can meander to my backyard and pick up a mountain lion to eat. Well, I guess, technically, I could, but that would be gross. Also, I'm not sure if vampires can actually live off animal blood. That could just be wishful thinking and stellar creative writing on the entertainment industry's part.

Still, I know what Adam risks by doing this. He only does it if I am unable to do it myself. Usually, I will pose as a hospital worker and steal two or three bags using my Jedi mind trick. That's what I call whatever it is that allows me to mesmerize people and get them to do whatever I tell them to.

This past week, I got stuck doing research for the next book I'm writing as a newly published author. My agent has been hassling me for a rough draft.

Still, it's no excuse not to get what I need to survive on my own. This has to be the last time Adam does it for me. No exceptions.

"Stop that," Adam says, looking at me sternly.

"Stop what?"

"I'm assuming you are thinking of all the reasons why you shouldn't be letting me risk my career to steal blood bags for you, right?"

"Umm, no."

*How does he do that?*

"Stop reading my mind," I say when he gives me an arch of his brow. "I'm the supernatural one, remember?"

"You are a person just like anyone else, and I took a vow to try to save people who need saving. I can't just watch you starve. You need blood to live, so I'm getting you blood to live."

"I thought you vowed to do no harm," I say.

He shrugs. "Same thing."

I finish the bag, slurping up the last bit of blood. "Well, thank you."

He salutes me, and then sighs, getting up from the couch and arching his back, like a stretching cat.

"I'm off to bed for eight hours of uninterrupted sleep," he says, making his way to the bedroom. "Please only wake me if you are dying, and since you are technically already dead, you should have no reason to wake me."

I snort out a laugh. "Got it. Wake you up in an hour to go over my latest Chewbacca and Rebel leader, Vice Admiral Holdo, fanfic."

"First of all, I am not feeling that ship, so that's a no," he says in a decisive tone.

Adam and I really got into Star Wars when I first came to him as a newly turned vampire. It was something we watched together to help keep me grounded during the daylight hours when I could no longer go outside. That was one of the hardest transitions for me. One of the things I mourn the most is the feel of the sun's rays on my face.

"Secondly," he continues, not privy to my internal thoughts. "If you wake me up for that, the next time I have to steal blood bags for you, I will lace them with LSD."

"I doubt LSD would even work on vampires."

"If you wake me up, you'll soon find out," Adam states as he blows me a quick kiss and then shuts his bedroom door behind him.

"You wouldn't even know where to get LSD," I call out to his already closed door.

I refrigerate the remaining three blood bags, then go to my room to swap my Charmander PJ bottoms for some pink and blue yoga pants and a matching pink V-neck shirt, and head out the door.

The sun set maybe an hour ago. Usually, at this point, I would either head off to Golden Gate Park and find one of the gardens to walk around in, or go to May's Diner to work on my novel.

But tonight, I've decided to clear my head on top of one of my favorite building rooftops in the Sunset District.

I reach the building in five minutes and use my speed and velocity to scale up the apartment's brick wall like a cross between the Flash and Spider-Man.

I love this rooftop. I assume one of the tenants here is a gardener. It's filled with a cornucopia of flowers. I've been looking for the names of the flowers with the help of Google: hibiscus, lemon verbena, marigold, cosmos and floss flower. They are protected by a homemade garden fence, but it's always extremely windy up here, so the smell is everywhere. It's like a floral funhouse. If I close my eyes, I can almost pretend I'm outside in a beautiful garden during the day.

I'm just taking a seat next to the lemon verbena when I hear something. I silently get up to perch over the edge.

There's a group of four vampires in the darkened alley below. I can see their fangs out, ready to feed.

For a split terrifying second, I'm scared they are here for me. *Has Mr. Leon finally found me?*

I get my answer when I hear them arguing about something unrelated to me.

"The first human we lure here is mine," says a woman with bright pink hair. "I'm tired of waiting for you three Neanderthals to have your fill before I can eat."

"Not a chance. I'm starving," hisses an older fella, licking one of his fangs in preparation.

I'm mentally preparing myself to save whatever poor, innocent person they are going to Jedi mind trick into the alley. I've only done this a few other times before.

The first time I saved a girl from being fed on by two vampires was the first time I realized how much stronger and faster I am than them, and every vampire I've come across since. It was also the first time I realized that we can't be killed by just simply ripping out the heart. No, it needs to be impaled by wood or be burned by fire.

I watch and wait for my moment to intercede.

As it turns out, I will not need to play superhero tonight. Not two minutes later, I hear a totally different and way more terrifying group—the vampire hunters.

# Chapter 2
# Sarah

I'VE MANAGED TO AVOID all contact with hunters since becoming a vampire. I can usually hear them before they hear me and see them before they see me. Tonight is no different. I do hear them first, but I don't run away like I usually do.

I know that I should bolt. Staying to watch vampire hunters do their thing, when I am in fact a vampire, would not be my smartest move. But another thought crosses my mind—my book. Desperate times call for desperate measures.

I'm currently working on book two of a sci-fi trilogy series about a made-up planet called Oricon.

The second book follows my main character, Cassie, a human, as she tries to dodge being hunted by the aliens, or Oriconans, amongst other plot angles I have yet to fully outline.

Which brings me back to my desperation.

I hope that by watching the vampire hunters in action, I can gain some inspiration for the hunting scenes in my book. What they wear, how they work as a team, things like that. Because at the moment, I've hit a slight writer's block.

I know I'm being a little risky, but to be honest, I feel pretty invincible. I suspect since I'm stronger and faster than most vampires that the same can be said about vampire hunters, right?

I sneak halfway down the building, posting on someone's fire escape to get a better view. The streetlights don't reach where all the action is about to take place, but it doesn't matter much because, lucky for me, vampires have excellent night vision.

I can't help but wonder why the vampires haven't heard the hunters yet. They've managed to creep up on the vampires so easily. Although their footsteps are as light as feathers, I can still hear them. One hunter does a little hand signal, motioning for two of them to go around, I'm assuming to ambush the vampires from both ends of the alley.

Three seconds later, one of the vampires shushes the others, and all four become alert at once. They finally hear the footsteps, but by then it's too late.

The hunters are on them so quickly. There are six hunters in total. I watch as they descend on the vampires. Their fighting skills have no parallel. It's almost like watching a dance. The way they move in sync with each other. They are all carrying various types of wooden weapons like stakes, daggers, and knives. One of them carries a crossbow, which at the moment is strapped across his back. Another has a bow and a quiver of arrows.

Each hunter is using their weapon of choice like it's an extension of their hand. It looks as though the hunters have been training with them their whole lives, which I assume is exactly the case.

The bow and arrow hunter is locked and loaded in less than a second. He aims and strikes the first vampire right through his back. The vampire falls dead before even fully turning around to face his killer. The hunter loads and shoots another arrow, but misses. The remaining three vampires are ready now.

The same hunter shouts, "Blue stance!"

The whole team splits into pairs.

As the shorter of the girls runs to be by his side, the vampire closest to her charges, pushing her against a dumpster. I watch as the male hunter sneers and maneuvers around the vampire, holding him in place while the girl quickly stands and runs to stab the vampire in the heart with a wooden stake.

The second pair, which has the only other female hunter, runs toward another vampire. The girl jumps and twists her legs around the vampire's head in a Black Widow-style move. Using her momentum, she throws the vampire at the male hunter she is paired with. He stabs the vampire in the heart with his dagger. I don't catch the last pair with the two males. By the time I look, the last vampire is already dead.

All four vampires are defeated within a minute. I'm stunned motionless.

*Wow.* I was not expecting that. Maybe staying to watch wasn't such a good idea after all. They are killing machines.

"Are you hurt?" I hear the man with the bow and arrow ask his partner.

The woman shakes her head. "I'm fine, Liam. I just scraped my arm against that metal sticking out of the dumpster. It's nothing."

Liam, who looks to be the oldest and the leader, gives the impression that he wants to reach out and touch her but holds back. He gives off a Clark Kent vibe, but in all black fighting leathers.

Leave it to a big city like San Francisco to be able to walk around looking like someone who walked out of a fantasy movie and no one takes notice.

They start working on gathering the vampire bodies, dragging and throwing them on top of one another. Liam lights a match and throws it at the heap.

The vampire corpses immediately go up in flames and burn for a moment before all turning to ash. Not even the smell of burning flesh lingers.

It's crazy how a vampire can just cease to exist, body and all, with just a little bit of fire. This is why I'm thankful for Adam's and my electric burner stove. Knowing me, I would be the vampire that died from accidentally setting myself on fire while cooking with gas burners.

"Kael, man, why didn't you let me have the redhead bloodsucker? You know I'm trying to bring up my nightly average," says the big, pale, brawny one with the crossbow. I notice he has a tattoo of a snake going up his left arm, and a full sleeve of tattoos on the other.

Kael shakes his head disapprovingly, and then suddenly stops.

"Do you guys feel that?" he asks.

They all instantly go on alert, looking around, each arming themselves with another weapon. Liam arms his bow with another arrow.

*Damn it.* I need to leave. I creep further into the shadows of the fire escape. This was definitely a bad idea... the worst.

"What is that?" asks the pixie-haired one who got hurt. "Feels like another vampire, but doesn't at the same time."

"It has to be another vampire, but I sense the weirdness, too," Liam says, looking around.

I don't move. I don't even breathe, not that I need to anyway. More habit than anything.

Kael, whom I can't stop looking at because he is, without a doubt, the most gorgeous guy I have ever set eyes on, starts eyeing his surroundings, too. Suddenly, he looks straight up at me.

Although I've hidden myself on the only fire escape that has a broken light connected to it, I can tell I've been spotted. Our eyes stay locked on one another for the briefest of moments before he narrows them, hatred blazing inside.

Time to run. I turn and quickly propel myself up the building to the rooftop. I don't know how, but when I look back four of the six hunters are scaling up the building as well.

Once I'm at the top I take off at a run, jumping from one rooftop to another. Somehow, the other two hunters figured out my next move because they are just making it up the second rooftop as I get to the end of it, cutting me off.

"Not good," I mutter under my breath, panic really starting to set in. *What have I gotten myself into?*

I see the big, brawny one lift his crossbow as he aims and shoots a wooden stake right at my heart. I step to the side and catch it with my hand at the last second, snapping it in half and flinging the broken halves to the ground.

"How the hell did she do that?" the brawny one yells, as he takes off barreling toward me.

*Think, Sarah, think.* How to get out of this mess?

I realize that I'm not far from May's Diner, so I burst into a run and jump off the side of the building adjacent to where the two hunters in front were. I turn at the last second to see the other four hunters who were behind me join the party.

"Damn, she's fast," one of the men says as they run to also jump off the building.

I know they will cease chasing me as soon as I am in view of humans. I run as fast as I can to the end of the alley and back on the main street.

Thankfully, there are people walking around, so as soon as I am back on the crowded street, I drop to a more human-like run. I chance a look behind me. They are still following, but they, too, have dropped their inhuman speed to a more natural one.

I don't stop running until I make it to May's Diner and hurry in. It's not too busy tonight, just an elderly couple and what looks to be their adult son sitting at a booth, and two gentlemen in their thirties at the bar. I walk to the far end of the bar to my usual spot and take a seat, placing my hands flat on the bar table to keep them from shaking. I let out a breath, again, more out of habit than necessity.

*Damn, that was a close one.* I don't know what I was thinking, staying behind to do research for my book by observing vampire hunters. Lesson learned. They are more dangerous than I gave them credit for.

Just then, my senses rise up as someone sits right next to me. The air suddenly too thick to breathe as I slowly turn to see who it is.

Sure enough, it's one of the hunters. Kael.

# Chapter 3
# Sarah

I SCAN THE DINER and see that the two girl hunters have also come in and have taken the table closest to the door, which leaves the brawny one, the leader, and the other slightly leaner man outside.

"You guys don't give up, do you?" I ask casually as I reach for a plastic menu. I take a quick glance at him and am once again taken aback by how gorgeous this guy is.

He's even better looking up close with his cinnamon-brown hair, warm beige skin, and vibrant green eyes. His black shirt fits snug on him, especially on his biceps. They look like they want to Hulk out of their sleeves. The tight leather vest on top only adds to his hot-guy-hunter vibe that has me squirming uncomfortably in my seat.

*Tame it down*, I tell myself. *Stop lusting after your wannabe killer.* It's been so long since I've lusted after anyone; the effect he's having just by being near me is a little unsettling. Since becoming a vampire, I've steered clear of all relationships save for Adam, and perhaps, the Mays.

"No," he says, answering my question just as casually. "So you can either come out now, or we'll wait you out."

This guy smells nice, too, which is crazy since he was just fighting and sweating. But he smells of cedar. I'm going to assume that's from the various wooden weapons he keeps hidden on him.

Do I try and pretend I'm not a vampire? Maybe I can pretend to magically be a super speedster. I internally shake my head at the thought.

*Of course, he knows I'm a vampire. He's a vampire hunter, and this isn't a DC comic book.* I've become quite the nerd these past few years, and it really shows.

"Hmm, if I walk out with you now, will you let me go for being such a cooperative vampire?" I ask, already knowing the answer.

"Why don't you walk out with me and find out."

I pretend to think about it for a moment before shaking my head. "Nah, I think I'll wait." I look at him and furrow my brow in confusion. "Are you not the least bit concerned that non-magical people might find you alarming walking around with all those wooden stakes and daggers strapped to you?" I gesture to his shoulder and waist holsters full of weapons, hoping to distract him enough so that he forgets he wants to kill me.

"They're charmed," he says.

"But I can see them," I point out.

He rolls his eyes. "Yes, but you are aware of what I am when you look at me. Human minds are more susceptible to seeing what is within the scope of their reality. You're a vampire, so obviously your reality mirrors mine, for the most part. So, you see the truth."

"Interesting," I say, truly fascinated by this fact.

Just then, an older, slightly heavyset Black lady with dark hair that has streaks of gray in it walks up to us from behind the counter. She gives me a warm smile, which I return easily.

"Sarah, honey, so glad to see you. I think this is the first time I've seen you without either Adam or your laptop with you. Where is Dr. Adam?" the lady asks as she sets down a glass of water next to me.

I try not to flinch at knowing the hunter now knows my name. "He's back at our apartment sleeping off an eighteen-hour shift from the hospital," I say, taking a sip.

I don't want to give too much information about Adam away. Not that I think the vampire hunter, Kael, would do anything to him. He's human, after all. It's me that I should be worried about.

"How's that second book coming, and who is this handsome fella with you?" she asks, turning to give Kael a welcoming smile.

"It's coming along slowly, Mrs. May, but I'm trying to get it going. That's what this gentleman is here for," I say as I turn to Kael. "He's helping me with some of the authenticity of the hunting scenes. He's somewhat of an expert in the field." Not totally a lie.

"Is that so?" Mrs. May says, looking at Kael with interest.

"Yes, ma'am," Kael says politely, but doesn't elaborate any further.

"Mrs. May and her husband own this diner," I tell Kael, making sure he realizes she is human. Not that he wouldn't already know. Do they have an extra hidden ability to tell them when they are looking at a vampire versus a human? I'm sure they would have to in their line of work.

"They have the best New Orleans soul food you will ever taste," I continue. "Anything you order from the menu will be the best you have ever eaten. Trust me."

"Now, Ms. Sarah here is being too polite, but she sure does love our food. She comes at least four times a week. What would you like George to whip up for you?" she asks me before turning back to Kael. "George is my husband and one of the cooks here while I handle the customers."

"They are the dream team," I say proudly. I glance down at the menu, already knowing what I will see. I know the menu by heart. "I will take my usual burger and fries."

Mrs. May writes down my order on her pad and turns to Kael. "And for you, honey?"

"I'm not eating," Kael answers.

"Oh, but you must," I say insistently. "Try their crawfish étouffée. It is to die for. Unless you don't eat meat or seafood, then get their veggie wrap or their vegan veggie burger. You'll love either one."

Kael looks at me quizzically and then at Mrs. May. "I'll have the veggie wrap, ma'am, thank you."

"And your drink?" she asks, writing his order down.

He looks over at my water, which she already knew to bring since water is the only beverage I order here.

"I'll just take a water."

Mrs. May smiles. "Coming right up."

Neither one of us says anything until after she sets down his water and walks away. Kael turns to look at me.

"What was that?" he asks in confusion.

"What was what?"

"You seem to have a relationship with this human. How is that possible? What did you mean about your roommate working at a hospital? Is he also a vampire?"

"First of all, her name is Mrs. May. She and her husband, Mr. George, are from New Orleans and the two sweetest people you will ever meet, and I am proud to call them my friends. It is practically impossible not to have a relationship with them."

I take a sip of water to calm my nerves before continuing. "To answer your second question, no, Adam is not a vampire. Could you imagine a vampire working at a hospital? Now that would be impossible. Well, except for Carlisle Cullen; he's vampire goals. I strive to be him one day."

He gives me another quizzical look.

"Carlisle Cullen from *Twilight*," I elaborate. Does he seriously not know who I'm talking about?

"I don't know what that means," he says firmly.

"It's a book turned movie about vampires. I'm a bit of a movie buff. Especially movies about vampires," I tease, trying to cut the tension with humor—a coping mechanism of mine. Though it only seems to confuse Kael.

He stares at me intensely, changing the subject by asking, "Why do you feel different, and act differently? What are you exactly?" He never takes his eyes off me.

*Holy guacamole.* His penetrating eye contact does unspeakable things to my body. Is this why they sent him in here to talk to me? Are they hoping that with one look at him, I'll swoon and tell him *cuff me, I surrender*?

His hair has that messy I-just-got-out-of-bed vibe, and yet, it looks unintentionally perfect. I want to run my hands through his hair, drag his face to mine.

I shake my head as if to clear it. *Get it together, Sarah. He's a vampire hunter. He is literally here to kill you.*

"Honestly, I'm just a vampire," I say in a soft tone so that no one overhears me. "And I don't really know what you mean by me feeling different since you have never touched me."

His eyes narrow a bit, and I definitely don't miss the quick scan of my body.

Something inside me stirs. It's a weird sensation. It feels a bit more intense than just physical attraction, but that could be just because I haven't felt anything physical, or otherwise, since becoming a vampire. Maybe this is how it feels to become... sexually charged as a vampire. All my other senses are heightened, why not this?

"That's not what I meant," he says somewhat hoarsely.

"Too bad," I say in a low whisper. But of course, he must have super hearing because he gives me a quick arch of his brow.

My cheeks heat, which has Kael frowning in confusion. I know I'm blushing, which, by the way, totally sucks. What kind of vampire blushes? I've never heard of such an absurd thing in my life, but here I am, cheeks warm and rosy.

To be honest, it's nice being able to have a good cry every now and then, makes me feel more human. The downside is that I apparently show visible signs that I'm getting all hot and bothered by the sexy vampire hunter sitting next to me.

It took months to figure out that my body pretty much functions the same as it did when I was human, except I need blood rather than food. Internally, the only thing that changed was my heart, which beats differently—slower since I first woke up from Mr. Leon killing me. Basically, it keeps the blood pumping but that's it. I don't even need to breathe if I don't want to. I do because it makes me feel normal.

I wish there were a way to learn more about it. Is there something about the heart that is now magical? Is that why a wooden stake to the heart is the only thing that can kill a vampire? Well, that and fire, but I guess fire would destroy everything including the heart.

Just as I'm about to die of embarrassment, Mrs. May comes back holding both plates. She sets them down in front of us, smiles and then walks to greet a young couple who just sat down at a booth.

Tucking a loose strand of hair behind my ear, I turn toward the food, glad for the distraction. I rub my hands together and grab my burger, taking a big bite. I look over, and Kael is still staring at me.

"Want a bite?" I ask, gesturing to my burger, my mouth still filled with food. *Why is he staring at me so hard?*

"No," he says. "Thank you," he adds as an afterthought.

Kael's ear starts talking, or more specifically, someone from an earpiece in his ear starts talking.

"You're not supposed to be getting to know her," says a male voice. It sounds like the one they call Liam.

Kael turns his head to look out the glass windows.

He's not the only one with super hearing, and I'm sure my vampire ears trump his, so I can make out what's being said pretty easily.

"I'm interrogating her."

"It looks like you're having dinner with her."

I turn and look toward the guys outside and give a big wave.

Surprisingly, Kael grabs my hand and forces it down.

Chills run through me at the mere touch of his hand on mine. He lets it go instantly, like he is just as surprised he did that as I am.

"Tell them you got the veggie wrap," I say teasingly.

I can see that Kael is trying to bite back his smile. I turn to look out the window again at the confused guys outside and notice the two girls in the booth are glaring at me. I turn in my seat so I'm no longer facing them.

"Listen, you don't need to talk to her anymore. We can surround the place and wait for her to leave and kill her then."

Kael flinches a little as he looks at me.

I give him big eyes, letting him know that I heard.

"Fine," is all he tells Liam before tapping his earpiece, making the others go silent. He pulls out some money to pay for the veggie wrap that went untouched.

I look down at my food as he gets up.

"Can I ask you a question before you go?" I ask softly.

He stops but doesn't respond.

In the corner of my eye, I can see the two girls exit the diner. I take his pause as a sign to proceed. "You guys don't kill vampires in front of humans, right?"

He looks at me questioningly. "Not if we can help it."

"Do you ever hurt humans who get in your way?"

"Never," he says, sounding almost offended. "That's not what we are about."

I nod. "Okay," I say and smile up at him. "It was nice meeting you, Kael."

He narrows his eyes at me. "How do you know my name?"

"I'm a special vampire," I say in a whisper. "With only one touch of your hand, I can know every thought you have ever had."

He gapes at me, his eyes widening in disbelief.

I can't help the laugh that escapes me. "I'm kidding," I say in between giggles. "I heard someone call your name back in the alley."

He nods, his eyes softening and mouth twitching at the corners like he wants to laugh too, but restrains himself.

He doesn't move for a moment, and I think he's about to sit back down, but then after another second he turns and walks out of the diner.

*Okay, Sarah. Time to get out of this mess.* I grab my phone and call Adam.

"Hello," he says groggily.

A pang of guilt fills my stomach... I know he is still sleeping.

"I'm so sorry to wake you, but remember when you said I'm allowed to disturb you if I'm dying?"

"Yeaahh." He sounds more awake now.

"Well, I'm in a bit of a pickle and can really use your help," I say, and quickly tell him about tonight, ending with the fact that they have six vampire hunters outside the diner waiting for me to leave so they can kill me.

Adam is awake and sounding panicked. "I'm on my way. I'll text you when I pull up."

"Thank you," I say apologetically. "I'm so sorry you have to do this. I promise to make it up to you."

"Don't worry about it. I'm not about to let my bestie be bested by some bullies."

Try saying that five times fast.

17

"I'm sure I could have taken down at least one of them before they finished me off," I say, knowing for sure I would not have wanted to hurt Kael, although I don't know why. It's the eyes, I think. Or the hair.

*Geez, what is wrong with me tonight?* It's like I've never seen a handsome, soldier-like man who oozes sex appeal before.

"I have no doubt about it," Adam says, taking me out of my reverie.

While waiting, I finish my burger and ask for a to-go box for the veggie wrap. No way I'm going to let that go to waste.

Adam pulls up twenty minutes later. He's looking around frantically as he enters the diner. He gives me a kiss on the cheek before searching the room once more.

"Did you see them outside?" I ask, realizing as I'm looking out that they have all disappeared, or so they want me to believe.

"Hard to tell," Adam says. "There is a young couple that seems to be in some sort of lovers' quarrel just under the streetlight. I guess they can be hunters, but they seem too much in their own personal problems to be paying much attention to what's going on around them. Are Mrs. May and Mr. George here?"

"Yes, I think they are both in the back," I say, taking a look around the diner now. I only see the other waitress in the front taking customer orders. "Let's go say a quick bye."

As we walk to the kitchen area, I can hear Mrs. May fussing over Mr. George.

"Stop being stubborn. Walter can handle the grill. You need to go home and lie down," Mrs. May says sternly.

"I know he can, but we still have two more hours until both our shifts are up. I can power through," Mr. George says just as sternly.

"Knock, knock," Adam says before actually knocking on the wall. "Mr. George, I hope I'm not hearing what I think I'm hearing? I thought I prescribed you light work for the next two weeks. You don't want to put too much strain on that recovering heart of yours."

Mr. George suffered a heart attack six months ago and had to have open heart surgery. Although he has been discharged from the hospital, Adam has been keeping up with his checkups.

They both turn and smile at us.

"You hear that?" Mrs. May says, nodding her head. "If Dr. Adam says to go home, then you have to go home."

"Vivian, I'm fine," George says tenderly, "but if it makes you feel better, I'll call it quits for tonight and head on upstairs and rest."

Vivian is Mrs. May's first name. I'm not sure why Adam and I have always called her by her last name and Mr. George by his first.

"Dr. Adam, Ms. Sarah, y'all come visit us soon, you hear?" he says sweetly.

"We sure will," I say, going over to him and giving him a quick hug. "We are taking off for tonight. We just wanted to say bye." I walk over and give Mrs. May a hug. Adam follows suit.

After we say our goodbyes, Adam and I head back to the front. It's perfect timing. The young couple that is at the booth in the corner is just getting up to leave as well. The four of us walk out of the diner together.

The universe loves me because the couple is parked right next to where Adam is, so we all start walking down the street together. The couple is too deep into their own conversation to really notice us though, so we try as best as we can to stay near them, without making it obvious, as we head to Adam's car.

"I got you a veggie wrap," I tell Adam as I lift up the to-go box to show him, trying to keep a light conversation.

"Yum," is all he says back distractedly, still looking around.

Once we are safely in the car and are pulling away, Adam finally releases a breath.

"Do you think they will follow us?" he asks, panic still etched in his voice.

"I'm not sure," I say truthfully, keeping my hands in my lap to keep from shaking. That was a close one. "Maybe we should park in the parking garage of the apartment complex beside ours, and sneak to our building, just to be on the safe side," I suggest.

He nods as he pulls onto the highway.

I take one last look around and I see them. They are all at the corner, hidden in the shadow of the streetlight.

Five angry faces are looking straight at me alongside one slightly bemused one.

19

# Chapter 4
# Kael

MY ALARM GOES OFF at noon, but I'm already awake so I silence it quickly and sit up. My mind is racing going over everything that occurred in the diner.

*What happened last night?* I don't know what came over me. Sitting, having "dinner" with a fucking vampire. It was unacceptable, but she was just so... different. Not like any vampire I've ever come across before. And beautiful. Her honey-colored skin and long, silky raven hair, and the cute little way she would tuck strands of it behind her ears every so often.

*Stop.* I can't think about her that way. I need a shower... a cold one. I grab my bag of toiletries and a towel and then head to the communal showers.

Most of the time, living at the Hunter's Academy is great. The kitchen is always stocked with food. Retired hunters prepare meals and snacks throughout the day for everyone. There is a state-of-the-art, twenty-four-hour gym that I spend a lot of my free time in. Plus living here is free. I get to spend my paychecks on my wants rather than needs.

The restroom and shower situation, however, are the fucking worst. I hate not having a personal bathroom. Thankfully, there are a set of bathrooms down every hall, and since each hall only contains two squads, I only share with eleven other people and not the entirety of the Academy.

I'm on Liam's squad. Who is, by far, the best squad leader at the Academy. Liam is smart, patient, and an amazing tactician.

I wonder if there is any way to avoid him today. I know he saw the relief on my face when Sarah got away. A shiver runs down my spine, and I mentally berate myself for it.

*Don't think about her name. Don't think about her at all. She is a vampire, not a person. If you ever come across her again, you will stab a wooden dagger through that fantastic chest of hers right to her heart.*

I repeat the mantra several more times while walking down the hall to the showers. *Kill the vampire.* It's the same mantra I repeated all last night.

Still, I know there has to be more to Sarah—fuck, I mean, the vampire. She seemed so kind. It's as though she still has her humanity left, although I know that to be impossible.

From everything I've been taught and know from personal experience of dealing with vampires, once turned, they lose the soul they once had. All humanity is stripped away, leaving a desire to kill and feed. This vampire is just good at tricking and deceiving.

I take an extra-long shower this morning and let the sting of the cold water knock some sense back into me. After twenty minutes I finish, wrapping a towel around my waist as I step out.

Shyann walks in as I'm starting to head out. The showers are coed. Her eyes go wide when she spots me. I watch her stare at my bare chest. Her gaze drops to my towel before she quickly fixes her eyes to mine. She blushes and gives a sheepish smile.

"Hi, Kael," she says with a small wave of her hand.

I smile back at her. "Morning, Shy."

I know she has a crush on me. She's had it for a while. Although, I can't tell if she truly likes me or if she is just infatuated with me.

I have a bit of a reputation here as a man whore, but really, I only seek those who plan to use me for meaningless sex just as I plan to use them. For many reasons, Shyann does not fit in that category.

I'm not against a serious relationship, per se; it's just that I would rather focus my time on hunting and killing vampires.

It's not that Shy isn't pretty. She's petite with strawberry blonde hair cut into a pixie style and has wide blue eyes.

I just don't know if she would expect more afterwards. Besides, Shyann is in the same squad as me, so I wouldn't want things to get weird between us.

The biggest reason, however, is that I know Liam is in love with her. He's my best friend. I could never, and *would* never, do that to him.

We stand there for a moment more before I gesture to the door she's blocking. "I'm going to go get dressed. I'll see you at breakfast?" I ask.

She nods her head frantically. "Yes, sorry. Oh, um, Liam wants us to have a meeting in the study after we eat. He put it in the group chat. I don't know if you saw it. It showed you hadn't read it," she informs me as she steps to the side so I can pass.

"I didn't. Thanks for letting me know."

"You're welcome," she squeaks a little too loudly before running into the shower closest to her.

*Great.* I wonder what this could be about. I hope it has nothing to do with last night. Although, why he would want a meeting about us not getting a vampire is beyond me. It's not like this is the first vampire ever to escape us. It's bound to happen every once in a while.

Unless that's not the thing he wants to talk about.

I think he was the only one that noticed my reaction to the vampire.

*What reaction? You didn't have a fucking reaction,* I scold myself. But even as I think it, I know it's a lie.

Either way, Liam wouldn't call a meeting if that's what it is about. He would just take me off to the side and talk to me. I breathe a little easier knowing that I'm right, and that it has to be about something else.

After grabbing my breakfast, some fresh fruit and a muffin, I glance around the dining hall. The only ones here are the squads that were on duty last night, Patrick's and Liam's. It's one-fifteen in the afternoon, so everyone else has just finished lunch, while we are just starting breakfast.

Hunting shifts don't end until dawn when the sun starts to rise and vampires are going back to their lairs for protection.

I go and sit with Kayda and Zach, two other members that are a part of my squad.

"Where's Carmack and Liam?" I inquire, popping some blueberries in my mouth.

"Liam is in the study talking with Aquila, and Nick is probably still sleeping. You know he doesn't like to wake until the last minute," Kayda informs me.

Kayda is wearing a sleeveless shirt, which showcases the three tattoos on her left arm. She just got one of them colored in, which looks great against her tawny skin. It's a tribal hummingbird that she colored in a mix of turquoise and pink.

She is one of the only single girls around here who has no interest in bringing me back to her dorm room for a one-nighter. She's the only one that I truly love like a sister and who loves me back like a brother, the way I wish Shyann would see me, too.

"Do you know what Liam's meeting is about?" I ask as casually as I can, giving my voice an air of indifference that I've come to master. I'm trying to fish out more information, but don't want to make it obvious.

"No idea," she says.

I look over at Zach, who is staring fixedly at his laptop.

Kayda follows my eyes and shakes her head. "Don't mind him; he's researching the possibility of different vampire species. I keep telling him there is only one kind of vampire species, the evil kind, but you know him, he has a one-track mind."

Zach looks up from the screen. "There was something off about that vampire girl last night. You know, the one that got away," he clarifies, looking over at me. As if he needs to remind me. As if she hasn't taken up ninety-nine percent of my thoughts since I laid eyes on her, but I don't voice that aloud.

"Why did she feel different? Kael, you were interrogating her. Did she seem different to you, or did her up-close presence feel more normal?" he asks, letting his scientist side take over.

"What does it matter?" Kayda questions, splaying her hands out in front of her in exasperation. "She's still a vampire who has probably killed countless people and will continue to do so if not stopped. That's all that matters."

"Not true," Zach says matter-of-factly. "What if vampires are starting to progress somehow? That could mean so much. I mean, did you see the way she caught Nick's wooden stake and broke it in half like she was snapping a pencil? Not to mention, she is the fastest vampire we have ever come across." He turns to me and asks, "Kael, after turning your comms piece off, did you happen to find out how long ago she was turned, or who turned her?"

"No, sorry man," I say as I think about what Zach just said about Sar—the vampire. *I've got to stop doing that.*

"So what if she caught my wooden stake?" Nick Carmack says as he joins us with a tray full of food. "And I can break a wooden stake in half, too. We all can. That doesn't mean she's some super vampire."

Zach shrugs. "I doubt we can snap a stake with one hand as easy as snapping a twig the way she did, and no vampire has been fast enough to catch one of your crossbow stakes before. All I'm saying is that it's worth researching. I know there is something off with the vampire girl. I just know it."

I know it too, although I'm not sure if I want to let on that I agree with Zach, so I keep my mouth shut.

***

Thirty minutes later, we all file into one of the three conference rooms in the back of the library. This specific room is decorated more like a lounge, with chairs, a loveseat, and a sofa arranged in a circle around a wooden coffee table.

Shyann and Liam were already here. Shy is sitting on one end of the loveseat, while Liam occupies one of the chairs. I grab the chair next to him while the others, Nick, Kayda, and Zach, sit on the sofa, with Kayda sandwiched in the middle.

"This won't take long," Liam says as we all quiet down to listen. "I just wanted to inform all of you that we are adding a new female member to our squad."

We all start speaking at once.

This is not a small thing he just announced. Usually, once we have our squad, that's it. It's the six of us until one of us dies or retires.

"I don't understand," Shyann says, shaking her head.

"Who is it?" Zach asks.

"I hope it's Vanessa from Annalise's squad," Nick says, rubbing his hands together like he's about to eat something delicious.

"Can you stop the transfer?" I question.

Only Kayda keeps quiet, waiting to hear more details.

Liam gestures with his hands for everyone to calm down. "First of all, no, Kael, I cannot and will not stop the transfer. It's not someone from this academy," he says, answering Nick's question next.

"Her name is Amberly Mitchiner. She's coming from Atlanta, Georgia. Aquila asked that we take her into our squad, and I already said that we would," Liam states, saying the last bit quickly before anyone can interrupt.

Aquila Young is a retired hunter and the person who has run the Academy for the last twenty years. I guess it's no surprise he would ask Liam to take on the newbie. Liam is probably the only squad leader that's kind enough to do so.

"Liam," I say in exasperation. "We are like a well-oiled machine. The six of us work well together; we trust each other. Adding someone else now will just screw us up."

Kayda clears her throat. "Kael's not wrong, Liam," she says, speaking for the first time. "You can't just expect us to trust this girl with our lives. We're hunters, hunting the most dangerous prey there is. We have to be able to know who we are fighting alongside."

"I know," Liam says with a sigh. "But this move can't be easy for her either. Not only does she have to adjust to a new squad, but also a new city. She's coming in two weeks, so that gives us plenty of time to adjust to the news.

"Once she's here, we will be spending some group time together as a 'getting to know each other' week. In that week, we will train with her and show her how we do things. We will have to go on some hunts with her. After a month or two, if we all feel like she's not working well with us, then I can ask Aquila to find her another squad, but we all need to try and adjust to having a seventh member on our team. It's strength in numbers. Having someone else with us might benefit us in the long run."

This is not what I was expecting when I came in here—a seventh member of the squad. We six have been together since we were ten years old, since the moment we were all selected to be a team together, back when we were all still training.

We all murmur grievances or agreements before moving on, but the meeting seems to be over. Everyone gets up to head to the training room. We train for at least three hours every single day.

I get up, and at the same time Liam puts a hand on my shoulder.

"Got a second?" he asks as everyone else heads out the door.

*Great.* I have a feeling I know what this is about. "Sure, man, what's up?" I say as I face him.

"Just wanted to make sure everything is okay with you," he articulates, clearly wanting to say more.

I narrow my eyes. "I'm fine."

"It's just last night. You seemed off. Zach seems to think there was something different about the vampire girl that got away from us. What are your thoughts?" he asks.

I shrug. "I mean, we can't deny she felt different," I say nonchalantly, not wanting to give away any more of my thoughts on her than I have to.

"She did. I'm not sure why. I talked to Aquila about how the vampire felt. To be honest, he seemed to know something, but was reluctant to give me any information about it. I think there is a chance that having a vampire that doesn't quite feel as dark as the others do might have happened before."

He squeezes my shoulder, forcing me to look at him. "In the end though, she is still a vampire. You took an oath. You have to remember that," he finishes.

"I know. I know she's a vampire, and the chances of us ever seeing her again are close to never. This is San Francisco, after all."

I don't mention the fact that I learned she's a regular at the diner we chased her to. I'm thankful it seems no one else caught on to that bit of information. For some reason, I don't want anyone to know.

Liam sighs. "I know. I hate when one gets away from us. I feel like all the humans she will kill after last night are on me."

"You know that's not true, right?" I say, hating that Liam always feels the need to hold so much on his shoulders because he's our leader. I guess that's the price of being a leader: taking fault when things fail or don't go to plan.

"I know... so," he says. After a beat he changes the subject to a lighter topic. "We're not scheduled to patrol tonight. Any plans?"

"Nah, maybe catch up on some sleep," I lie. I know exactly where I'm going tonight, and I definitely don't want anyone coming with me.

***

We make our way to the training room, or rooms, I should say, because it is in fact, made up of two large rooms. One is the gym, and the other is the weapons and training room.

The weapons, mostly made of wood, take up the back wall, and standing opposite that wall are targets. The center of the room is a wrestling mat for combat practice.

Aquila is training a younger group of vampire hunters who haven't ascended yet. We called them tyros.

Aquila has almond-colored skin with long, jet-black hair that he keeps in a ponytail. He has one long scar across his cheek that he received a long time ago during battle. It must have been a very nasty wound; hunters don't scar easily. I should know. I have a similar one on my chest.

Ascending to the status of a vampire hunter allows us not only the heightened senses, speed, and strength of a vampire, but also fast healing.

Amongst the tyro students Aquila is currently training is Shyann's twelve-year-old brother, Benjamin Karman.

Ben's face lights up as soon as I walk into the room. He is tall and slim. He looks a lot like Shyann with his blue eyes, light skin, and strawberry-blond hair, although Ben fixes his hair to match mine. I know he looks up to me, so I try to be on my best behavior when he's around.

Ben is a little too eager to become a vampire hunter, but I think he has too big a heart to ever truly be any good at it.

"Kael, Kael, man, you missed it," Ben says excitedly, running over to Liam and me. "I was practicing with Roger over there,"—he looks over at a redhead kid sitting on the sidelines drinking from his water bottle— "and I was able to pin him to the ground. You should have seen it. I can't wait until I turn eighteen so I can ascend."

"It'll come before you know it," I tell him. "For now, just keep practicing and aim to be the best tyro in your class."

"I will." He turns to see Aquila ushering him back over. "I have to go. See you later," he says as he rushes back to the younger students.

"Are you guys done bromancing?" Nick asks as Liam and I walk up to the rest of the team.

"What the hell is bromancing?" I ask, brows lifting.

Liam rolls his eyes. "Apparently, they have given a name for when you and I have our heart-to-hearts," he jokes.

"Bromancing," I repeat the word as if testing it. "I like it."

"I knew you would," Liam says with a smirk.

Nick shakes his head. "Can we get started on training or what?"

# Chapter 5
# Kael

I MAKE IT BACK to the Academy by midnight. The vampire didn't show up at the diner tonight. I don't know why I thought she would, and I ignore the ever-growing question of why I want to see her so badly.

*It's just so I can kill her.* I need to finish the job so I can move on, I remind myself, not willing to examine how much of it is a lie.

I can't sleep, so I decide to get an extra hour in the training room to help tire me out. I take a shortcut, passing through the study, where I notice Zach sitting at one of the tables in the library.

I head over to him. "Hey man, you're up late on your night off. Still researching?"

He looks up as if surprised to see me and then looks down at his watch. "I didn't realize the time, but yes, I am still researching," he says, beaming. "You won't believe what I found."

I take a seat, eager to hear what he has to say. "Is it about Sa—the vampire girl?" I ask, mentally cursing myself for almost using her name in front of him. He doesn't need to know just how interested I am in her.

"Yes, well I found a few cases in which a vampire might be different," he says, pushing his glasses up the bridge of his nose, wearing them more out of habit than necessity. "Did you know that vampires can procreate?"

*What the fuck?* "That's impossible," I say. There is no way vampires can have babies. We would have heard about this before now.

Zach shakes his head, a broad grin on his face. "Not if the mother is a non-vampire but of a magical line. For instance," he says as he sets the laptop he is using off to the side and pulls one of the many open books sprawled all over the table.

He taps on the page. "According to *The History of Vampire Kind,* a male vampire and a female fae can procreate. We just never seen a half-fae, half-vampire because they would have been banished with all the other fae folk."

"So, you think this vampire chick is half-fae?" I ask incredulously. I'm having a hard time believing that Sarah is half-fae. She doesn't seem like she's from a different realm, and wouldn't her ears be pointed?

Zach shakes his head again. "Actually, I think my other finding is more likely, and it would explain why she felt so different," he says, lifting a finger and glancing around the table. He swaps out the book he's holding, reaching for another one. He flips to a bookmarked page.

"Take a look at this," he says, gesturing to two small paragraphs at the top of a page in a hunter's codex I've never seen before. Vampire hunters have several books telling of our history and fight against vampires. The chapter is titled:

Validus

A Validus is a vampire that has kept their soul after transforming, allowing their humanity to stay intact. A Validus vampire would not have the same darkness as other vampires, because their soul is still unbroken, thus allowing for a lighter aura.

To become a Validus, one must come from a vampire hunter bloodline. One must also transform into a vampire before the hunter's ascending ceremony. Due to having hunter blood still running in their veins, the Validuses are known to be stronger, and faster than all other vampires. Other unknown abilities are said to manifest, although none are recorded, making them one of the strongest creatures on Earth.

There are only twelve cases of known Validuses on record.

This is it. This is her. I look at the book that he found this information in more closely, but I don't recognize it.

"Where did you find this? I never saw it in the library before," I ask.

Zach looks sheepishly at me. "That's because I found it in the attic. It was one of the books they banned from teaching here."

Confused, I ask, "Why?"

I didn't even know we had banned books, let alone where to find them. Leave it to Zach to know.

"I assume because there are certain things they don't want us to know about. This being one of them," he replies, gesturing to the book. "Maybe to some, the temptation of being that strong and still having your wits about you would be too much to resist. Can you imagine being one of the strongest creatures in the world?"

I shake my head. "Wait, that means that if the girl from the other night really is a *Validus*, then she would have to be from a vampire hunter family."

He smiles in delight. "Yes, isn't that crazy? I kind of wish we could see her again. I would love to ask her questions, assuming that we wouldn't have to kill her. Although I doubt Liam would approve of letting her go."

I flinch. "If she has a soul, maybe we don't need to kill her," I say, knowing that's a lie even as I say it.

Zach shrugs. "I guess it would depend on her humanity."

"What do you mean?"

"Well, if she was a bad person in life, then she would still be a bad person as a vampire, with the added bonus of being one of the most powerful vampires on the planet."

"You're right," I say, thinking hard. I need to find this girl now more than ever. "Have you told anyone what you found out?"

"No, not yet."

I grab him by the shoulders, forcing him to look at me. "Can I ask you a favor and maybe keep this just between us, at least for now?"

Baffled by my intensity, he nods. "Of course I can. Is it so we don't panic the others?"

"Yes... and I don't want them hunting her down," I say truthfully, and then curse myself. *Why did I tell him that?*

"Why not?" he asks.

I close my eyes and shake my head. "I can't explain it, but please, let's keep this information between us."

"I won't say a thing," he assures me.

I know I can trust Zach. If he says he won't say anything, then he won't, but why am I asking him to keep secrets from the rest of the team to begin with? That is something I need answered, and there is only one person who can help me figure out what I need to know.

# Chapter 6
# Sarah

I SAUNTER TO THE open door of the bathroom where Adam concentrates on applying his eye makeup in the mirror for tonight, his mouth partially parted, as he leans forward a bit over the sink. The smell of his cologne mixed with cosmetics wafts out of the bathroom.

"Do you like it?" I ask, modeling my costume for him.

I'm dressed in tight, black leather pants, black boots, a black leather vest, a trench coat, and a black fedora. Perfect for slaying vampires.

Adam looks over at me, making fish lips as he scans my costume. "You can just as easily be Kate Beckinsale's Selene, from Underworld," he tells me.

"Nuh-uh," I say in defense. "Selene doesn't wear a vampire-slaying fedora. Also, she doesn't have this." I bend down and grab the big plastic crossbow that came with the costume, which I kept just out of Adam's sight for dramatic effect. I pose with it as if I'm ready to shoot a vampire.

He smiles. "Do you think with the recent events that have transpired that dressing as Van Helsing, the vampire hunter, is appropriate attire for the Halloween party?"

I shrug. "Why not? The real vampire hunters didn't get me, and it's not like I'll ever see them again." The thought of never seeing Kael shouldn't bother me. I don't even know him. *It doesn't bother me.*

Besides, I've been purposely staying away from the diner now that Kael knows I frequent there. I wonder if the other hunters picked up on Mrs. May and I's conversation, too. Let's hope not.

He nods in agreement. "Fair enough," he says as he turns back to the mirror, scrutinizing his makeup. "What do you think?" he asks, lifting up a lipstick tube. "Matte-black lips or keep them bare?"

I think about it for a minute before saying, "Definitely, go with the black lips. After all, you are going as a vampire; you have to think dark and creepy."

"Right," he says playfully, knowing that I, a vampire, am the exact opposite of dark and creepy. Still, he turns and applies the lipstick.

There is a knock on the door letting us know the first guests have arrived. Adam runs to his room to get his vampire cape. I take one last look around the apartment, which is decorated with a vampire lair theme in mind.

I smile at the thought of how different vampire "lairs" actually are after spending a short amount of time at Mr. Leon's coven's lair than those depicted in folklore. The room I was kept in was modern and actually quite comfy with blacked-out windows. We, on the other hand, have cobwebs in the corners, sticker bats covering one wall, fake coffins propped up lining another wall, and dozens of red and black candles scattered around the living room and kitchen.

I wanted fake-flamed candles, but Adam argued that it wouldn't look authentic and that we needed real-flamed candles. After reminding him that one drunk person knocking a candle on me would have me burning to ash faster than a stack of hay during a drought, he conceded. Besides, there is always the chance of someone accidentally burning the apartment down after hours of partying and drinking.

People trickle in slowly throughout the night. It's all Adam's friends from the hospital or med school. To all of them, I'm known as Sarah Summers, Adam's roommate, which is fine. It's better this way.

Adam is the only friend I allow myself to keep after the transformation. It's too dangerous being my friend, because whether I like it or not, I am different now. I'm the thing that goes bump in the night, and anyway, it was way too hard to explain to my friends why I can't ever go out during the day, not even for a coffee. Adam is my one selfish guilty pleasure.

I never intended for Adam to learn the truth about me. It was just a hard time for me back then, and I needed a safe place to crash for awhile before figuring out my next steps. Leave it to Adam to practically force me to tell him what was going on with me. I'm so grateful for him now. He's literally my lifesaver. He helps keep me tethered to my life before I was turned, and his friends always treat me as if I'm part of the group when I'm with them.

Some even try to hit on me; I always politely turn them down. Others invite me to hang out during the day, but I always fake an excuse.

*Sorry, can't. I have to work on my book. My editor has been hounding me for the next chapter.* That usually does the trick. They don't push me about it. They are Adam's friends, after all, not mine.

After several hours of dancing, mingling and making small talk, I decide to take a break and head to the roof. Everyone is starting to get pretty tipsy, aside from the on-call residents, and me, of course. Alcohol has absolutely no effect on vampires.

I stand on our roof, soaking in the view, which is only okay. As far as rooftops go, this one is definitely not making the top one hundred. It's sandwiched in by taller buildings on either side and to the front is a view of warehouses.

I wonder if I can make a short, five-minute trip to the garden rooftop without anyone noticing. I guess there is only one way to find out. I look around to make sure I'm alone and then make the jump to one of the bigger buildings.

*Guilty truth.* I don't really mind being a vampire. The strength, the speed, the heightened senses make me feel powerful in a way I never did as a human. The fact that I can jump twenty feet in the air or leap over buildings in a single bound, makes me feel like I can fly.

I make it to the garden rooftop within minutes. I lie down next to the hibiscus and breathe in the beautiful, familiar floral scents. Although the need for breath isn't necessary anymore, it's times like this I love my heighten sense of smell.

I want to be buried here. If reincarnation is a thing, I definitely want to come back as one of these flowers. I wonder, vaguely, if maybe in a past life I was a gardener. Of course, now, in this life, I couldn't even keep a cactus alive. *RIP Clifton.*

To be fair, I was kidnapped and turned into a vampire within weeks of getting Clifton. Still, his death is a guilt that I carry with me. Thank goodness Abby didn't get me an animal. I shudder when remembering the goldfish I got my first semester of college. *RIP Shelby.*

What made Abby, my old colleague and friend, buy me a cactus as a congratulations-on-getting-a-promotion gift, I'll never know. I wonder about her sometimes and how she's doing since I left. We promised we would stay in touch, and, of course, I broke that promise. I wonder vaguely if Abby knew about Mr. Leon the whole time, or like me, she didn't know who she was really working for. I immediately scratch out that line of thinking. There is no way Abby knew the truth. Still, I bet some of the workers there know. Maybe the higher-ups?

I breathe out a sigh, letting my mind wander to lighter things. I'm in the middle of contemplating whether or not to go as Ahsoka from Star Wars or Garfield, the lasagna-loving cat, next year for Halloween when, suddenly, I hear a noise.

A slight shuffle of feet. If I didn't have super hearing, I would have missed it. I sit up and look around but see nothing.

*Maybe I imagined it?* I get to my feet, brushing off the dust from my pants. I guess it's time for me to get back to the party anyway.

As I start making my way back, I hear the sound of feet moving again. Okay, this time I know I'm not imagining it. Someone is following me. I turn back to try and catch this mystery person, but again, there is no one around.

I continue on my way home. Whoever this person is has to be of the supernatural sort. That's the only way they would be able to keep up with me, or maybe I'm completely paranoid after the hunter incident, and no one is following me at all.

Mr. Leon's face pops unbidden in my mind. I shake my head. "No, Sarah," I say out loud to myself. I haven't seen or heard from him in two years. For all I know, he has forgotten all about me.

I don't head straight home. Instead, I scale building after building until I'm sure I've lost whoever was following me, if anyone.

I finally make it back to my own rooftop and am about to head down the stairs to rejoin the party when my inner Spidey sense kicks in.

Everyone has it, or at least, I think everyone does. That feeling you get when you know someone is watching you.

I turn around, and sure enough, someone is standing at the edge of the roof, and it's not Mr. Leon or another vampire—it's him. The hunter.

# Chapter 7
# Kael

I FINALLY ALLOW HER to see me.

She's so much faster than I am. I nearly lost her several times. Only her aura kept me on her trail.

I was hoping that she would lead me to her vampire coven. At least, that's what I'm telling myself. I've been telling myself so many lies lately that I can't tell the difference between what I really feel, and what I want to feel.

*I was only hanging around the diner where we sat together because I want to finish what I started.* Of course, she wasn't there, so I decided to try lurking around the rooftop where she was the first time I ever laid eyes on her, all so that I could kill her. I have to kill her. I repeat the sentence over and over again in my head. It is now the new mantra of my life.

Now, it looks as though she's led me back to her personal apartment building instead. She must be a rogue vampire. Is it because she is a *Validus*?

It doesn't matter if she is a *Validus*. I have to kill her. I took an oath: hunt them, kill them, burn them.

Frankly, I was surprised to see her on the rooftop laying between a row of flowers, just staring at the sky. What vampire does that?

Unfortunately, my memory of her doesn't do her justice. Staring at her now, she is the most beautiful woman on the planet.

What is she wearing? I can't keep my eyes off her. She has on a body-hugging, little black outfit with a long coat over it. Damn, her thick thighs look good in those skin- tight pants, not to mention that toned stomach leading down to those fuckable hips.

*Focus.* I'm here to kill her, not objectify her.

She gives me a look that lets me know she is aware I was just checking her out. My eyes fix on hers, and damn, she has the most beautiful dark-brown eyes.

"It's a costume," she says, as if to answer my unspoken question.

Her statement reminds me that it's Halloween, so at least the outfit makes sense now.

"I'm Van Helsing," she continues when I don't say anything.

I arch an eye at her in confusion. *Am I supposed to know who that is?*

She smiles. "The famous vampire hunter."

I chuckle in spite of myself and it comes out sounding more like a croak than anything else. The fact that this vampire is dressed like a vampire hunter is hilarious; maybe she is going for irony.

I try to recover quickly, schooling my face to one of masked anger. It's not hard. My anger is what has consistently driven me for the last five years. Ever since yet another family member died at the hands of these soulless monsters there's been this unquenching need for vengeance that fuels me until I'm overflowing with rage, looking for vampires to unleash it on.

"Never heard of her, and hunters don't wear such cheap material to hunt in," I say with a sneer.

She frowns and looks down at herself. "Van Helsing is a dude, and I bought the costume at the It's Halloween Time store, so of course it's going to be cheap material. Although the costume still cost me eighty bucks, so a little endearment wouldn't hurt."

"Did you know I was following you?" I ask, changing the subject. I can't let her distract me.

She purses her lips. "Not you, specifically," she says under her breath.

"Kind of dumb of you to allow me to follow you home, don't you think?"

She shrugs. "Who says this is my home? Maybe it's just a random building I stopped at because I knew someone was following me."

I narrow my eyes, trying to decide if she's playing me or not when she nods toward me. "What are you dressed as for Halloween?"

What is she talking about? These are my normal hunting leathers. She knows this because this is the exact thing I was wearing the first time she saw me.

A lightbulb clicks. She's being funny. She *is* a *Validus*, which means she has a soul. Apparently, that soul likes to make jokes at my expense. Not that I mind in the slightest.

Kayda's words run through my mind. *She's still a vampire, who probably has killed countless people, and will continue to do so if not stopped. That's all that matters.*

It doesn't matter that she's a *Validus*. I have to kill her.

"A vampire hunter," I say in a menacing tone, answering her question as I pull out a wooden dagger. The time for games is done. I want her to be afraid. I flip the dagger in my hand, warming up my wrist, letting her know I fully plan on plunging it into her heart tonight.

I have to do this. I have to kill her. This is what I came here for. The reason why I was searching for her. Maybe after she's dead, I won't think about her all the fucking time.

"Well, from one hunter to another, this territory is taken. I assure you, I'll take care of all vampires that come in this vicinity," she teases.

"Enough games," I say calmly. "Any final words?"

She gives a ghost of a smile. "That's very sweet of you. Do you always allow your victims to say their goodbyes?"

"I guess not," I say as I charge for her, though not fast enough, giving her the slightest chance to dodge me. Not that she needs it. She is extremely fast and makes it to where I was just standing in an instant.

*Don't hold back this time*, I tell myself as I charge for her again. This time she tries to side-step me, but I anticipate her move and kick out, my boot meeting the back of her knee.

She falls to the ground with a thump, throwing out her hands so she doesn't face plant the concrete.

I jump on top of her, flipping her over so that we are face-to-face. I don't hesitate as I jab the wooden dagger down, aiming straight for her heart.

She grabs my hands, stopping the dagger from landing the killing blow. The tip is piercing through her skin just enough to cut through her shirt and draw blood.

Her eyes fill with fear, and for the first time since I've met her, the fun, carefree vampire is gone. In her place is a terrified, trembling girl, all because of me.

I hate seeing this new version of her, more than I care to admit, but I don't stop trying to force the dagger to finish its job. I need to do this now, before I change my mind. I can already feel the doubt pricking at the corners of my conscience. Her fear turns to anger as she fights to keep the dagger from penetrating her heart.

*Fuck, she's strong.* I'm using all of my might and, still, she is able to force my hands back.

"Get off me," she screams as she wrestles out from under me.

I don't let her get on top. Instead, I roll to the side and jump to my feet.

We circle each other for a moment. We are both trying to decide our next move. I'm trying to decide how I want to finish her off, and she looks like she is trying to figure out her best chance of escape. Little does she know, I don't plan to let her leave my sight alive.

"You're strong," I tell her. "Surprisingly."

She doesn't smile or say anything back. Serious, terror-filled eyes glare at me. I guess she's done with the back-and-forth banter that I've come to know and love. I hate that I want it now.

I lunge for her knowing that she will try to avoid my advance. I reach for her at the same time she tries to run away. My hand clutches her arm for only a second before her speed and velocity have me losing my grip. She stumbles but doesn't fall, and when she turns around to look at me, her fangs are out, and she hisses.

This time it's she who charges me. I let her force me to the ground, but before she can secure her weight on top of me, I wrap my right leg around her left and push her sideways so I can maneuver myself on top. I pin her arms down with my legs so she can't fight me again as I raise my dagger to plunge into her heart.

I'm about to bring it down on her when she cries out in fear.

I don't know what makes me hesitate. I have her. I fucking have her right where I want her. The kill would be so easy, but I can't.

They say that the eyes are the windows to the soul. Every vampire I've ever killed looked at me with nothing but empty rage and bloodlust in the moments before I took their life. That moment always solidified my resolve, gave me that extra nudge to finish the job. I always knew there was nothing behind those eyes but evil. But as I look down at Sarah, I see fear in those big brown eyes of hers. I see regret, sadness... human emotions. Or am I making this up?

"Please," she cries. "Just let me go, I won't hurt anyone. I promise. I don't hurt people."

My hands clutching the dagger relaxes for a second, hesitating, but that's all it takes. One second, I'm on top, and the next, she wrestles herself out and flips me on my back.

I growl as I try, and fail, to break free. I'm an idiot. How could I have let this happen? She's not the first vampire to plead for their life, so what made me waver this time?

I struggle once more to get out from under her, but she is using strength that I didn't even know vampires had to keep me in place as she grabs my hands and pins them down over my head. Her face inches from mine, her deep brown eyes staring at me, with lashes so long they practically touch her eyebrows. Her long, raven hair falls around us, like a silky curtain around our heads.

I stop struggling. I want to stare at her for hours, learning every inch of her beautiful face. Her body on top of mine feels... I grind my teeth. It can't feel like anything. It just can't.

"I'm not a bad person," she says softly. Her lips are so close to mine and it takes everything inside me not to lift my face to meet hers. "If I let you go, will you try to kill me?"

"Yes," I say instinctively, even though I know I'm lying.

She rolls her eyes and sighs. "Seriously, so what, are we supposed to just stay like this forever?"

I keep quiet.

Damn, she smells good. I can smell the apple and honeysuckle of her shampoo.

"OMG, what have we walked in on?" a drunk male voice calls out.

We both look at where it came from.

A man with caramel-colored skin, dressed in a comical vampire costume and a pale woman in a slim-fitting police officer outfit are standing by the door that leads down to the apartment building.

He looks vaguely familiar. Is he the one that she got in the car with the other night?

"Looks like we interrupted something," the girl says through giggles. They both sound drunk, their voices high-pitched, their words slurring.

The vampire on top of me looks at me and smiles. "They're human. You can't kill me in front of humans," she says triumphantly as she releases me, jumping to her feet.

"Adam, this is not what it looks like," she starts to say.

I hold back my own smile, looks like she lives in this building after all.

He shakes his head, taking a step back toward the exit. "No, no, no, don't let us interrupt. I'm glad to see you having a good time, Sarah. Lord knows it's been a while."

"Adam," she shouts. I can see she is embarrassed by his last statement. How long has it been, I wonder.

"This is a vampire hunter," she says a little roughly. That seems to sober Adam up quickly. He straightens up, alert, and his jaw drops in understanding as he stares at me.

Who is this guy, and what is his relationship with Sarah? I remember her mentioning a roommate. This must be him. I think I remember her saying his name was Adam. Is the girl with him his girlfriend? I hope so, although I don't know why that would matter. *It doesn't matter.*

I can see that he knows I'm an actual vampire hunter, which means he must know that Sarah is a vampire. Doesn't she know that telling humans about our world is forbidden? But I guess vampires don't have to play by our rules, do they?

"Cool, you came as a vampire hunter, totally badass," the girl says, eyeing me up and down. She is clearly oblivious to what I am. "You look so hot in all that leather. Hey, Sarah, if what we walked in on wasn't what we thought, can I have him?"

Okay, so not the girlfriend.

I hear Sarah let out an irritated huff. "He's not an object, Meg."

Meg laughs. "Fine," she says, looking at me. "Do you want to come down to the party with me?"

"No!" Sarah shouts at the same time Adam says, "I don't think that's such a good idea."

"Whatever, Sarah, if you're into him, just say you're into him," Meg says, a hint of annoyance in her voice. "Unless, it's not mutual." She turns her glazed, drunken stare straight at me again. This time with a glint in her eyes.

"Ew, Meg. Let's pretend to have some class, shall we?" Adam says distastefully.

"I only came for her." I nod toward the vampire. I refuse to say or even think of her name again. I can't afford to get any more attached than I already am.

She looks at me and I can't read the expression on her face. She licks her lips, and I swear for a millisecond she looks as though she wants to take a step toward me. Electricity flows between us. I can't deny that. It sizzles, sending shock waves throughout my body.

I stare at her now-wet lips a little too long. I clench my hands into fists at my sides to help keep all my blood from rushing to one area. She's the enemy. I can't forget that.

Adam comes up and grabs her by the arm, tugging her back toward the stairwell.

A boiling sensation takes root inside me. I need to know their relationship. Are they just roommates or something more?

*Stop. It doesn't matter. You're not jealous.*

"Well, she's busy," Adam tells me. "We have a party to dual host, so we best be on our way."

The vampire locks eyes with me for a second more before turning and walking back with the others.

As they head down I can hear the girl, Meg, say, "This is so awkward, are we really just going to leave the hot guy on the roof by himself?"

"He'll be fine," I hear the vampire retort back with a little irritation in her voice. I'm getting under her skin, and knowing that has me excited. "He knows what he's doing." That last part is said with a hint of admiration, if I'm not mistaken.

I turn and head home, knowing the humans are safe, my mind and heart battling for dominance on what to do next.

*Do I keep hunting her down until I can finally kill her? Can I even kill her at this point?*

She's more human than I was expecting. Maybe it's time to bring in the team, so that the choice isn't on me.

I curse myself for my own weakness because I know that I'm not going to do that. No, I'm going to keep her my little secret... for now.

# Chapter 8
# Sarah

CASSIE OPENED HER EYES wearily. She took in a shaky breath, and then another. Sitting up, she looked curiously around the room. *Where am I?*

It was a large room, if you can even call it that. The walls were a blue-green cave rock. Glowing crystals hung from the ceiling.

Cassie found herself on a huge, soft bed in the center of the room. Nothing looked familiar, but she was alone; she had a chance to figure things out. She rolled off the bed and landed on the floor with a thud. Her body felt so weak. Not trusting her legs, she began to crawl her way forward when Caspian walked into the room.

"You're awake, finally," he said with a hint of irritation as if he'd been waiting for far too long.

Seeing Caspian, all Cassie's fear came coursing back through her, and then anger—red hot, untempered anger.

"Where am I? Bring me back to Basille right now," she demanded.

"I can't," he said dismissively. "You are in my city now, far below the sea's surface."

Cassie stared at him wide-eyed. *This can't be. I can't be in the underwater city. Not with him.*

Caspian frowned. "I promised Basille I would keep you safe for now."

Cassie stood up on shaky legs and marched over to Caspian. "Please, I need to get back to him."

Something strange passed through Caspian's face. Cassie couldn't quite put her finger on it. It was there and then gone in a flash. Maybe she imagined it.

Caspian gave her a wicked grin. "You love him," he said.

It wasn't a question. A statement. Undeniable. "I get why you do; he rescued you and all that. What baffles me is why he loves you back. You're quite painful to be around."

"Screw you," Cassie shouted.

Caspian's eyes scrunched up in confusion. "Screw," he said the word slowly, pronouncing each syllable. "Is a type of fastener. That can't be right," he muttered, mostly to himself. "We must not have a word of the same meaning here. My translator is not picking up your intended use of the word."

Cassie knew that these aliens spoke a different language, that they had built-in translators allowing them to communicate with other species. She also knew, from her many conversations with Basille, that they didn't translate all human sayings or lewd phrases.

Cassie rolled her eyes. "It means I don't like you and that I think you are an asshole."

"Ah, yes, those words I do understand," he said cheerfully, looking rather pleased with himself.

"But Basille has promised to help me with something I desperately need, but only if I keep you safe, so I will do just that," he continued to say. "Now come, you must be hungry. I will show you where to eat."

Cassie wanted to argue and refuse to go with him, but unfortunately her stomach decided to pick that moment to growl loudly, proving his point. She followed him out the door into the most beautiful hallway she had ever seen in her entire life.

The floor and ceiling were made of gold, and the walls were glass allowing Cassie to see straight into the glowing green sea around them. She watched as a school of fish with silver and blue scales passed right by.

Beyond that, she could see the city.

Golden towers were spread out all around her. Glass skybridges connected one tower to another all along the sea floor. The water was emerald-green with a bioluminescent glow, much different than the blue water she was used to on Earth.

"Beautiful, isn't it?" Caspian asked, coming up behind her. "I couldn't imagine living anywhere else."

"Yes," she admitted. "I've never seen anything so beautiful."

"I have," Caspian said, looking down at her.

Cassie blushed, although he couldn't possibly be talking about her, could he?

"Have you?" she asked in a whisper, all anger gone, leaving only fear. This fear, however, was vastly different than the one she felt earlier. This fear was exciting and new and pulsed all the way down to her toes.

"Yes—you," he stated as if it were the most well-known fact in the world. His hand reached up as if to touch her face before falling back down. "You are the most beautiful thing I have ever seen. Maybe that is why Basille loves you." There was something like admiration in his eyes when he looked at her, but his features quickly slipped back into their neutral indifference. "Too bad your horrible personality contradicts your beauty. Now come along, I don't have all day."

He turned from her.

Cassie rolled her eyes, the anger once again floating to the top of her emotions.

And then, without warning he grabbed her by the waist and pinned her to the wall. Caspian was all hard abs and broad shoulders as he pressed his body up against hers. He leaned in and bit her bottom lip. Cassie gasped in shock and delight. That's when he went in for the kill, pressing his firm lips to hers in an endless yearn of passion.

*Ping.*

My phone goes off for the third time. I sigh as I close my laptop. It's just as well, I was starting to project certain feelings and fantasies about a broody hunter in my writing that weren't supposed to be there. Not yet anyway. I will definitely have to delete that last paragraph. I don't even think "yearn of passion" makes sense.

Next time, I will have to continue my rule about keeping my phone in a different room or on silent while writing.

I tap on my screen and see that it's Adam letting me know he is staying at the hospital tonight. He is one of those texters who presses send after each sentence.

Adam: Staying at the hospital tonight.

Adam: One of my patients isn't doing too well.

Adam: Will have to watch him overnight.

Really, all of that could have been sent in one text, but no. I shoot him a quick text saying I hope everything works out before deciding I need some fresh air.

Night is just falling, so I make my way to Mile Rock Beach. It's a small, rocky cove that's covered with logs. It's high tide, so my terrain is narrower with the ocean taking up more land than at low tide. I find a good place to sit, picking a large rock far enough away from the ocean so my shoes don't get too wet.

I lean back and close my eyes, breathing in the smell of the salty sea. The sound of the tide drifting in and out is so soothing. I can stay here and listen to its calming melody forever.

It's been a while since I've been here, but tonight I needed a change in scenery to help clear my head; it doesn't work. My head is anything but clear. Meeting up with Kael the other night has me reeling. Is it by chance that he found me, or was he looking for me?

I shake my head. *Get a grip, Sarah. He wasn't looking for you; he was hunting you, very big difference.*

However, thinking back, he had the chance to kill me. He had my arms pinned so I couldn't defend myself. All he had to do was plunge the dagger into my heart, but he didn't. *That* fact has my head reeling for a whole different reason. I really need to get him out of my head.

I hate how attracted I am to him. It's not just his looks, but his smell, that mixture of cedar, sweat, and men's shampoo. I even like the way his lips quirk up ever so slightly when he is trying to hold in a smile. His touch makes me feel things I haven't felt since becoming a vampire.

Maybe Adam is right, I really do need to get laid. It's been far too long, and I'm getting all hot and bothered by a man who wants to kill me. It's not the healthiest of choices. Anyway, Kael would never want me in that way. To him, I'm just a soulless vampire.

Since becoming a vampire two years ago, this is the first time I really wish I wasn't one. It's true, given the choice, I would pick being human and alive again, but being a vampire isn't all that bad. I'm not sure exactly what happened during the transformation that allowed me to still be me and not turn into a soulless monster like all the other vampires I've met, but I just count my blessings and try not to think about it too much.

Still, if I weren't a vampire, then Kael would have no reason to hate me. Maybe we could have even met in a totally normal, non-hunting encounter. We could have run into each other while both turning a corner in some sort of meet-cute. He could have knocked my bag to the floor, spilling the contents all over the pavement. We both could have scrambled to the ground, gathering my things, him mumbling his apologies before our eyes finally met, both filled with curiosity and desire.

I lean into the fantasy, daydreaming about different ways Kael and I could have met. The more I do, the less real my life feels, carried away by the waves gently crashing onto the shore. Vampires, hunters, coven politics... all of it fades away until I'm floating in a made-up world where I can walk around in the sun and Kael and I eat dinner by candlelight each night after work.

Eventually, and reluctantly, I force myself back into reality and decide it's time to start heading back. Enough make-believe for one evening. I slowly make my way back up to the Lands End Coastal Trail that leads down to this secluded beach when I hear someone behind me, stopping me in my tracks.

"A rogue vampire," a male voice says.

"This is coven turf, you are not allowed to travel through here," says another male. "Doing so is punishable by death."

I turn around to see two vampires steadily approaching me from a little ways off the path. It's a windy night and their scent travels to me with the breeze. The smell of fresh blood swirls around me. They just fed. One of them didn't even bother to properly clean the red stain off his chin or the sides of his mouth.

I scan the area. Is the body, or bodies, close by? Are they still alive? My heart aches because I'm pretty sure I know the answer to that question.

"I'm not hunting," I tell them.

They are upon me now. Two guys who look like they used to be bouncers at a nightclub before becoming vampires.

One looks familiar, although where I've met him eludes me at this moment. He seems to have the same thought in mind because he narrows his eyes at me, trying to figure out how he knows me.

We both seem to figure it out at the same time. His eyes grow wide in recognition. His name is Taylor, and he is one of Caesar Leon's bodyguards.

He was there the last time I saw Mr. Leon before they went overseas.

Taylor's mouth falls open at the sight of me. "You're alive?" he says in shock.

"Technically, no. Your boss saw to that," I say stiffly.

"We were told you died," he says. "A final death. That you ran out into the sun."

"Ew, I did no such thing," I tell him. That must have been what the vampires told Mr. Leon after failing to keep me prisoner.

Taylor gives me a look. "Obviously. The boss will be happy to hear that you are still alive."

"Tell your boss he can go to hell," I say, trying to sound strong and fearless, although I'm feeling anything but. This whole time, Mr. Leon thought I was dead. No wonder he never came for me.

Taylor laughs. "How about I take you to him and you can tell him yourself?"

"Or I can kill you both now and not have to worry about it at all." I don't know what's come over me. I'm not looking for a fight. I know I can't take them both, but I'm fast. I just need to find an escape window. Other vampires have a bad habit of underestimating me, which often works out to my benefit.

"You always did like doing things the hard way," he says as he cracks his knuckles.

Without another word, Taylor lurches toward me. I side-step at the last second, which makes him lose his balance and fall to the ground.

He hisses as he spits out sand, fangs showing. I run and jump on top of him, but he grabs my neck and flips me sideways. The sound of wood snaps as I land on logs and rocks.

I hear the other guy coming from behind.

"We can't kill or hurt her," Taylor instructs the other vampire. "Boss wants this one."

The other one grunts in acknowledgement. He grabs me from behind, lifting me to my feet and giving me a bear hug, pinning my arms to my sides.

Using all my might, I lift my arms up and break out of the embrace. I kick Taylor, who is trying to bind my feet, hard in the gonads. He lets out a loud grunt as he stumbles back and falls over several rocks.

I'm only free for a second, but that's all I need. I quickly take off running. There is no way I'm going to get the better of these two vampires. They are trained to fight.

Luckily, I found my escape window, and I'm much faster than either of the two. Although I can hear them chasing me, the sound of their running footsteps is getting fainter and fainter before it disappears altogether. I don't stop running until I make it back to the city, where I quickly scale a building and run and jump from rooftop to rooftop. I take a few scenic routes to make sure I've truly lost them before heading back to my apartment.

So much for clearing my head.

# Chapter 9
# Kael

I'M MOVING STEADILY THROUGH Golden Gate Park. It's a beautiful, clear night, and as I gaze into the darkness, a cluster of shooting stars chase each other across the sky.

The rest of the squad is patrolling nearby, their conversation a distant muffle coming through my earpiece.

I know Nick spotted a vampire and is on the hunt. I'm circling the Shakespeare Garden, hoping to cut off the undead monster before it tries to run away.

I'm about to jump over the side of the gate that's hidden by foliage when I hear shuffling. I see someone land on their feet, having just jumped down from the very gate I was about to jump over.

I run to their side and push them against the shrubbery, one hand braced against their chest, the other holding a wooden dagger ready to make the kill.

The woman's face is a mask of utter shock. It takes me less than a second to realize I almost killed, and definitely just scared the shit out of this human.

I curse myself for not staying as completely focused on the hunt as I should be, and that I didn't register the lack of darkness from her that I know I should feel when being in close proximity to a vampire. I blame the meteor shower and this sudden human's appearance in an unlikely spot.

"I have pepper spray, you perv, and I'm not afraid to use it," she shouts.

I look at her hand, and sure enough, she is feverishly gripping a small spray can, her finger on the trigger button.

I quickly sheathe my weapon and take a step back, my hands raised in surrender. "I'm sorry. I thought you were someone else," I tell her soothingly. I don't want to scare her any more than I already have.

Her eyes narrow. "You thought I was someone else that you would slam against a fence?" She shakes her head as if to clear it. "You know what, I'm not here to judge. If that's how you and your girlfriend, or whoever, get your jollies, then by all means, I'll get out of your hair."

I laugh. She's surprisingly funny. "That's not what is going on here."

"Kael, we just spotted a second vampire," Liam comes in through the comms. "Stay with the human girl and keep her safe until we deal with them. I don't want her running into one of them."

"Copy that," I tell him, and then tap my earpiece to turn it off for a moment. I don't know why, but I want to have some privacy with this intriguing human.

She looks at me in confusion.

"Sorry, I was on the phone with someone when I... uh... ran into you," I explain.

She smirks. "And you were going to let someone listen in? Wow, feisty, roughness in a public place, and vocal spectators. I see I'm living life on the vanilla side."

I laugh again. Who is this funny woman, and where did she come from? "I told you that's not what was happening here. I saw you jump over the gate and... How did you do that, by the way?"

Maybe she is more than human after all.

She looks at me with big, brown eyes, and then at the gate that is several feet taller than either of us. "I didn't jump. Do I look like Mario to you? I climbed over, like a normal human being."

"Right," I say. So, definitely human. Her snarkiness excites me. It's like a challenge. "You know the garden closes at night? It could be dangerous for you to be out this late, especially alone."

"Tell me about it," she says as she rubs her chest where I used my arm to pin her. "I'm not sure how I feel about getting judged by Mister 'I let people listen in on me'."

I ignore her comment as my eyes travel down to her chest, which she was just rubbing. Damn, she's hot.

"If you're checking for bruises, I'm sure I'll be fine," she says teasingly.

My eyes shoot up to hers. Fuck, Kael, stop acting like a teenage pervert.

"Sorry," I say sheepishly. "So, what brings you here tonight, breaking and entering the Shakespeare Garden?" I ask, wanting to change the subject quickly.

"There was a meteor shower tonight, and I wanted to see it," she replies.

"Ah, yes, I think I glimpsed some shooting stars earlier."

She shifts on her feet a little and asks, "What about you? Why did you feel the need to thrust me up against a wall?" When she looks back up at me, her gaze roaming my body, there's a desire lingering in her eyes, as if the memory of our encounter is one she'll be thinking about for a while.

Thankfully, she is human, therefore unable to see the many weapons magically glamoured on me.

Trying to think of a good cover story as quickly as possible, I say, "I'm practicing a reenactment play with some friends. I thought you were one of them when I saw you."

She smiles. "That sounds fun."

I hear the others approach from behind me. The girl notices too and looks over my shoulder at them and then back at me.

"I guess it's time for me to go so you all can finish your reenactment," she says kindly.

I nod and as she turns to leave, I ask, "What's your name?"

She turns her head in my direction and says, "Sarah."

I wake up at the sound of my alarm. My sheets are a crumpled mess, kicked to the foot of the bed during the night. A sign of my restless sleep. I press the silence button in a rush, wishing I could return to the dream.

What wouldn't I give for it to have been real? It would be so much easier if I had met Sarah as a human. I wouldn't have to try so hard to hate her, or feel guilty for wanting to be near her, to touch her. What I wouldn't give to be able to admire and pursue her openly.

One thing is for sure, I have to see her again.

\*\*\*

Every night that I'm not patrolling, I'm lurking outside the diner we sat at together the first time we met, hoping to see her again. I'm starting to feel like a desperate stalker, but still, I find myself making my way to the diner after another lie to Liam about what I'm up to tonight.

The truth is, I need to get her out of my head. I can't keep camping out at this diner hoping she'll show up. It takes all my willpower not to stalk outside her apartment building, although if she doesn't come by the diner tonight, I know I will end up perched by her building waiting for her to emerge. I've become obsessed with her, might as well play the part well.

The smart thing to do is give up, but I know it's too late for that.

I round the corner to the diner, and there she is.

It's been a week since I've seen her. *Damn it.* She's just as beautiful as I remember, and I can only see her profile from this angle. Her dark, wavy hair is a silk waterfall down her back. For a moment, I'm wondering if I'm seeing things. But, there she is sitting alone with a glass of water, a half-eaten apple pie, and laptop in front of her.

Her fingers fly over the keyboard like she is trying to get everything that's on her mind down on the page as fast as possible. I take a minute to just stare at her before getting the courage to walk inside. The place is mostly empty, just as it was the last time I was here, with only a few people in some of the booths by the windows.

I go and stand by the empty bar chair next to hers.

She immediately stops typing and looks at me with those big brown eyes of hers. They're like vortexes, ready to swallow me whole. I feel nervous and uneasy all of a sudden.

*Focus, Hart.* I can't let her lure me in anymore. She's the enemy.

"What... what are you doing here?" she asks me in horror. She looks around the diner and then outside on the street.

"I came to find you, vampire," I hiss as I take a seat.

She points to herself. "Sarah," she says, assuming I don't remember her name.

If only she knew how many times I've whispered her name this week.

"This is starting to feel a little stalkerish," she says, forcing my thoughts back to the present.

"It's called hunting," I correct.

"Where are your friends?" she inquires, looking around.

I shake my head. "They're not here."

She seems to relax a little at my words. "So, Kael... What's your last name?"

I smile despite myself. "Hart. Kael Hart." I'm not sure why I'm answering her questions. It's like I want to make her happy, which is really fucking stupid.

"So, Kael Hart, are you planning to try and finish what you started on Halloween? Just so you know, I'm not your average vampire. I'm much stronger, and I was taking it easy on you the other night."

I know she's lying about the latter part of her statement. If anything, I was the one holding back, but her mentioning that she is stronger than most vampires has me intrigued.

"So, you truly are then?"

"What, a vampire? Yes, Kael, I'm a vampire," she whispers teasingly, cupping her hand on the side of her mouth to emphasize the secret.

"That you're a *Validus*," I say amusingly.

She looks at me quizzically. "I've never heard of that. What does it mean?"

I narrow my eyes, choosing to ignore her question and ask her another one. "Are you not part of the San Francisco coven?"

She turns back to her laptop, clicking away casually, but I can tell my question bothers her. "No, I was asked to join, but said no. Being a part of the creepy vampire club isn't really my thing," she informs me, looking a little uncomfortable. I can tell she is holding onto more information, but I opt for another question instead. I plan to coax more out of her about the clan later.

"How old are you?" I ask. She talks as if she is my age. Most vampires can't seem to keep up with the times and speak like the time period in which they were turned.

"I was twenty-two when I turned. I would be twenty-four now."

"So, you've only been a vampire for two years now?" I ask, a little surprised. I don't think I've ever met a vampire so young before. "Do you know who turned you?"

She refuses to meet my eyes but answers anyway. "Yes, his name is Caesar Leon."

Caesar? Why does that name sound so familiar? Then it hits me. I've read about a Caesar in our history books.

"That can't be right," I tell her. "He's an ancient. Caesar is in our kind's history books as one of the oldest known vampires. He hasn't been seen for almost half a century. Are you sure that's who turned you?"

She shrugs. "I mean, that's what he goes by. I guess he could have been lying, or maybe he hasn't been seen by hunters, but I worked for him for six months before he turned me. I saw him almost every night. There is a chance we are talking about two different Caesars entirely."

Caesar... Caesar... Lebeau. That's his last name. In *History of the Ancients* Caesar Lebeau is said to be the first ancient to cross the seas to make his mark on the new world. This can't be the same vampire, could it? How easy would it be to alter your name throughout the centuries?

This vampire who turned Sarah isn't even on our radar. The thought that he has his eyes on the woman sitting next to me is disturbing—and enraging.

"I'm going to need you to tell me your story right now," I demand, my words coming out more harshly than I intended.

She stops clacking around on her laptop, and with a sigh she turns, narrowing her eyes at me. "Not until you give me some answers. I've answered all your questions, and you haven't answered any of mine."

"That's not how this works," I bark back, although I'm not sure why I'm being so rude. Am I angry at her, or for her? Maybe it's just that I'm not used to talking with a vampire so casually. There's usually minimal conversation between all the chasing and stabbing stakes through hearts.

I admit, when I first approached her tonight, I couldn't help but give her a once-over. She's wearing shorts, and those honey-colored legs leading up to her curvy hips have me whirling. Why does she have to be wearing fucking shorts? We are in November, for crying out loud.

A tall, dark, good-looking man approaches us from behind the bar, shaking me loose of my inappropriate thoughts.

"Can I get you anything?" he asks me sharply.

"No, I'm fine," I snap back, just as sharply. I need him to leave so I can continue my interrogation.

"Sarah," he says, turning his eyes to her and softening a bit. "Is this man bothering you?"

A twinge of jealousy passes through me. *They know each other?* Of course they do. She seems to know everyone in this damn diner.

I don't like the way she smiles up at him.

"No, Sam, I'm fine," she says sweetly to him. "This is a friend. He's helping fact-check some things for my book. We're just having a bit of a disagreement on how to proceed in this next chapter, but I'm reminding him that this is my book, and we are going to do things my way."

He smiles at her, showing off his pristine white teeth.

"Thatta girl," he says, never taking his eyes off her. "I'll be close by if you need backup."

She gives a small nod. "Thanks, Sam."

I roll my eyes when he leaves. "Can we go talk somewhere else? Preferably somewhere we can't be interrupted by your boyfriend," I ask, still annoyed at this Sam person, and wondering precisely what their relationship is.

"He's not my boyfriend. He's my friend," she clarifies. "And why would I go anywhere with you? For all I know, your hunter friends are waiting in the alley out back so you all can ambush and kill me."

I flinch at the thought of her dying, although I don't know why. "I told you before, I came alone. You can trust me."

She scoffs. "I don't trust you. I don't even know you. All I know about you is that you're a hunter who kills people like me, and that you're rude."

I sigh. She's not wrong. I have given her every reason to stay away from me. All I've done is try to kill her. She doesn't even know that she drives me crazy, that she confuses me beyond comprehension. I want her. But I shouldn't. Instinct tells me to drive a stake through her heart, but every nerve inside my body is screaming to touch her, to hold her, to make her squirm beneath my fingers, and not out of fear.

I find her staring at me, studying my expression as if she's trying to decipher the thoughts flittering across my mind. Before I can stop myself, I say, "You're right. I don't mean to be rude. I'm finding it hard to concentrate because you are, without a doubt, the most beautiful woman I have ever met, and the only thing I want to do to you in the back alley is push you against the wall and learn what it feels like to have those lips on mine."

Silence.

*What the fuck is wrong with me?*

Her jaw actually drops, and I can't help but feel pleasure at the reaction I'm getting from her for my sudden outburst.

Still, I can't be with her like that. No matter how much I might want to.

"Kael," she whispers a bit breathless. The way she says my name sends jolts of electricity through my body. "You cannot just say things like that to me—or to anyone. It's illegal."

I smirk. I can't help it. Everything about her is addictive. I crave this. "Is it?"

"If it's not, it should be."

Maybe this is the way to get the answers I want. That's the only reason I have for doing what I do next. I lean into her, so I can whisper in her ear. "If I promise not to kill you or kiss you, will you come take a walk with me?"

She swallows hard. "And you promise to answer my questions?" she inquires softly.

"Yes, you answer mine, and I'll answer yours."

She shuts her laptop with a slightly trembling hand.

"Okay, we can go for a walk, but I'm still swooning over what you just said, so if I fall, you'll have to catch me," she says as she gets up from her chair. She slowly starts packing her laptop into her bag and secures the strap across her chest.

Her transparency is exciting. I smirk. "I won't let you fall; I promise."

Now that she's standing, I give her a full once-over. This is the first time I've seen her standing up so close to me without us fighting.

She's several inches shorter than I am. I guess about five-five to my six feet.

Her hair falls around her face as she adjusts the strap of her bag. I wait for what I know is coming. Sure enough, she reaches and tucks one side of her hair behind her ear.

I don't want to notice these intimate details about her, yet at the same time I want to learn more—everything.

*Fuck. I'm in trouble.*

# Chapter 10
# Sarah

*WHAT IN THE SEVEN hells was that?* Kael telling me what he wants to do to me in the back alley will be in my dreams tonight—and every night for the rest of eternity.

I like him, which is so not in my best interest. My body tingles when he gets near me. Is that a vampire thing? The only person with whom I have any physical contact is Adam. Of course, Adam and I are all hugs, high fives, and platonic cuddles. I definitely don't feel this intense longing when Adam touches me.

It's like my whole body came alive the few times Kael and I have touched.

I can't help but glance toward the alley as we walk by. *Oh, wall, what I wouldn't give to be sandwiched between you and Kael?*

I wonder if he was serious, or if he just said that to distract me? If it's the latter, then it worked.

"Hey."

I turn to Kael. He clearly just said something to me. Crap. "Umm... sorry. I didn't hear you. We just passed the alley," I say with a point of my finger, biting my lower lip. "Trying not to swoon."

He narrows his eyes. "We can put the talking on hold if you want," he says with a suggestive raise of his eyebrow.

*Stop that,* I chastise him in my mind. I didn't think this beautiful, chiseled man even made jokes.

"No, no," I say. "We barely know each other. I don't know how much of an 'up against the wall' kind of girl I am. That"— I gesture to the alley with the wave of my hand— "would not be a good idea. Stop distracting me. I want to know what being a *Validus* means."

He gives a devilish grin before nodding. He tells what he knows. My brain is spinning after he's done talking. Apparently, he just learned it himself, having heard it from one of his hunter friends the other night.

I'm vaguely aware that he is leading me to a nearby park.

He gives me a moment or two to take it all in. "Are you okay? What are you thinking about?"

*Everything*, I think to myself, but what I say out loud is, "I'm thinking that the phrase *Vampire with a Soul* would be a great title for the first book of a new vampire series I'm considering writing." Even though that is just a small part of what I'm really thinking.

He smiles. "What is the new book going to be about?"

"A vampire and a werewolf fall in love. Your classic forbidden-love story."

"So, you're an author? Do you have any published books?"

I nod, "Yes, just the one, but it did well enough that I'm writing my second one now. It will be a trilogy in the end. My turn, that was three questions in a row I just answered," I say quickly. I can tell he's used to being the one in charge. Making decisions. Taking conversations where he wants them to go. A man in control. I try not to let the thought of all the other ways he might like to take control sizzle in the back of my mind.

He sighs, but says, "Alright, shoot. What's your next question?"

"So, to be a *Validus*, you have to have hunter blood in your veins, but I'm not sure that I do. I'm adopted, so I don't know who my birth parents are. My mom and dad, my adopted mom and dad," I clarify, "died in a car accident seven years ago, so I can't really ask them about it. The humanity thing seems to track. I know that I feel just as I did when I was human. I still love and care about people. I'm not a murderer."

"I'm sorry to hear about your parents, but none of what you just said is a question," he tells me, not unkindly.

"My question is, is there a way to find out who my birth parents are? Do you have any hunter family trees I can go through?"

Do I even want that? I've been secretly angry with my birth parents for giving me up. I always told myself that I didn't need to find them. I had two parents who actually loved and wanted me. But this *Validus* stuff changes things. If my birth parents are hunters, then maybe they gave me up for a reason?

He thinks for a moment. "I'm not sure, to be honest. I'll have to get back with you on that one."

I'm both relieved and disappointed by his answer. I'm not sure how much I'm ready for the truth. I've spent years in one perceived reality. This new information could shatter that reality into pieces. Then what?

He jumps right into his next question, taking me out of my thoughts about my heritage. "Have you ever killed someone?"

I look over at him. I can see that he's been wanting to ask me this particular question for a while now.

"No," I say, shaking my head, wondering how different his reaction would be if I said yes. "I have never killed a person. I've fed off people when I first turned, but I've always been able to stop well before any damage can happen. Now, though, I drink from blood bags."

He gives me a questioning look.

"I steal them from hospitals," I say sheepishly. "I know. I know. I'm a horrible person. I just don't like to risk drinking from people. So much can go wrong. What if I take too much, or what if they try to tell others what happened to them? I know vampires have the Jedi mind trick thing, but it doesn't last forever. And isn't supernatural secrecy like the number one rule for all of us?"

He nods in agreement. "I guess. The mages tend to deal with keeping the humans from knowing too much. They have their own council and everything. Although hunters have a seat on the MC, it's run by the mages," he tells me.

"MC?"

"Mage Council," he says. "Did you not know about them?"

I shake my head. "Definitely not. I've never met a witch or warlock, or a werewolf. Are faeries a thing?"

"Seriously, vampire?" he asks. "It's like you were created yesterday. How do you know so little of our world?"

"First of all, my name is Sarah," I inform him for the second time tonight. *Why does he keep doing that?* Is he refusing to call me by my name on purpose, or does he think me so far beneath him that he doesn't even bother remembering it?

"Second of all," I continue, "it's true, I don't know much about our world. I've always felt stuck between two worlds, somehow unable to fully step into either. I'm a vampire who isn't evil. I didn't ask for this. It was forced on me. It's not like I'm just going to go and join VampireTok online or anything."

He pauses, his Adam's apple bobbing before asking, "What's VampireTok?"

Something in his eyes tells me that's not what he wanted to ask, but I give him a questioning look anyway. "Obviously, I'm kidding. I doubt there is a VampireTok. It's like TikTok, but for vampires."

He shakes his head.

"Never mind," I say. "I guess hunters don't really live in the real world, either."

"Our world *is* the real world. It's humans who don't truly know the world they are living in. To answer your question, yes, faeries are real. We call them the fae, and they're just as dangerous to humans as vampires are. They have magic beyond what mages have, and they used it to trap and torture humans. Luckily, they are now stuck in their own lands, underground, away from ours, as are all other supernatural creatures aside from vampires and werewolves."

"The faerie lands are underground?" I ask, intrigued.

"No, that's more of a saying. It's like a realm adjacent to ours."

"Is there a way to get there?"

He shakes his head. "No. A thousand years ago, the MC and hunters banded together and trapped them in the faerie underground so that they could no longer travel between realms. The few that were left on our side were hunted down to extinction.

"Of course, vampires were supposed to be trapped in the faerie courts as well, but someone with magic created more vampires here in this realm. Those vampires started creating more of their kind at a rapid pace and soon the mages realized that they would never be able to extinguish the vampires fully."

"What about the werewolves?"

"The werewolves don't pose a threat to humans in the way the fae and vampires do. Their curse is more of a genetic thing passed down from generation to generation. They only turn once a month, and in their werewolf state, they only hunt their mortal enemy—vampires. That's why we don't have werewolf hunters. If anything, they help us rid the world of your kind."

I nod. "Sweet spear of Ares, that's a lot to take in." Thankfully, I've never come across a werewolf before.

He side-eyes me and smirks, but doesn't say anything.

We arrive at the park. It's well past midnight, so we are the only ones here. He leads me to a set of swings, and we each take a seat side by side. If the circumstances were different, this might be considered a cute first date.

"I think it's my turn now," he says, as he gently sways back and forth on the swing, his feet never leaving the ground.

"Why didn't you ever join the city coven? Wouldn't that have made things easier for you? Just stay with the one that turned you?"

I take a moment to consider my answer. From his perspective, it would have made things easier for me. But I doubt he truly understands what it's like to be a vampire with a soul. I barely do. But, I knew I couldn't entirely give up my human life. Human feelings and urges and desires still stir within me. "Because I didn't want to. They, apparently, don't have souls, and I do. It makes more sense why I didn't fit in there. I guess, in reality, Mr. Leon turned me, but I think of it more as he murdered me. I'm technically dead because of him. Why would I want to be in his coven?"

It's clear by the furrow of his brow that he's shocked by my declaration. "That's a good point," he says slowly, like this way of looking at it is just occurring to him.

Neither one of us says anything for a short while, but I don't want him to get up and leave, so I continue on with the questions. "Okay, I think it's my turn now."

"Ask me whatever you want," he says, this time with no sign or hint of annoyance.

"Are you going to kill me?" I ask, though I'm scared to hear the answer.

He flinches ever so slightly, which I take as a good sign. "No," he says firmly, which fills me with relief. "Although, I can't make that same promise about other hunters," he adds. "I already told you I wouldn't try to kill or kiss you tonight."

"The fact that kissing was ever on the table means you don't have a girlfriend?" I'm shocked by my own question, but it's out in the open now, hanging in the air like a suffocating toxin.

He arches a brow at me, rubbing his fingers over his bottom lip before saying, "No. My line of work leaves little room for committed relationships. To be honest, I usually just stick with staying casual in all my romantic relationships."

"Oh," I say, unable to hide the disappointment in my voice. "Casual isn't really my thing."

He nods. "Yeah, I kind of figured that out on my own."

I want to slap myself. As if he cares what my thing is or not. It's not like he's interested. Attracted to me, maybe, but not interested.

"Oh, God," I say a little too loudly. Something horrible just occurred to me. "If I have hunter blood in my veins, does that mean we could be related?"

Kael laughs. "I doubt it. There are thousands of hunter families all over the world. Is there a particular reason being related to me would be so terrible?" He gives me a knowing smirk that makes me think he knows exactly why it would be terrible.

*If we were related, I would have to go wash my brain out with soap.*

I shake my head. "No reason. Your turn to ask me a question," I say quickly, trying hard to move on from this sexually awkward-on-my-part moment.

Thankfully, he doesn't press further and asks me some random questions about my life since becoming a vampire.

We stay in the park talking for hours. He asks more about my published book, about my upcoming book, my parents, and Adam. I, in turn, ask about his life as a hunter. He tells me about the Academy.

It's an hour before sunrise when we finally start to say our goodbyes. Kael tells me that he won't try to hunt me anymore. There's a weird finality hanging between us. I become acutely aware that this might be the last time I see him.

There's no more reason for us to interact, and the realization leaves me feeling somber.

"So, I guess this is it," he says solemnly. "See you in the afterlife, vampire." And with that, he turns and vamp-speeds away. Technically, I guess, for him, it would be, vamp-hunter-speeds away.

Kael has opened up my world in just one night. *A Validus?* What does that truly mean, and could I really be one? Can I truly be descended from a vampire hunter line?

There are so many things I need to wrap my head around. One being that Kael Hart, the vampire hunter, is no longer a threat to my life, but Kael Hart, the gorgeous, mysterious man, is dangerous for me in more ways than one.

# Chapter 11
# Sarah

To my surprise and delight, Kael found me the very next night at the diner again. In fact, he has come to find me three more times in the past week.

I waited at the diner every night in anticipation of seeing him again. He didn't always show, having to hunt with his squad some nights.

When he did show, he always had more questions for me. Some started to get personal. He wants to know all about the week after I was turned, how I coped, what I've learned from trial and error.

I've wanted to tell him more about my time with the coven, but I'm not sure if I'm ready to dive back into that part of my life. I've answered the best I can, without going into too much detail. Still, I know I'm not giving him enough. But, that may be the very reason he keeps coming back to find me, and I'm not ready to truly say goodbye yet.

He realized that I know hardly anything about this supernatural world I now live in. So instead, I've started asking him questions, which he seems not to mind. He's told me a little more about mages, werewolves, and the latest hot topic, faeries. But sadly, those are the ones he knows least about.

"Obviously, I've never seen one, and we don't spend much time learning about them now that they are banished to another realm and extinct in this one," he told me.

I convinced him to meet me at a Mexican restaurant and bar for tonight's round of questioning, eager to keep this going. Kael is my only connection to the world of vampires, and I've been enjoying his company as much as learning more about my kind. I also wanted to meet somewhere other than the diner. Mrs. May and Mr. George might start asking questions if they keep seeing us together.

I'm waiting at the table when he walks in. He isn't wearing his usual jeans and black T-shirt that I've grown used to seeing on him. Ninety percent of the time, when he's not wearing his hunting leathers, he's wearing jeans and a tee, mostly black, but every once in a while, he'll change it up with a different dark color: hunter green or dark gray.

Tonight, however, he's wearing black jeans and a royal-blue cashmere sweater. The sleeves are rolled up to the elbows. I don't know why, but there's something deliciously enticing about exposed forearms. It's an aphrodisiac for me. I feel like a Victorian man seeing ankles for the first time.

With Kael's sleeves rolled up, I have to squeeze my legs together and hope I don't spontaneously combust in an orgasmic explosion.

Several people take notice of him as soon as he walks in. Girls start taming their hair and adjusting their bras, hoping Kael will pick them to entertain.

He takes a quick scan before spotting me. I wave as he approaches.

"What made you decide to meet here?" he asks as he takes a seat across from me.

I shrug and take a small sip of the water I ordered when I first got the table. "It's dark and misty, and it's not too crowded on weeknights."

He gives a small smirk and says, "I don't know if misty is considered a perk."

"Misty is fine. What you don't want is a place to be murky."

Kael rocks his head back in laughter, and I can't help but join in. I love his laugh. It's deep and throaty, and I feel as though I'm getting something rare from him.

Our server comes over and reintroduces herself, her attention immediately on Kael. She's about my age with piercings on her ears, nose, eyebrow and chin, along with tattoos covering every visible part of her body.

She didn't seem too happy that all I ordered was water, and I'm sure she is hoping now that my dinner companion has arrived, we will order properly.

"What can I get started for you, hun?" she asks him.

When he just orders water, she gives him a devil's glare and stalks away.

I look at him questionably. "Aren't you going to order something? I can pay for it, if that's the reason you aren't ordering," I say, hoping that offering to pay doesn't offend or step on his man-toes in any way.

"No, that's not the reason. I'm just not hungry," he tells me. "Besides, this isn't a date. This is business."

I give him an exasperated look. Every time we've met up, he's made it a point to clarify that our encounters are for "business purposes." Whether he does it to remind himself or me, I'm unsure. Either way, it's getting old. There is no way I'm the only one enjoying us being around each other. No way the attraction and intrigue are one-sided. But, it's like one minute we are having fun and he's letting his guard down, and the next he's snipping at me and calling me vampire. Like I'm the most disgusting creature on the planet.

"Okay," I say, crossing my hands over my chest. "What is it that you need to ask me now?"

"I want to know the story of how you were turned and how you escaped," he says in a stern and demanding voice that instills no argument. We've been dancing around this topic for a while, and I can see he's tired of me dodging the question.

I furrow my brow. "How is that going to help you any?"

"I just want to know," he tells me. "Please."

His "please" does me in, and besides, I want him to know. Keeping this part of my origin story a secret has weighed heavily on me. It would be nice to share the burden. And I can't deny that I want him to know everything about me. I want him to see all of me. Maybe it's some fucked up test. Maybe I finally want someone to know the real me. "Fine, but it's not an interesting story," I mutter.

"I'm okay with that."

I let out a breath, tucking a strand of hair behind my ear. *Here goes nothing.*

"Okay well, two years ago I got a job for this company that buys out other companies to... well, I'm not sure what they do with the companies once they own them. I worked in a small cubicle on the fifth floor and was the assistant to one of the sales leaders."

Kael nods along, as if waiting for the real story to begin, but I'm the narrator. I will tell this story how I see fit. He's just going to have to strap in for the ride.

71

"Anyway, the company throws a big Christmas party every year on the top floor of the building. That was the first time I'd ever seen Mr. Leon. I'm not sure what I did to make him notice me, but he did. He asked me to dance, which I did. I was not about to tell the man who signs my checks 'no.' Plus, I was a little less strong-willed as a human. Becoming a vampire changed me in that way. Made me more confident."

Kael smirks at that, which surprises me. I didn't think he would like me admitting anything good about becoming a vampire.

"So, he asked if I wanted a promotion to be his personal assistant, which I of course said yes to. It felt like I was moving up the corporate ladder. Before I knew it, I moved from Leon Tower to his personal penthouse, which is where he worked from. I spent my nights going there to essentially follow him around and schedule his meetings. He told me he had a skin disease that didn't allow him to work during the day. I didn't think anything of it at first."

My voice drops down to an almost whisper. I'm afraid it would shake too much at reliving this particular part of my story. "I only worked as his personal assistant for a month before he attacked me. That was the night I died. When I woke, I was a vampire."

# Chapter 12
# Sarah

## Two Years Earlier

"Ugh," I groan as I open my eyes, rubbing my tender neck. I look at my surroundings and groan again.

Still here. I was hoping to wake from this nightmare. It's been exactly twenty-four hours since I was put into this room. No one has come to check on me, or tell me what's going on. The door is locked, and no matter how much I bang on it, no one comes.

I'm aware that something happened to me. I get flashes of Mr. Leon attacking me and twisting my neck before everything went dark. Maybe I'm still in shock, or maybe this is some crazy drug-induced nightmare. Kinda hoping for the latter. Although, being kidnapped isn't exactly best-case scenario. Being dead but not at the same time is unimaginable.

As far as prison rooms go, this one is quite extravagant. It's bigger than my whole studio apartment with a California King bed, which has the softest duvet ever, and a wooden four-poster bed frame with intricate carvings. Thick, floor to ceiling curtains cover the windows, and huge hourglass-shape, stone base lamps stand in the corners while decorative crystal bowls sit on the side tables. Seriously, this is the most expensive room I have ever stayed in. It's a perfect mixture of vintage and modern.

I get up and make my way to the bathroom. There is a nice, oversized whirlpool tub in the corner, which, under different circumstances, I would want to drown in for hours until my fingers and toes wrinkled, but these aren't different circumstances.

I make my way to the sink, splashing cold water on my face to help clear my head. My throat burns, and I'm hungry. It feels like my stomach has begun eating itself, and the hunger has turned to nausea. I need to get out of here.

I hear the doorknob turning in the bedroom, which has me running out of the bathroom, but I lose balance and go crashing into the wall instead.

*Bloody hell, what just happened?* One second, I'm in the bathroom and the next... It's like I was The Flash. *How did I run so fast?*

My boss, Caesar Leon, rushes in and is by my side in an instant. "Sarah, my darling, you must be cautious of your new abilities. Don't worry, in time you will learn to control them."

He offers me his hand and I shakily take it, not really knowing what's happening.

"You killed me," I say frantically. Voicing it out loud is frightening, making it seem too real.

Every fantasy book I've ever read comes crashing into my mind.

"You're a vampire, aren't you, and you made me a vampire too?" I ask in a half-shout.

I wait for my pulse to quicken, but it doesn't. I don't even breathe heavily. It's strange; getting upset and not having my body respond accordingly, except, I can still feel my cheeks heat.

He guides me to the bed and sits beside me, gently brushing the hair away from my face. I pull away from his touch.

He allows it, lowering his hand to his lap. "You were always so intelligent, Miss Greenwood. Yes, I've turned you into a vampire, like myself and everyone else in this penthouse, but unlike everyone else in the penthouse, you are special. I want you by my side as my queen, Sarah. You and I will do extraordinary things together."

I flinch at his words. He sounds delusional, and I want to tell him he's batshit crazy if he thinks I will submit like this after what he's done to me. But at the same time, I'm acutely aware that this man could kill me again in a heartbeat if he wanted to. Permanently, this time.

"And if I refuse?" I ask carefully, lifting my chin in defiance.

"You won't," he says. "It may take time, but you will come around." And with that, he stands up, straightens his suit, nods to the guard at the door who followed him in, and then leaves, leaving me with a million unanswered questions.

I'm not sure if I'm happy to see him go, or angry. I rush to the door just as it slams shut in my face, getting there faster than I wanted to. All I did was look at Mr. Leon exit, with a desperate need to follow him, and before I knew it, it's like I transported from the bed to the door. It takes a second for my mind to catch up to my body. My hand flies to the door handle, but it's once again locked. In frustration, I twist and yank on the doorknob with all my might, and to my utter surprise the doorknob breaks; the wood around the knob splinters and cracks.

No time to dwell on that now as I kick the door off its hinges. The rush of power is exciting. Two men are standing right outside my door, looking frustrated with me.

"Great," one of the men scoffs. "Now we have to get that fixed. You're not allowed to leave the room."

"Like hell I'm staying in there one more night," I bark back, trying and failing to get around him.

I hear the other one sigh behind me. "I got this."

Before I can turn or respond I feel his large hands cup my face, and I feel a sharp pain, before everything goes black.

*** 

I test my strength on the second night when I again break down the door in an attempt to escape, but, as I soon find out, Mr. Leon has bodyguards posted outside my door at all times. The next day, the door is replaced once again, as if nothing had ever happened.

I try jumping from my window the next night, but more vampire bodyguards are stationed right outside. Apparently, they are all over this place.

My failed escape attempt outside, however, is how I found out that I'm not in the city anymore, or at least not at the penthouse. I'm in a mansion surrounded by a field of wild flowers... somewhere.

I finally learn my lesson on trying to escape after the third day. Every time I do anything to piss off the guards, they break my neck rendering me unconscious for almost an hour. I've stopped trying because I don't like the idea of them grabbing or touching me while I'm knocked out.

Mr. Leon waits six days before visiting my room again. At least I think it's six days. I'm starting to lose all sense of time, more importantly, how much of it has passed since I was locked in this room.

Mr. Leon enters wearing an expensive suit, as always, looking like the CEO to Leon Tower, which, until nine days ago, was all I knew him to be.

Now when I look at him, I see the man who has kidnapped me and stolen my life by turning me into someone like him—a vampire. I'm still adjusting to this information. It's a lot to take in.

He walks over to the bed and sits next to me. I want to move away, but don't want to show weakness, so I just stay put.

"Good evening, Miss Greenwood. Taylor here tells me that you've been giving the guards a bit of a hard time?" he asks, a slight smirk etched on his lips.

I look over at the big, burly man standing just inside the door. He was the same one who came in with Mr. Leon the first time. I turn back to Mr. Leon and shrug.

"I just want to go home," I tell him.

He sighs heavily. "You are home, my dear. Are you ready to accept your fate and join me by my side, Sarah?" he asks in a cold voice.

"Umm, no, I'm not interested. So, if you can just please let me go," I bite out, letting anger win out over fear.

He smiles like I've said something amusing. "Sarah, darling, you have such fire in you. This is why you are perfect," he says as he strokes my hair. I shy away from his touch, but he doesn't seem to notice, or he does, but ignores it.

"Why me? I'm nobody," I say softly. *What use am I to him?*

"You are more special than you even know," he says, reaching over to grab my hand. I quickly yank it away.

He stands and straightens his suit. "I have to go away for a while. Perhaps, when I return, you will be ready."

"Where are you going?" I ask, getting to my feet.

"Overseas," he tells me.

"What?" I say in horror. "How long will you be gone?"

I hate this man for what he did to me, but he is the only person who talks to me in the place. Will I just be trapped alone in this room until he returns?

"A few years," he answers nonchalantly, like it's no big deal.

"Years?" I say with a squeak. "I'm just supposed to stay here for years waiting for you to return?"

"My darling, Sarah. You are immortal now. Years are but a grain of salt in the ocean of life you have," he says, softly brushing his fingers along the side of my cheek.

I recoil from his touch, but he just smiles and walks away.

"You can't leave me here," I shout, but it's no use. He walks out the door without a second glance.

The next few days go by in a blur.

Two days after he leaves, some vampire bodyguard shoves a crying human girl into my room and shuts the door quickly. By now, the hunger has become unbearable, and just at the sight of her, my fangs involuntarily pop out. They've been doing that on and off, mostly when I'm thinking of my hunger, which is definitely now.

I can feel her heartbeat, hear the delicious blood running through her veins as loud as a waterfall. I watch her scurry to the farthest corner of the room and curl up in a ball.

I can't do it. There is no way I can feed off this terrified girl, but holy Count Dracula, does she smell good. My throat feels dry and scratchy, and when I swallow there is a burning sensation that I know will be soothed by her thick blood. I vaguely wonder what will happen to her if I bite her. Will she turn into a vampire like I did? Is that all it takes? Mr. Leon bit and killed me, so maybe just biting isn't enough, but will it kill her?

I close my eyes to help fight these new instincts of mine. The need to bite into her flesh and taste that salty, thick liquid. The thought of drinking blood should repulse me, but it doesn't. Not even close.

I run at full speed into the bathroom and lock the door behind me, like that'll do anything. One swift kick and the door would come crumbling down. Still, the distance helps a little. The smell is less pungent here, less overwhelming.

She's someone's daughter, sister, and friend. I remind myself this over and over again. I give her a name. Hope. She looks like a Hope. Hope is scared and just wants to go home. Hope might even have a boyfriend or girlfriend waiting for her. Let's not forget that Hope is going to college to be an environmental scientist. She is going to save the world someday.

But if I kill her, then all that goes away. All her hopes. All her dreams. Which is why I'm going to stay in this bathroom. I will not think about blood. Only Hope.

At some point she stops crying, and hours later I hear someone walk in, probably shocked to see the girl still alive. I hear them take her out without a word, and I can't help the tears that begin streaming down my face. Did I do anything but prolong her life for a few hours? Deep down, I know that Hope is lost.

Days go by at a slow, agonizing pace before anyone steps foot inside my room again. I'm going wild with thirst. It's all I can think about. Can a vampire die if it never feeds on someone? Thankfully, I don't have to find out.

On day number eight, or maybe it's day nine of Mr. Leon leaving, the door opens and a different male guard ushers in a middle-aged white man in a cheap suit. This man does not need to be dragged or tossed in like the young woman. He walks right in like it's his room.

"Are you the girl?" he asks excitedly. "You are so beautiful."

"Umm, what do you think you are here for?" I ask quizzically. Did they trick him into thinking this is something else?

I see the ghost of a smile on the vampire bodyguard as he closes the door, leaving me and the human man alone in the room.

Immediately, my mouth starts to water. The scent of his blood hits me like a truck. I'm losing control over my senses. There's nothing but the hunger.

"You're going to suck my blood, are you not?" he inquires, striding over to me. He begins unbuttoning the cuffs of his shirt.

Okay, so this man definitely knows why he's here. When he starts unbuttoning the top of his button-down, I quickly throw my hands out to stop him.

"Whoa, mister, what in the seven rings of Saturn are you doing?" I shout, my fangs coming out without my permission at the sight of his jugular, pulsing and ready for me.

He looks at me curiously. "I'm taking off my shirt so you can bite me," he answers, like it should have been obvious. "Do you prefer my neck or wrist? If it's all the same to you, I would like you to suck from my neck."

Somewhere in the back of my mind, I know this man is crazy... or disgusting. But I'm so hungry it's hard to care. "So, you're not at all scared that I'm a vampire?"

The man shakes his head and looks at me with a tinge of hope and awe glinting in his eyes. He's not afraid of me one bit. "No, I've always wanted to be bitten by a beautiful vampire. I would love to be made by you and hopefully mated."

"Mated?" I ask in horror. I've grown to hate this word. But as he steps closer, my desperation takes over. He's so close. The blood coursing through his veins so tempting. I can feel how weak I've become, and I'm really not in the mood to find out how long vampires can last without sustenance.

I narrow my eyes and take a step toward him. "I don't want to kill you, but I need blood."

He nods feverishly. "Yes, yes, of course, it's why I'm here. What's your name?"

I shake my head. "No, no," I say sternly. "No need to exchange names."

I can't believe I'm about to do this. The second he offers up his wrist, I can't hold back a second longer. Without another word, I yank his hand up to my mouth. I take a deep breath and then instantly regret it. The smell of his blood is overwhelming. I pierce my fangs through his skin right into his veins.

He lets out a small yelp as blood gushes into my mouth. I feel a sensation I've never felt before. It's euphoric. I drink and drink and drink. After a long moment, I can hear someone yelling to stop, begging even, but I don't care. The voice seems to be coming from a distance, an echo compared to the all-encompassing ecstasy

79

reverberating through me right now. I can feel every muscle getting stronger with each ounce I gulp down. I've never felt power like this before. It's intoxicating.

"Please," the man cries. He starts fighting me, but it's like an ant trying to fight an elephant for all the good he's doing. Still, something in me finally registers that I'm taking too much blood from him, and I jump back like someone has lit a match between us. I'm on the other side of the room in an instant.

"I'm sorry," I say quickly, wiping at my mouth, blood staining my hand. "Are you okay?" My mind is clear now. All thoughts aren't centered around my ebbing hunger.

He sinks to the floor, clasping his hand to his chest. For a second, I'm worried that I took too much blood, but he turns to me and gives a toothy smile.

"That was amazing. Should we have sex now?"

*So gross.* How is it that he's the one who was bitten and drank from, but I'm the one who feels violated?

I scoff and yell at the door. "Okay, vamp guards, you can take him away now."

The door opens, and one of the two men guarding the entrance walks in. He goes straight to the crazy fetish guy and begins to haul him away. The man struggles, yelling something about how this isn't what they promised him.

I don't know what comes over me. Maybe it's the sudden powerful energy boost that drinking blood for the first time gives me, but I'm behind the vampire in a second. I grab his neck and twist hard. I'm not sure if I'm doing it right, but sure enough, his lifeless body drops to the ground. Well, they've done it to me enough times. A little payback is in order.

The creepy guy is incapacitated by shock.

The other vampire turns and shouts, "What's going on?"

I'm by his side in a second, breaking his neck in that same moment. The sound of bones breaking resounds through my ears as he hits the ground. Surprise is definitely on my side, because neither of the guards had time to shout or react in any way.

I run out the door at top speed, not stopping to think about anything but getting out of here. Someone in the heavens loves me, because it's just turning dusk outside. There doesn't seem to be any guards on patrol yet, maybe because just minutes ago they might have burned from daylight.

I vaguely hear someone running after me, but I pick up my speed and run toward the woods that I see in the distance, which I don't remember being there in my last escape attempt.

After about an hour of non-stop running, I realize I'm not being chased anymore, but it doesn't matter. I keep going and don't stop. I'm not sure where or what is supposed to happen next.

# Chapter 13
# Sarah

KAEL STAYS SILENT THROUGHOUT my story. Only the subtle shifts in his face, or the clenching of his jaw, let me know he is affected by my words.

"I changed my name from Sarah Greenwood to Sarah Summers, moved out of my apartment, and found Adam. We only kept in minimal touch since college, so I knew no one at the company would know that he and I knew each other. He let me move in with him. I kept the secret from him for a while, but he started questioning why I never left the apartment during the day, so I ended up telling him the truth."

I let out a heavy sigh. "And now two years later, here I am. No Mr. Leon in sight. Although, I expect he will come and find me one day. Time doesn't seem to be a big thing for him." I'm not sure what holds me back from telling Kael about my recent encounter with Taylor, Mr. Leon's personal bodyguard. Like ignoring it will make the whole thing go away.

Surprisingly, Kael reaches for my hand and I let him take it, noting that this is the first time we've ever touched in such an intimate way. I hate how much I love it.

"I'm sorry that happened to you," is all he says.

I shrug. "What's done is done. I don't plan to ever see him again. I'm kind of hoping he's forgotten about me." It's a fool's hope. I know from running into Taylor that Mr. Leon is back. Taylor would have told him that he saw me. I don't know much about Mr. Leon, but I remember how desperate he was to make me his queen. Now that he knows I'm alive, how far will he go to get me back? Or has he found himself another queen?

"Well, I'll help you kill him if he hasn't," Kael tells me.

I give him a small smile. "Thank you, I think. Is it weird to be grateful someone is willing to help murder another person with you?"

"He's not a person; he's a vampire."

"So am I," I tell him, hurt by his comment, but it's not like I didn't know that this is how he feels. He's made it very clear that he despises vampires.

He pulls his hand back, the ghost of his touch still lingering. I miss it already.

He stares at me for a moment without saying a word. I can't take it any longer and I say, "We should probably head out. The server keeps giving us the evil eye, since we're just sitting here."

He nods slowly, and together we stand. I pull out my wallet and place a ten-dollar bill on the table, which makes Kael arch an eyebrow.

"What are you doing?" he questions.

"I'm leaving a tip," I inform him. "It's not her fault that we didn't order anything, and you know she lives on tips. I would feel awful if we sat at her table only drinking water and didn't leave her anything."

Kael stares at me, with a new look that I can't quite decipher on his face. "I never thought about that before."

"Of course *you* didn't," I say teasingly. "You're a hunter. Your job is to protect the humans, but you don't really live amongst the humans."

"But you thought about it, leaving a tip for the waitress."

I look at him in confusion. "Yeah, so?"

He shakes his head. "It's nothing." He takes out his wallet and puts another ten on the table, which makes me smile.

As we walk out the door, two guys are walking in. I don't look at their faces, so it surprises me when I hear my name being called.

"Sarah?"

I look at the one calling me and see Jared, my ex-boyfriend. The same ex-boyfriend whom I dumped two years ago because I had just been turned into a vampire.

He and I were about to hit our one-year anniversary when it happened. I felt awful about it. Still do, actually, but there was nothing I could have done. I became a vampire, so unless I was willing to tell him the truth about what I had become, I needed to end things.

I didn't see him taking that particular news well. Plus, I was still adjusting and coping with it myself.

"Jared, hi," I say, surprise evident in my voice. I have to look up to see his face because he's ridiculously tall, like six-three. I stand on my tippy toes as he bends down to meet me, giving an awkward two-second hug before pulling away.

"How are you?" he asks, looking at Kael, then back at me.

"I'm good," I say, taking an imperceptible step to the side, allowing me equal distance from both Kael and Jared. "How are you?"

"Good, I just finished my dissertation at Berkeley, so I'm meeting up with friends to celebrate," he tells me.

"Wow, Jared, that's amazing. I'm so happy for you," I say with excitement that I truly feel.

Jared was the best boyfriend. He was kind and smart, and although he never quite gave me the leg-tightening feels the way one look from Kael does, we were good together. I know he was heartbroken when I ended our relationship suddenly. It was a painful time for both of us.

"Thanks," he says and then looks over at Kael again. "Hi, I'm Jared. It's nice to meet you," he says, offering up his hand to Kael.

Kael takes it a little too roughly. "Kael. Nice to meet you. How do you two know each other?" he asks in a way that, if anyone on the outside was watching, they would assume he was a jealous boyfriend.

"We used to date," Jared tells him. Standing up to his full height, Jared is almost three inches taller than Kael. "But that was, of course, before you two..."

"We're not dating," I say quickly, scared at how Kael would respond. I don't want Kael to get all weird in front of Jared. I know the last thing he would want is for anyone to think he and I are dating.

Kael looks my way and gives me an arch of his brow. I don't meet his gaze. I'm just hoping he lets the moment pass without saying anything too harsh, like "I would never date anyone like her" or something of equal humiliation.

"Oh," Jared says, a little too happily. "Umm, Sarah, does that mean you're free to join me for drinks?"

Kael stiffens beside me. "She's busy," he growls.

"I'm sorry, Jared. I can't," I tell him apologetically, ignoring Kael's rude comment. "I'm consulting with Kael on a book I'm working on. We aren't quite done yet."

He smiles and shakes his head. "No worries. I best be going. The guys are waiting for me at the bar," he says, gesturing to the three guys just getting their drinks from the bartender. "It was good seeing you again, Sarah."

"It was good seeing you, too, Jared, and congratulations again. Next time I see you, I'll have to address you as Dr. Jared Gould."

He laughs. "Let's hope we run into one another soon. My number is still the same, if you ever want to catch up."

I smile and nod, but don't say anything further as Kael opens the door for me and I step outside. He and I start walking down the street together in silence.

"Old boyfriend," Kael finally says after several seconds.

I nod.

"He seems nice," Kael says flatly. "A little boring, but nice."

"He is nice, and Jared is not boring," I say, wanting to defend poor Jared, who, I have to admit, can be a bit boring at times, not that I would ever tell Kael that.

"Seems like he is still into you. Why did you two break up?"

*Why do you care?* I want to ask, but instead I say, "I broke up with him a week after I escaped. I didn't think it was fair for me to keep dating him. He deserves to be with someone alive."

"Right, makes sense."

I can see he wants to ask more questions, but seems to rule against it. We continue walking, neither of us talking, not ready to say our goodbyes just yet.

He stops suddenly, near a darkened alley.

"Listen, I think this is the last time we should meet up. There is nothing more I'm going to learn from you. To be honest, with you being so new to this world, I know way more about your kind than you do, so... This is goodbye."

Of course, he's saying that he's not coming back. He always says that.

He also has yet to call me by my name. I'm not sure what that's about. Is he scared that saying it will give me power over him, because I'm pretty sure that's Rumpelstiltskin, and it would be Kael that would have the power over me, not the other way around. I am also sure Rumpelstiltskin is a faerie, not a vampire, though I'm not one hundred percent sure of that fact.

I nod in understanding. "Okay, well, here," I say and pull a piece of paper from my pocket with my number on it. "This is just in case you think of any more questions for me." I've wanted to give him my number for days now.

He doesn't reach for it. "I'm not going to contact you," Kael tells me, his voice coming out a bit rough.

"Just in case," I say, shoving it in his hand and quickly taking a few steps back so that he can't put it back in mine.

He looks at it for a moment before putting it in his pocket. "Goodnight."

"Goodnight," I say softly and turn to leave, not wanting to linger in silent awkwardness. He's done this before, I remind myself, but somehow this goodbye feels more final than the others. There's a chance that I really won't see him again.

*Don't cry. Do not do it.* I scold myself. *Just keep walking.*

Suddenly, I feel him grab my arm and twist me toward him. His mouth finds mine like a magnet.

Kael angles his face downward, his lips consuming me with hunger and need. He moves us gracefully into the dark alley and pushes me up against the wall. My hands move to his waist, sliding up his cashmere sweater over his rock-hard abs to pull him to me. Turns out, I am most definitely an "up against the wall" kind of girl.

Strands of my hair get caught between our lips as they glide over each other, and he gently brushes them away, securing them behind my ear before resting his hand behind my neck. His other hand squeezes tightly on my hip as he pushes closer to me.

Arching my head up to give him better access, I let out a moan as he slides his tongue in to caress mine, my hands grabbing a fistful of his shirt.

I don't know if it's the heightened sense or if it's just him, but I feel—everything. His touch sends shockwaves of pleasure straight down my lower belly, pooling between my legs.

The sexual tension is almost too much to handle. My fangs feel as though they want to pop out, but I easily will them to stay away. This is not the time for that. The sudden urge to bite him elevates tenfold, but then his hand squeezes my hips once more, and the thought is replaced with the fact that I want him to touch me—everywhere.

I've never felt such desire and lust before. Is it like this for all vampires?

"This is a bad idea," he says in between kisses.

"The worst," I agree in a breathy whisper, even though that's furthest from the truth. I can't imagine anything feeling more right.

He bites my bottom lip before plunging his tongue inside my mouth once more. I moan against his mouth again, not being able to help it.

He growls. "Baby, if you make that sound again, I'm going to forget that we are in a public place and take you right here, right now."

I gasp. Hearing him call me baby has me instantly wet and ready. "I would be willing to partake in some indecent exposure," I tell him as his lips travel down to my neck, his teeth grazing my skin.

He laughs, the feel of his warm breath on my neck sending waves of pleasure all the way down to my toes. His lips find mine for a final time, but it's just to give me one last kiss before releasing me completely. Suddenly, I feel empty and cold.

What is he doing? He cannot just end it. I am far from wanting this, whatever *this* is, to be over. I want to close the distance he has put between us, but instead, I try to compose myself.

"That was..." I whisper, not really sure what that was.

"A mistake," he finishes for me. "We—I can't be with you. You know that, right? Not even in a casual way."

I flinch at his words. They cut deeper than a knife. "Yes," I say, my heart breaking just a little.

We stand there in silence for a moment.

"I should go," I say. I don't know why, but I want to leave him before he leaves me. Like it means I get to hold on to my dignity. I turn and quickly run at full vamp speed away from him.

# Chapter 14
# Kael

I CLOSE MY EYES from the sting of staring down at my phone for so long without blinking. *I could just text her. Just to see how she's doing.*

I shake my head. I can't text her. I'm done with her. No more going to find her. No more thinking about her. No more wanting her. Last night was the end of it.

*Vampire. She's a vampire.* Who has a kinder soul than most humans.

I exhale loudly. *Fuck it.*

Just as I start to write out a text, I hear a familiar voice from behind.

"Hey, man," Liam says.

I quickly delete the message and shove my phone in my pocket.

"Hey, Liam."

"Need a spotter?" he asks, gesturing to the weight bench I'm standing by.

I've been thinking about Sarah nonstop since our kiss last night. The way she tasted, the way her lips felt against mine.

Seeing that Jared guy brought up some hyper-jealous emotions that I didn't think I was capable of.

I went too far last night, but damn did she feel good pressed against me. There is just something about her that has me feeling like the sky will cave in if I'm not near her. I want to claim her, make her mine.

I inwardly sigh in frustration. This is why I came to the gym in the first place. I need to release some of this pent-up aggression. I need to take my mind off Sarah.

"Yeah, thanks," I tell Liam.

He nods, coming to help me set up the weights. Most of us hunters bench press between one to two thousand pounds. Whoever used it last did a thousand.

"How much?" Liam asks.

"One on each," I tell him.

Together, he and I get through our set before moving on to weighted squats. Thirty minutes go by, and we're both sweating, having tossed our shirts halfway through the workout.

I grab my towel and water bottle, wiping my face before taking a drink. "Where's our patrol tonight?" I ask because, although he had already mentioned it during our briefing, I wasn't paying attention.

Liam takes a seat on the bench as I hand him his towel. "Golden Gate Park. There is supposed to be a concert, so they're keeping it open late. We'll head there as soon as it's over," he informs me.

I stiffen, remembering the dream I had about the park and Sarah.

"Hey, Kael. Hey, Liam," Stacey from Annalise's squad greets us she walks in wearing workout shorts and a sports bra, showing off her toned legs and lean back. Her auburn hair is pulled up into a high ponytail.

"Hey, Stacey," Liam and I say together.

"Kael, I think you and I are both off tomorrow night if you want to come by my room," she says, adjusting the hem of her bra.

I know what she's asking, and by Liam's hiding smirk as he takes a sip of water, he knows, too. It's not uncommon for women to invite me over for the night, but somehow, it feels different—less appealing.

I can't understand why it feels wrong now, but it does.

"I can't. I'm busy," I tell her.

Her lips curve down. "Oh, are you and Carrie..."

She lets the sentence trail off. Carrie was the last hunter I was seeing casually.

"No, not because of Carrie. I'm just busy," I tell her, adding a little venom to my tone. I want this conversation to be over.

She doesn't look stunned by my roughness, just disappointed. Then again, why would she be surprised? I'm not known for my kindness.

Stacey looks at Liam, who I watch give her a sympathetic smile before she turns and stalks away.

"Sweet as ever," Liam teases as soon as Stacey is out of earshot.

I give him a stern glare that lasts about two seconds before I smirk. Liam is someone I rarely get annoyed with. He's one of my favorite people in the world.

"So, if it's not Stacey and it's not Carrie, who are you seeing on your free nights?"

I take another drink of water just to have something to do. "Who says I'm seeing anyone?"

Liam shrugs. "I just figured. Every time I've asked you if you're free on our nights off, you say you're busy. I just assumed you started seeing someone. It's not Leslie again, is it?"

"Hell no," I say. She was a disaster, promising she didn't want anything serious and then doing a complete one-eighty after spending one night together.

"Reshia?"

"Oh, for fuck's sake, will you drop it?" I demand.

It's not as though I'm the only one who likes to bed hop. We are hunters. There is no guarantee that we will survive our next patrol. Most of the adults in the Academy sleep around. I just happen to do it a tad more than others.

Liam laughs, lifting his hands in surrender. "Okay, okay. I'll stop. So, are you really busy again tomorrow night, or did you want to hang out? You clearly aren't getting laid. Unless, it's Courtney?"

I throw my towel at him. "I've never slept with Courtney. You're confusing me with Carmack."

Instead of catching the towel, Liam turns his stance so that the towel hits his shoulder before falling to the ground.

"I'm not busy tomorrow night," I tell him, my mind instantly going to Sarah. The urge to see her is growing, and I need to do something about it before I give in. "I'm free to do something."

"Awesome," Nick says. I turn to see him, and the rest of the team heading our way. "What are we doing?"

***

It's just past ten o'clock as our squad splits up and fans out through the dying crowd exiting the concert venue. Events like this are the perfect opportunity for vampires to lure tired and inebriated humans to secluded parts of the park.

"We're sensing a vampire over here," Liam informs us through the comms.

I look at Zach and he shakes his head.

"Do you want us to head your way? We're getting nothing here," I tell Liam.

Zach and I are near the Japanese Tea Garden, while Liam and Shyann are closer to Polo Field. I think Kayda and Carmack are somewhere near the Dutch Windmill at the corner of the park. We're not usually spread so thin, but Annalise's squad was called off to Geary Boulevard, where rogue vampires were sighted.

"For now, stay where you are. I think there is more than one," Liam instructs.

Zach and I are silent as we listen while scouting the area.

It's so quiet that Zach jumps a little when we hear Nick curse over the comms.

"We have three here," Nick shouts. "And a human."

"Shy and I are coming," Liam says in a rush.

"Let's go," I tell Zach, who is already running toward the fight. With our unnatural speed, we can make it there in a few minutes.

I stop short when I feel the familiar cold prickles runs across my senses, letting me know that there is a vampire nearby. It's not just any other vampire—it's her. I can feel the difference. It comes easily to me now that I've spent so much time with her; the lightness and warmth in her aura is unmistakable.

*What is she doing here?*

I've managed to refrain from using the number she gave me last night. I've made plans with the team for tomorrow night to get dinner and hang out on the Academy roof. I've done everything I possibly can to distract myself and keep my mind off Sarah, and now here she is, in danger for how close she is to my team.

*Damn it.* Zach has stopped running, too, looking around. "There's one here," he says and then tilts his head, no doubt noticing the difference. "It may be the rare one."

Kayda screams through the earpiece, making both Zach and me blanch.

"Fuck, three more appeared," Nick yells.

"We're here," Liam announces, clearly just joining the fight. With Liam there, I know they will be okay. The man is formidable in battle.

"Go," I tell Zach. "I'll take care of this one."

He looks unsure as the team continues to battle it out without us. "Are you certain?"

"Yes, go," I demand, taking out a wooden dagger from the sheath at my side.

He nods, and then he's off. *Thank God.* I take off running in the opposite direction, following Sarah's aura to the center of the Japanese Tea Garden.

I spot her lying back on a boulder, looking up at the sky, but before I fully emerge from the trees, she flashes to her feet, vigilantly looking around.

She must have heard me approach. She doesn't wait to see who found her as she takes off running. I run after her, using my hunter instincts to anticipate her next move, and ultimately cutting off her retreat by slamming her against a nearby tree. I'm careful to cushion the blow by securing my hand to the back of her head.

Sarah starts to scream, but I smash my hand against her mouth, using the hand that's holding the dagger to turn my comms piece off.

"Hush," I hiss. "What the fuck are you doing here?"

Her eyes, which are wide with fear, calm a little as she takes me in. Her whole body relaxes against the tree.

She starts to talk, but my hand is still covering her mouth. I release it, but stay pressed against her, my dagger hand moving to her waist.

Sarah doesn't even seem to care that I'm holding a weapon meant to kill her as she flexes her jaw. The trust she has in me is overwhelming. And intoxicating.

Her eyes move to my lips and settle there for a beat too long before slowly traveling up to meet my eyes.

My free hand moves to her neck as I release the dagger so I can grip her waist. *God, do I want her.* It's like a primal need deep within me. Her flushed cheeks and the pressing of her thighs tell me she wants me just as badly.

Sarah licks her lips before saying, "There was a concert here tonight."

"Yeah, I'm aware. Did you really come here for a concert? You're a vampire."

That has her lusty, hazy eyes clearing, morphing to anger. "Vampire, not recluse," she retorts.

*God damn, this woman drives me crazy.*

"You can't be here, Sarah. Do you have any idea what's going on? Are you so lost in your own world that you haven't noticed other vampires around?" I ask. Her naivety is frustrating. Other vampires could find us. Zach and the team could be heading this way any moment.

Her breath hitches, and she gives me an open, heart-wrenching smile. "You said my name."

Her joy at hearing me call her by her name for the first time thaws the thick wall I had spent so long carefully building up. I close my eyes for the briefest of moments before opening them again.

"Fuck it," I say, and slam my mouth to hers.

# Chapter 15
# Sarah

KAEL PUSHES ME HARDER against the tree as he invades my mouth with his.

The bark of the tree bites into my back, but I don't care. I welcome the pain as long as he stays crushed against me. His tongue presses long, hard strokes against mine as I kiss him back.

Kael's unrelenting in his assault, and I want more. I can take more.

I wrap my arms around his neck, my fingers traveling up and combing through his hair.

His hands are all over me, gripping the nape of my neck as the other snakes up under my shirt to cup my breast over my bra. His lips leave mine and make their way across my jaw, down my neck, all the way to my collarbone.

I arch into his touch. "Oh, Kael," I moan, loving the feel of him exploring my body with his hands, his mouth.

"You are going to be the death of me, woman," he growls.

"Please, don't stop," I beg, not wanting him to pull away like last time.

He lets out a dark chuckle against my ear. "I don't think I can. I'm not sure how much longer I can keep denying myself when it comes to you," he admits.

"Then don't," I whisper, before I grab his face and bring it back to mine.

He kisses me back, eager and wholly, his hands traveling up my body to cup my face.

"Kael, where are you?" I hear a male voice call out in the distance.

"Shit," Kael hisses, whipping his head back.

We look around but don't see anyone.

"They're coming from the Polo Field," he says in a rush. "Run that way," he points in the opposite direction. "And please don't stop until you're out of the park. Promise me."

"I'll run straight home, I promise," I say. It's the least I can do, seeing as he's helping me escape certain death.

He nods, accepting my vow. "I'll distract them," he says, grabbing my face and kissing me one final time. "Go."

Kael grabs his fallen wooden dagger and then reaches up and turns his comms back on. "I lost the vampire. I think it's headed toward the Boathouse."

He spares me one final glance before he runs away.

Just as promised, I dash all the way back to the safety of my apartment, where I proceed to spend the next several hours meditating over our kiss.

It's not until I'm slipping into bed, having just showered and brushed my teeth that I get a text from an unknown number.

Unknown Number: Did you make it back safely? This is Kael.

I smile from ear to ear as I sit up in bed. Kael is texting me. If I had a regular beating heart, it would be hammering its way through my ribcage, but alas, my heartbeat will keep it's slow steady pace no matter what I do or how excited I get. And right now, I'm way more excited by the fact that Kael is texting me than I should be.

Me: Yes, I'm home. Are you done hunting for tonight?

Kael: No. We patrol until sunrise. We're just taking a break.

An instant reply. *Wow, he's a fast texter.*

Me: Vampires are on the loose, and you're taking breaks?

Kael: Easy, tiger. Even seasoned hunters, like myself, have to eat.

I laugh at Kael's teasing text. I'm captivated by him and his many moods.

Me: Okay, but just know that as you sit and eat your burger and greasy fries, a vampire is draining the life of an innocent human and coating their clothes red with the blood of their prey.

Instant regret. That might have been too dark a joke for him. Especially coming from me. Maybe I'm not allowed to make vampires-eating-human jokes.

At least he doesn't keep me in suspense long, as he replies in seconds.

Kael: You know, for a pacifist vampire, that was pretty graphic.

Kael: And I'm eating tacos.

I sigh in relief at his carefree response.

Me: I'm a writer. I live for being graphic. On paper, at least.

Kael: Break's over. I'm off to hunt and slay vampires.

Me: Be careful.

```
Kael: I always am. Except when it comes to you.
I'll text you tomorrow.
```

I set my phone down, feeling buoyant and slightly in over my head. I'm not sure what I'm getting myself into, becoming so close to a hunter. Someone whose sole purpose in life is to kill creatures like me. I just know that I'm in far too deep to stop.

***

Kael makes good on his promise and texts me just before sunset the next day.

```
Kael: Did you sleep well?
```

Should I admit I was beginning to worry that he regretted what happened last night when I didn't hear from him all day?

*Nah.* Best to keep those insecure thoughts to myself.

```
Me: Good. And you?
```

```
Kael: Okay, I suppose. Thoughts of you kept me up.
That and some tyros thought it would be funny to
run down the hunter quarters banging on walls and
screaming like adolescent assholes.
```

*Thoughts of me kept him up? How am I supposed to think of anything else now?*

```
Me: Tyros?
```

```
Kael: It's what we call trainees who haven't
ascended to full-fledged hunters.
```

Me: Right. Because, although you are born with hunter blood in your veins, you still have to ascend in order to get the supernatural powers.

I remember that from the many nights we would question each other back and forth. Back when Kael thought he could learn something from me about Caesar's coven. *Boy, was he sorely disappointed.*

Kael: Exactly.

Me: So, when you say thoughts of me kept you up. Are you saying that you regret what happened last night?

I couldn't help it. Might as well rip off the Band-Aid and figure out where we stand.

Kael: Not at all. Just the opposite, in fact. I was thinking I can't wait to do it again. Preferably, at a place where we can't get interrupted. That has a bed.

*Holy Thor's hammer. What am I supposed to say to that?*

Me: Easy tiger, moving a little fast there.

I smile as I send it. Hoping he laughs at me using his words from last night.

Kael: Am I? Are you saying you wouldn't want me in your bed?

*Hell, yeah, I would.*

Me: Do you want to meet up later to discuss this further?

Kael: Can't. I promised the squad that I would spend tonight with them.

Me: Tomorrow night?

Kael: Patrolling.

I frown. I guess he isn't so eager to do a repeat after all. He isn't exactly trying hard to see me again. I'm about to text him to forget about the whole thing when another message comes through.

Kael: Sorry, I know it sounds like I'm trying to brush you off. I promise I'm not. My next night off is Saturday. Do you want to meet up then?

I set my phone down and take a deep breath. I don't like that I'm falling in too deep with him already. This isn't like me. Jared and I took it slow for months before we progressed to relationship status. Even when we were seriously in it with each other, I never felt like my world would crash if I didn't see him every day. Meanwhile, Kael says no for two nights in a row, and I'm ready to cry thinking he's trying to cast me aside. I need to get it together.

Kael: I have to go. The team is calling me. Tell me you'll say yes to Saturday. I want to see you.

I bite my cheeks to hold in a smile.

Me: Yes, Saturday sounds good.

Kael: Great. I didn't want to have to hunt you down, but I would if I had to. See you Saturday, Sarah.

*Sarah.* He said it again. Well, texted it. Whatever. This side of him, the more vulnerable, honest side, is beyond enticing. He was all "I want to kill you but also kiss you" at the start, which was hot, I won't lie. But this, now... It feels like I've cracked his armor a little, and I'm getting a peek into the real Kael. So far, I'm liking what I see. Is this still an incredibly stupid idea? Absolutely! Am I going to go for it? You betcha!

I wonder if Kael would be willing to do a little roleplaying, where he hunts me down, but instead of killing me, we do other things if he catches me.

I shake my head. That's definitely not something I thought I would be into, but I don't hate it.

I grab my laptop and dress to go to May's Diner. Adam is working tonight, so I'll take this time to work on my book.

***

I walk into the living room the next night and take a seat, cuddling up next to Adam. I feel like it's been forever since I've seen him. He sinks a little further into the couch so that my head can rest comfortably on his shoulder.

He's reading from his iPad mini, some sort of medical article, it seems.

"Studying?" I ask as I lean in close to get a glimpse of the title, but it's no longer showing because he has already scrolled too far down.

"Yes, I'm reading up on a medical journal about transplants," he tells me as he sets it aside. "But, I feel like I haven't seen you in days, so now I'm taking time to catch up with my soulmate."

I clap my hands together. "I love catch-up time. Should I go first, or you?"

"You, I have nothing new to tell, well, except that Steve and I broke up."

"What? Why? I liked Steve."

"He kept getting mad at me for going hours without texting him back, and I was like 'Hello, I'm a surgeon. There will be times when I'm too busy to text back!'" He shakes his head. "Whatever, he was getting too clingy anyway."

I snuggle in for a hug. "I'm sorry, Adam."

"What about you? Have you been working on your book? Cassie and Basille better have sex in this book. Please don't wait until book three. I will lose my mind."

I laugh. "Yes, I'm working on it, but not as much as I would like. I've been distracted." Adam catches onto my tone and shifts to look at me, one brow raised. He doesn't even need to say it. I spill the tea, everything that's happened since the Halloween party almost three weeks ago.

Adam eyes me suspiciously, never interrupting, letting me get it all out before he takes a breath. "The hunter? I don't know if it's a good idea for you to be gallivanting with a vampire hunter, Sarah."

"It is weird that I'm crushing on someone who may or may not want to kill me at any given moment, isn't it?" I ask defeatedly.

"Yes, you are quite the desperate shit-show, with a possible secret masochism kink that you never told me about."

"Technically, it would be an Autassassinophilia kink. That's when a person gets their jollies by the risk of being killed," I correct him, trying to avoid taking responsibility for the situation I've found myself in.

This is what happens when I sink down a rabbit hole of kinks after reading sci-fi smut books. My favorites are the ones where women are abducted from Earth and hunky aliens come to their rescue.

He looks at me with a blank face for a long moment before saying, "I don't normally kink shame, but it's deeply disturbing that you know that."

"Agreed, let's move on," I say and then add, "But for the record, I don't get turned on by the thought of being killed."

He waves his hands back and forth. "We are moving on," he says determinedly. "Are you seeing him again tonight?"

"No," I say with a sigh. "He's hunting tonight. I'll see again tomorrow night."

"Well, his loss is my gain. I'm off tonight, want to go watch a movie?"

I perk up instantly. I love nights out with Adam. "Yes, please."

# Chapter 16
# Sarah

ADAM AND I ARE laughing as we step out of the theater.

Movie night has always been a great excuse for Adam to binge on candy, popcorn, and soda. In college, he and I would buy four different kinds of candy to share every time we went to the theater, which was as often as our schedule allowed. We are the ones people shush because we can't stop talking and laughing throughout the movie.

After the movie, we pop into a bar for drinks. It's past midnight by the time we are walking back to our apartment.

I don't feel the effects of alcohol because—well, vampire. Adam, however, is a little tipsy and is currently oversharing a story about a time he dated a Beanie Baby enthusiast for three weeks.

I'm laughing so much my cheeks are starting to hurt. "Did she really have that many Beanie Babies?"

"Floor-to-ceiling bookshelves full of them. That's 'bookshelves,' plural," he says with a slight slur. His bracelets create jingling noises as he makes over-dramatic hand gestures.

We continue to casually walk on a busy side street, but as we round the corner to the main street that leads to our apartment building, I notice lights up ahead from police cars, fire trucks, and ambulances. They have the road blocked off, as well as a large section of the sidewalk.

"What do you think happened?" Adam says, sobering up in an instant. "I wonder if they need help."

"You've been drinking. I don't think you are allowed to help in your state," I remind him.

"Damn it, you're right," he says with a huff. "It's too far away; I can't see much, except the flashing lights."

"Looks like a car drove onto the sidewalk. I can see two people being loaded into the ambulance. They must have been hit by the car." Suddenly, my mouth begins to water, and my hands fly up to cover my nose. "We should take a backway home. I can smell their blood. It's making me hungry," I say a little shamefully, although I know deep down there is nothing to be ashamed of. I'm a vampire. I can't help what I crave.

Adam nods in understanding. "Right, let's go this way." I know he hates the fact that he is walking away from people who possibly need his help. But he also knows he's not supposed to offer any medical assistance when he's been drinking.

I let him guide me away from the accident and down the first alley we come across. I'll have to drink a blood bag tonight. It's been a few days. My hands begin to tremble a little, and I try not to think about all the blood I saw on the road.

"Are you okay?" he asks.

I look sideways at him and smile. "I'm fine now, thank-" I stop midsentence and stiffen. The hairs on the back of my neck stand to attention.

I might have spoken too soon. One male and two female vampires suddenly appear using unnatural speed through the fog in the back of the alley.

They clearly were on their way toward the accident, having smelled all the blood. The three look rough, with layers of torn clothes and wild, matted hair. They look dirty and savage. Not at all like Taylor and his companions by the beach, who looked... well like they'd just got off work at the office.

I wonder vaguely if they are rogue, coven-less vampires like me.

"Well, well, well, look what we have here," one of the females says, her eyes jerking from side to side as if she has no control over them.

*Cheese and rice! This cannot be happening.*

"We were just passing through," I say firmly.

The second female takes a step toward us. "Mmm, how unfortunate for you. I like your boy toy over there. Was he supposed to be *your* snack?"

Adam tenses beside me. I take his hand and move him behind me.

"He's mine," I declare with as much venom as I can muster.

"I want him, he looks tasty," voices the female with the jerky eyes.

"My sisters always get what they want," the male says, speaking for the first time, his voice hoarse and throaty. I wonder, vaguely, if it's from lack of use.

I glare at him. "Well, *sisters* aren't getting what they want this time."

"Be smart, girl. Leave the boy and run away. There is no reason why you should both die tonight," the second female says.

Adam clears his throat, but still, there is a slight shake to it when he says, "She's right, Sarah. You don't need to die for me."

"Shut up, Adam. No one is dying tonight," I say over my shoulder to him, never taking my eyes off the vampires. Then I give a devilish grin and say a bit louder, "Well, you and I aren't dying tonight."

I'm able to keep my voice hard and steady, even if I'm trembling inside. How am I going to keep Adam safe from three vampires? I can take him and run, but I would have to run and jump over several buildings with him in my hands. Can Adam's body handle it? What good would it be to save him from the vampires just for him to have a heart attack in my arms? Besides, these are vampires; they can track Adam's scent to our apartment. I have to finish this here.

The second sister laughs. "Kill her," she demands of the other two. "I want the male."

I release my fangs, getting ready to fight. The male vampire comes charging first. I stand my ground, waiting until he reaches me, then I bend and grab him, lifting his whole body over my head and throwing him as hard as I can toward the second sister.

Then I charge toward the first sister. She lashes out at me, but I'm too quick and dodge her attack. I seize a fistful of her hair, pulling her down toward me. With my other hand, I strike and force my fingers inside her chest and rip out her heart. I run and slam it down against the jagged edge of a broken wooden pallet lying haphazardly against the alley brick wall. The wood pierces the heart through and through.

Fire or wood through the heart are the only two ways to kill a vampire—well, that and sunlight.

"Sister!" the second female cries out.

I run, casting the remains of the body aside as I start toward the second sister. Before I can reach her, however, the male vampire tackles me from behind. He's on top of me in a second, sinking his fangs into my neck and pinning my arms to the ground.

I cry out, more in frustration than agony. The vaguely familiar sting of another vampire's venom isn't painful, but it is unwelcome.

In the corner of my eye, I see the second sister jump on top of Adam. He's where I left him, frozen in fear. She sinks her teeth into his neck as she tackles him to the ground. The fedora he was wearing falling in a small puddle beside him.

I curse out loud, knowing that her venom will be momentarily paralyzing to him. I remember when Caesar bit me, the venom was both intoxicating and agonizing. It took a moment to resist the intoxication and fight back. Not that it did me any good in the end.

With a wave of fear for my friend's life, I yank my hands free, lifting the male vampire's head off my neck. He's strong, but I'm stronger. Using my whole body, I push him off me. I jump on top of his back, gripping his head between my hands and twist, snapping his neck. I know that won't kill him, but it will knock him out for several long minutes, buying me enough time to save Adam.

I'm off the male vampire before his body hits the cement and run toward the second sister. She is still feeding off Adam, too bloodthirsty to even notice or hear me approach. I grab her so tightly by the jaw that I hear a bone break, forcing her to eject her fangs from Adam's neck.

I quickly pull her off him and throw her several yards away. She's up in a second, hurtling toward me. I wrestle her to the ground. With one hand, I squeeze her neck, and with the other I reach into her chest, my fingers cracking through her ribcage to get to her heart. Her face goes pale as my hand closes around it. She knows she's done for. With a yank, I rip her heart out and go to shove it down onto the same protruding makeshift spear where her sister's heart lies, dripping with blood.

When I'm done, I quickly seek out Adam. He's bleeding. *Fuck!* My own hunger is raging to the surface. The adrenaline of the kill and the smell of Adam's blood throw me into a frenzy I'm struggling to fight. I have to turn away for a moment to clear my head and force my fangs to recede back into my gums.

"Adam, are you okay?" I ask, counting to three before turning back and kneeling beside him, my throat still burning with need.

I help him sit up. Shakily, he lifts a hand to his throat where two fang marks are dripping with blood. "I don't know," he says unsteadily. "Am I going to turn into a vampire?"

I shake my head. "No, of course not," I assure him. "It's a certain type of venom we inject when turning someone, and then you would have to die with that vampire venom in your system." Not that I've ever used *that* venom, but I feel it, like a switch inside me, if ever I wanted to use it.

"I feel weird," he admits.

I nod, giving him a small, sympathetic smile. "I know what you're feeling. It'll pass in a moment or two. The venom used when feeding tends to put its prey in a hypnotically aroused state."

He gives me a look that almost has me laughing. "So, your venom is an aphrodisiac?"

"Umm, kind of. I guess. I've only bitten a handful of people, as you know, but that's what I've gathered from the few encounters."

"Well, if I start humping you, know it's not my fault," he says, as he starts to get up from the ground. I breathe a sigh of relief. Humor is good. Adam will be okay.

"I won't hold it against you," I tease and quickly stand to give him a hand. That's when I notice the large gash on his arm. I knew I smelled more blood than just the fang punctures. I'm not sure what caused it, but it's bleeding a lot and looks like it might need stitches.

*Don't breathe,* I tell myself. Should be easy. I only breathe out of habit.

Adam follows my gaze. "It's fine. It's not deep. I won't even need stitches," he tells me, almost as if he read my mind.

"That's good," I say, looking around for something I can use to stop the bleeding. I run to the first sister and rip off a long piece of her worn shirt.

"May I?" I ask.

He inclines his head, knowing what I'm asking, and I wrap his arm tightly.

"Are you okay?" he asks.

I give a shaky nod. "Yes, but I'm thirsty. I need to get home and drink. Now."

"Of course," he says knowingly. "What you did, just now, was both terrifying and badass."

I bark out a laugh. "Thanks."

Something catches Adam's eye as he looks behind me and stiffens. "Sarah, more vampires."

I'm on my feet and in a fighting stance in a split second, prepared to take on more vampires.

*Damn it,* I should have grabbed Adam and run while I had the chance.

The three figures approach. I curse to myself, fear finally taking center stage over the adrenaline coursing through my body.

"Those aren't vampires," I say to Adam as I eye the various wooden weapons strapped to each person. "They're vampire hunters."

# Chapter 17
# Kael

I'M INVESTIGATING THE FIRE escapes for vampires. Liam split us up into two groups. He, Shyann, and I are down one alley, while Kayda leads Zach and Nick to scope out the adjacent alley.

I'm trying my best to give the hunting patrol one hundred percent of my focus, but I'm finding it hard to concentrate.

I keep thinking about her—Sarah. I gave up trying not to think of her. If I'm being honest with myself, I gave up on staying away from her the second I kissed her again in Golden Gate Park. I want to be with her so fucking bad, despite all my training telling me this is a bad idea and damn near impossible.

Why didn't I text her today? I should have. I keep rereading our text exchange over and over again. She's sweet and funny. I love waiting to see what she'll message next. *God, she's turned me into such a softy.* I'm not used to this feeling—the excitement, the anticipation of talking to her, seeing her again.

I know I'm well past just wanting a physical relationship with her. I want more. I want everything with her—the physical and emotional parts.

Before, the hunt and my revenge have always been the most important things to me. For others, like Liam, Zach, and the rest of the squad, hunting vampires is a duty. Something they do to keep the world a little safer. For me, it was always about justice for my family.

Now, my single-mindedness has... shifted. *She* is all I think about.

I shake my head to help clear my mind. I can't think about her right now. My team relies on me to have their backs. *Focus on the hunt.*

Liam leads the way, with Shyann in the middle, and me holding up the back.

"Anything?" Liam asks over the comms.

"No, nothing yet," I hear Kayda announce through my earpiece.

"Keep your eyes and ears sharp," Liam directs all of us. "There is definitely a vampire nearby."

He doesn't really have to say it. We can all sense the darkness. A second later, I hear Nick yelling in my ear.

"We found it, just one by the dumpster, facing north."

"You, vampire, step away from the human," Kayda demands.

Liam, Shyann, and I all look at each other. Liam signals for us to go around back so that we can sneak up on the vampire from behind.

"Is the human still alive?" Liam asks as we all make our way to the end of our alley to loop around to the back street where Nick and the others are.

"Yes," Zach answers, and then adds, "It's the *Validus.*"

I freeze for a split second. I know Zach says that just for me.

"*Validus*? What's that?" Shyann asks, but Zach doesn't say another word.

I vaguely hear Nick saying, "The human must be under persuasion. It's trying to protect the vampire from us."

I take off at full speed. Sarah—but that can't be right. I definitely sense a vampire. A normal vampire around. Sarah doesn't feel like this. Her aura has always been lighter, less dark than that of normal vampires. Although now that I'm feeling for it, I can sense her too.

*Fuck. This can't be happening.*

"Thanks, hunters, but we won't be needing your services tonight," I hear someone say through my earpiece. I recognize the voice as the man from the rooftop the night of their Halloween party. Adam.

"Human, we won't say it again. Step away from the vampire," Nick demands harshly.

"First off, hunter, I'm not stepping anywhere. And secondly, this vampire just did your job. If I had to wait for you all to save me from these three vampires, I would be dead by now. Really, you should be thanking her. Do you guys get paid for this shit, because it seems like she deserves your pay for tonight."

Another voice joins in the conversation.

"That's a bit much, Adam. I don't think us asking for their money is going to help any. They already think I'm a murderer, I don't want to add mugger to their list of reasons to off me."

I recognize that beautiful second voice. It's definitely Sarah.

How many hundreds of thousands of people live in this densely populated city, and we keep hunting down Sarah? It's like now that she's been introduced into my life, I find her everywhere. Even when I don't want to—like now.

I make it around to the alley first, taking in the scene before me. Sarah is closest with her back turned to me. There is a human with her; definitely the same guy from a few weeks ago. The roommate, Adam. He, too, has his back to me. They are both staring at Nick, Zach, and Kayda.

Nick and Kayda both have their weapons aimed and ready to kill, but Adam stands between Sarah and my fellow hunters. Zach is the only one who doesn't have his weapon drawn, staring fixedly at Adam.

There are two female vampires on the ground with their chests ripped open, their hearts pierced and bleeding from a broken pallet lying against the side of the building. A male vampire is lying a few feet away, face down.

Liam and Shyann arrive seconds after me. Liam raises his bow to shoot Sarah from behind.

"No!" I yell as I grab Liam's hand and jerk it upward, causing the arrow to pivot from its original trajectory, which was Sarah's heart. Instead, it flies a foot over her head.

Sarah turns, her eyes landing straight on me.

"What are you doing?" Shyann shrieks at me.

Not thinking about anything but Sarah, I run and stand in front of her. She is now sandwiched between Adam and me.

"What the fuck is going on here?" Nick shouts.

Liam gestures for everyone to lower their weapons. I don't turn to see if Nick and Kayda follow orders. I'm staring straight at Liam.

"Please, I can explain," I say, hating the look of confusion and betrayal on Liam's face.

"What's going on, Kael?" he asks roughly. "Why are you protecting a vampire?"

"She's not just any vampire. I can explain everything, but we have to let her go," I plead.

"Umm, the big lineman is coming toward us like I'm holding a football and he needs it to win the Super Bowl," Adam informs us with a screech.

I turn. "Stay away from her," I growl at Nick as he tries to get around Adam to Sarah. I grab Sarah and yank her to my side, and then pivot so she's now sandwiched between me and the building wall.

"You've got to be fucking kidding," Nick shouts back.

"Back up," I demand.

"Stand down, Nick. That's an order," Liam commands, using the full force of his authority.

Nick shakes his head, but does as he is told.

Liam sighs. "Kael, we can't just let her go. What's going on?"

"And I can't let you hurt her," I say, turning back to face Liam.

Liam's eyes widen in shock.

Zach approaches, stopping to grab what I assume is Adam's cloth-looking hat. He brushes off dirt collected from the ground as he hands it back to Adam. "Did the vampire girl really save your life tonight?" he asks Adam.

I'm not sure how Zach knows the hat belongs to Adam, but I guess he made an educated guess by what Adam's wearing. He's in skinny blue jeans, a fitted dark-gray shirt, and a zipped-up black leather vest with a scarf tucked in. His eyes are heavy with black makeup. The hat appears to match his outfit. The only thing that looks off is the bloody scrap of cloth bandage around his arm.

I watch Adam turn to look at Zach, giving him a once-over before taking his hat back and saying, "Yes, she's my friend. She took on three vampires all by herself. All to save me, and if she wasn't here, I would be dead."

"She truly is a *Validus*," Zach says, looking at me. "Fascinating."

I nod, although now is not the time for Zach to get into one of his scientific zones.

Just then, the male vampire rises from the ground. He cracks his neck and charges at Kayda, tackling her against the opposite wall.

"Kayda," Shyann shouts, running to her.

I can see Kayda start to push back. Nick and Zach become distracted by the male vampire.

I turn to Sarah. She is shaking her head, looking over at the fight. "I forgot to finish him off. I just snapped his neck."

The fact that I couldn't feel Sarah as easily makes sense now. I think the darkness of the male vampire was masking Sarah's lighter aura at first.

I take her hand and pull her to me. "Can you not stay out of trouble for one night?" I hiss.

She snaps her head to me. "You are the one who's always hunting me."

I roll my eyes. "You have to go, Sarah."

Her eyes light up as she smiles. "You said my name again," she says quietly, and with unfiltered joy.

*Fuck.* Sometimes I feel as though I need Sarah like I need my next breath.

My hands slide behind her neck as I pull her forehead against mine. "Yes, baby girl, but now is not the time to swoon, okay," I joke. "Right now, I need you to take Adam and run."

She gives a small giggle, but nods in agreement. "Right."

When we break apart, I turn and meet Liam's cold and confused glare.

Sarah walks over to Adam and sweeps him into her arms like he weighs no more than a toddler and takes off running. Liam let's her go. In a second, she is gone from sight.

*Damn, she really can run fast.*

She disappears from view, not a moment too soon. The others are just finishing off the vampire and didn't notice her escape. Liam looks as though he's in shock. I have a lot of explaining to do.

***

Liam calls it quit early tonight as load back into the van in silence. Nick is fuming as he jumps into the passenger seat. I slide all the way to the back, next to Kayda, who looks more confused than pissed.

114

"Are you okay?" I ask, looking over her for any injuries.

She rolls her eyes but smiles. "Of course, I am. This kind of thing happens all the time." She is silent for a beat and then asks. "Are you ready to explain what happened back there?"

"I don't give a fuck if he's ready or not. I want to know why we let a vampire go," Nick barks out.

"And Zach, you're not off the hook either. Don't think I didn't notice that little exchange you and Kael had back there. You know something," Kayda adds, leaning over to bump his shoulder where he sits in the middle seat with Shyann, while Liam starts the van.

"That's my fault, too," I quickly add, defending Zach. "I told him to keep what he knew about Sarah a secret."

"You know her name?" Shyann asks in disgust.

"Sarah is a *Validus*," I inform the group, ignoring Shyann's remark. "It means she has a soul, and her humanity. She descends from a line of hunters, although she's not sure which family because she's adopted. She's thoughtful, smart, and cares for humans. I've seen it firsthand."

"I think we've all seen it firsthand," Zach adds. "We all saw her help that guy she was with, defending him against three other vampires. That's pretty impressive."

Thank heavens for Zach; him defending Sarah, too, makes this a little easier.

"Why didn't you tell the rest of us about this?" Liam questions. "Why keep this to yourself?"

I'm silent for a beat. "I just wanted to get to know her a little more. I wanted to see for myself what kind of person Sarah was before... hunting her. She's never killed a human."

"She's told you this?" Kayda probes.

"Yes."

"And you believe her?"

"Yes," I say, without hesitation.

Kayda stares at me for a long while. She searches my eyes for any doubt, a hint of hesitation, but I offer none. When she seems satisfied, she shrugs. "Okay, I trust you. If you think she's someone who is good, then I vote that we don't kill her."

"Agreed," Zach joins in.

I look up to Liam, knowing that his vote counts the most as our leader. He stares at me for a second in the rearview mirror. "Okay," he says finally. "We won't kill her—for now, but this isn't over."

I let out a breath. "Thanks." I'll make Liam understand. I just need time with him.

"Whatever," Nick spits out.

Shyann doesn't say anything, but I can see the hurt in her eyes. I know my behavior is out of character. I know they all know there's more to this, but I've only just begun to admit my feelings about Sarah to myself. I'll need time before I can really speak to anyone else about it.

Still, I feel like Shyann deserves to know, but what would I even say?

*Hey, I know you have this crush on me, but I only see you as a friend. I think, instead, I might be falling in love with a vampire.*

No, I definitely can't say that.

# Chapter 18
# Sarah

WE MAKE IT BACK to the apartment with no more interference. I help Adam properly wash and wrap his arm in a bandage.

"Your poor fedora," I say, holding his gray, wool felt hat up to examine it. It's all dirty and bent.

Adam shrugs. "I'll see if I can get Ramon dry cleaned."

I smile, almost forgetting that Ramon was the name he gave his fedora. I set it down as Adam finishes throwing away the bloody gauze.

"Thank you, Sarah, for saving my life tonight," Adam says as he turns to look at me.

I start to wave him off. Of course, I would do everything in my power to save my best friend.

"No, let me get this out," he argues, and I nod for him to continue, already feeling a well of emotion forming in my eyes.

"What you did was scary and dangerous. I'm so grateful to you," he says before going over to the fridge and grabbing a blood bag. "Here, drink this. I know you need it."

I take the bag with no argument. I really do need it. Just the sight of blood has my fangs popping out and my throat burning.

"I love you, Sarah. You are my family. I'm alive tonight because of you, so thank you."

I sip up the last of the blood bag before wiping my mouth. "I love you, too. We are family. You are literally all I have in this world."

I guess that's not entirely true anymore as Kael's face flutters through my mind.

"I guess your hunter man is not so bad," he declares, as if reading my thoughts.

I smile. "Yeah, he's pretty great. But I wouldn't say he's 'my man.'"

Adam gives me an incredulous look. "I wouldn't be too sure about that. Did you see the way he jumped in to protect you from his kill squad people?"

He did defend me to his fellow hunters. Something I never thought he would do. Does that mean he cares about me? He has to care a little bit, otherwise, he would have just let them kill me, right?

I know there is something between us. I just can't put into words what it is. It's not like we can date, not that he even wants to date. Even if he did, I'm a vampire and he's a vampire hunter. We are not exactly compatible.

I'm supposed to see him again tomorrow night. I make up my mind to get answers then.

"Not to mention he's hot as hell," Adam says, continuing with the conversation, unaware of my newfound plans.

I nod emphatically as Adam and I sit together on the sofa. He reaches for the remote and starts navigating to Disney+.

"Right?" I agree excitedly. "Merlin's beard, I could just stare at him forever."

Adam smirks. "Try not to use one of your little Sarah-sayings in front of him."

When I don't say anything, he laughs. "Never mind. I can see by the look on your face that you already have."

"He didn't notice," I say confidently.

"Oh, I'm sure he did and just didn't know how to comment on it."

I stick my tongue out at him playfully. We end up watching a few of our favorite episodes from the Star Wars animated series, *The Clone Wars,* before Adam starts yawning and we decide to call it a night.

He takes pain relievers, bids me goodnight, and slips into his room.

I head straight for the bathroom, taking my time and using up all the hot water.

Tonight was crazy, but Kael defended me. Against his hunter squad, nonetheless. I wonder how hard a time his crew is giving him at this very moment, or even worse, if they are convincing him to kill me.

I don't know what I would do if Kael tried to kill me now. I would die, both figuratively and, well, literally.

When I return to my room, I can see that I have a text from Kael, and my chest swells with anticipation. Is this it? The "goodbye forever" spiel?

`Kael: Sorry about what happened. Can I c u tonite?`

Immediately, I sigh in relief. But it's been a long night, and as much as I would love to see him, I'm exhausted and want to get some sleep, even though I usually wouldn't go to sleep for at least another few hours.

`Me: I'm pretty beat. Would it be okay if we waited until tomorrow night?`

It takes him a minute to reply. He must have been thinking about what to say, because he usually replies within ten seconds.

`Kael: I need to c u tonite.`

I sigh and look down at myself. My panties and night cami are definitely not appropriate attire.

`Me: Okay, you can come over now if you want.`

I text as I head over to my dresser.

`Kael: That's perfect. Drop your location.`

I furrow my brow. He's been here before. Why would he need the address? Then I remember, he's only ever been to the roof, not my actual apartment.

`Me: Oh, you mean my apartment number. It's 305.`

A minute goes by before I get his response.

```
Kael: That's what I meant. Thnks.
```

*Okay, that was weird.* He doesn't sound like himself. The way he's texting is weird. Something feels off. I put on some yoga pants and a Finding Nemo T-shirt. That seems like it would be an appropriate outfit for a night in my own home.

I'm anxious to see why he needs to talk to me so badly. Will he want to come into my room for the first time? I start to straighten my already clean room, fluff my pillows, and organize my Star Wars memorabilia on my nightstand, before deciding to shove everything into the attached drawer.

I look around for something else to clean. I'm pretty well organized. I make my bed every afternoon when I wake up. I don't keep dirty clothes just lying about.

I am regretting the Han Solo in carbonite bed sheets just a little bit, but I guess unless he pulls back the *Star Wars: The Empire Strikes Back* comforter, he won't see my sheets.

*Note to self: Buy sexy adult bedding online ASAP.*

Thirty minutes later, I hear a knock at the door. I guess the apartment building door was open since he didn't have to be buzzed in. That happens too often.

I close my shopping app, having added three different types of bed sheets, two different blankets, and four different comforter sets to my cart. I'll have narrow it down further until I have just one picked out tomorrow.

A little nervous about Kael being in my apartment, I take a deep breath and unlock the chain and deadbolt to open the door.

It's not Kael.

Nick and Shyann—I think that's the girl's name—are standing at the door. As soon as I open it, Nick stabs me with a wooden stake.

Sharp, searing pain shoots through me. He missed my heart, *thank God*. Still, it hurts so much that I stumble back falling on a side counter and knocking over Adam's and my Darth Vader lamp before dropping to my knees. My phone flies from my hand and skitters across the floor.

Shyann stalks over to me and takes my head in her hands. The stake has weakened me, but not enough. I push her off me with as much force as I can muster. She goes flying across the room, tumbling over the back of the couch.

I grab the stake and yank it out of me. I bite back a scream and struggle to get to my feet just as I feel another stab from the back, this time in my lower spine.

This stab sends tingling vibrations from the point where the wooden stake impaled me, all the way down to my toes, and then my lower half goes numb. I'm momentarily paralyzed.

"This time, stay down," I hear Nick whispers in my ear from behind me.

I don't cry out this time, hoping that Adam's white noise machine helps to drown out all the chaos happening out here. I don't want Adam waking up and running out of his room. I know that they aren't supposed to hurt humans, but something tells me that these two might make an exception.

I fall to the ground as Shyann approaches. She grabs me by the hair and lifts me a little. I seize her hand. If she were a vampire, I would have just reached into her chest and yanked out her heart, but she's human so, instead, I just twist her hand until I hear a pop. She lets out a cry of pain. I don't want to kill her. I don't even want to hurt her, but right now, it feels like her life or mine.

"Nick," she cries out angrily. "A little help here."

The sound of my own neck breaking is the last thing I hear as everything goes black.

# Chapter 19
# Kael

LIAM DOESN'T SAY MUCH on the walk to the graveyard the next day. Hunters have their own special graveyard a little way past the track behind the Academy.

We're headed out there now to put flowers on his baby sister's headstone. This is something he usually does once a month with his mother, but she and his father are currently overseas.

He asked me a few days ago to join him. That, of course, was before the events of last night, but since I was up and ready to go with him this morning, he didn't send me away.

As we walk up to the headstone, I read:

Here Lies Sarah Bell
September 26th, 2001
Beloved daughter and sister

Just reading the name Sarah sends a wave of warmth through me. I forgot that's what Liam's little sister was named, although she died at birth. I imagine a little coffin buried underneath. Poor Danielle and Client. This tragedy has weighed heavily on them, Liam too.

He would have been a great big brother. I know this for a fact because he's a guiding light for the rest of the team—especially me. He and I have always had a special bond. A closeness not shared with anyone else.

Liam replaces the dead flowers on top of the headstone with the fresh bouquet. We stand there quietly for a moment.

Finally, Liam turns to me. "Why did you keep this from me?"

I knew this was coming. I don't answer right away. I don't really know how to put it into words.

"I don't know," I ultimately admit. "I guess I was worried that... Well, first, I was worried that I could be wrong about her, and that she is just a normal, evil vampire. Then, I guess, I wanted to figure out why she was different on my own."

I stare at the ground, not daring to look him in the eyes. "I found her again on a rooftop and then several more times at that diner that we chased her into the first night we saw her. She was friendly and kind to some of the workers there. Apparently, she is a regular, and all the workers there love her." I say that last part with a bit of venom, remembering not liking the guy she called Sam, and how he looked and smiled at her.

"Then she started talking about things she loves, people she loves. Sarah is even writing a book. She's an author with a published book and everything. It's like she's a vampire living a normal life. I didn't get it at first. Every vampire we have ever come across was not... human, but she is.

"Then Zach told me about how some vampires can be a *Validus*, and it all made sense. It's why we don't feel the same aura around her as we do the others. It's because she doesn't have the darkness that's in all other vampires."

I stop and wait for Liam to say something.

"But why did you keep it from *me*? We're supposed to be best friends. You could have told me this," he says, betrayal still evident in his voice.

Shame hits me like a running bull. "We *are* best friends, but you are also the leader of the squad. She's a vampire. I didn't want to put you in the position to lie to the rest of the squad about something like this. Besides," I add, getting a little defensive. "It's not like you tell me everything that happens in your life. Were you ever going to tell me how you feel about Shyann?"

I know I'm not being fair, and that Sarah is a different situation entirely, but I can't help it. I'm not the only one who has kept secrets.

Liam looks genuinely startled. "How long have you known?" he asks after a long beat, not even trying to deny it, not that he would. Liam doesn't lie to me.

"For a while."

"Right," he says, like he should have known. "Does anyone else know? Does Shy know?"

I shake my head. "I don't think anyone else has caught on, or if they have, they haven't talked to me about it. Shyann definitely doesn't know."

"She's too wrapped up in you," Liam says with a self-deprecating smirk.

I was thinking the exact same thing, but didn't want to say it out loud.

"She doesn't really like me. You know she doesn't," I say.

Liam shrugs his shoulders. "Maybe, maybe not."

"Have you ever thought about telling her how you feel?" Her getting over me and moving on with Liam would help all of us, and Liam deserves to be happy.

"To be honest, I kept waiting for you to open your eyes and see the light," he says truthfully. "I was never going to say anything because I didn't want to be the reason you two didn't work out."

"I don't see her that way," I say with a finality that I hope he believes.

Liam nods. "I see that now."

We turn to start slowly walking back to the Academy. "Just as I saw the way you looked at Sarah last night." He says it matter-of-factly, not accusingly. I don't respond. He doesn't need me to. We keep walking in silence.

Looking up at the beautiful, blue sky, with splashes of big, puffy, white clouds, I close my eyes and let the sun hit my face for just a moment as I continue walking.

To think Sarah can't feel the sun's warm embrace anymore. This huge thing that we all take for granted every day has been stolen from her. Sadness and rage wash over me. Sadness for Sarah, and rage toward the person responsible for it, Caesar Leon.

"I was planning to try and get you to change your mind on this walk," Liam says guiltily, bringing my thoughts back to the conversation. "Remind you of the oath you took during your ascension ceremony. Hunt them, kill them, burn them."

It's the shorter version of the Hunters' Oath we take to complete our ascension and gain the strength and speed of a vampire to aid us in our never-ending conquest.

*Hunt the ones that hide in the shadows. Kill the ones that surrender their souls. Burn the ones that drink the blood of the innocent.*

I open my eyes and look over at him. "I won't change my mind about her."

"You getting close to a vampire might not be the best thing for any of us."

I sigh and struggle with the words I'm about to say, but Liam deserves the whole truth. "I'm falling for her, man."

Liam stops in his tracks, his eyes growing wide. "I've never heard you say that about a woman before."

"That's because I've never felt this way about a woman before. I don't know what it is about her. She is smart, funny, kind, and beautiful both inside and out. She makes me laugh without even trying. I can't stop thinking about her." I stop talking before I start really rattling off like a love-sick teenager.

Liam laughs and gives me a playful shove. "I guess then it might be time for me to meet her," he says slowly. I can see that he is still unsure about everything, and I can't blame him. It took me a while to wrap my head around Sarah. He deserves the same.

I smile to reassure him. "I would like that. I think you will really like her."

"Of course, we couldn't bring her to the Academy."

"Definitely not," I agree, and then add, "Maybe we can all go have dinner or something. Well, you and I would have dinner."

Liam laughs. "It would be funny to see a vampire eat real food."

"Actually, she's done it several times in front of me already. Every time I've met her at the diner, she was eating something small. She doesn't want to just sit there and not order anything, and she doesn't want the owners there to think she doesn't enjoy their food, so she just eats it."

"Wow, that's... considerate of her," Liam says, a little surprised. "Does she like it? I mean, is she still able to taste the food?"

I shake my head. "Sarah explained it to me once. She said that she can still remember what it tastes like, but that it doesn't taste like food to her. It would be like us eating paper or grass. We can do it, but it doesn't taste good."

Liam nods in understanding. "Interesting."

We continue our walk to the Academy. Liam coughs uncomfortably then says, "What if there was another place that would be safe for Sarah to visit?"

"What do you mean?" I ask.

"I was thinking that maybe—I've been thinking about moving out of the Academy. I'm twenty-five now, so I'm thinking it's about that time for me."

"Yeah, but you don't have to move out," I say, not wanting him to feel like he has to move out just because he's getting older. "I'm twenty-four and still living there, and besides, there are others who are older than you and still living there. Patrick and his squad are all in their thirties. It's not like Aquila will kick us out or anything."

"Yeah, I know," he agrees. "But I want to get my own place. It'll be nice to come home to a place that's not swarming with hundreds of other people all the time. A place to wind down."

"You're right. Having a little peace and quiet does sound nice."

We pass the track and see a bunch of young tyros in training, running laps. It helps prove the point that this is an Academy, not meant to be a permanent home.

"Let me know if you want a roommate," I say teasingly.

"Actually, I do," he says to me, and then quickly adds, "Not just any roommate. I was going to ask if *you* want to be my roommate."

We stop walking just outside the back entrance to the Academy. I look over at him in shock. "Really? You really want us to get a place together?"

He rolls his eyes. "Well, when you say it like that," he says with a smirk.

"No, no. I just mean—I mean yes. I think us moving in together sounds good. It'll be nice having our own place. Is there an opening in Kroger Place?"

Kroger Place is the apartment complex closest to the Academy. Most hunters who leave the Academy get an apartment there. Sid, the landowner, is a retired mage with a soft spot for us hunters. He rents out the apartments to us at a discounted rate.

There is also the option of moving into the subdivision adjacent to the Academy, but typically only those starting a family purchase those houses.

Liam nods, "Yeah, I talked to Sid already. He said that a two-bedroom will be available the first week of January, and it's ours if we want it."

"Let's do it, man," I say excitedly.

He smiles. "I'll text Sid and tell him to put us down for it."

He goes to open the back door, and as we walk inside, I ask, "Oh, by the way, do you still have the key to the van? I think I left my phone in there. I can't find it anywhere."

"No, I put it back in the key cabinet last night," he tells me.

"Okay, thanks."

I head to the key cabinet in the small office by the main entrance.

The Academy provides squads with large vehicles to patrol in so that all hunters can ride together while out hunting. I grab the van key from last night.

It takes me a minute, but I find my phone under the back seat where I was sitting.

*Great.* It's at eight percent battery life. I make my way to my room to charge it. Looking at my phone, I see that I have one new message from Sarah and seven from an unknown number, plus eight missed calls from that same number. I open Sarah's text first.

`Sarah: Where is Sarah?`

*What the fuck?* Confused, I navigate to the other number I don't recognize and open the unread messages.

`Unknown number: WHERE IS SHE? This is Adam.`

`Adam: You better not hurt her.`

`Adam: Why aren't you answering your phone?`

Adam: If you don't answer me, I'm calling the police.

Adam: Just because the police think I'm crazy doesn't mean I will give up on her.

Adam: I won't ever stop, so you might as well talk to me.

Adam: Damn you, hunter.

The last text was sent just a few minutes ago. *What the hell is going on?* What does he mean "I better not hurt her?" I call Adam immediately. He picks up on the second ring.

"It's about time, asshole. Where is she?"

"Adam, what's going on? I haven't seen Sarah since last night in the alley," I tell him. "How long has she been missing?"

"Since last night."

"Is there a chance that Sarah might have spent the night at a friend's house?" I ask, hoping that Adam isn't her only human friend and that she is safe at someone else's house. I'm also hoping it's not another male friend, although that's not the most important thing at the moment.

"No, I'm all Sarah has. I woke up this morning to find our living room a mess, broken shit everywhere. She's not in her room, and when I called her phone, I found it ringing under the sofa. If she left willingly, why would she leave her phone under the sofa? I got worried and unlocked it to see that you were the last one to text her last night, and that you came over. I swear to God, if..."

"Wait," I say, cutting him off. "I never came over to your place last night."

"Umm, not true, I'm literally looking down at the message exchange as we speak."

I look down at my phone and go to Sarah and my text, but the last conversation I see is us making plans to see each other today.

"I'm headed over there, text me your apartment number," I say, grabbing my personal car keys and heading out of my dorm door. "I want to see those messages in person."

"Fine," he says, hanging up with no further comments.

I'm almost to the main door when I turn and decide to go find someone who I know might be of help.

# Chapter 20
# Kael

W E MAKE IT THERE in thirty minutes with me speeding the whole way, zig-zagging in and out of traffic while Zach gives me evil side eyes.

"You know we won't be able to help anyone if we wreck and die," he shouts as he grips the door's armrest to steady himself.

"We're as strong as vampires," I remind him. "We don't die so easily." Truth is, I don't really care. I need to get to Sarah's. I need to find out what happened to her.

Adam already has the door open after buzzing us in when we reach their apartment, and he's wearing a colorful robe that swishes behind him as he impatiently waits for us to enter. He starts talking the second we step over the threshold.

"I want to warn you that I have a hidden camera recording us, and it is scheduled to email my parents if I don't turn it off in the next hour, so I wouldn't try anything if I were you," he warns us.

I look around the room. *Is he serious?* It's hard to tell, but something in his face tells me he's not lying.

I notice him glance over at Zach, clearly expecting me to have shown up alone.

I clear my throat and quickly introduce them. I don't need to give Adam any more reason to be difficult. "I brought some help. This is Zach Owen. He's good with tracking people," I explain.

"Nice to see you again. I wish it were under better circumstances," Zach says kindly, his tone soft.

Zach's shy demeanor is a godsend. I'm sure Adam's first impression of vampire hunters isn't the greatest, but by the way his eyes are eating up Zach, I'm feeling like we've got a shot at redemption.

"So, he's the beauty and the brains," Adam says, giving Zach a wink before turning back to me. "What, pray tell, are you useful for in your group?"

I see Zach blush a little at the compliment.

"Can I see Sarah's phone?" I ask, ignoring Adam's ridiculous question. He hands it to me, and he's right. Her phone has a small text exchange that my phone does not.

2:02am Me: Sorry about tonite. Can I c u?

I hate when people don't write out their words. It takes an extra second to do so. But I know someone who does text like this. Shyann. It drives me crazy.

2:02am Sarah: I'm pretty beat. Would it be okay if we waited until tomorrow night?

2:03am Me: I need to c u tonite.

2:03am Sarah: Okay, you can come over now if you want.

2:04am Me: That's perfect. Drop your location?

*Drop your location?* Whoever did this didn't even try to sound like me.

2:05am Sarah: Oh, you mean my apartment number. It's 305.

2:08am Me: That's what I meant. Thnks.

I'm shaking my head. "I never texted her any of this," I tell them, trying to stifle the panic bubbling up inside. I'm starting to get a bad feeling.

"You did sound kind of needy," Adam notes.

I ignore him and ask Zach, "Is there a way someone could have written out these messages and made it look like it came from me?"

"Yes, but I doubt that's what happened," he answers. "You don't have a computer that's connected to your phone. It's more likely that whoever did this probably stole your phone to do it. You did say that you didn't have your phone all night last night."

"Yeah," I agree. "But it was under the backseat of the van all night."

"Or someone wants you to think that's where it was all night," he counters.

*Fuck.* He's right. He has to be right.

Zach is looking around the room as he speaks. I take a look around, too, for the first time.

I see a wooden stand by the door. It holds a glass bowl with keys in it, and there is a picture frame that has been knocked down. It's of Adam and Sarah at Disneyland in front of the castle at night. They are both wearing Mickey ears. She looks so happy in it.

There is also a broken lamp of a black masked head broken into several pieces, just like Adam said. There is another picture hanging on the wall above it. It's of a younger Sarah and Adam in front of a college campus. It's daytime, so I know Sarah was human when that picture was taken.

She looks so beautiful with the sunlight illuminating her face and hair. A pang of sadness hits me. I'll never know her like this. Human.

"There was definitely a struggle here," Zach continues. "But I'm sorry Kael, I don't think I'll be able to track Sarah down. Maybe if she had her phone with her, we could have tracked that, but..." He lets the rest of his sentence float into oblivion.

"It would seem that the next move is to talk to your fellow hunter friends and see which one would have possibly done this," Adam suggests, like it is the obvious thing to do.

"My team wouldn't do this," I say, closing my eyes and rubbing my temples, trying to ward off the headache I feel coming.

"No? So, Sarah going missing the same night we finally meet your little death squad is what... a coincidence?"

My eyes shoot to Adam. I know what he's saying makes sense, but I just can't see any of the team going against Liam's orders. Except maybe... "Carmack," I blurt out, thinking out loud. This is something he would do. I start to pace back and forth; hands clenched tightly at my sides.

If it is him, I'm going to kill him.

"Who?" Adam asks.

"Nick Carmack is one of our squad mates," Zach answers. "Do you honestly think Nick could do this?" Zach questions, but not in a *Nick would never do such a thing* sort of way, more like *this scheme would have been too complicated for Nick to pull off* sort of way.

"Is that the lineman?" Adam asks. "I didn't get good vibes from him."

I turn without another word. I have to get back to the Academy. Now.

"Hold up," Adam says quickly. I look to see him walking over to the laptop sitting up on the coffee table. It's positioned so that the back is facing us, but I can see now that there is a webcam set on top of it, which is also facing us.

I guess he was serious about recording. He turns off the camera and looks at us. "Okay, I'm ready."

"You're not coming, human. You'll only slow us down," I say harshly, but I don't care. I'm only thinking of Sarah.

Adam gives an arch of his eyebrow and frowns. "First of all, just because you are a hunter doesn't mean you're not also a human, unless you consider your kind beastly animals. Secondly, you may address me as Dr. Patel and nothing else. And lastly," he says unrelentingly, pointing his finger at me. "I don't trust you, so I'm coming."

"He could help us. He does know Sarah best," Zach points out.

I flinch. I know Zach didn't mean anything by it, but it still stings a little knowing that I'm not the one who knows Sarah best. I want to change that, but I have to find and save her first.

She's in this mess because of me. The idea that my own team, my own family, would betray someone I cared about sets my skin on fire. My fists will have some words for Nick.

"Fine. Let's all go."

When we get down to the car, Zach blocks my way so that I can't enter the driver's side. He holds his hand out.

"What now?" I say through clenched teeth.

"I'm driving back," he demands. "You are in no condition to drive us."

"Are you fucking kidding me?" I shout. "We don't have time for this."

"Then you'd better hand the keys over to me quickly. You and I might be as strong as vampires, but Dr. Patel isn't," he says in a commanding voice I'm not used to hearing from him. "If you get in a wreck because you aren't thinking clearly and kill him, then when we do find Sarah, I don't think she will be too happy about the news."

He's right. But I'm angry. I cast a growling glare at Adam before shoving the keys at Zach and making my way to the passenger side. Of course, Adam pops in first, shutting the door firmly behind him.

"I guess I'm sitting in the back seat of my own fucking car," I mutter to myself.

If I weren't in such a hurry to get back to the Academy, I would have thrown both of them out on their asses.

# Chapter 21
# Sarah

I WAKE UP WITH a jolt.

*Mother nature's screaming toddler*, my neck hurts. This whole waking-up-after-repeating-broken-necks thing is so two years ago. I don't miss it, and it makes me hungry. My jaw is killing me, and I can feel my fangs aching to come out.

*Where am I?* I look around and see that I'm in a big room full of dusty boxes and old furniture covered in sheets. There is a boiler a few feet away from me. The whole place smells of furnace ash and mothballs.

I'm in a basement. That much, I'm sure of. I can see the stairs leading upward, but whose basement, and why?

*Caesar Leon! Did he finally find me?*

So far, every time I've woken up, someone's been here snapping my neck before I could get a good look at them.

I'm alone now. I try to get up, and that's when I notice I'm chained to a wall, both my hands and feet. *Really?* Did whoever did this to me really think chains could hold me?

I yank at the chains, expecting them to tear like paper, but to no avail. I try my feet, but it's the same thing. *How is this possible?*

I know I'm strong enough to break chains. It shouldn't even be a struggle, but this little bit of effort has already drained me. Maybe I'm too hungry and weak after last night.

Last night.

Memories crash through me like a tidal wave. The big one, Nick, and the blonde pixie-haired girl, Shyann, did this to me. I wonder if I'm at the Academy Kael told me about.

Why would he let them do this? Where was he, and why didn't he show up last night? Could all of this really have been his plan all along to get me to trust him and then have his hunter friends kidnap me? Was I just a prized kill all along?

I shake my head as if to clear it. No, that doesn't make any sense. I doubt hunters are in the kidnapping business anyway.

Unless this has something to do with the fact that I am a *Validus*. What are they planning to do, experiment on me or something, like some mad scientists?

The disappointment kicks in then. I haven't known Kael long, but what I'd felt for him was real. I thought that he was feeling it too. Maybe I never really knew him at all.

*No time to worry about that now, Sarah.* I can cry over him with a pint of blood-covered ice cream when I get out of this mess. I tug and pull on the restraints until I'm blue in the face. "Argh, come on," I hiss.

These must be special vampire-proof chains or something, because I'm having zero luck with them. But I can't give up.

I keep trying to break free. Finally, one of the foot shackles starts coming loose from the wall. With all my remaining energy, I pull once more, and the chain breaks free, taking chunks of the wall with it.

I slump back down too tired to keep standing.

I force myself to get up. I know I have no time to rest; someone could come down at any moment.

As if my thoughts summoned them, I hear footsteps start coming down the stairs.

But out of all the people I thought it was going to be, a kid of eleven or twelve was not it. Man, these hunters start out young.

No, that can't be right. I know from Kael that they don't become official hunters with all the strength and speed of a vampire, until they are eighteen. Before ascending, they are called tyros.

This kid must still be a tyro trainee. He slowly walks up to me like I'm a rabid beast that will pounce at any moment. Which, to him, I guess, I am.

"I knew I saw Nick and my sister bringing someone down here. Are you a vampire?" he asks in awe.

Shyann's little brother, great, just what I need. Still, he doesn't seem as disgusted by me as Shyann appeared to be the couple of times I've come in contact with her.

"I am," I say weakly.

He cocks his head to the side, almost like a chicken. "Where are your fangs then?"

I smile. I guess some vampire killers in training start out cute and innocent. "They aren't always out. They mostly pop out when I'm feeding or angry."

"Oh," he says, deflated. "I was hoping to see some fangs. I've never met a vampire before."

"I think the fact that you haven't met a vampire before is a good thing."

He nods, although I can see he disagrees with me. "I guess, but you don't seem so evil, or ugly and fat like my sister said."

*Really? Body shaming?* I internally roll my eyes. So she's definitely not a girl's girl.

"It seems like your sister said some mean things." It takes all my self-control to keep my tone calm and steady. *This is a teaching moment,* I remind myself. "Beauty is subjective, and about so much more than what you look like on the outside. Your sister, for example. Her rude comments have made her very ugly in my eyes. You wouldn't want to grow up being a misogynistic a-hole, would you?"

The boy shakes his head adamantly. "No, ma'am."

I can't help but crack a smile. *What a cutie.* "Good."

It should be Shyann giving these life lessons to her little brother, but apparently, Shyann watched *The Devil Wears Prada* too many times. She also doesn't care to teach her younger brother how to respect women, but I digress.

"I'm also not a normal vampire," I inform him. "Something happened to me, and I was able to keep my humanity, but other vampires aren't like me. So, you can't go around chatting with any vampire you come across, okay?"

"So, you're a special vampire, cool," he says, believing me so easily. His gullibility is both adorable and concerning. The life of a vampire hunter has no room for it. I suddenly fear he's going to have to learn this the hard way one day.

He cocks his head at me again. "You don't look so good. Are you sick?"

"No, I'm just hungry," I say truthfully. "Does anyone else know I'm down here?"

"I don't think so. I was getting a glass of water when I saw them bring you in. It was super late at night, and everyone was still sleeping. Well, except for Geralt's and Annalise's squads. It was their turn to hunt, and they were still out patrolling. Besides, no full-fledged hunter would have seen you anyway. They brought you through the tyros' wing of the Academy. I guess it's because we haven't ascended and can't feel vampire auras yet," he says with a shrug.

So, I'm far enough away from full-fledged hunters for them not to pick up my scent or aura, or whatever. That's both a relief and a disappointment. I wonder if this kid knows Kael. He should, since this is Shyann's brother and all.

"What's your name?" I ask, hoping to keep him talking.

"Ben Karman."

"Hi Ben, I'm Sarah," I say kindly. "Since you're Shyann's brother, that must mean you know Kael Hart, right?"

Ben's face lights up. "Yes, I know Kael. He and I are really good friends. He sometimes helps train me."

I can tell by the way he speaks of Kael that he is fond of him.

"Believe it or not, Kael and I have become friends, too." This has to work. *Please let this work.* "Would you mind going to get him for me?"

Ben's eyes narrow. "I don't think Kael would be friends with a vampire. Even though you are a really nice vampire. He hates them more than most."

The words feel like shrapnel in my ears, and I try to stay focused on the task instead of succumbing to the sorrow of everything between Kael and me being a lie.

"Do you want to see my fangs?" I ask, trying a different approach.

"Yes," he says, practically jumping up and down with excitement.

138

I sit up on my knees and make a big show of getting ready to show him. "Okay," I say after a breath. "I'll show you, and then afterwards, you have to go get Kael for me. Just tell him I'm here, and if he doesn't want to come and see me, then that will be up to him. How about that? Do we have a deal?"

Ben contemplates for a few seconds before nodding. "Deal."

*Yes!* Sarah for the win. It's a testament to how truly weak and awful I feel that I'm this excited about having outsmarted a preteen boy, but whatever. I'm still taking the win.

I put my head down and will my fangs to come out. They slide out with ease; all I have to do is give in to the hunger. I lift my head up and keep my mouth open, showing off my fangs.

"Whoa, that's so cool." His eyes look as if they're about to pop out of his head.

I give two thumbs up, the chains rattling as I do. "They are pretty cool, aren't they?" I slur out. Talking with my fangs out is not the easiest.

I let him look at them for a few moments before pulling them back in. "Okay, now your turn."

"Okay," he says with a shrug. "I'll be right back." And with that, he turns on his heel and runs up the stairs.

*Thank goodness.* Relief, followed by immediate panic courses through me as a dark thought crosses my mind.

Doesn't Kael already know I'm here? He's the one that I sent my apartment number to in the first place. Dread threatens to drown me, but before I have time to question my actions, I hear voices and the door to upstairs opens.

# Chapter 22
# Sarah

THAT WAS QUICK. A little too quick.

"Are you sure you remembered to erase all of the messages before putting the phone under the seat, and to clear out the location app?" I hear Shyann ask as two sets of footsteps make their way down the stairs.

*Neptune's beard*, that's not Ben coming back with Kael.

Did I just hear right? Maybe Kael didn't send those texts; maybe he didn't have anything to do with them taking me. Hope blooms in my chest, a relief I didn't know I needed coming with the realization. I close my eyes and shake my head. I can't think about that right now. I'm still chained. Still in danger. First, I have to figure out a way out of here.

"Yes," Nick says, exasperated. "I'm not a total idiot like you all think."

"What about her phone?"

They make it downstairs but still haven't looked my way.

"What about her phone?" he asks, stopping to look over his shoulder at her.

She huffs. "We have to get rid of it. Where is it?"

"How the hell should I know?" he yells. "I'm the one who carried her downstairs and into the van. Why was it also my responsibility to make sure I had her phone?"

I see Shyann roll her eyes. "Fine. Forget about her phone. Let's just kill her. I don't know why we haven't yet already."

"Because Liam ordered us not to," he reminds her.

Liam is their leader and Kael's best friend. I remember Kael telling me as much. Did he really order them not to kill me? Was it on Kael's behalf?

I watch Nick and Shyann warily. They are obviously going against the rules by having me here. Nick meets my gaze.

"Yes, she's awake."

Shyann makes a disgusted sound. "Why is that a good thing?"

Nick is rubbing his hands together excitedly. I don't like the look on his face.

"Because it's daylight. I've been keeping her knocked out all night, but now I want to see how she responds to the sun. I've never seen a vampire get exposed to sunlight before," he says, a little too giddily.

My eyes grow wide as panic threatens to consume me. *Oh no, please God, no.*

I don't say anything. I'm sure as hell not going to beg. I just need time to think of a way out of this mess.

"Seriously," Shyann demands. "I just want to get this over with. I don't care what a vampire looks like when killed by daylight. Besides, how are we going to get her upstairs and outside without anyone seeing us?"

"Relax, we don't need to bring her all the way outside," he states. "We just need to move her where the light from the cellar doors shines through." Nick signals toward five steps leading to two big wooden doors. "What do you say, vampire? Ready to get crispy?"

I ignore him and start tugging at the set of chains still holding my other foot prisoner. *Come on. Come on. Just break already.*

"You're wasting your time," Nick tells me. "Those chains are spelled by a mage to keep vampires from breaking out of them."

He walks over to me, and I hiss at him, showing my fangs. "Stay away from me," I yell.

"How the hell did you break one?" Nick asks in disbelief. "That shouldn't be possible. I guess you are as powerful as they say." He shakes his head. "I guess we will have to do this the hard way." He takes out a gun and, without hesitation, starts firing at me. Four shots. To the stomach, the arm, the leg, and the last one straight to my forehead. The echoes of the shots die out and give way to my screams. Somehow, the worst part is his mask of indifference. Not a single hint of guilt or shame. Shyann just watches from several feet away, a bored look on her face.

With shaky hands, I yank out the bullet lodged in my forehead—both it and my hand come back bloody. Getting a closer look, I see that they are wooden bullets.

Despite my earlier promise that I won't beg, I do. "Please, stop," tumbles out of my mouth before I completely fall to the floor.

Ignoring me entirely, he finishes off the rest of the rounds in his gun, avoiding my heart. Every gunshot is agony, like fire zipping through my veins. I can barely move, and even if I could, I'm still shackled to the wall.

No sooner than the thought crosses my mind, Nick walks over and starts unhooking the chains from the wall, but leaves the shackles secured to my limbs. He fixes it so that all he has to do is tug on the chains like I'm a dog on a leash.

He leads me across the room. My feet feel like lead. I can't seem to stand up straight, so he has to drag me to the first step leading to the wooden double doors blocking out the sun from outside. Every movement sends debilitating pain shooting through my body, and once they get me outside, it's only going to get worse. My hair is sticking to my face with blood and tears.

This is it. I can't believe I'm going to die like this. At this point, however, I'll welcome death. Anything has to be better than the pain I feel now.

"You ready?" Nick asks me like we are about to embark on some thrilling adventure together.

If I weren't so weak, I would give him the finger.

Nick starts up the steps to unhook the doors when Ben comes running down the other set of stairs leading to the Academy.

I look over to see that he's alone. My heart drops as the small glimmer of hope I was holding onto slips away.

Ben skids to a halt and looks at me in shock and horror. I see my torture reflected in his eyes, and I wish I were able to shield him from this gruesome sight. What I must look like to him... Bloody, weak, covered in bullet holes.

"What's happening?" he asks in a small child-like voice. He's holding a plate with a sandwich on it and a bottle of water.

My heart warms a fraction. He was bringing me food because I told him I was hungry.

Nick curses out loud. "Shyann, what the hell is he doing here?"

Shyann throws up her hands. "How should I know?"

She quickly runs over to Ben, grabs him hard by the elbow, and starts trying to usher him up the stairs. "Ben, you shouldn't be down here! Go to class."

"It's Saturday," he says, trying to peer around her to look at me.

"Why are you here?"

"I-I was just looking around," he lies, yanking his elbow free of her grip.

"Well, you need to leave," she fusses. "We are doing adult hunter business."

He nods in a daze, and his eyes find me one last time. I muster up whatever strength I have left and give him a reassuring smile before gesturing that he get the hell out of here. Ben's mouth presses into a thin line, and he rushes up the stairs and out the door.

So much for that. No one is coming to my rescue. I hate the thought of even needing rescue. I'm a powerful vampire. I should have been able to take them on, but I didn't.

Nick turns to me as soon as Ben leaves. "Now, where were we?" he asks. "Aww, yes. The sunlight. How about some fresh morning air, huh, vampire?"

"We have to hurry," Shyann demands. "Who knows if Ben will open his big mouth."

Nick brushes her comment away with the wave of his hand and pushes open the wooden doors. He must have already unlatched it from the outside, because they creak open easily.

I brace myself, shutting my eyes, waiting to feel Icarus's demise, but nothing happens. Finally, I dare a peek and see that the sun's angle at this time of day isn't as ideal as Nick had hoped. Only the top two steps have sunlight hitting them, and I'm on the bottom step.

"Shit," Nick curses. He yanks on my chains for me to come up the steps, but I hold fast, using the last of my strength to fight back.

Nick turns to Shyann, "Shy, grab her and—"

"I'm not touching her," she says with revulsion.

Nick gives an exasperated huff.

"Fine, I'll do it myself," he yells as he comes behind me, grabbing me under my armpits, pushing me up the stairs.

But, it's not working because I drop my weight, refusing to move a single inch. He gives up trying that way and comes around to grab my arm, pulling with all his strength. My struggle is futile. He's able to get me to the third step, but he still has my arm, and it alone touches the light.

I scream.

My hand feels as though it's been kissed by fire. It's like the sun itself grabbed me by the arm and is holding on for dear life, slowly, agonizingly sizzling my skin straight down to my bones.

"Damn, it's like her arm is getting barbecued," Nick says, his nose wrinkling in disgust. "Look, Shy, it's turning black and is starting to smoke."

"I can't look," Shyann says from somewhere behind me.

"What the hell is going on down here?" I hear a female voice say behind me.

I'm in too much pain to even notice, or care, who it is.

Nick lets go of my arm and I yank it back quickly, staggering back as far from Nick and the sun as I can.

I start to fall down the last two steps, but someone from behind catches me. I immediately thrash and kick out. I've had enough of these sick fucks trying to test how many ways to barbecue a vampire.

Whoever caught me, quickly stands me up and turns me around to face them. It's not Kael, but I already knew that. I brace for a fight, one I'm certain I will lose. I'm already swaying on my feet. Black dots are beginning to cloud my vision, but I hold onto consciousness. If I pass out, I know I won't be waking up. The girl steadies me instead. I flinch at her touch, and she quickly removes her hands, giving me a once-over.

It's the other girl hunter.

"What the fuck are you guys doing?" Kayda shouts. I think that's her name, Kael's mentioned her before.

"I just wanted to kill her," Shyann says, defensively. "It's Nick who wanted to see what would happen if he put her in the sun."

"Kael won't forgive you for this," Kayda snarls.

"Ben, go get Liam," she says over her shoulder.

I look and see that Ben, no longer holding the food and water, is cowering on the steps, too afraid to come any closer—my hero.

"Kael," I manage to rasp out.

"I couldn't find him," Ben says to me. His voice is shaky, like he's on the verge of tears. I want to thank him. Tell him he did a good job, but the words are trapped in my throat.

"Kael's not here," Kayda informs me. "He came and got Zach earlier from the study. They left about forty minutes ago. It sounded like he needed Zach's help with something, but he was too in a rush to explain why. I'm now guessing it might have something to do with you. And with these dumb dumbs." She shoots Shyann and Nick an angry glare.

I look at her and take a deep breath, finding my voice. "You aren't going to kill me?" I ask, my eyes stinging, but trying my best not to cry. The words come out garbled and slurred, but it's all I can muster.

"No," she says kindly. The dam of panic within me shatters, and I'm flooded with relief. My knees finally give out, and I tumble toward Kayda, who catches me quickly and pulls my arm over her shoulder, taking most of the weight. "I'm sorry they did this to you," she says and nods at Nick. "Where's the key to get her out of these chains?"

"Seriously," Nick yells. "We can't just let her go."

"Let's hurry and kill her now," Shyann says. "Kael will get over it. She's just a vampire."

"The fact that you believe what you're saying shows how little you know Kael," Kayda states, still holding me up. She looks over at me. "We have to get these wooden bullets out of you."

"What do you mean?" Shyann says, sounding worried.

Kayda sits me down on the ground gently, before turning to face Shyann. "I mean, you are so infatuated with him, but you don't even really know him," she shouts angrily at Shyann. "Kael stood between us and this girl last night. You think he would do that for just anybody, especially a vampire?" She allows a moment of silence, as if giving Shyann a chance to use that useless brain of hers.

"No," Kayda roars, answering her own question when Shyann just stares at her. "Which means she means something to him. I'm not about to lose Kael over one vampire. A vampire that Zach explained has all her human emotions intact, so when she told Kael she never killed anyone, she was probably telling the truth."

Kayda pulls out her phone and takes a minute to, presumably, send out a text.

"The key, Nick," she demands again after shoving the phone back in her pocket. "I need the key to the shackles."

I watch as she approaches Nick, who has his arms crossed against his chest defiantly.

"No, we're not letting her go."

Just then, the door that leads to the Academy opens and Kael, Zach, and Adam all come running down the stairs.

# Chapter 23
# Sarah

*A*DAM IS HERE.

"That was quick," Kayda says to Zach.

"We were already inside the building when I got your text," he states.

My eyes fall first to Adam and then to Kael.

He stares at me with such intensity, taking me in, assessing. I know what I must look like, and I suddenly want to cover up, to hide.

He's immobile for only a second before he is at my side, kneeling beside me.

"Who the fuck did this?" he says through gritted teeth, addressing the room.

No one answers.

Adam is by my side now, too. "I need to take these bullets out of you," he says with the gentleness of the doctor he is.

"You came," I say, tears starting to fall down my face at the sight of him.

Adam smiles. "Well, someone broke our Darth Vader lamp, and I want to know who owes us fifty dollars."

My heart warms at the comment. Like me, Adam tends to use humor as a defense mechanism. We're both so good at it.

I give out a weak laugh. "It was the lineman."

"I'm really starting to hate that guy," Adam says.

"You hate him? What about me? He's been talking so close to my face all morning, and I don't know what sort of combination he had for lunch, but his breath smells like tuna mixed with garlic," I say in disgust.

Adam laughs. "Well, then I think Stinky Breath is a much more appropriate name for him."

"Let's patent it," I say.

Kael watches us for a moment, and then he says, "How about we save this conversation for later?" He turns to Nick, and in a much harsher tone, he asks, "Where's the key to get her out of the shackles?"

"He won't give it up," Kayda tells him.

Kael's eyes turn from anger to full-on enraged. It's definitely one of those *if looks could kill* moments.

"Adam, watch Sarah," he demands as he rises to his feet and storms over to Nick. Without warning, Kael cocks his fist back and punches Nick square in the nose.

"What the fuck, Hart?" Nick barks as he stumbles back, clutching his nose between his hands. Blood starts pouring like a faucet down his face.

Kael seizes Nick by the shirt and slams him to the wall, "I'm not going to ask again, asshole, where is the key?"

Nick shoves Kael away from him and starts swinging. The two men start fighting, each landing punch after punch onto one another.

"Oh, my," Adam whispers to me. "We seemed to have found ourselves in the basement of a fight club."

"It's in his pocket!" Shyann yells. "Stop fighting."

They don't stop. They just keep beating each other to a pulp. I'm so focused on them that I don't even notice when their leader, Liam, comes barreling down the stairs.

"That's enough," he shouts, and his words shake every atom in the room. Liam oozes authority and leadership, especially in the way he steps in between the two boys, grabbing Nick by the neck. Zach is there too, holding back Kael.

Liam holds out his hand to Nick. "The key, Nick, now!"

Nick grabs the key from his pocket and reluctantly hands it over to his leader. "This is bullshit," he spits, as he nurses his bloody nose.

Liam looks at Kael and tosses him the key.

Kael is by my side in a flash. He quickly frees me from the chains that bind me.

"Oh, my gawd, it's like he's Superman," Adam whispers to me in awe, staring straight at Liam. "He even looks like Superman."

148

He's not wrong. Liam's broad chest, dark hair, and hazel eyes would make him the perfect fit for a Henry Cavill stunt double.

Liam quickly turns his head away from us, but not before I see a ghost of a smile cross his lips, letting me know he heard the Superman comment.

"Right," I whisper back, shifting a little and immediately regretting it. My body feels like one giant bruise.

Kael notices and leans toward me as if to protect me from the rest of the world. He reaches out a hand, but hesitates to touch me, probably because he doesn't know where he can touch me without hurting me.

"You're bleeding," I say softly to Kael, looking at his busted lip, all other people and distractions vanishing in an instant. I lift my unburned hand to brush the edge of his lips.

The room goes eerily silent all of a sudden, and I feel everyone's eyes on me, or maybe they are all looking at Kael, but I don't care.

"Don't worry about me," Kael voices gently, leaning into my hand and kissing my palm. "How do we get the bullets out of her?" He's still inspecting me, but addressing Adam.

"I can get them out, I just need..." I can see that Adam's thinking about what they might have around the Academy that they could use.

Zach comes and kneels next to us. "Dr. Patel, we do have a medical bay. We have supplies and equipment in there. If you like, we can take Sarah there. I'm sure it'll have everything you need."

Adam smiles at him. "Thank you, Zach."

Kael lifts me in his arms and follows Zach and Adam out. Just his touch helps cool some of the pain I'm in.

It's a long walk from the basement to the medical bay. I don't even know if anyone else is following. I'm still in so much pain, but that's not even the worst of it.

The hunger. I'm so stinkin' hungry. And now that my body is trying to heal, the hunger is getting worse. I have to consciously keep my fangs from emerging as Kael carries me. I have to concentrate on not wanting to sink my teeth into everyone here.

My head is level with his neck, and I can hear the blood pulsing through his veins. I can smell it, too, from the cut on his lips. And I'd be lying if I said it didn't smell fucking delicious.

*Mother of all that's good and holy, please do not let my fangs come out.*

I move my head back so that I'm as far away from his neck as possible. Kael notices. He looks down at me.

"It's going to be okay, Sarah," he assures. "No one is going to hurt you again."

I give a small smile and nod, not trusting myself—or my fangs—to speak.

Finally, we enter a room. It's clean and white, and looks like the inside of an operating room you would see on TV medical dramas. Gauze and bottles of liquid are stacked up on the counters, and the operating table is in the center of the room. Several beds line the back wall.

Kael brings me over and sets me down gently on the center table. Zach and Adam enter the room and close the door. I'm assuming Liam is busy handling his wayward team members.

*Thank goodness.* I'm really not up to having too many people in here, especially because I know what Adam's about to do.

Kael must sense my unease because he grabs my unburned hand between both of his and gives a tender squeeze.

"I'm right here, Sarah. I promise I'm not going anywhere," he vows and lowers his lips to my hand. Electricity pulses through me at this intimate gesture. It draws my attention away from the fact that my limbs feel like shattered glass. That my chest feels heavy, like it's filled with rocks. That my singed arm has begun to lose feeling now that my nerves have fried off.

Kael stares at me with those gorgeous green eyes of his. This is the first time I've noticed he has specks of gold on the outer rim of the intense green.

I'm suddenly wondering how much of a mess I look like right now. It's vain of me, but I can't help it.

I can hear Adam walking around the room, grabbing stuff.

"Zach, can you be a dear and bring over that stand?" Adam asks, talking to the hunter like they are well acquainted. *Are they well acquainted?* I highly doubt it, but Adam can be that way sometimes. Outgoing and talking to strangers like old friends.

Zach brings over the stand as instructed, and Adam drops what he's holding onto it with a clatter. He goes over to the sink located at the back of the large room, takes off his colorful kimono, placing it on the countertop, and washes his hands thoroughly.

When he's done, he walks over to us and turns to Kael. "I suppose there is no point in asking you to wait outside?"

Kael gives him a death stare.

"Yep, that's what I thought," Adam says.

I can tell by the hard look on Kael's face that he wouldn't leave my side even if Selena Gomez were waiting for him in the lobby. Although, in his defense, he probably doesn't even know who SelGo is. Hunters seem to live in their own special world of all things supernatural.

Adam huffs his defeat, puts on some blue nitrile gloves, and clears his throat. "Sarah, I will begin extracting the wooden bullets now, okay? I would give you morphine to ease the pain, but you aren't affected by it, so that's out. Unfortunately, so is alcohol for the same reason. Feel free to use all your vampire strength to squeeze Kael's hand as hard as you like."

I want to laugh because what he's saying sounds so like Adam, but he is saying it in his most doctorly voice, which makes it that much funnier. I like seeing Adam in doctor mode. I rarely get to see him this way. He's much more authoritative and attentive.

Taking a deep breath, I say to him, "I'm ready."

He also takes a deep breath, grabs a big tweezer-looking thing and says, "Let's begin."

I shut my eyes, waiting for the sensation, the pain. At first, there's nothing. Then I feel sharp, thin metal dig into the hole in my arm.

"Holy rollie pollie, that hurts," I cry out.

Adam looks at me. "Sarah, please don't make me laugh while you're in pain. It doesn't look good on me."

"Sorry," I say through gritted teeth.

I try to keep quiet for the rest of the treatment. The next thirty minutes are torture. The last two bullets are wedged deeper than the others, causing my already faltering bravado to crumple to bits. My fangs come out after the first one is taken out. I try to will them back in, but they refuse, along with my will to hold in my cries.

After Adam finishes, Kael looks at me and frowns. "Sarah, why aren't you healing?" he asks. His voice is as desperate as his concerned eyes.

I look down in shame. "I'm too hungry," I admit a little awkwardly, talking with the fangs still out. "I need to drink and then, I'll heal."

Kael nods in understanding. "Right, of course. I'm sorry, I didn't think of that." He lets go of my hand for the first time since coming in here, and offers me his arm, wrist up. "Go ahead, drink."

My eyes widen, and I hear Zach take in a breath.

"No," I half shout, pushing his arm away as if it were a vicious snake. "Are you crazy?"

"She can drink from me," Adam says, removing his gloves after tossing all the bullets in the trash.

"No," I demand. "That's very kind of both of you, but I'm not drinking from either of you. I can't—I'm too hungry. I might not be able to stop," I confess a little shamefully.

Zach walks over to us. "Kael, she can't feed from you, remember? It will only hurt her."

"Damn it, you're right," Kael says defeatedly.

Confused, I look at Kael and then at Zach and finally at Adam, who just shrugs.

It's Adam who asks the question we are both thinking. "What do you mean, it will hurt her?"

I wait for Zach to make a face of annoyance that he has to explain himself to a vampire and a human, but the exact opposite happens. He actually pipes up a little, adjusting his glasses on the bridge of his nose like he's excited about being able to teach someone something. He reminds me of a handsome schoolteacher with his features softer than those of his fellow hunters—hot professor vibes.

"Hunters, during the ascending ceremony, have to drink a potion which allows them to become as fast and strong as vampires, but it does more than that. The potion we drink turns our blood to poison, essentially. If a vampire were to bite us during battle, they would become weaker once our blood entered their body."

He turns his attention to me, addressing me for the first time. "Miss. Sarah, my name is Zach Owen. Forgive me for not properly introducing myself earlier. May I ask, what is it that you usually do to umm—feed?"

I smile at him. "It's just Sarah, and I usually drink from a blood bag. I have some at home." I turn to look at Adam. "Are you ready to go?"

Kael frowns. "Sarah, it's only one-thirty in the afternoon. The sun won't set for a while. Maybe Adam can go and get it for you."

"NO," both Adam and I shout at the same time.

I look at Adam. "Please don't leave me here," I beg.

"My thoughts exactly," he assures me, and then turns to Kael, "I'm not leaving her here alone in a building filled with vampire killers."

Kael flinches, and I immediately feel guilty. It's not that I don't trust Kael, because I do. I know he wouldn't hurt me, but he's just one person in an Academy of vampire hunters.

Still, I don't want to hurt his feelings. "I'm sorry," is all I manage to say.

He shakes his head. "Please don't apologize. You have nothing to be sorry for. I'm the one who should be sorry. It was my fr—coworkers that did this to you," he says, his tone hard. Kael's angry. It's obvious in his stiff posture. His jaw set. But I know he's not angry with me.

"Please tell me what I can do to help. I can go and get your things from your apartment, or Zach can," he turns to Zach. "I don't want her here without me."

Zach nods. "Of course, I don't mind."

I close my eyes. I don't really want Zach, a stranger, albeit a, very kind stranger, but a stranger, going through my things. Kael is the only hunter I fully trust to be on my side while I'm stuck here.

I sigh, knowing the only logical solution. "Adam," I say, looking at him. "You can go and get the blood bag, and maybe something for me to change into?" My current outfit is covered in my blood.

He starts to argue, but I cut him off. "Don't worry, I'll be fine. Kael is here now. I trust him to keep me safe."

"Well, I rode with him, so unless they want to pay for my Uber."

Zach steps up. "I'll take you," he says. After a beat he adds, "If you don't mind, Dr. Patel. I mean, I don't mind taking you to your apartment in Kael's car, and then you are free to follow me back in your vehicle—if you prefer."

Still not sure, Adam sighs, coming over and grasping me gently by the shoulders, "Promise me, you will kill anyone who tries to hurt you again."

I purse my lips. "Adam, I can't. It would be murder."

"Sarah, they used your humanity against you. Don't let that happen again. I know you could have taken them if you tried, and you know it, too."

I look down at my hands in my lap, now dried with blood. "I've never killed a human before, and besides, they're hunters. They're trained killers. I wouldn't have won even if I tried."

"But you didn't try, did you? And lucky for you, they don't consider themselves humans."

I smirk. "What, no, that's silly, just because they are hunters doesn't mean they aren't human. What are they, aliens?"

Adam snorts and looks at Kael. "That's a good question."

I turn in time to see Kael roll his eyes. "Just go. I'll take Sarah to my room. No one will hurt her there."

"Sounds good," I say in my most cheerful voice, although by Adam's frown, he sees through my artifice.

We say goodbye to Adam and Zach. Kael scoops me in his arms again and starts heading out the door.

"Kael, I can walk this time," I tell him.

"You sure? I kind of like carrying you."

*And I like being carried by you,* I think, but don't say. Instead, I smile. "I'm sure." Actually, I'm not a hundred percent sure, but I keep that to myself, too.

When he sets me down, I stumble just a little before righting myself. "I'm okay," I assure him when he reaches for me.

"Sarah, you are still weak." Kael sounds so gutted, like my pain is his pain. He reaches for my hand, and I let him, closing my eyes for a brief moment.

"No, I'm okay, really," I say again, now trying to convince both him and myself. "Lead the way."

# Chapter 24
# Kael

HOW WE MANAGE TO get to my room without a hitch is a miracle. The only people we pass are some second-year tyros.

They stared open-mouthed at Sarah, but didn't stop us or say anything, which I'm grateful for. I don't think Sarah can handle any more confrontations.

She looks so bruised up. It's hard to look at her without wanting to burn the world down, or at least Nick and Shyann for doing this to her. I hate them for what they did. I still can't believe they would stoop to kidnapping someone—especially someone I care about. They're lucky if I let them live to see tomorrow. Every time she cried out during the bullet extractions felt like a bullet to my own heart.

I know Sarah is scared to be here. I just don't know if she is scared of the place or me as well.

I watch her take in my room, which is pretty bare. I'm a minimalist. There's a bed, nightstand, and dresser. I don't keep pictures or sentimental items; all my dirty clothes get put straight into my clothes hamper on the side of my dresser. The only thing that looks rumpled is my bed.

I never make my bed. I see no point in it. I'm just going to mess it up again when it's time for me to sleep. It's not like anyone ever comes in here but me, and *I* don't care if my bed is made.

It dawns on me that Sarah is the first girl that I ever brought back to my room, always preferring to have my hookups in their room instead.

"Umm, you can sit on my bed if you like," I say, gesturing to the queen-size bed against the back corner. My sheets and blanket all have the same matching blue plaid design. "Sorry, I don't really have anywhere else to sit."

She stays standing, seeming a little unbalanced, like she will collapse at any moment. I know she's still in pain. I can see it on her face. I wish I could take it away.

I need to apologize to her somehow. This all happened to her because of me, because we couldn't stay away from each other—because I couldn't stay away.

"Sarah," I say at the same time she says, "Kael, listen."

We both stop.

"You go first," we both say simultaneously.

She mirrors my smile.

"Sarah," I say after a moment, realizing she wants me to go first. "I'm so sorry about what happened to you. Words can't even describe how truly sorry I am."

I walk over to her and place my hand gently on her cheek.

"You don't have to be sorry," she whispers. "It wasn't your fault."

"It was my fault. They wouldn't have been able to do what they did if I had just left you alone like I was supposed to, like I'm supposed to do now."

She swallows. "What if I don't want you to leave me alone?" I can feel the urgency in her voice—the longing.

I close my eyes and lower my forehead to hers. "Sarah," I say desperately.

She quivers a little and uses my shoulders to steady herself.

My eyes shoot open. "You have to feed."

"Nonsense, I'm just swooning over you saying my name. Usually, I don't care for my name. I always felt it kind of plain, but when you say it..."

"Sarah," I say again, wanting to help her through this pain, but hopeless about how.

She smiles and says, "Yep, I have the best name in the world when it's coming from your lips."

I don't smile back. I can't joke and flirt with her when all I think about is how much pain she is in. I hate looking at her like this.

Sarah's still the most beautiful woman I have ever laid eyes on, even when she's covered in bruises and bullet wounds. Her hair, which is usually a silky waterfall of perfection, is knotted, and some parts are sticky and matted together, probably

157

from dried blood. Her honey-colored skin lacks the luster that I now associate with her.

The arm that Nick exposed to sunlight looks worst of all. It looks raw with its shiny red and pink skin going halfway to her elbow. It's hard to imagine Sarah not having any physical scars even after she feeds.

She'll probably have emotional ones, that much, I'm sure.

"I'm sorry you can't feed from me," I say honestly. "If you could, you know I would let you in a heartbeat."

A smile creeps onto her lips. "I believe you," she says, wobbling a little as she speaks.

How is she still standing, or a better question is, why is she still standing? I wonder if it's because the thought of sitting on my bed is unnerving for her.

"Is there anything I can do to help?" I ask.

"Do I need to worry about a bunch of hunters busting down the door with pitchforks?"

I sigh, but take my time to answer, because, honestly, I have no fucking idea. I don't want to tell her how worried I am about the people here at the Academy doing just that, substituting the pitchforks for various wooden weapons.

The only thing on our side is that Sarah does have a different aura around her than every other vampire I've ever come across. That might confuse hunters that just so happen to walk by, and tyros who haven't ascended yet lack that extra ability, thankfully.

"I think we are okay for now," I say after a pause. "Don't worry, I won't let them hurt you, I promise."

She gives me a side smirk. "Are you that talented a fighter, Kael Hart, that you can fend off an Academy full of hunters?"

"I can if I have to," I assure her.

She nods and looks around the room again.

"Sarah, do you want to sit on the bed, that way you can rest up a bit?" I offer for the second time.

"I don't want to get your bed dirty," she says, gesturing to herself and her bloody clothes.

So that's why she doesn't want to sit. "Don't worry about that. I can always wash my bedding afterwards."

I go and sit on the bed, gesturing for her to do the same. She comes and sits next to me, leaving us at arm's length from each other. She winces as she sits.

*Damn it.* I hope that Adam comes back soon with the blood bags.

She takes a few deep breaths before saying, "Can you tell me something to help pass the time while waiting for Adam?"

"Like what?"

"Anything," she says, turning her head to look at me. "Tell me how vampire hunters came about. Do you know? Were you always around?"

"No, we weren't always around," I tell her. "However, we have been around for hundreds of years now. Jamin and Joel are the names of the original hunters."

Sarah turns her body fully to me. "I'm intrigued."

I give a slight grin. "Okay, but I've never told this story before. I only hear others tell it, so I might leave parts out," I warn.

She gives a small incline of her head and gestures for me to proceed.

"It all started a long, long time ago, when vampires were starting to overrun the population. There was an abundance of lives lost. History books blamed it on war, famine, and plagues."

I try to recite the story just the way Aquila does.

"There was this one small village that a group of four vampires came to. They were entering huts and cabins, killing everyone they came across.

"While everyone else was running scared, these two brothers stood up to fight the vampires. They approached one vampire who was feeding off the wife of the village's pastor. The vampire laughed at the two humans who thought they could stand a chance against him.

"Little did it know that Jamin's girlfriend was a mage. She was watching from nearby and saw her beloved attempting to fight one of the bloody beasts. She cast a spell of protection and strength to help him and his brother succeed.

"The brothers, Jamin and Joel, were great fighters and very wise, and with the added strength the brothers were able to defeat the vampire, by stabbing a sharp wooden stake through his heart. They were able to defeat another one by striking it with a flaming torch.

"Jamin and Joel saw how quickly the creature burst into flames, turning to dust moments later. They hunted down the last two vampires and were quickly able to defeat them, striking them at a distance with flamed spears.

"Jamin's beloved told an elder mage how she was able to help the brothers defeat the blood beasts. The elder went to them and told them that she could make them just as fast and strong as the vampires they defeated, for the rest of their days, if they pledged an oath to use that strength to hunt and kill vampires. They agreed, and so began the first ceremony to become a vampire hunter.

"The mage made some kind of potion, adding sage, which was thought to weaken vampires, and cast a spell on it, binding it with the brothers' blood. Jamin and Joel drank the potion and became the first vampire hunters.

"The elder mage also told them that the spell she cast allowed it so that their children and children's children would have the blood of a hunter, and if they would choose that life, all they would have to do is perform the ceremony, take the Hunters' Oath, and they too would ascend."

"The Hunters' Oath?" Sarah asks.

"Hunt the ones that hide in the shadows. Kill the ones that surrendered their souls. Burn the ones that drink the blood of the innocent."

When I finish, I look over at Sarah, who is staring at me in amazement.

"Wow," is all she says.

"Aquila tells the story better," I say, not sure if the "wow" was because of the story, or the oath, or both.

"Who's that?"

"He's the head of the Academy, kind of like our headmaster."

She nods in understanding.

"And how would he feel about me being here?" she asks, eyes cast down.

"Let's hope we don't find out," I say, and then add in a lighter tone. "I'll just have to keep you in my bed until nightfall."

She smiles and looks like she is about to say something when there is a knock at the door.

# Chapter 25
# Kael

"Should I hide?" Sarah asks, standing up in a hurry. "Just in case it's pitchforks and stakes on the other side?"

Before I can respond, Zach's voice comes from outside.

"It's just us," he calls out.

I quickly unlock the door, letting him and Adam in.

Adam is wearing a backpack that he quickly swings off his shoulders and unzips. He hands Sarah a blood bag. I see her fangs immediately pop out. She's about to bite into it when she looks at me and then at Zach.

"Would you like us to step out, Sarah?" Zach asks, obviously picking up on her discomfort the same time I do.

"Umm, if you don't mind," she says sheepishly. "It will only take me a moment."

I want to argue that I don't mind her feeding in front of me, but I don't want to delay her feeding any longer by trying to argue my case. Instead, I nod and follow Zach and Adam into the hallway.

"Any trouble while we were away?" Zach asks.

I shake my head. "No, none."

Zach looks surprised, and to be honest, I'm just as surprised as he is. Kayda comes walking down the hall as Sarah opens the door.

*That was quick.*

"Is it okay if I join you?" Kayda asks as Zach and Adam stride back into the room.

"I'm not sure how many hunters Sarah is willing to be around," I say.

"It's okay," Sarah says from behind me.

I turn to look at her and am amazed at how much difference one blood bag can make. All of the bullet wounds are gone, and her complexion is healthier. I look at her arm and, it too, is back to normal.

She smiles, looking at Kayda. "Thank you for today. I know standing up for a vampire must not have been easy for you."

"Let's bring this inside," Zach says from already inside my room. "We don't want Sarah to be spotted."

We all pile inside and lock the door behind us. I've definitely never had five people in my room at one time. It's getting a little crowded in here.

I can't stop staring at Sarah. She's far from the victim on the verge of death she was a few moments ago. Only her bloody clothes give away the trauma she went through. Now that Sarah's feeling better, I want to kick everyone else out and have a little alone time with her. Help her change out of those clothes. See if there's some way I can make her forget all that happened today.

"You're welcome," Kayda says to Sarah. "If Kael trusts you, then that's enough for me."

I smile at Kayda, thankful for her being on my side. "Sarah, this is Kayda Parker. She's one of the smartest people alive. Well, aside from Zach."

Zach gives a shy grin. "I'm just book smart. Kayda is universally smart."

Another knock at my door cuts off whatever Kayda was going to say in reply.

"Seriously, who is it now?" I ask, a little frustrated. I don't think I can fit yet another grown-ass adult in my room.

"It's me," Liam answers, obviously hearing me.

I unlock the door, letting him in. He looks over at Sarah and gives a polite smile.

"You're looking much better, Sarah. I'm glad to see you are alright." Turning to look at me, he adds, "Aquila knows about her. He wants to see you. I've been trying to explain things to him, though when I mentioned the word *Validus*, he seemed to know what I was talking about, and now he wants to see her."

"Well, he can't," I say defiantly, knowing that I'm arguing a losing battle. No one says no to Aquila.

Liam sighs. "I'm sorry, Kael. He insisted."

I turn to look at Sarah. Everyone else is frozen in place, not knowing what to say.

"Pitchforks time?" she asks.

I nod sympathetically. "I'm still not letting anyone hurt you. I promise," I reassure her.

"Would it be okay if I got dressed in new clothes first? I'm going to assume asking for a shower would be out of the question."

"I don't think taking a shower in the communal bathrooms would be the wisest thing," Kayda says.

I agree.

"Sarah, if you would like, you can take a shower in my room before we go see the headmaster," Liam offers.

I sometimes forget that Liam, as the leader, gets an upgraded room with its ensuite bathroom.

She turns to me and I nod, giving the assurance that Liam can be trusted.

Sarah smiles at Liam. "That would be nice, thank you."

Liam hands me the key to his room. "I'll let Aquila know that you both will head to the library in twenty minutes." Without waiting for an answer, he opens the door and walks out.

Kayda offers to take Sarah to Liam's room instead of me, saying something about Sarah needing girl time or some shit like that.

Sarah agrees. I walk with them to Liam's room, but the door is slammed in my face before I can even attempt coming in.

I remind myself that it was Kayda who found and texted me about Sarah. I know I can trust her, but I really don't want to leave Sarah's side right now.

Zach offers to take Adam to wait in the study. Although, I don't think Aquila will like a human there, or rather an ordinary human.

Surprisingly, I like Adam, even though he seems to hate me. I can see that he loves Sarah like family and wants to protect her, so I could never really dislike him. We're on the same side.

He demanded that he be a part of the conversation with Aquila, and Sarah agreed. I think she needs him there for emotional support. Again, I hate that I'm not that person for her. God knows, I want to be.

I wait right outside Liam's door. I don't dare leave them to walk the halls alone. Kayda mentioned that Clara, one of the girls on Patrick's squad, approached her and wanted to know if it's true that I brought in a vampire.

Strictly speaking, I did not bring in a vampire, Nick and Shyann did, but I would rather everyone know that Sarah is associated with me. It may have them second guessing themselves on whether to approach her. I'm not known for my kind and friendly demeanor around here, unless you are in the same squad as me.

The girls take about fifteen minutes before walking out of the room. Sarah is dressed in colorful yoga pants and a black V-neck shirt; her hair is washed, dried, and back to its beautiful, dark waves down her back.

*Fuck, she's sexy.* I reach out for her hand, and she lets me intertwine our fingers. I smile a little; she smells like the men's shampoo and body wash that I usually associate with Liam.

"Ready?" I ask.

She shakes her head. "No, but I don't think I have a choice in the matter."

I frown. "I'm sorry about this," I say. "If you want to, we can go back to my room until they come to find us, which might give us a little more time."

She laughs. "No, no, let's get this over with now. I would rather know about the pitchforks sooner rather than later so that I have time to prepare."

Kayda looks at us in confusion. "Pitchforks?"

We explain the joke while walking to the library. Apparently, word has gotten around that Sarah is in the building because we come across several tyros hiding behind doors and plants trying to get a glimpse of the vampire we are allowing to walk freely.

Kayda and Sarah seem to be getting along well, which I like. I'm hoping they all grow to love Sarah now that I've decided to never let her go.

After today, I'm no longer going to fight my feelings for her, or try and stay away. I love her. *I'm in love with her.* I feel it with my whole body. The thought of her being in trouble, of her dying, filled me with fear I'd never felt before in my life. My team, my friends, the people I thought I would do anything to protect... I would have killed them in a heartbeat if it meant saving Sarah. I don't care if she's a vampire and I'm a vampire hunter. I'll find a way for us to be together if that's still what she wants.

I know I need to talk to her about how I feel and what I want. I'm a little scared to hear what she will say to it all. Everything that has happened to her today is because of me.

Even though she doesn't blame me at this moment, will she still be forgiving when she's had a night to stop and think about it? I can't be sure, and to think, it's not over yet. We still have Aquila to deal with.

Sarah is asking about Kayda's tattoos, of which she has several. They are all Adinkra symbols, or symbols of magic. Unlike Nick, who has just a sleeve of tattoos down one arm and a snake on the other, Kayda's tattoos are spread out on various parts of her body.

I've already seen all her tattoos, well, all her visible ones at least, so my mind wanders off to other things, like what Aquila wants with Sarah? I hope this doesn't come to a fight, but if it does, how many people am I fighting off to protect the woman I love?

"And this one is called Unity in Diversity," Kayda says, pointing to her collar bone where a tattoo of intricate black designs forms across mid-clavicle, finishing at the start of her neck. "My next one will be of strength."

"That's amazing. Do you have a picture?"

"No time," I interrupt. "We're here."

"I'll show you after," Kayda whispers to Sarah.

We walk in, and the whole team is there, in the middle of an argument.

"We can't kill her," Zach shouts. "She has a soul; it would be like killing a human."

"She's a vampire," Shyann says in disgust.

I clear my throat, although I know they already knew we were here. Shyann would have sensed Sarah as soon as we walked in.

"Why are they here?" I growl out with as much rage as possible, gesturing to Shyann and Nick.

I see Shyann flinch.

*Good.* I want her to know how much I've come to loathe her in the passing hours.

Aquila steps forward. "I was allowing them to discuss several options, but now that you are here—" he turns to look at the others— "please give us the room. I will keep all options in mind. Thank you." He says it in such a dismissive tone that it leaves no room for argument.

Shyann and Nick leave right away, giving us a wide berth as they pass. Zach and Kayda both hesitate a moment before slowly walking out. Liam lingers, and Adam folds his arms over his chest and plants his feet firmly on the ground.

Liam walks up to Aquila. "If it's okay with Sarah, I would like to stay."

That's when Aquila turns and looks at Sarah for the first time—and gasps.

# Chapter 26
# Sarah

THIS OLDER GENTLEMAN WITH almond-colored skin, and long jet-black hair pulled up in a ponytail, stares at me for a moment like he just saw a ghost. I know he is already aware that I'm a vampire, so why does he look so shocked?

"It can't be..." he whispers.

"Hello," is all I can think to say. I give a little wave of my hand. "It's fine by me if Liam wants to stay." Not that I would have a say in the matter.

Apparently, my voice seems to trigger another shock from him. This time he manages to hide it better, but I have super hearing, so I heard the jump of his heartbeat when I spoke.

Aquila turns to look at Liam and then back at me, and then back at Liam, and then back at me.

For all I know, he's always like this when he meets new people, but by the confusion on Kael's and Liam's faces, I'm guessing probably not.

"A *Validus,*" he whispers to himself. "Of course, she would have to be."

"Aquila? Is everything okay?" Liam asks, his brow furrowed in concern.

Aquila shakes his head, finally recovering from whatever crisis he just mentally went through.

"Of course, sorry." He looks at me. "Sarah, I'll make an announcement to the other hunters to leave you alone. At sundown, you are free to go."

I'm in shock. He's letting me go just like that? I thought I was going to have to fight my way out of this building. I'm having a hard time believing that it could be this easy.

"Umm, thank you, sir," I tell him, still not entirely sure what is happening right now. I don't want to let my guard down. This could be a trick.

He gives me the ghost of a smile and bows his head without saying another word to me. "Liam, may I speak with you for a moment?" Aquila asks, turning away from the rest of us.

"What in the ninety-five Jupiter moons just happened?" I ask in dismay, looking up at Kael, who looks as confused as I feel.

"Well, that was easy," Adam states, walking over to me. "I was ready to throw down, and by throw down, I mean call the authorities, because you know," he says, gesturing to himself.

Aquila and Liam step into what looks to be a conference room, but with my heightened hearing, I can still make out what they are saying. All it takes is a little concentration.

*"Your mother, is she still overseas meeting with the London Academy?" Aquila asks Liam.*

*"Yes, she and my father will be out there for another two weeks, I think."*

*"Call her and tell her she needs to come back right away," Aquila says, and then quickly corrects himself. "On second thought, I'll call her. I need to speak with her."*

*"Aquila, are you okay?" Liam asks for the second time tonight. "Earlier, you seemed to agree with Nick and Shyann about what we should do about Sarah. I thought we would have to fight you more to keep her alive. Don't get me wrong, I'm glad you are letting her go, for Kael's sake, but I'm curious... Why the change of heart?"*

*"There is much you don't know, and much I am not at liberty to share with you at this time. I'm sorry."*

"Sarah?" Kael asks, cutting off my concentration on the conversation in the other room.

I look over at Kael and he is staring at me in concern.

"Are you okay?"

"Yes," I answer, although I'm not completely sure that's the truth. It doesn't make sense that they would let me live, right? Maybe because I'm a *Validus,* that means I get the benefit of the doubt?

Kael lifts our intertwined hands to his lips and presses a gentle kiss on my knuckles. "I'm glad there will be no fighting, but I hope you know, I would have fought this whole fucking Academy to keep you safe."

A shiver runs through me at his words. I'll never get enough of him.

***

It's decided that we'll spend the remaining daylight hours in Liam's room, since it's bigger than Kael's. Kael tried to hint that he would prefer it be just the two of us in his room, but Adam refuses to leave my side.

Secretly, I think Liam doesn't want to leave Kael alone with a vampire. Zach and Kayda are hanging around, too. Although, by the quick glances toward Adam, it seems that Zach's staying has more to do with his own personal reasons than anything that has to do with me.

I'm a little on edge still. Sure, they seem pretty chill. As long as Nick and Shyann don't show up, the extra company is kind of nice, but they are still hunters. And they still don't really know me.

Kael seems to notice my uneasiness because he doesn't keep his hands off me for the next few hours, whether it's holding my hand, squeezing my knee, or putting his arm around my shoulders. Every once in a while, he will lean down and whisper in my ear asking how I'm holding up, or if I'm okay.

It's sweet, and it grounds me, my discomfort tempering with every touch.

Liam and Kayda keep giving us weird glances. I'm not sure what it's about. Are they weirded out because I'm a vampire, or because they aren't used to seeing Kael with someone?

When it's finally time to leave, Kael escorts me to Adam's car. But at the entrance, two women are walking in as we are walking out. Both give me curious glances. Not in a hard "I know what you are" kind of way. The older lady looks as though she wants to say something, but must think better of it.

Aquila appears out of nowhere and greets them. "I'll explain," he whispers to the older lady.

Everyone seems to forget that I can hear them, even if they whisper. The other one looks about our age. She is a curvy girl with deep, ebony skin, her hair in long braids down her back.

"Umm, nice to see you again, Kael." She says his name with a bit of rising inflection, as if she is asking a question rather than greeting him.

Kael lifts his chin in a curt acknowledgment. "Hi, Dana." Then adds, "I'm on my way out. I'll catch up with you next time."

Then, without another word, he ushers me out the door.

He must sense that I want to ask because he whispers in my ear, "They're mages. The older one is the Academy's main healer but helps with MC business from time to time."

I nod in understanding. "Do they come here a lot?"

"Yes," he answers. "We work with them to help keep the world safe from vampires. Aquila is on the council, too, even though he isn't a mage. The city's alpha werewolf also has a speaking voice and is allowed to attend bigger meetings, but I don't think he is permitted an actual seat on the council. He has to report to them if any of his pack kills someone during a full moon."

"What then?" I ask curiously, as we make it to the car. We have some time, because Adam was hungry, so Zach offered to show him to the kitchen to grab a bite to eat. I sent him a text to meet me at the car.

"The council deliberates on what will happen to the werewolf who has committed murder," Kael states.

"Wow, that's—organized. They don't allow the alpha to handle his own pack?"

"No, I mean he gets to say his piece, but in the end, it's the MC that hands out all sentencing."

I narrow my eyes. "So, they run the show? Sounds kind of tyrannical."

He shrugs dismissively. "This is how it's always been. I don't really get into it much. I just hunt and leave the politics to the others. Liam, however, will have a seat on the council one day. I'm sure of it."

Just then, Adam and Zach walk outside, deep in conversation with one another.

Kael pulls me in for a hug. "I'm glad you're okay, Sarah. I'm sorry about everything that happened today. Are you sure you don't want me to go with you?" he asks.

"No, I'm okay. I just really want to be home alone to process everything," I say truthfully. "I want to lie in my bed and not get up for the next few days."

Kael leans in and presses our foreheads together. "Let me know if you change your mind. I can't wait to see that bed of yours."

I get an immediate tingling in my heart and my inner thighs, but before I have time to swoon, Adam clears his throat. "As much as I would like to watch whatever sexual tension is about to unfurl here, I too, am ready to go home."

Kael groans, giving an agitated glance at Zach and Adam. "Does he always act this way or just around me?"

I laugh. "If you mean, is he always awesome? Then the answer is yes."

Zach snorts, trying to hold in a laugh while Adam gives Kael a smug grin. We all say our goodbyes before Adam and I get in his car and drive off.

As soon as the Academy is in our rearview mirror, I feel like I can finally relax, slumping into my seat. It's like my whole body has been in fight or flight mode the entire time I was there. No offense to Kael, but I hope I never step foot in the Academy again. I didn't want to break down in front of him, but now that it's just Adam and I, finally making our way home, the lump that's been hiding in the back of my throat begins to rise. The first few tears slip down the sides of my face, and as soon as I clock it, I completely break down. My emotions are like a sea surge crashing down on me from everything that has happened in the last twenty-four hours.

Adam doesn't say a word. He lets me cry it out, knowing that I need this. On the way, he stops and gets a pint of chocolate chip cookie dough ice cream for us to share. Technically, I know I can't even taste it, but it's the principle of the matter. Besides, I still like the coldness of the ice cream; I might just drizzle some blood on top to make it a real treat.

# Chapter 27
# Sarah

I TAKE A FEW days for myself. The shock comes in waves, so do the tears. And so, I spend my time alternating between staring at my ceiling and going through a pack of tissues. In between, I'm sleeping and drinking blood. I'm consuming more than usual; Adam's had to make some extra trips to the blood center.

Kael texts me the day after the ordeal to ask how I'm doing. I tell him I'm fine, but that I need a few days to recover. I know he wants to come over, but processing what happened is taking me a while. I almost died. I was tortured. By the people who work and live with the man I have this intense connection with. But if him and I had just left each other alone, this would have never happened. I wouldn't have put Adam in danger. I wouldn't be feeling like this.

And still, when I think about him, warmth blooms in my chest. It's confusing as all hell. As much as I want to be near him, I don't want him to see me this way, hair messy, in my pjs, drinking blood bag smoothies.

He respectfully, albeit reluctantly, keeps his distance. Texting me every day to tell me that he hopes I'm recovering okay and that he's thinking about me. I never feel any pressure to reply or be attentive. And slowly I begin to remember his touch, how good it feels to have him close. I remember the way he kissed the back of my hand, how he was willing to burn the whole Academy down for me. His home. His friends. He'd put me first.

It's now been three days, and I'm dying to see him. Kael has become my addiction, and I'm having withdrawals. I'm jittery and antsy and won't be able to think straight until I see him again, but not tonight.

Tonight, Adam and I have plans. Adam knocks on the apartment door as we arrive at Mr. George and Mrs. May's place.

"Sarah, honey, did you get yourself enough food to eat, dear? Would you like seconds?" Mrs. May asks, forty minutes later.

I shake my head. Swallowing down the last bite. "No, Ma'am. I'm stuffed," I lie, but patting my belly to embellish my untruth.

To be honest, I don't really feel anything when it comes to eating actual food. It's like eating perfumed mush to me. "But thank you so much for dinner, it was delicious as always."

"Hmm, she's right, Mrs. May. I cannot get enough of your food," Adam says, still eating from his big bowl.

We are in their apartment above the diner. They invite Adam and me once every few months to come eat ever since they found out that Adam's parents moved back to India after he graduated high school and mine are deceased. I think they took it upon themselves to try and give us some parental presence closer to home. I've grown to love dinner nights with the Mays.

Their one-bedroom apartment is small and quaint, with dozens upon dozens of pictures lining every wall, corner table, and shelf. The two of them on their wedding day. Another of them, young and all smiles on vacation at the beach. Then later on in life, Mrs. May holding her oldest daughter, Tania, at the hospital. Mr. and Mrs. May buying the diner downstairs, of them cutting a small red ribbon lining the door on opening day.

Then, it's Tania's school pictures and Tania's wedding, Tania holding her baby boy, Sam. Lastly, Sam's school pictures, them and Sam at the park, Sam working in the diner downstairs, Sam graduating college. It's a beautiful love story of memories and happiness.

"Oh, make sure you leave room for Vivian's peach cobbler," Mr. George tells me, gesturing to the oven. "Best in the world."

"Absolutely," I say.

"See now, this is why I can only afford to dine with you two every couple of months," Adam says sternly. "It takes so much time to recover."

"Nonsense," Mrs. May tells him with the wave of her hand as she fills his cup up with sweet tea before sitting back down. "You are too skinny anyway. You need to put some meat on those bones."

Adam scoffs and puts his hand to his chest. "You know I've got to stay looking sharp. My twenties won't last forever, and I plan to make the most of them."

Mr. George laughs. "I'm sure you attract attention everywhere you go," he says, eyeing Adam's clothes.

"Mr. George," Adam exclaims in mock horror. "Are you making fun of me?"

Adam is wearing baby-pink chino pants, with a low-cut, fitted, silk white shirt tucked in, and a matching pink and blue ascot tied around his neck.

"Now, you don't listen to this old fool, ya' hear. I think you look very nice, Dr. Adam," Mrs. May says, getting up to take the peach cobbler out of the oven.

"Thanksgiving is this Thursday. Are you flying out to see your aunt again this year?" she asks me.

"Yep, got my flight booked," I lie.

They've invited me, along with Adam, for the last two years. I've made the excuse that my Aunt Margaret insisted I fly out to Seattle to spend Thanksgiving with her.

Not being able to go out during the day really sucks.

I actually do have an Aunt Margaret, but she has never asked me to visit her. Apparently, after her brother, my dad, died, she decided an adopted child was not flesh and blood. As soon as the funeral was over, I was no longer a part of the family.

I've never minded the disownment. She has always been an awful person. My dad never talked to her when he was alive. He always said life is too short to try to make room in our lives for people like her.

"Well, safe travels," Mrs. May tells me, bringing me back to the present.

"I, too, will not be able to make it this year," Adam confesses. "I'm working in the ER that day. People can't seem to keep themselves out of trouble, even during Thanksgiving."

"I'm sorry to hear that," Mr. George says earnestly. "We will miss you Thursday. I know Sam likes having you here. Otherwise, he's here all by himself with a bunch of old people."

"I think you meant to say 'awesome people,'" Adam corrects. "Oh, what the hell, bring on the peach cobbler."

Mrs. May grabs fresh plates from her pantry. After serving all of us a piece, and refusing help from either Adam or me, she sits down with us and looks over at me.

"Now Miss. Sarah, I've noticed that young man come and join you at the diner a few nights in a row. Is that someone special to you?"

I smile. "Maybe, the jury is still out on that one," I say truthfully.

I'm not sure what Kael is to me. Something has definitely changed between the two of us since he found me in the Academy basement. I'm just not sure exactly what it is, but I can't wait to find out.

We spend another hour sitting around the kitchen table, talking and catching up, before saying our goodbyes and making plans for our next dinner night.

***

Ten minutes later, Adam and I make it to our apartment building and are walking down the hall arm in arm to our door, when we both stop short.

The hunter, Zach, is waiting by the entrance.

"Umm, hi," I say awkwardly. He is the last person I would expect to show up at my apartment.

Does Kael know he's here? Sudden doubt pricks at me, and I clutch Adam a little tighter. I know Zach was one of the people who helped us, but I stay vigilant just the same. Fool me once, as the saying goes.

"Can we help you with something?" I ask skeptically.

"Right, sorry to intrude with no warning," he quickly says, and then holds out Adam's colorful kimono. "You forgot this at the Academy the other day. I figured you would want it back."

*Ohhh*, a lightbulb clicks inside my brain. He's not here for me. I breathe a little easier as I try to hold in my grin, my eyes flicking to Adam to read the look on his face. Pulling the old *bringing back an item so that he has an excuse to see Adam trick. Oldest one in the book.*

Adam seems frozen, his mouth slightly agape, his brain clearly processing the epiphany I just had.

"That was very considerate of you," I say when, after five seconds, Adam still hasn't said a thing, or moved. I turn to Adam and squeeze his arm a little, willing him out of his funk. He finally moves to look at me, and I give him a shit-eating grin.

Adam ignores me and takes his kimono from Zach, his motor functions working again. "That *was* very considerate. Thank you. I thought I lost Rolo forever."

At the confused look on Zach's face, I elaborate, "He names his more prized pieces of clothing. Would you like to come in?"

"I don't want to impose," Zach says shyly, and now that his hands are free, he shoves them into his pants pockets.

He's handsome, with his sandy brown hair and steel blue eyes. Although he is the slimmest of the males in his group, he, like the rest of the hunters, is lean and fit. He's wearing glasses tonight with jeans and a chestnut, knitted sweater that has his hot professor vibes going off in full swing.

I gently elbow Adam in the ribs to signal that it's time for him to step in. He's not usually so silent.

Adam coughs before finding his voice. "You're not imposing," Adam assures him. "I would like it if you stayed. Maybe you can have a drink with us." Then adds with a roll of his eyes, "well, not Sarah—obviously. She wouldn't be drinking, unless she is in the mood to make her own special cocktail, the Bloody Sarah."

Zach gives a quizzical eyebrow bunch. "The Bloody Sarah?"

"Yeah, it's like a Bloody Mary except with real blood instead of tomato juice," Adam explains.

Zach's shoulders shake with silent laughter. "I would love to stay for a drink."

"How are you feeling?" Zach asks me as we head to the kitchen. Adam gathers the ingredients and tools he needs to make him and Zach a martini.

"I'm good, no scars to speak of, only the emotional ones," I joke.

He grimaces.

I wave my hand and give a reassuring smile. "I'm kidding. I'm okay, really." I don't add that I've had nightmares of being left out in the sun for the last few nights, but he doesn't need to know that.

Adam, having either not heard our exchange or choosing to move on from it, says, "Unfortunately, I have run out of sour apple schnapps to make an appletini." Then, with the shake of his head, he adds, "That's what I get for not vetting the bartender we hired for the Halloween party using my two-page interview guide. I do not think he was using the jiggers I specifically asked him to use, but what's done is done. Would you like a Gibson or a dirty martini?"

Zach looks blank-faced at Adam like he's speaking a different language. I take pity on the bashful hunter and whisper, "Do you want an olive or an onion in your drink?"

"Oh," he says in understanding. "An olive, please."

Adam makes both of them a dirty martini, his extra dirty, and then joins us at our small kitchen table.

"Thank you, Dr. Patel," Zach says as he grabs his drink and takes a small sip.

Adam waves his hand. "You can call me Adam. I was being, understandably, extra that day."

"Understandably," Zach agrees.

We talk for a while, trying to find topics to converse about, from the weather to Adam's work at the hospital. We sprint through books, movies, and social media outlets quickly since Zach isn't well educated on any of those subjects. His lifestyle and area of expertise is more closely tied science and history for both the human and supernatural worlds.

We avoid the obvious topics. What's life like as a vampire hunter? How long has he been killing my kind?

I excuse myself after an hour, feigning tiredness.

"Oh, yes, well, I guess I should go," Zach softly says, a little defeatedly, getting to his feet.

I eye Adam, who jumps in and speaks. "You don't have to go. I won't bite when Sarah leaves, I promise."

Zach gives a sheepish grin before sitting back down, and I head to my room feeling rather proud of my wingwoman skills.

# Chapter 28
# Kael

I'M PACING BACK AND forth in my room, just like I've been doing for the last few days.

I don't know how long I should give Sarah before asking to see her again. How much space is too much space? I don't want to push her, but I also don't want *this*, whatever this is, to be something that just fizzles out due to lack of contact. Sure, we've been texting, but it's not enough.

I'm scared she may be having second thoughts about me. She has gone through a lot just because of knowing me, and yet I'm too selfish to stay away. I can't. I want her, need her.

I pull out my phone.

```
Me: How are you feeling?
```

Five minutes go by with no response. A ping finally lights up my phone, but I feel a twinge of disappointment when I see it's the squad's group text, and it's from Liam.

```
Liam: Meeting in five. Meet in the conference room.
```

Almost everyone is here by the time I arrive. I go to sit next to Kayda on the loveseat. Zach hasn't arrived yet, so while waiting, Kayda leans over to me seeing Sarah's name at the top of my phone. She's asked about Sarah only once since the rescue.

"I like her," she says, giving me a slight knock on the shoulders.

I smile. "She's pretty great, isn't she?"

"Yes. The roommate is perfect. I hope to see him from time to time."

I sigh. "I'm pretty sure Adam hates me," I admit.

"He might just need more time to get to know you. When he called you the brooding Greek god the other night, I seriously almost peed myself laughing."

I scoff, remembering Adam's off handed name-calling toward me the day we all spent in Liam's room. "I don't brood."

"Oh, you so do brood," she tells me. "But it's okay because you're super-hot and it looks good on you."

I arch a brow at her. "Kayda, are you starting to crush on me?"

She barks out a laugh. "Get over yourself," she says as she pushes my shoulder again.

I catch Shyann's eye for a second, before quickly looking away. I'm nowhere near ready to talk to her or Nick yet, probably not for a while. Or ever again.

Zach comes running in and plops down in a chair, apologizing for running late. None of us are surprised that he is late. Whenever he's researching, which is what he's doing ninety percent of the time, he won't pay attention to anything else.

This time, it's the usual meeting, talking about our upcoming patrol schedule for the next week. Liam is in the middle of our routine map layouts when my phone vibrates letting me know I got a message.

I quickly look down to see it's from Sarah, and my heart jumps in excitement.

Sarah: Hey, sorry it took so long to respond. I had a treat-yourself online shopping night two days ago and bought this amazing memory foam pillow, which I used for the first time last night. It works a little too well. Put me in a sleep coma.

Another text comes in a second later.

Sarah: I'm feeling much better. How about you?

I smile.

Me: I'm good. I'll be even better if I can see you.
Any chance you'd be up for a date with me?

Sarah: How do I know this is the real Kael this
time?

I frown. *Fuck*. She's right. I wouldn't trust texting, either, after what she went through. I put my phone on silent and quickly take a selfie while Liam's back is turned, then send it. I catch Kayda's smirk from the corner of my eye, but I ignore it.

Sarah: This picture could have already been on your
phone. How am I supposed to know that it was taken
just now?

Me: Because that is the first selfie I have ever
taken. Believe it or not, I'm not a big selfie-taking
person. Well, of my face, anyway.

I grin as I press send.
Three dots... three dots... three dots.

Sarah: Oh boy. I really have no comeback for that
last comment. Please give me a second and I'll come
up with something.

I hold in a laugh. I can't seem to stop smiling down at my phone.

Me: So, what about that date?

I immediately see the three dots appear.

`Sarah: Is Kael Hart asking me out on an official`
`date?`

`Me: I am. And just a heads up, I plan to ask you`
`to be my girlfriend by the end of that date.`

I see the conversational three dots appear and then disappear. And then reappear again. I might burn a hole through my phone if I stare at it harder, but still, I can't seem to look away.

"Seeing as how both Kael and Zach are a bit distracted today, I guess we can go ahead and end the meeting here," Liam shouts playfully.

The sound of my name breaks the death-stare contest I'm holding with my phone. I glance over at Zach, who is putting his phone back in his pocket with a guilty look.

"Sorry," he says sheepishly.

I briefly wonder who he was texting before focusing my attention on Liam.

"Yeah, man, sorry, I was..."

Liam smiles and waves me off. "It's fine. I was mostly done anyway, but I do have one more announcement. Amberly has been delayed coming here until the start of the new year. She will be here the first week in January."

It takes me a moment to even remember why I know that name, and then I recall us getting an unwanted addition to our squad. The news that upset me a few weeks ago almost has me relieved now.

A new member might not be so bad, considering the state of our squad. Maybe this girl can provide some much-needed distraction to Nick and Shyann. I wonder why her coming here is delayed?

As he wraps up and everyone is dismissed, I finally get a ping on my phone.

`Sarah: I thought you didn't do the girlfriend`
`thing?`

I frown. That's not what I thought she would say. Does she not want to be together? Would I blame her if she didn't?

Me: If you agree on going on a date with me, we can talk about it in person.

Three dots and a few seconds later...

Sarah: I most definitely agree to go on a date with you.

Me: Tomorrow night?

Sarah: Can't wait.

***

The next night, I'm knocking on Sarah's door and stunned into silence when she answers.

Sarah is wearing a short red dress that ends just above of her thighs. It's one of those dresses that's loose at the bottom. I can easily slip my hand up the dress to have full access to her if I wanted, and damn, do I want to. She's in heels, which I don't usually associate with Sarah. Every time I've ever seen her she's been wearing Converse.

"Do you like it?" she asks as she gives a little twirl. "It's an off-the-shoulder chiffon ruffle dress."

"I have no idea what any of that means, but yes, I like it," I say, and reach for her hand to pull her to me, breathing in her deliciously sweet apple and honeysuckle scent.

She giggles as she wraps her hands around my neck. Before I can think better of it, I kiss her.

The second our lips connect, I lose all thoughts except for how desperate I am to taste her. To touch her. I suddenly want to glide my hands all over her body.

She reacts to my desire instantly, like I've unlocked it in her. She's kissing me back, sliding her tongue in to massage with mine. Our kiss is frantic and hungry. We're both clawing and pulling at each other, willing the other to be closer. I lift her slightly, taking a few steps into the apartment so I can kick the door closed behind us.

I pull my head back to ask, "Is Adam here?"

She shakes her head feverishly. "No, he's at work."

"Good," is all I say before sliding my hands to her thighs and lifting her completely up. She obediently wraps her legs around my waist.

I back her up against the wall, never taking my lips off hers. Her fingers slide up and fist in my hair, causing me to go instantly hard. I make my way to her neck, down to the tops of her breasts, pressing open-mouth kisses to every part I can reach.

Sarah's head falls back as she moans. She starts to move her hips in a dance around my waist.

"Fuck, Sarah. Do you know how long I waited for this? How much I want you?" I whisper in her ear as I slide my hands up the back of her legs, under her dress. I feel her shudder beneath my touch; it's intoxicating.

"Show me," she rasps. I don't know how things got so intense so quickly. Maybe it's because we haven't been around each other. Maybe it's because we've been building too much tension, and the time apart has brought it to a boiling point. I usually don't do this on a first date. Then again, I usually don't date. All I know is that this feels right. And she's making it very clear that it feels right to her, too.

Her words have me guiding her to the sofa. With a gentle hand on her lower back I lay her down and settle myself on top of her, right between her legs, so she can feel exactly how much I want her.

"Is this what you want me to show you?" I ask, grinding my hardness into her.

Her body arches at the sensation. "Yes," she manages to huff out as she wraps her legs around me once more. She must have lost her heels during the move because she is now barefoot.

I love seeing her like this. So free, so sensual, not afraid of telling me or showing me what she wants. Who am I to deny her? "We're supposed to be going on a date right now." I remind her playfully, nibbling at her ear.

"I don't care. I don't want to stop," she urges. Her fingernails are digging into my back through my charcoal Henley shirt.

"My eager Sarah," I say as I sit up on my knees, her legs falling on either side of me. I push her dress up to her waist. My breath hitches as I look down at her. Sarah is a fucking masterpiece.

She's wearing black silk panties, and her legs... I'd happily let those thick thighs suffocate me.

"Beautiful," I say in awe. My hand starts at her knee, gliding up her thigh until I get to the hem of her underwear. She sucks in a breath as I slowly slip my hand inside, cupping the base of her. I use my fingers to spread her and slide one finger inside, then two.

I can feel her tighten around me immediately, and she closes her eyes, letting her head fall back. "You're so wet for me. My fingers are practically soaked." I praise her as I let my fingers move.

"Yes," Sarah utters, moaning as I stroke my fingers inside her a few times before moving up to rub soft circles around her clit.

Her moans grow louder as she rides my fingers. "Right there, don't stop," she demands, clutching the sides of the sofa for control.

I take my time, watching and feeling, figuring out exactly how she likes to be touched by her whimpers and moans. Sarah is so expressive, she's vocal, and I love it. I love the sounds she makes, the way her face scrunches up when I hit a spot inside her that's been begging for attention. Her body writhes and moves as I play her like an instrument. Her slickness aids my caress until I feel her whole body tense up, and she cries out in an orgasm, her back arching, her core pulsing around my fingers. I hold pressure, riding the orgasm, stroking her more gently through the comedown.

"Wow," Sarah says breathlessly after a moment, staring at the ceiling, letting one arm dangle off the side of the couch. She makes eye contact with me as I pop my still wet fingers into my mouth one at a time. She immediately turns red. Her lips break into a smile, and she quickly covers her face with her hands. I think I made her shy.

The feeling of euphoria I got from getting her off is all-consuming. I slide her panties back into position and lower her dress before leaning over her. I pull her hands aside and look right into those big, brown beautiful eyes. My lips find hers softly, and when I pull back, we both let out a little laugh. *Damn, that got hot and heavy real quick.*

I give her a moment to regain her equilibrium before slowly sliding off, and extending my hand to help her up.

She looks at me in confusion. "Are we moving to the bedroom now?"

I want to. Oh, how badly I'd love to carry her to the bedroom and sink into her over and over again until the sun comes up. But another part of me wants her to be fully mine first.

When we do finally get alone and naked I want the sky to shatter, I want her to shatter. And for that, I'm going to need to release some tension. I smirk. "No, we still have a date to go on, remember?"

"What about you?" she asks shyly.

"Sarah, baby, watching you cum by my hand is plenty for me right now. Besides, I plan to get mine tonight after you agree to be my girlfriend," I say with a wink and pull her in for a quick kiss.

"How are you so sure that I'll agree?" she teases.

"Did my incentive not work?" I tease back and lean in to capture her lips once more before slowly dragging my mouth down her neck and shoulders. "I tend to get what I want," I say in between kisses. "And I want you. In fact, I don't think I have ever wanted anything or anyone as much as I want you. I've become quite obsessed."

Sarah takes in a breath and lets outs a soft moan. "That's unhealthy."

I pull back and smile. "My obsession is just getting started. Now, as much as I love the way you look in those heels, my plans for tonight require more athletic footwear."

She looks at me in surprise. "Should I change?"

"No, keep the dress on. I'm not done looking at you in it just yet," I say, sliding my hand up the dress to squeeze her ass.

She jumps, giving a little yelp in the process, and she playfully slaps my hand away.

"If you keep doing stuff like that, I'll refuse to go anywhere with you but the bedroom," she teases. "I'll be right back," she tells me, before running to her room to change her shoes.

# Chapter 29
# Kael

I DRIVE US TO the Baker Beach Sea Cliff Access. It's a hiking trail with rocky terrain mostly along a cliff leading to the ocean. You can see the glow of the Golden Gate Bridge in the distance.

The ocean sings its calming lullaby as waves hit against the rocks and wash up on shore.

Thankfully, we are the only ones here right now, with our date starting so late at night. I reach for her hand as soon as we get out of the car. I love the feeling of our fingers intertwined. There's a primal need inside me that constantly wants to touch her. I'm not sure if it's normal to feel the way I do, but I don't care. She seems to enjoy it, too.

"I'm surprised you were able to bring me on a date tonight. Adam said that Zach told him he was patrolling tonight," Sarah says curiously.

I arch a brow at her. "I didn't realize that Adam and Zach were keeping in contact with each other."

"Oh, hmm, yes," she says guiltily. "I thought you knew. They have been texting each other since the night after the *incident*."

I flinch, my hand tightening around hers at her words. *The incident,* meaning when Nick and Shy kidnapped and tortured her. It's only been a couple of days. The memory of how she looked when I found her in the basement is still too fresh in my mind.

"I hope I didn't just out Zach or got him in trouble," Sarah says softly.

I shake my head. "No, it's fine. I mean, I know Zach's gay, if that's what you're worried about. He came out years ago, and I guessed that Adam was as well. I just didn't know they were talking," I tell her.

I'm not surprised I didn't know. Zach is a pretty private guy, so it's not like he would go around broadcasting anything about his personal life. Usually, I have to specifically ask Zach what's going on in his life to ever learn anything. I kind of feel bad that I've been so wrapped up in my own shit that I didn't ask.

"Adam is actually bisexual. Besides, I think it's still in the beginning, flirty, getting-to-know-each-other, stage," she tells me.

"I see," I say, nodding my head and giving her hand a gentle squeeze. "And what stage are we in?"

Sarah smiles, biting her lip. The act alone has me wanting to say to hell with the date and go back to her place.

"Hopefully, we will know after tonight," she says bashfully, "but you didn't answer my question. Why aren't you out hunting tonight? It doesn't seem like the kind of job where you're allowed to take the night off."

"Actually, I am taking some time off," I tell her.

I'm not sure if I want to admit to everything that's been going on since I last saw her. Should I tell her that I asked to switch squads because I can't trust Nick and Shy anymore? I can't even look at them without contemplating murder.

Liam, instead, asked that I take time off before deciding on something as big as switching squads. I know it hurt him when I asked. I hated the look on his face when I did it, but I can't work with Nick and Shy. Although, I would hate to give up working with the others.

"I just need a break from some of my teammates right now," is all I decide to say.

Her face fills with sorrow. "Oh, I see," she says, obviously picking up on the what and why of my statement. "I'm sorry."

"Don't be. It's not your fault. Now come on. We are almost there," I say, changing the subject. I don't want to ruin our date by getting angry thinking about what happened.

It's not until we step onto the dirt trail heading for the view of the bridge that I let go of her hand.

"The reason I brought you here tonight is to see what you're really made of," I tell her with a grin. "First one back wins?"

Sarah's face lights up in excitement. "A race? Are you sure you want to race me? You know I'm faster than you."

"Bring it on, Sarah Summers," I dare her.

"Oh, you are going down, Kael Hart." She's practically giddy with eagerness. "What do I get *when* I win?"

"*If* you win, is what I think you meant to say," I tease. "What do you want?"

"Hmm," she says, mulling it over. "I'm not sure. Do you know what you want if you win?"

"If I win, you have to agree to be my girlfriend," I say, hoping I'm not actually pressuring her by continuously bringing it up, but her smile tells me I don't have to worry about that.

"And if I win, you have to make me feel as good as you did on my couch at least one more time tonight and then agree to be my boyfriend."

*Fuck*. I love her. I know it. I feel it deep in my bones. I've never felt this way about anyone ever before.

"You got yourself a deal."

We both turn and face the trail ahead of us.

"Now to decide how much of the trail we want to race," I say.

"What? Can't handle running around the whole bay?" she teases.

"It's like three hundred miles around."

She shrugs. "Suit yourself."

I smirk. "I was thinking of going up and taking the Richmond Bridge to loop back around."

That's around seventy miles total, giving me plenty of time to really let loose all this extra speed that, for the most part, I never get to use to the max. Hunters have been gifted with the speed of a vampire. Since Sarah isn't an ordinary vampire, I'm curious to see what she can really do when using everything she's got.

"Got it," she states, digging her feet into the ground, ready to sprint. "On your mark."

"Get set."

"Go!" we shout at the same time as we both take off at a run.

HUNTED

We keep the same speed for about thirty seconds before Sarah laughs and says, "See ya at the finish line." Then she bolts as if she pressed some sort of inner turbo button.

"What the..." I smile, impressed and encouraged by the challenge she's pushing. I try to pick up the pace, but I'm already giving it all I've got.

There is a spot in the trail that reaches all the way up to the edge of the small cliff, and straight down is the ocean. Some boulders are protruding from the water there, some yards away from the edge.

I watch as Sarah runs and jumps off the cliff, aiming for the boulder. It's like watching an extraterrestrial parkour jumper as her feet bounce off the boulder, making it back to the trail all within three seconds. Incredible.

I ignore the sand grit that's found its way into my shoes as I try, once again, to catch up to her. It's no use. Sarah really is much faster than I am, and I'm one of the fastest hunters at the Academy.

*What else is she capable of?*

I can just about make out her running across the Golden Gate Bridge as I reach it, and by the time I'm circling back using the Richmond Bridge, I've completely lost her. Sarah found a secluded spot and is waiting for me when I finally reach our original starting point.

"That was so much fun," she shouts happily. She runs and practically jumps on me. I catch her and allow our momentum to hurtle us to the ground, her on top of me.

I'm sweating, but she doesn't seem to care. Sarah, however, is not even breathing heavily.

I guess that's a vampire thing. The only clue that shows she was running at all is her winded hair, but even so, it still looks and smells amazingly sweet.

"I'll take my prize now," she whispers seductively in my ear.

My pants immediately tighten. "Right here?" I ask in shock.

I slip my hand under her dress. I know she made a joke about sex outside once before, but I didn't really think she would be down for it if the time ever came. Not that I wouldn't fuck her right here, right now.

She giggles. "No, the thought of..."

But I'll never know what she thought, because I cut her off with my finger. My body goes tense as I sense the darkness—a vampire.

The second she stops talking her eyes widen. Sarah is off me in a flash, looking around frantically.

"You can sense it too?" I ask in surprise as I get to my feet. I didn't think vampires could sense other vampires the way hunters can.

She shakes her head. "No, but I can hear and smell them. They just fed."

Right. Sarah can smell the blood.

"They?" I question. "How many?" I reach behind my back and grab a hidden dagger I strapped to my waist, hoping Sarah doesn't get offended. It isn't for her, but I never go anywhere without at least one or two weapons on me. It's just how I was trained, thankfully. It looks like I will need them now.

Before Sarah can answer, I see them.

"Well, well, well, look who we have run into. We've been looking for you," says a male voice as three vampires step out of the fog into the clearing.

Sarah stiffens beside me. *Does she know these vampires?* I thought she didn't hang around with her kind. But by the sound of it, these aren't friends.

I slip out my phone; none of the vampires are even looking my way. I press the alert button, which will send a distress signal to the others along with my location. I wish I had thought to wear my comms earpiece tonight just in case, but I didn't. Something about it felt inappropriate for a date. Hopefully, the others get here in time.

"Taylor," Sarah says in shock. "How did you find me?"

"The boss has eyes everywhere," he states.

I'm so confused right now. Are these men here to hurt her?

"Sarah, who are these vampires to you?" I ask coolly.

"They work for Caesar Leon. They're his minions," she whispers to me, and then louder, she asks them, "What does Mr. Leon want with me? Why can't you leave me alone?"

Caesar Leon. The vampire that turned Sarah. She did mention that she thought he would come looking for her, back when I was still getting to know her. There is no way I'm going to let anyone hurt Sarah. Not in a million years.

"We don't ask questions," barks the only female vampire in the group. "We follow orders. The boss man wants you brought to him alive, and that's what we'll do."

"Spoken like a true minion," Sarah says in her usual calm, joking way. I can sense she is trying hard to keep her voice normal, to not show any signs of weakness. "Why don't you quit? Sounds like the job is pretty crappy. Do you even get dental?"

The guy she called Taylor laughs. "It's not that kind of job," he hisses.

It dawns on me. "Is Caesar Leon the vampire coven leader?" I ask. Now that I say it out loud, it's so obvious. I can't believe I didn't connect the dots before.

I was so upset over Sarah's heartbreaking story that I didn't see past the injustice that was done to her.

It would make sense as to why Leon has vampires doing his dirty work, and why they can't refuse. Coven leaders have power over their coven. A leader can demand something of one of their subjects, and they can't refuse. It's like their free will is taken from them, allowing for total submission.

Taylor looks at me for the first time, sliding a glance at my wooden weapon. "What do we have here? Is that a vampire hunter?" He looks over at Sarah and then back at me. "With a vampire... How interesting," he says and then, with a shrug continues, "but no matter. Miss Greenwood, you'll be coming with us."

"Over my dead body," I say.

Taylor smiles. "That can be arranged." He snaps his fingers, and the two with him start coming forward. "Kill the hunter. I'll take the girl."

I brace myself. Fighting two vampires without any other squad member to assist is risky, but nothing I can't handle.

I'm about to start attacking, when Sarah suddenly charges for the nearest vampire in the group, a pale man with ghostly white skin. She is so fast, like a blur. Sarah grabs the vampire, lifts him up over her shoulders, and throws him across the yards of grass and trail over the cliff.

Everyone is stunned into stillness. That should not have been possible to do. The cliff isn't anywhere near close enough to have thrown a grown man, even with our added strength.

"How did you do that?" Taylor asks in horror. He's not as confident as he was a moment ago.

I'm the first to recover and charge at the female vampire. She also recuperates in time to fight back. In the corner of my eye, I see Taylor launching for Sarah.

She's dodging him, but I'm not sure how long she can keep it up. I can see that she's all strength and speed, with little skill. But, I already knew that from the time I fought Sarah on her apartment rooftop. Even back then, I didn't really want to kill her, purposely pulling my punches and hoping she'd get away.

Taylor, on the other hand, is trained and organized in his fighting. He doesn't seem to be fighting Sarah, only trying to apprehend her. I'm distracted, paying too much attention to Sarah, that I don't see or hear the female vampire come at me from the side. She wraps her hands around my head and sinks her teeth into my neck.

A sharp but measurable sting emerges from the puncture, but she just made a terrible mistake. The female vampire pulls back quickly, crying out in pain. She takes several steps back, clutching at her throat. I know my blood is singeing her insides like fire. This isn't the first time I've been bitten, so I know it'll keep her in pain long enough that I can focus and make the kill. Thankfully, vampire bites don't affect hunters the way they do humans. I feel the initial sting of pain, but that's it. I don't succumb or have to fight off the momentary trance like humans do.

Before I can stab her through the heart, however, the vampire that Sarah threw over the cliff knocks me to the ground, having made his way back up. His clothes are all wet, and he is angry, his fangs out as he hisses at me.

He spears me to the ground, slamming my head against a jagged boulder. Pain shoots from the point of impact. I see stars for a moment before grabbing his neck as he goes to bite me. If I was thinking clearly, I should have let this vampire bite me too, but I stopped him on instinct.

Instead, he uses his long nails to scrape my torso from chest to navel. The pain is blinding. I felt him scrape bone. Suddenly, my chest tightens as crimson stains my shirt.

When he pulls his hand back, I notice they are styled into points like claws, and they are dripping with my blood.

I curse loudly as I release his neck and seize his hand to keep it from clawing at me again.

I lift my leg and reach for the wooden dagger secured to my ankle strap. Bringing it up, I stab the vampire in the back. He stills for a moment in shock, and I use the time to push him off me. I yank the dagger from his back and stab him again, this time straight through the heart.

When I look over, Sarah is still fighting, but Taylor is getting the better of her. To be honest, if he were allowed to kill her and was not just trying to capture her, she would probably be dead already. He grabs her from behind, locking her in his grip. He looks as though he's about to take off with her. After all, he got what he came here for.

The thought has me running toward them. I tackle Taylor to the ground, Sarah along with him. As we all fall, Sarah uses the moment to escape his clutches.

I've lost my second wooden dagger somewhere on the ground, so stabbing him is no longer an option.

Sarah is by my side in a flash. Taylor looks at us both, and then to the female writhing in pain some yards away. He must know that he's been beaten, because he runs to the female vampire, puts her arm around his shoulder, and together they dash away.

I want to chase them but I'm suddenly feeling woozy. I stumble, finding it hard to stay on my feet. The last thing I hear is Sarah calling out my name, but her voice feels so far away...

# Chapter 30
# Sarah

I catch Kael before he hits the ground. He's covered in blood. I lay him gently on his back as I search for the source of all the bleeding. I don't need to search long. His whole torso is covered in blood, and my eyes go to his shirt which has several long slashes through it. It's as if a bear came and ripped his shirt from top to bottom.

Kael's hurt. He's hurt because of me. Those vampires were after me. I take a deep breath. The simple human act helps to calm my nerves. I don't have time to wallow in self-pity. I need to help him.

"Kael, Kael, are you okay?" I ask in a panic.

His eyes flutter open. "Sarah, I'm fine," he assures me, but I don't believe him for one moment. "Are you okay? Did he hurt you?"

"Don't worry about me right now," I tell him. "And please don't talk. You have to conserve your energy."

Just the little talking he did, has him drained of color. His face has taken on a pale, sickly-green that has me panicking even more than I already am.

I grab his torn shirt and rip it clean off him. I use the scraps to wipe away some of the blood, enough to see four gashes starting from his chest down to his stomach. They are so deep that bone is peeking through the mangling flesh. It's clear that every one of them will need stitches.

"Kael, your stomach," I say as if he doesn't already know that he's injured there. I use the remains of his shirt to press against the gashes to help stop the bleeding.

Then it hits me—the smell. My goodness, the smell of all this blood is making me hungry. My fangs are still out from the fighting, but it's hard to school them back in with all this blood. It would be like trying to keep your stomach from grumbling when you're hungry. Impossible.

As I press the shirt to his torso, I notice that blood is also coming from the back of his head. *Another injury? Damn it. That's not good.*

Headlights appear, turning from the street to shine right at us. The vehicle comes to a screeching halt only a few yards away. Kael's hunter group jumps out of the van.

*Great. Where were they five minutes ago?* They seem to have an act for showing up right after all the fighting is over.

"How did they even...?" I start to ask.

"I sent... a distress signal," Kael coughs out as they all appear before us.

"Get away from him!" Shyann shouts.

*Seriously*? I have half a mind to slap her but resist the urge, mainly because I'm still putting pressure on Kael's wounds.

"What happened?" Liam asks as he runs to kneel beside Kael.

"We were attacked by vampires," I tell him.

"Liar," screams Shyann. "She probably did this to him. We should have killed her."

Kael's eyes harden at the statement. "No," he yells and practically throws himself on me. "It's not her fault. You can't hurt her."

I have never wanted to maim another person the way I want to maim Shyann right now. The adrenaline from the fight is still pumping hot in my veins, and rage is burning through me like a drug. But then I remember that Kael is hurt. He matters more.

"Kael, stop," I say, pushing him off me and lying him back down on the ground. "You are losing too much blood."

"Don't let them hurt you again, Sarah," he coughs out.

"We won't hurt Sarah," Liam states, shooting a warning glare Shyann's way. "But we need to get you to the medical bay now."

"We need to get him to a hospital," I argue.

Zach comes and lays a hand on my shoulder. "Sarah, hunters have fast healing. Not as fast as vampires, but still, too fast for human doctors to look at him. We have mages who we call in healing emergencies like this."

"Fine," I say through gritted teeth. I help Kael up to his feet. He is pinning almost all his weight on me. Zach quickly steps in to throw Kael's other arm over his shoulder and shifts half of Kael's weight onto him. I shoot him a quick, grateful look. "I'll ride next to him and keep pressure on his chest."

"Like hell she is," Shyann says.

Liam huffs in annoyance. "Enough Shy," he barks out and reaches into Kael's pants pockets to extract his keys. He throws them to Nick, who has been awfully quiet with his remarks tonight. "You and Shy drive Kael's car back."

Nick nods and looks around before spotting Kael's car on the opposite end of the parking lot. "Copy that," is all Nick says, which, once again, shocks me.

I vaguely wonder if Liam or Kael talked with him. Although Kael admitted he's been avoiding Nick and Shyann, so I doubt it was him.

On the way to the Academy, Kayda calls the mage healers to let them know they are needed in the med bay. I want to stay with Kael while they work on him, but Zach explains that it's not possible. The mages will not want to be around vampires, and won't come near Kael if I'm there. So when we get to the Academy, I let Zach and Liam take Kael to the med bay, while Kayda leads me to Kael's room to wait.

I can't believe I'm back here again. I vowed never to set foot in this building for the rest of eternity. So much for that.

Kayda assures me that Kael will be fine.

"The mage healer will perform a spell to supercharge the speed healing. He'll be good as new in no time."

Still, there is no way I'm leaving without knowing if Kael is okay. I need to see for myself.

I'm fighting every nerve in my body, telling me that being here is not a good idea. After going to get me a change of clothes that doesn't have Kael's blood all over it, Kayda sits with me in silence on Kael's bed, which I'm grateful for. I don't think I have it in me to explain what happened, even though I'm sure she is dying to know.

I like this about her. She seems to know when to push and when to back off, because I need a moment. I wonder if she is this perceptive about everyone. Something tells me she is. This must be one of the reasons Kael likes her so much. Every time he mentions Kayda, it's with such genuine respect and admiration. I see why.

I'm fidgeting and bouncing my leg on the bed, impatiently waiting to hear about Kael, when there is a knock on the door. I'm on my feet in an instant. The person at the door is one of the last people I want to see—Nick.

"What are you doing here?" Kayda asks, and not in a kind way.

Nick holds up his hands in surrender. "Whoa, easy. I was just bringing Sarah her phone. It was in Kael's car." Sure enough, he's holding my phone in one of his hands.

I narrow my eyes at him. "Why would you do that?"

"What, bring you your phone?" he asks in a playful innocence. "Because, Sarah, despite me trying to kill you the other day, I am a gentleman."

I can almost feel Kayda roll her eyes. She steps toward him and takes the phone. "Okay, you returned it. Now I think you should leave," she states, gesturing to the door. It seems like Kael isn't the only one who's on bad terms with Nick and Shyann.

"Wait," he says, holding out his hands, his tone suddenly serious. "I've also come to apologize to Sarah for what I did the other day. Seeing you control yourself around Kael, with all his blood oozing out..." I blanch at his choice of words, but he continues. "I realize now that you do indeed still have your soul, and I pledge from this day forward to never try and kill you again," he promises, holding one hand to his heart and the other up at his side, as if taking an oath.

I scoff. If he thinks he can just apologize for kidnapping me, torturing me, and attempting murder, he has another thing coming.

"Fine," he gives in with a shrug. "I can see you may need a little more time to come around to my charm, but make sure you tell Kael I did this. I'm tired of him icing me out."

"Right, because you returning Sarah's phone and apologizing will make up for you almost killing her," Kayda says sarcastically. I am so grateful that Kayda is brave enough to say exactly what I'm thinking. It has more weight coming from her, too, I'm sure. Nick looks between me and Kayda.

"I'm hoping it's a start. I don't like Kael mad at me," he says, mumbling the latter under his breath. I'm not sure if he even meant to say it out loud. He turns and leaves without another word.

The sad part is, he doesn't seem like a bad guy. Funny, even. I'm finding it hard to hate him, but then I remember him dragging me and forcing my arm into sunlight so he could watch me burn, and the hate comes back in full force.

It's another twenty minutes of pacing back and forth before Liam ushers Kael into the room, holding him by the waist and helping him walk. I'm at his side the moment he steps through the door.

"Are you okay?" I ask.

I can tell Kael is shocked to see me here. He lets out a sigh and pulls me into his arms. "I wasn't expecting you to still be here," he says as he holds me tight.

I melt into his arms. I can't help it. When he holds me like this, it's like nothing else in the world matters or even exists.

"I was not leaving until I knew you were okay," I tell him.

He pulls back and kisses me hard on the lips. It's a quick kiss, and yet I still feel it reverberate through my body. "I was worried about you."

"I'm all right," I assure him. "I'm not the one who got hurt, you are. Kael, I'm so sorry."

I look him up and down. He's bare-chested with white bandages wrapped around his torso and head. The smell of blood mixed with the slight smell of mint and antibiotic ointment permeates around him.

"It's not your fault," he says and then winces.

"Kael, you need to lie down," I say at the same time Liam says, "You should be resting."

Kael looks like he wants to argue, but one look from me to Liam and he nods and makes his way to his bed. With my help, he sits down, pressing his back to the headboard.

I notice the tip of an old scar peeking out of the bandage over his left pec. It's perforated and has a light pink coloring, letting me know it's an old wound and not one from tonight's events. And then my eyes begin to wander.

Even with the bandages, Kael shirtless is a sight to see—a body fit for the gods.

*Focus, Sarah.* Kael is hurt and needs to be taken care of, not ogled after. He notices me staring at his chest, and his eyes darken. With great effort, I keep my eyes trained on his before I completely swoon.

Kael eyes my attire. "Changed your clothes?"

"Oh, yeah," I say, tugging at the flowy oversized T-shirt, suddenly a little self-conscious. I'm a few sizes bigger than Kayda, so she had to go with what she found in their lost and found stash, which was an extra-large shirt that says "Zombies Rule" on the front and a pair of ratty gray sweatpants. Not my best look.

"The dress was covered in blood, so Kayda was kind enough to find something for me to change into."

Even with the less-than-desirable outfit, Kael's eyes are still full of hunger. He looks like he wants to devour me.

"I'm fine now, guys. No need to stay any longer," Kael says to the others suddenly, his eyes never leaving mine.

"Actually, we still need to know what happened tonight," Liam states as he looks between us.

# Chapter 31
# Sarah

I SIGH WITH INDIGNATION and—weariness. "I'll tell you."

I start from the beginning, leaving nothing out. Well except maybe making out with Kael on the ground. Kael flinches when I get to the part about Caesar Leon wanting me.

Kael only interrupts once to add that he thinks Mr. Leon might be the city's vampire coven leader, which has Kayda gasping and Liam and Zach looking dismayed.

I watch Zach open his laptop and type Caesar Leon's name in the search engine. Several articles pop-up. He starts to click on one.

"Do you know why an ancient vampire, who might also be the city's coven leader, wants you, Sarah?" asks Liam, forcing my attention back on him.

I shrug. "I honestly don't know. He did say something to me, a few days before I ran away, about being his queen, but I can't imagine why he hasn't given up by now. I mean, really, we barely knew each other. Even when I was working directly for him, we only spoke about work stuff, nothing personal."

"He might feel that you are mated to him because he sired you," Zach informs us, looking up from his laptop.

Kael growls. "Sarah is not mated to him."

Zach looks placatingly at Kael. "I'm just saying that could be an explanation as to why he isn't giving up on Sarah. If he feels like she is his mate, he would be drawn to her by an unmovable force. Although, it is strange since Sarah clearly doesn't reciprocate."

I wrinkle my nose in disgust at just the thought of feeling anything toward Caesar Leon. The only unmovable force I feel is toward Kael, although I haven't let myself dive too deeply into that force, scared of what I might find.

Zach continues his thought process. His voice getting more animated the more he hypothesizes. "Perhaps someone that old and powerful feels as though he can imprint on Sarah. I've read of an imprinting between vampires once. An ancient, such as Caesar, officiated a bond at the creation of another. A metaphysical link was forged. If that were the case, it would be nearly impossible for Caesar to sever that or to simply forget about her. It may have dulled over the years when he thought she was dead, but that strong determination to have her probably never went away. He might not ever stop until he has her."

*Never stop.* This cannot be happening. I don't want to live in fear that one day Caesar's minions will snatch me up and bring me back to him.

What if I'm with Kael and he gets hurt again because of me, or worse, what if I'm with Adam? He's normal and human. He wouldn't heal fast the way I, or even Kael, can.

Anger flares to life inside me. *I hate him.* I made a life for myself despite what Mr. Leon did to me. Adam became family, and I found Kael. Caesar Leon is threatening to take that all away. Rage consumes me. I can feel it ignite and build as I press my nails into my palms, letting my thoughts spiral.

"Sarah?"

I shake my mind from the dark path I was tumbling down and look up at Kael who is looking at me with lines of concern steeped into his brow.

"I'm okay," I lie. I am far from okay. The people I care about are in danger simply by being near me. What am I supposed to do about that?

"We'll go and give you two some alone time," Kayda says. She's also looking at me in concern and, once again, must sense that I need some time to process.

"I have to go update Aquila," Liam says.

They all file out of the room. Zach gives me a reassuring smile before carefully closing the door behind him.

"Come here," Kael says in a gentle tone that I'm not used to hearing from him.

I walk over and sit next to him on the edge of the bed.

"It's going to be okay, Sarah, I promise," he says as he strokes my back. The smells of medical ointment and mint are almost overpowering. I'm guessing it's something the mages cooked up and rubbed on his chest and head for healing.

"How do you know that?" I ask.

"Because," he says tugging me to him, and I move so that I'm sitting against the bed's headboard just like he is. He wraps his arm around me as I rest my head on his shoulder. "I'll kill him myself before I let Leon or anyone take you. You are mine now, and I'm not letting you go."

I wait for my feminist side to flare up at a man trying to possessively claim me like I'm an object rather than a person, but instead, warmth fills my body at his declaration.

I thought I was immune to the age-old misogynistic belief that men have some sort of dominance over women. Which to be fair, I still am, but the way Kael said "You are mine" has my Stepford wife avatar doing a victory tap dance over my ovaries.

How is it that I've known this man for only about a month, and already, I'm in this deep with him? Kael is like a meteor that came crashing down on me. He's the only one who sees the real me. I don't have to hide any part of myself from him. And through his eyes, I see myself as free. I'll never be the same again. My heart will always have fragments of Kael's embedded into it.

I just can't stand the thought of him getting hurt again because of me. I feel like it's selfish to stay with him when I know being with me is putting him in danger.

"It's not safe to be with me, Kael," I whisper, hoping he doesn't hear the crack in my voice.

Kael pulls back, forcing me to lift my head from his shoulder. "Look at me."

I do as he asks, his intense green eyes piercing me to my very soul.

He grabs my face between his hands. "The way that you're feeling right now, I felt exactly the same way a few days ago when Nick and Shy did what they did to you. But those days without you were agony. Because I'm starting to realize that I have your back, like you have mine. You hear me? I'm not going to let anyone hurt you."

I don't doubt him. If anything, he's right. We complete each other. I'm just scared it won't be enough. If Mr. Leon is as powerful as they fear he is, then we are fighting a losing battle.

"I believe you," is all I say.

He sighs, rubbing my cheek with his thumb, no doubt seeing the worry in my eyes. "I got you," he promises, leaning in and softly pressing his lips to mine. Softly, at first, taking little nips of my mouth with his. My thoughts tear from my troubles and lock in on him, and the way it feels when he finally presses his lips firmly against mine. He takes his time coaxing my mouth open with his. It's a long and deep kiss that sends butterflies to my stomach. I let out a soft moan as he bites gently on my bottom lip.

My whimpers must spur him to action because Kael moves one hand to grasp my neck, his tongue playing with mine. With the other hand, he slides to the small of my back, pressing our bodies together.

He lets out the slightest wince, barely noticeable, but I do notice. I pull back immediately.

"Oh my goodness, Kael, I'm so sorry. Did I hurt you?"

"No, it's fine," he says with an air of trying to brush off the pain. He reaches for me again, but I don't budge.

"Kael, no, you're hurt. You need to rest," I say.

He shakes his head. "I need your lips on mine. Now." He goes to reach for me a second time, but I place a hand on his chest, careful to avoid the bandages. I give a little push so that he's lying back against the headboard, and I sit on his lap, straddling him. Instantly, I feel him harden beneath me. My body reacts immediately, grinding against his hardness, and he lets out a groan as he reaches up to hold me.

A rush of bravery washes over me. I smile and pin him back in place once more. "I think this time you need to let *me* take care of *you*," I say, sliding my hands along the rim of his jeans and undoing the button.

Kael's jaw practically drops when he realizes what I'm about to do. I can feel him twitch excitedly between my legs. I'm not sure what's come over me. I'm not usually so forward. I've never felt the urge and passion to even try, but Kael has me wanting to reenact every smutty book scene I have ever read.

"Fuck, Sarah, baby," he says, a little throaty, as he wiggles under me. He shuts his eyes tight and shakes his head, like he is having some sort of internal battle with himself.

Finally, he says, "You don't have to, Sarah. You've been through a lot tonight, and I don't want to take advantage of..."

I stop him with a finger to his lips. "I can see where you are going with this, but enough. I want to. Kael Hart, are you going to make me beg?" I lean into him, pressing my breast against him ever so slightly, careful not to disturb his wounds. "Please," I whisper.

Kael gives me a wicked grin, and I know I've just discovered a preference of his. He likes it when I say *please*.

I move down him, positioning myself between his legs and slowly unzip his pants. I push down his boxer briefs. His lengthy, thick shaft springs free, and I gulp.

*Wow.*

Whoever crafted this god-like creature pulled out all the stops. I summon my courage and lick him from base to tip to help lubricate all of him, just in case I need to use my hand to help out.

He sucks in a breath as I take him into my mouth, massaging his hardness with my tongue. I bite back a gag as I force most of him in, eyes watering as I relax my throat.

Kael lets out a groan and gently places one hand on my head. He doesn't try to push my head down, just sort of rests his hand, letting it go up and down to my rhythm.

"Oh, fuck," he moans.

I work him for a while, my tongue massaging and my teeth gently grating. One hand is squeezing his thighs tightly. My other hand is stroking what I can't fit in my mouth.

"Sarah, if you don't stop, I'm going to cum in your mouth," he says breathlessly. The idea of him spilling into my mouth suddenly feels like a reward. I want to know what he tastes like. I pick up the pace, just a fraction until he groans, letting me know it's happening, and then proceeds to burst inside my mouth. I let the warm, thick liquid slide down my throat, but don't stop until I've sucked him clean.

"Holy shit, Sarah. That was amazing."

I slowly release him, stopping at the tip to give him another light suckle. He shudders, letting out a low hiss. I still have the taste of him on my tongue when he pulls me up and gives me a deep kiss.

After a moment, he tugs back. "It's your turn."

I smile. "You need to be resting. You already gave me my turn earlier tonight, remember?"

"If you think I'm going to let you leave this room without you sitting on my face, you have another thing coming," he says as he strokes my cheek with his hand. "Besides, it's only my tongue I'll put to work while I'll let you fuck my face. I'm dying to taste you." His words have wetness pooling between my legs instantly.

I'm not sure what alternate reality I've stepped into where this is my sex life now, but I'm all for it. I've never had this sort of heat and intensity with past boyfriends before.

I've only had sex with two other guys before Kael. The first guy, my first real boyfriend in my freshman year of college, didn't know how to make sure I was satisfied before finishing himself. He thought I was done when he was. I spent a lot of nights nourishing my own needs in the bathroom after he fell asleep.

Jared was the second. He was different. Our nights together were more intimate, but we were always more friends than lovers. The sex was sweet. Gentle.

With Kael, however, just the way he talks to me has me soaked. I've never felt such passion, such desire, and such comfort all in one package. Just when I'm about to give in and let Kael do whatever he wants to me, there is a knock at the door.

*Wow.* Talk about bad timing.

"Go away," Kael yells, not even bothering to ask who it is first.

"Aquila wants to have a meeting with us now." It's Liam. "He wants Sarah to come, too. You would know this if you read my text five minutes ago."

Liam texted Kael? Either his phone is dead or on silent, or I was so involved in what I was doing five minutes ago that I didn't hear his phone go off. I wonder if Kael did?

"We're not going," Kael barks back.

"It's important."

"Unless an asteroid is headed straight for us in the next few hours, go away," Kael shouts, frustrated.

"We are trying to help you protect Sarah," Liam says calmly. "Do you really want to put whatever you're doing in there before her safety?"

My face heats. The thought of Liam guessing at what we are doing in here is enough to make me die of embarrassment.

Kael drops his head back and sighs. I can see by the look on his face that Liam said the one thing that would get him to change his mind.

"We're coming," he tells Liam. "Give us a few minutes."

"Meet us in the lounge conference room," Liam says. A second later, I hear his footsteps retreating.

Kael tugs playfully at my hair. "To be continued?"

I laugh. "Definitely."

He touches my heated cheeks. "I love that you blush," he says. "I didn't know vampires could."

"Oh, I don't think others can," I say. "Just another way being a *Validus* makes me different. Though this particular thing is quite mortifying." I say the last part under my breath.

I know Kael heard me because he laughs as he reaches for my hand.

# Chapter 32
# Kael

EVERYONE IS ALREADY SEATED at our usual meeting area in the conference room when Sarah and I arrive.

I'm surprised to see Nick here. I want to protest, but decide against it. Liam told me that Nick is trying to make amends. Plus, if we are here to discuss helping Sarah, then I'll take all the manpower I can get.

He did try to talk to me earlier today, before my date with Sarah, but I refused. I still can't forgive him and Shyann for what they did to her. Thankfully, Shy seems to be absent from this meeting, which I think is best. She still can't be trusted.

Aquila gives Sarah a weird look before schooling his face into his practiced look of indifference. It was quick, and maybe I just imagined it, or it could be that he is still getting used to having a vampire in such close proximity to him. Sarah's unusual vampire aura should help, since it's lighter than that of normal vampires.

I've become so acquainted with Sarah's aura; I crave it now.

Sarah and I sit together in the open love seat. I reach for her hand and give it a gentle squeeze. I know she isn't at all comfortable being here in this building with so many hunters around. Not that I blame her. She has every right to hate the Academy.

It's a testament to Liam's professionalism that he looks at us with a straight face as he says, "I'm glad you could join us."

I'm ninety percent sure he knew what he was interrupting when he knocked on the door. I'll have to remember to give him hell for it later.

Just the thought of what he interrupted has me hardening. The way Sarah sucked my cock was perfection. The satisfying moans she made while doing it, letting me know she was enjoying herself as much as I was, made everything a hundred times better.

*Fuck.* I'm getting too excited just thinking of it. I make a slight adjustment to my pants, hoping no one notices. Now is not the time to be thinking about this.

*Focus on what's important at the moment.* Finding a way to make sure Caesar Leon doesn't get anywhere near Sarah is my main priority.

I'm grateful when Aquila starts. "It has come to my attention that we may have found the city's coven leader, which until now has always been a mystery to us. But if it's true that Caesar Lebeau could very well be in our city, and worse, the coven leader, then we must find a way to destroy him."

What does he mean *if it's true?* Does he not believe that Caesar Lebeau, now Leon, is really in the city?

"Sarah didn't lie," I shout, feeling an irrefutable need to defend her.

Aquila holds up his hand, gesturing for me to calm down. "That's not at all what I meant, Kael," he says evenly. "I just mean that there may be many vampires out there posing as Caesar Lebeau. He's an ancient. He could be anywhere around the world, or even dead. We haven't heard anything that would suggest that Lebeau is here in this city—until now, that is, which is why we need to investigate. Zach, can you show Sarah the sketch we have of Lebeau, please?"

Zach nods and brings over a book he is holding. There is a bookmark sticking out two-thirds of the way through. Zach opens up to the bookmarked page.

"Sarah, this is a book on all the ancient vampires we have on record. We don't have an actual picture of him, but ancestors were able to sketch Caesar Lebe—Leon." Zach turns the open book to face us and points to a headshot drawn picture of a white male in his mid-to-late thirties. He has angular features and high cheekbones. I've seen this picture before during one of our vampire history classes.

Sarah studies it for just a moment. "That's him, just more modern looking now, if that makes sense. Also, he has a tattoo on the left side of his neck. It's like a creepy, long-tailed cross with curved T's in the shape of fangs. At the time, I thought it was kind of cool and bold for him to get a sizable neck tattoo. Afterwards, I was like 'Well, now I get the whole fang part of the tattoo at least.'"

The coven leader symbol. Why did I not think to ask Sarah about it?

Zach gives Sarah a small smile at her rambling. I wonder if it's a sign of her nervousness.

"That's not a tattoo, Sarah," Aquila informs her. "That's the coven leader symbol. Every coven leader gets a mark on their body. It doesn't always show up on the neck, but it is always the same mark. It's said to hold the power that allows them control over their coven. Once a vampire pledges to a coven, the present and future leaders have control over the vampires for the rest of eternity in exchange for the protection that being in that coven provides. Unfortunately, we've never gotten close to a coven leader to have accurate pictures of it."

That proves it. Caesar Leon is definitely the city's coven leader, and he's after Sarah. I realize a small part of me still hoped that Sarah was wrong. Not only having an ancient after you, but the city's coven leader, is a pretty big deal. This guy will be impossible to kill and have a whole coven of vampires at his disposal.

I squeeze Sarah's hand. I can't lose her. I won't. I'll find a way to get to Leon and kill him myself.

I look over at Sarah, and she seems to be taking the news well. Maybe because none of this is technically new news to her.

"So, now that we know who this guy is, does anyone have any ideas on how we get to him?" Nick inquires.

"I can give you the address of the building where I worked. He's the CEO, although I'm not sure how he pulls that off. Also, I can give you the address to his penthouse," Sarah offers.

"That would be great, thank you, Sarah. We will have to get with the other squads and plan an attack, but first, we should do a reconnaissance mission," Liam responds.

"If there is a way to get inside, I can plant a camera so we can gain information. We might even get the location of the coven's lair," Zach says enthusiastically.

Within seconds, the team begins strategizing on how best to handle the new information Sarah has provided. I'm listening and throwing in ideas as well when Sarah finally speaks again.

"I know when we can for sure run into Mr. Leon. At the company's annual Christmas party. He shows up every year. That's where I first met him. He asked me to become his personal assistant not long after that."

"Perfect," Nick booms. "Fuck a recon mission. Let's just kill the bloodsucker at the party."

Liam lifts a hand to silence Nick. He turns to Sarah and asks, "This party, can you figure out when it will be held?"

"Yes, I can get with an old coworker of mine and see if she still works there. She might even be willing to put me on the guest list as her plus-one."

"You are not going without backup," I immediately chime in.

Sarah waves her hand dismissively. "I know, but I just need to get close to the bouncer so I can use my Jedi mind trick to get you past the door as well."

"Bitchin," Nick says, pumping his fist in the air. "Is that what you call it?"

"It's referred to as persuasion," Zach informs Sarah.

"Nah, Jedi mind trick sounds cooler," Nick declares. "Sarah, I didn't know you watched Star Wars. I love Star Wars."

"The things you miss when you are trying to kill someone," Sarah says sarcastically.

"You are going to be one tough nut to crack," he teases.

I don't know why, but their banter has jealousy coursing through me. "Don't talk to her, Carmack," I yell at Nick. "You've lost your right to ever speak to her."

Nick rolls his eyes. "Roger, roger," he says in a robot voice and gives a salute.

Sarah snickers beside me. She places a hand over her mouth like she didn't want to laugh but couldn't help it. I arch my brow at her in confusion, but she just shakes her head, giving no explanation as to why that was so funny.

We talk through several plans of action and strategize on what to do the night of the Christmas party. The meeting wraps up with Sarah promising to let us know as soon as possible when the party will be.

I offer my bed up for Sarah to finish the night here with me, but she politely declines. She points out that a vampire spending too much time at a vampire hunter academy is not in the best interest of the vampire, which, of course, I can't deny. Still, I'm disappointed, but instead of showing it, I offer to drive her home.

Everyone argues that I'm not allowed to be doing anything but resting in bed, so Zach ends up driving her instead, and I reluctantly bid her goodnight at the door.

# Chapter 33
# Kael

S ARAH MAKES GOOD ON her promise, and within a week, she has the date of the Christmas party. It's also been a week since I last saw her. I hate it.

Liam insisted that I follow our mage healer, Orla's, strict orders to stay in bed and let my quick healing do its magic.

Apparently, the knock to the head resulted in a concussion, and the scrapes on the chest were dangerously close to my heart and intestines. So, Orla's being extra cautious in not clearing me until she comes back over to inspect the wounds herself. Even though everyone can clearly see that I'm fine now. The scars on my torso are a lighter shade of pink than the permanent one going down my sternum.

It was my bad luck that I got Orla. She is always more cautious than the other mage healers. Any of the other healers would have released me days ago.

Since the Academy isn't Sarah's favorite place to be, we have been communicating strictly via video chats and texting.

On Thanksgiving, my mom spent an hour with me on video chat. She had also shipped me some chocolate chip cookies, because she knows they're my favorite.

The hunters all got together and made a big feast in the Academy cafeteria. I stayed in my room, not really feeling up to going to the cafeteria to get questioned by other squads about Sarah. By now, word has spread that I'm in some way connected to a vampire, even if not everyone knows how or why.

Kayda and Liam end up having Thanksgiving with me in my room. They've been visiting me on and off all week, bringing me all my meals and helping change my bandages.

Thankfully, Shy hasn't even attempted to come visit me. She can stay the fuck away. Somehow, the longer I don't see her, the angrier I get, and the less I want to see her face. Nick tried once, but I kicked him out. I'm not ready to forgive him yet either. Zach only comes in short intervals. I'm kind of jealous of him because he, apparently, has been visiting Sarah's apartment frequently. It's to see Adam, but still.

Yesterday, Sarah included him and Adam in the video chat, in which Zach already looked like he's part of their group dynamic. It's strange to see, but I badly want to be a part of it, too.

The good news is that now that we have the Christmas party date coming up, Liam has asked us to get together for another strategy meeting. Sarah will be attending, so I'll get to see her today, but first, I head to the med bay to check in with Orla.

To my surprise, the mages Dana and Cynthia are present when I walk in. The squad and I are closest to them more than anyone else at the Magisterium, which is sort of like an academy for mages. They often visit the Academy to hang out with us.

However, they don't usually hang around the med bay. Neither Dana nor Cynthia is training to be a healer. I'm pretty sure Cynthia is more into the offensive and defensive spells of mage training, while Dana does more research and development. She reminds me a little of Zach in that way.

"Hey, you two," I greet. "What brings you here to the med bay?"

Dana shrugs. "We heard you got hurt and wanted to come see how you were doing," she says nonchalantly.

I smile. I don't always see eye to eye with the mages about certain things, but I've always been able to call Dana and Cynthia my friends.

Dana has changed her hair since I last saw her. The long braids down her back are gone, replaced with small cornrow braids starting from the ends of her bangs, and ending in the middle of her head. The rest of her hair fluffs out in tight ringlet curls.

"I'm fine. Thank you for checking on me," I say.

Orla, a no-nonsense Irish lady, and my personal healer for this accident, walks over to me, gesturing for me to lie back. "I'll be the judge on whether you are fine or not, lad. Now, you hold still while I cut your bandages off," she instructs. A hint of her Irish accent peeks through her words.

"Yes, ma'am," I say, doing as I'm told.

With the back side of her hand, Orla pushes back a strand of bright red hair that has fallen loose from the tight knot on her head. She pulls tighter on her blue nitrile gloves before getting to work cutting the old bandages off. She washes the area carefully and studies the almost healed wounds, deciding if I need more healing ointment.

While the spell supercharged my speed healing, the ointment worked to instantly relieve pain. It smells of mint and herbs and is cold to the touch, but it's a miracle worker. I don't know what I would have done these past few days without it. I don't need any of it anymore, though. I already know this before she has to say it.

She examines my head next. "It's healing nicely. In a day or two, they'll just be nasty-looking scars, but that too'll fade away with time. You are free to return to your hunts."

I sigh in relief. It's about time. I'm more than ready to get out of this building. I can finally spend time with Sarah at her place.

"Thanks, Doc. I appreciate it."

"Uh-huh," she says with a grunt. "Next time don't let a vampire get the better of ya."

"Don't plan to," I mutter.

Orla finishes up and heads out, leaving Dana, Cynthia, and me alone in the room. I'm buttoning up my shirt when Dana finally speaks again.

"Is it true?" she asks.

"Is what true?"

Of course, I know what she's asking. I've been getting asked the same question the last few days by those brave enough to approach me.

"Boy, don't play games," she says with a scoff. "You know what."

"It's not what you think. She's different."

"Pah, please, she must be a real sight for sore eyes for you to be hooking up with a vampire," Dana says with disgust.

"It's not just her looks. She has a soul. She's amazing inside and out," I say defensively. I've had to say these very lines about half a dozen times, and it was pissing me off that they were starting to lose meaning. Because they were true. "You don't have to like it. I'm not asking you to date her."

"How did you even find out that she had a soul?" she shouts with a mocking cackle. "What, are you vetting your vampires on these hunts? You're supposed to just kill them. Not get to know them."

*I've heard enough.* "Listen," I yell, that all too familiar feeling of anger rising to the surface. "I don't tell you how to do your mage shit, you don't tell me how to hunt."

I start to leave, not wanting to spend any more time in Dana's presence, but Cynthia blocks the doorway, her hands up. Speaking for the first time since the start of this trap disguised as a visit. "We didn't mean to upset you, just trying to figure out how this happened, right, babe?" she asks, looking over at Dana.

The two of them have been dating for six months now. Dana's always been uptight, but Cynthia has a natural calm about her, and Dana instantly softens under Cynthia's gaze.

"I didn't mean to get into an argument," Dana agrees, taking in a deep breath. "We just wanted to warn you. If the council finds out that you are dating a vampire, which they will if you keep trotting her around here, you are going to get in a lot of trouble." She lowers her voice to an almost whisper, like she is scared someone will overhear. "And it wouldn't just be you; there would be consequences for Aquila and Liam as well."

That gets my blood boiling. "They have nothing to do with this," I grit out. I'm clenching my fists at my side, trying to calm myself down.

"I don't give a shit who the council is, and I don't care what they think about me dating a vampire. They better not come near any of us," I threaten.

Dana's eyes widen in disbelief. "Kael, you need to watch what you say," she pleads. She almost seems scared for me. "Are you crazy? You do realize that we are the ones who give you your abilities? The council can take them away if they feel you are no longer fit to have the powers of a hunter."

Her words hit me like a wrecking ball. I never thought about someone taking away my hunter abilities. I guess I never even thought that was possible. I am not sure who I would be if I wasn't a hunter.

Cynthia sighs when I don't speak. "Just be careful. It's not only your future at stake here. Is the vampire really worth all this?" She doesn't wait for my reply as she pats me on the shoulder before reaching out her hand for Dana to grasp, and they turn to leave.

She opens the door to find Zach, Adam, and Sarah approaching; the three of them are talking and laughing together.

Hopefully, they were so lost in conversation that Sarah or Zach didn't overhear us. I look at Sarah. She's laughing at something Adam just said. Her face is lit up in delight. Looking at her now, there's not a doubt in my mind that I'm supposed to be with her. I can feel it in my gut. I can't quite explain this unnatural feeling. There is a gravitational pull inside me, and she is my North.

If the mage council punishes me for it, then so be it. I just have to find a way for them to spare Liam and Aquila for my actions. Has there ever been a hunter who quit and had their abilities taken away from them?

My mom stopped hunting after my dad died, but she still has her abilities. I'll have to talk to Zach about it when we are alone. If anyone knows, it'll be him. Hopefully, he can help me figure this out. Quitting isn't something I ever thought I would even consider. Being a hunter has been my whole life up until this point. I'm not sure who I am without it.

Zach stiffens at the sight of Dana and Cynthia. "I saw Orla driving away. I thought it was safe to bring Sarah here. I'm sorry." He turns to Sarah. "Let's go to the library and wait for everyone there."

Sarah looks over at me and then at Dana and Cynthia. She narrows her eyes and says, "Barbara Ann?"

Cynthia shrieks. I never heard Cynthia shriek in my life. "Sarah!"

# Chapter 34
# Kael

"SARAH!" CYNTHIA SHOUTS, RUNNING to give Sarah a hug. Then she sees Adam and goes to hug him too. "Adam!"

"Gurl," Adam says, hugging her back. "What are you doing here?"

"Cynthia, are you a vampire hunter?" Sarah asks, all smiles.

Cynthia shakes her head, her long bangs falling into her eyes a little. Cynthia always keeps the same hairstyle, choppy short hair with long side bangs. "No, I'm a mage."

Adam gasps, placing a hand to his chest. "Is that how you kept pulling off those magic card tricks, by using real magic? I knew it."

"Can someone explain what's happening?" Dana asks and then looks toward Cynthia. "And why did she call you Barbara Ann?"

We all usher into the med bay, feeling awkward standing around the door frame. Cynthia lifts her long sleeves up to her elbows as she explains. "I met these two about, damn, I guess about two years ago now, at a gay bar. I tried hitting on Sarah, but she turned me down."

"Excuse me?" Dana interrupts, just like I was about to.

I'm not sure why, but I instinctively reach to grab Sarah's hand like I'm some sort of territorial caveman. She looks at me with a small, amused quirk of her lips.

"Babe, it was the night you told me that we could never be together. I was hurting and looking to forget for just one night," Cynthia tells Dana, wrapping her arm around Dana's waist.

Dana looks down at the ground when she says, "I wasn't ready back then."

"I know. I'm not mad at you or anything. It was just hard to hear, and I needed a night away to just be in my feelings."

Dana sighs. "I'm sorry about that. I won't ever let fear keep me from you again," she tells Cynthia, giving her a quick kiss on the lips. "But that doesn't explain the Barbara Ann thing."

Cynthia's smiles. "I'm getting to that. Anyway, so Sarah starts telling me how she's really straight and just broke up with her boyfriend and was feeling sad too."

I give Sarah's hand a hard squeeze. I bet it was that asshole from a couple of weeks ago. *God, I hate him.* I also hated that Sarah was so quick to tell him that I wasn't her boyfriend. Somehow, that had grated on me. Maybe that's what led me to finally kiss her in the alley. I wanted to prove that she was mine, even back then.

I hold in a deep breath. I have to remind myself that this is all before me. I can't be jealous of Sarah's past relationships, no matter how much they bother me. I definitely have to stop reacting at just the mention of anyone else with or near her.

I'm not the jealous type, or at least I didn't think I was, but that may have been because I've never cared for anyone like this before. Every other woman I've dated was just to fulfill my sexual needs. With Sarah, I apparently get jealous of anyone who looks at her too long.

"And then," Cynthia continues, oblivious to my internal crises, "she introduces me to her friend Adam, who is part of the LGBTQ+ community, and the reason she was there. He'd also just broken it off with a guy. So, there we were, three people down in the dumps, looking to escape. That's when the real fun began."

"What Cynthia is failing to mention is that this gay bar is also a karaoke bar, and we all decided to drink four tequila shots in a row," Adam adds.

"Hence, Barbara Ann," Sarah finishes.

I look at her still confused. She gives me a scoff. "Kael, please tell me, you've heard of Barbara Ann from The Beach Boys?"

I shake my head. "I'm assuming it's a song."

"Yes, it's a song," she shouts and then starts singing to the beat that is vaguely familiar.

Adam and Cynthia join in repeating the lines, and together, the three of them make their way through the chorus of the song.

I feel like I'm delusional. What is this coincidence? And after Cynthia and Dana tried to give me this warning as well.

"And I don't want to brag," Adam says when they finish, "but we nailed it."

Sarah shakes her head. "As I'm the only one who, unfortunately, stayed sober, I can tell you that we sounded horrible, but it was so much fun."

Sarah did sound high-pitched but still cute. I couldn't keep my eyes off her.

"Right," Cynthia says, her brow furrowing, instantly becoming serious. "So, you're a vampire. You were a vampire that night too?"

For a split second there, it seemed that Cynthia completely forgot that Sarah is a vampire. Not that I can blame her. When I'm with Sarah, I can almost forget that fact, too. She's just so—human. Plus, mages can't sense vampires; only hunters can.

Sarah looks a little bashful. "Yes, I had just turned into one, maybe a month before. Another reason we wanted to go out that night. Take my mind off my life changing so drastically."

Cynthia lets out a loud sigh. "A vampire. I hung around with a vampire that whole night and didn't even realize." She looks at Adam, a little edge to her voice. "What about you? What's your deal? Are you anything special?"

I can tell by Adam's face that Cynthia said the wrong thing.

Adam looks at her with indignation, "Anything special?"

"Oh, no, I didn't mean—" Cynthia starts.

"My deal," Adam says with self-assurance, cutting her off, "is that I am a playboy, fashionista, with an MS and an MD, the top transplant surgical resident at Mary Birkin's Hospital, and reigning champion of trivia night at Ace's Bar for the last year and a half."

I notice Zach is just staring at Adam with admiration. I've got to give it to Adam; it takes a lot of confidence to be the only regular human surrounded by all the super-humans in this room.

"Don't forget Star Wars enthusiast," Sarah adds.

Adam points to her and nods as if she made a good point in adding that to his list of achievements.

"Adam," Cynthia says, a little less hostile. "I'm sorry, I didn't mean to offend you. I'm just processing. Sarah should have told me that she was a vampire."

"Oh, well, excuse me," Adam says, his hand on his chest. "We must have missed your sign telling us you weren't a muggle, and isn't it your big supernatural law that Sarah *not* go around advertising she's a vampire?"

"I'm not sure what a muggle is, but everything else Adam said is right," I say. "Sarah did nothing wrong."

Cynthia sighs again. "I know," she admits, and turns to Sarah. "A vampire with a soul, huh?"

Sarah shrugs and gives a sheepish smile. "I was thinking of getting that tattooed on my arm."

Cynthia laughs, and I give Sarah's hand another encouraging squeeze. Cynthia looks at me and says, "Dana and I will try and help keep Sarah off the MC's radar. Vampire or no vampire, you got yourself a good one."

"Thanks, Cynthia, I appreciated it. You too, Dana," I say, looking over at her.

She nods, seeming to have given in to Cynthia, but then says, "I still don't understand how this happened." She looks at Sarah. "You have a soul which makes you a *Validus*, but if you have hunter blood in your veins, then by all accounts, you should have died before transforming. All hunters go through a ceremony that prevents them from ever turning into a vampire at birth."

Sarah shrugs. "I'm adopted. I don't know who my birth parents are."

"It's strange that they, whoever they are, would not perform the ritual on you, even if they were giving you up for adoption. It is the law," Dana tells the room.

"Well, if I find them, I'll tell them to turn themselves in," Sarah says jokingly, but I can see that talking about her birth parents might be a bit of a sore spot.

I announce that we have to be on our way, and we say our goodbyes to Dana and Cynthia.

Sarah, Adam, Zach, and I all head to one of the conference rooms in the library. Unfortunately, the lounge room is taken, so we have to use the study which has just a rectangular table and chairs.

The meeting was supposed to start twelve minutes ago. We're late, but we aren't the only ones. Liam and Aquila aren't here yet, either. It's just Kayda, Nick, and Shy seated around the table.

"Where are Liam and Aquila?" I ask Kayda, navigating to the two chairs next to hers.

She shrugs. "No clue. I thought you all were together. It's not like Liam and Aquila to be late to their own meeting."

Sarah and I take a seat next to each other. She looks at me and asks, "How are you feeling? I didn't get a chance to ask earlier."

I tug her arm, pulling her out of her seat to sit on my lap. The second she is close enough I bury my head in her hair. The smell of apples and honeysuckle fills me.

*God,* I missed her.

"Healer Orla cleared me today," I tell her. "I'm all yours tonight. Can I sleep over at your place?"

"I love sleepovers," she says, biting her bottom lip just to tease me. I'm about to kiss her, but Adam's voice stops me.

"Just want to remind certain people that they are not alone in this room, and all PDA and sex talk are, although not frowned upon, maybe a tad inappropriate," Adam calls out, pretending not to be talking straight to Sarah and me.

Nick barks out a laugh across from us. I roll my eyes and intertwine Sarah's hand with mine as she sits back down in her own chair.

Liam and Aquila enter the study a few seconds later, followed by Danielle and Client. What are they doing here? I guess they are back from their trip overseas. Aquila and Danielle are clearly in the middle of some sort of argument.

"We have a meeting we must conduct first, Danielle. We can talk afterwards," Aquila pleads with her.

"Mom, what's going on?" Liam asks in confusion. "Why are you so upset?"

"I want to see her," Danielle says sternly.

"See who?" Liam asks.

Danielle ignores him and looks around the room. Her eyes land on Sarah, and they immediately begin to water.

Sarah looks at her and then around the room in confusion. She looks at me for help, but I'm just as confused as she is. I'm not sure what Danielle wants with Sarah.

Did she find out that Liam has befriended a vampire? Although, friend is a bit of a stretch. Liam and Sarah have barely spoken to each other. Just the rare times that Sarah has come to the Academy.

Danielle starts walking toward us, taking me out of my reverie. I quickly stand up, angling myself to try and shield Sarah. "Don't come any closer," I say harshly.

She narrows her eyes at me. I'm definitely not used to talking to Danielle this way. Liam's parents and I usually get along well. They treat me as one of their own—usually. Still, I'm not letting anyone hurt Sarah.

"Kael, watch your tone with my wife, young man," Client, Liam's father, says firmly, coming to stand beside Danielle.

"Tell your wife to stay away from my girlfriend," I say, never taking my eyes off Danielle.

I feel Sarah stand beside me. "Should I go?" She, too, is staring at Danielle, but asking me.

"Yeah, I'll go with you," I say, grabbing her hand.

"No!" Danielle shouts, her hands up and ready to block us from leaving.

Aquila walks up. "Let's reschedule the meeting for tomorrow night. The Christmas party isn't for another two weeks, so we will have plenty of time to go over details at a later date. Sarah and Liam, if you don't mind staying? Everyone else you are excused."

"I'm not leaving Sarah," I say firmly. Stubbornly, I know.

Confused, everyone starts to trickle out.

Zach and Adam come to our side. "If there is going to be a fight, I would rather stay and help defend Sarah," Zach declares.

Sarah and I both look at him. I see Sarah reach for his hand. "Thank you, Zach." The friendship they've forged seems genuine.

When Zach looks over at me, I give him a grateful nod, which he returns before facing the others.

"And I'm not normally a violent person," Adam adds, "but if you have a problem with Sarah, then you have a problem with me. I'm very good at using my fighting words."

"No one is fighting," Aquila informs us. "I promise, it's just to talk. Sarah is perfectly safe."

Adam looks at Sarah for approval to leave, just as Zach looks at me for the same approval.

I like that both would be willing to stay and help Sarah no matter the cost, but I trust Aquila to tell the truth. I give Zach another nod, letting him know it's okay. I look at Sarah, who is giving the same nod to Adam.

"Thank you," she mouths to them, before they turn to leave.

Aquila sighs. "I guess there is no way to convince you to leave," he says to me.

"Nope." I cross my arms over my chest.

"Very well." He turns to Danielle. "The floor is yours. I'll give you all some privacy." He leaves, closing the door behind him, leaving Sarah, Liam, Danielle, Client, and me alone.

"What's going on?" Liam asks. I can tell by the frustration in his voice that he has asked this question several times and hasn't gotten an answer.

Danielle, never taking her eyes off Sarah says, "Sarah is my daughter."

# Chapter 35
# Kael

EVERYONE IS STUNNED INTO silence. Whatever I thought she was about to say, it sure as hell was not that.

Why Danielle thinks that Sarah is her daughter is beyond me. Liam's sister's grave pops into my mind. Danielle did have a daughter named Sarah, who died during childbirth. Liam and I visited the grave not too long ago. Is Danielle losing her mind? A wave of sympathy washes through me for her.

Liam must have come to the same conclusion I did, because he walks over to her and gently places a hand on her shoulder. "Mom, Sarah died," Liam says slowly. "I know you miss her, but this isn't her."

"It is her," she says a little too aggressively.

I've never seen Danielle like this. She usually treats Liam like her golden child.

"Umm, not to mention the elephant in the room, but going just from looks, it doesn't seem possible for you two to be my parents." Sarah looks at her hand, obviously recognizing her darker skin color and then pointedly looking at their paler ones.

Client walks up to his son and wife. "Maybe you should start from the beginning, Dani."

She nods her head. "Should we sit?"

I squeeze Sarah's hand. I know this must not be easy or fair to her. She shouldn't have to listen to an unstable woman claiming that Sarah is her dead child. This must be bringing up unresolved grief for both of them. Still, we all take a seat around the table.

From what Sarah has told me, she never knew her birth parents. Her adoptive parents loved her so much that she never felt like she was missing out on anything by trying to find them. If I had to admit, now that I'm looking for it, Sarah does resemble Danielle a little. I can't point out what about Sarah reminds me of her exactly, maybe the shape of the eyes, even though Danielle's are hazel while Sarah's are chestnut brown. Not to mention Liam, Sarah, and Danielle all seem to have the same shade of raven hair.

Danielle keeps looking at Sarah. It's like Sarah is the only person who exists for her. She clears her throat a few times before she is able to speak.

"When I was—" She chokes up, clears her throat once more, and tries again. "When I was about your age, I was a hunter here at the Academy. I was captain of my squad. Client had his own squad he was captain of." She looks away from Sarah for the first time to smile at Client and then at Liam. "I guess it runs in the family. Liam was just shy of turning two. He was the cutest little toddler, running all over the Academy."

Liam gives her a small smile before she turns her attention back to Sarah.

"In my squad, there was a man named Hector Martinez. He was a good fighter and an even better man. We..." She pauses as if she doesn't know how to continue.

"Dani, would you like me to step out? Will that help?" Client asks quietly, only to her.

"No," she says, shaking her head. Danielle reaches for his hand. He takes it in both of his. "Please stay," she asks before turning back to Sarah once more.

She says the next part quickly, seeming to want to get it out before she loses her nerve. "Hector and I had an affair, which resulted in a child. I was young, and I made a terrible mistake one night. I got pregnant. I was scared of losing Client if he were to find out, so I planned to have an abortion." Danielle shuts her eyes as she says the last part, not wanting to look Sarah in the eyes. I can see Client squeeze Danielle's hand.

"But then Hector, your father, found out and begged me to keep you. He wanted us to run away together. I told him I couldn't. I loved my husband and wanted to stay and make it work with Client. On that same night he found out about the baby, Hector died. A vampire killed him on a hunt."

She's silent for a long moment, so long that I think she might be done, but then she adds, "I had to have the baby after that. I—I had to keep a piece of my friend alive. Client was willing to tell everyone that it was his and we could raise the baby together, but I knew it would be obvious that you weren't his. With the help of Aquila, we found this nice human couple, Joe and Donna Greenwood, who had always wanted a baby."

Sarah gasps at the sound of their names. She is squeezing my hand so hard at this point it's starting to become painful. Although Sarah never mentioned her adoptive parents by name, I know, by her reaction, it has to be them.

So, it's true. Danielle is Sarah's mom, which means Liam and Sarah are half-siblings. *Holy shit, this is crazy.* I look over at Liam. His face has turned ghostly white, and he looks as though he's going to be sick.

"We covered it up by saying that I lost the child at birth," she continues. "Joe and Donna were humans who knew of this life but promised to raise you as a human. Liam informed me of what happened to them. I'm so sorry to hear. They were lovely people."

"But we go to the grave every month," Liam says in a whisper.

"I mourn the daughter I never got to know, never got to watch grow up," Danielle clarifies.

Liam's face grows hard like something just occurred to him. "You cheated on dad," Liam states, jumping to his feet. "How could you?"

Client chimes in, "Son, it was a long time ago. Your mother was young—"

Liam cuts his dad off. "Stop," he shouts. "Mom was twenty-two when she had me, so she would have been maybe twenty-four when she had the affair. That's old enough to know right from wrong."

"Liam," Danielle pleads. "Honey, I'm sorry if this causes you pain."

Liam holds up his hands. "I'm not in the mood to hear any more of your excuses. I'm..." He looks over at Sarah and me. "I'm sorry. I need time to process all this. I'm going to go."

I watch as he turns without another word and storms out of the study. A part of me wants to rush after him. He's my best friend, and I know he will need me, but Sarah will need me more. A single tear falls down her face. She quickly brushes it away.

"Are you okay, Sarah?" I ask softly.

She shakes her head rapidly. "No."

"Sarah," Danielle says. "I'm sorry. I know this is a lot to take in. When Aquila called, I didn't want to believe it myself, but you are the spitting image of Hector. You have his eyes. I'm so sorry I wasn't there to protect you from this world. I thought I was doing the right thing by you. But you're a vampire. My baby girl turned into a vampire. The one thing worse than becoming a hunter."

Tears start pooling in Danielle's eyes. She doesn't even bother wiping them away as they begin to cascade down her cheeks.

I'm about to argue that Sarah is amazing, vampire or not, when Sarah says, "I'm not your baby girl." Her tone is stiff and full of venom. "My mother was Donna Greenwood, and for the record, I've made my peace when it comes to me being a vampire."

"Oh no, I didn't mean to make you feel ashamed or—"

"I'm not ashamed," Sarah says, standing up and cutting her off. "And just so I fully understand what happened. When you were around my age, you had an affair with what I'm assuming was the hot Spanish man on your squad. Maybe to sow some wild oats of yours, but then you got pregnant. You told him you weren't going to keep the baby and that you didn't want to be with him. After which, you sent him off to fight vampires with a broken heart and broken spirit. He then dies, and you felt guilty and decided to have the baby, but not guilty enough to *keep* the baby, and now what? You want to... What exactly do you want from me? Why tell me all this?"

Danielle stands and straightens, finally wiping away her tears. "I thought you deserved the truth about who your birth parents are."

Sarah nods slowly. "Is that all?"

"No, I-I would also like to get to know you." Danielle pauses for a long moment. When Sarah doesn't say anything, she continues. "I understand, of course, that you will need time. It's a lot of information to take in. I'll go. But before I do..." Danielle takes a deep breath. "I can't take back what I did. I regret the decision I made, and if I could go back, I'd make a different choice. Kael has my number if you want to get in touch."

Sarah doesn't answer her. Instead, she looks at me. "I would like to go home now." Her eyes are glossy and I know she is trying hard to keep tears in.

"Of course," I say quickly. I nod to Danielle and Client as Sarah and I walk past them without another word.

# Chapter 36
# Sarah

I T'S QUIET AS KAEL drives me back to my apartment. I'm grateful he is giving me the space to be alone with my thoughts. Of all the ways I thought this night was going to go, finding out about my birth parents didn't make the list.

This is a supernatural soap opera drama. My head is reeling with the weight of it all.

Firstly, my birth mom is also Liam's mom. I can't even wrap my head around that particular bit of info. I have a brother. I'll have to save that tidbit to ponder over when my brain can handle it.

Secondly, she didn't want me. I don't know why I'm upset by the information. I was adopted. Obviously, there was a big chance that my parents didn't want me, but the fact that she wanted to abort me. That stings a little bit differently than just wanting to give me up. She didn't want me to exist.

Lastly, my birth father is dead. He died thinking that I was never going to be. I don't even realize I'm crying until Kael wipes away the tears falling down my cheeks. I look around to see that we are parked in the parking lot of my apartment complex. I vaguely wonder when we arrived here.

"Thank you for bringing me home," I say in between sniffs.

"Is there anything I can do?" he asks softly.

Kael has been amazing tonight. He stayed by my side the whole time and even stood up to Liam's parents when he thought they were trying to hurt me.

"Can you stay with me tonight?" I inquire. I know we already agreed that he would spend the night, but after everything that transpired, I just want to be sure.

"I was hoping you would ask," he says softly, tugging a strand of hair behind my ear as he presses his palm to my cheek.

Kael ends up holding me all night long. I wake up the next afternoon, earlier than usual, around one. I reach out for Kael, but he isn't in bed.

*Did he leave?* I wouldn't blame him if he did. Last night was a crazy mess. I cried on and off for hours before finally falling asleep with my head on his chest. I get dressed and make my way to the kitchen, where I hear the guys talking.

Kael didn't leave after all. *Thank the heavens.*

"Good afternoon, Sarah," Zach says, taking a sip of his coffee and reading something on the laptop perched in front of him. He's dressed for the day, wearing jeans and a tan sweater. I've noticed that Zach tends to wear neutral-colored shirts. All browns, beiges, grays, whites, and occasionally black.

It's so different from the vibrant reds, oranges, and purples that Adam wears. I can see why Adam is so smitten with Zach. There is a gentleness about him that's rare in the world we live in. It was love at first sight for them two.

At the moment, Zach is wearing glasses, looking down at the laptop. I wonder if he wears contacts the rest of the time, or if he only wears glasses when reading. Adam once commented that when Zach wears his glasses, his sexy professor vibe is much more overpowering. He's not wrong.

"Good afternoon," I greet back.

Adam is working days at the hospital, so for the last two mornings and afternoons, it's just been Zach and me at home. It's funny because I would have thought that without Adam here, Zach wouldn't stay. I assumed it would have felt awkward, but I've now come to realize that Zach can be a bit scatter-brained. He gets so lost in whatever he is reading or researching that he doesn't even notice his surroundings.

He has to set reminders on his phone for just about everything. When to train, when it's time to get ready for a hunt, even when to eat. Otherwise, he would get lost in the world of information at his fingertips.

We fell into this comfortable routine, he and I. I make him breakfast, which he always appreciates. It's nice to have someone who also sleeps during the day and works at night. He doesn't mind having breakfast food in the afternoon.

But now Kael is here, too. He is sitting on one of the four barstools we have next to the kitchen island, which he gets up from to come kiss me good morning.

"How did you sleep?" he asks, cupping my cheek.

My, oh my, does he look good in the morning. His hair is all ruffled and bed-worn. He's wearing pajama pants and a white tee that shows off his incredible biceps. He's also sporting a five o'clock shadow, and even that looks good on him.

I lean into his touch. "Good," I answer.

Sleeping with Kael is a one-of-a-kind experience. The way he wraps me in his arms makes me feel safe and wanted. He has ruined me from ever sleeping without him again. After only one night, I'm officially addicted.

I turn to start cooking breakfast. I keep it simple, preparing to make each of them an omelet. "Kael, do you have an omelet preference, or are you allergic to anything that I need to be aware of?"

He looks at me quizzically. "Why are you making breakfast? You don't have to do that."

Zach snorts. "Don't bother," he warns Kael. "I've tried telling her she doesn't have to make breakfast for me, especially when Adam isn't here, but she wouldn't have it." He looks at me with a smile. "Adam says you became obsessed with cooking because of Food Network." Turning to Kael, he adds, "It's an entire channel for cooking shows."

I shake my head, bemused at the fact that he has to explain to Kael what the Food Network is.

"I will not confirm nor deny that statement, but I will say that becoming a vampire really put a damper on my dream of owning my own restaurant. I also wanted to start my own vegetable garden after watching two seasons of Down to Earth on Netflix, but vampires can't go out in sunlight, so there went that dream as well," I admit. "Thankfully, I love writing and can still write books as long as my publisher allows me to do all our meetings remotely or via email, which she does."

"Her omelets are the best by the way," Zach informs Kael.

"I can't wait to try one," Kael says. "I have no allergies, so I'm good with whatever you decide."

I give a thumbs up. "Great."

I gather my ingredients: eggs, onions, tomatoes, Canadian bacon, cheddar cheese, and place them on the counter. I chop my toppings and start whisking my eggs for thirty seconds. I'm in the process of pouring the eggs into the hot pan when I feel Kael's arms wrap around my waist.

"I didn't realize you knew how to cook," he whispers in my ear. "It's sexy."

My God, this man gives me all the feels. I lean back into his embrace, wanting to breathe all of him in.

"I'm going to swoon from you touching me, and then you won't have any breakfast at all," I say.

He laughs and releases me, taking a step to the side. "Can I help?"

"Yes. Can you get two plates from the cabinet there?" I ask as I point to the cabinet that holds the plates and bowls.

He follows my instructions, and I watch him. When he reaches up to grab the plates, his shirt lifts up just enough for me to see the deep lines poking out from beneath his waistband. I can feel the saliva pooling in my mouth.

*What a work of art*, I think to myself. *I want to lick every—*

"Sarah, your eggs are burning," Zach tells me, amused.

"Son of Krypton," I shout, focusing my attention back to my cooking.

"Did you just say 'son of Krypton?'" Kael asks, holding back a laugh.

"No," I tell him. "I said son of—a bitch, like a normal person would when faced with a cooking crisis of their own making."

He saunters over and kisses me on the cheek. "You're adorable," he tells me as he puts the plates on the counter next to the stove.

I finish cooking their omelets, trying not to have a goofy grin on my face the whole time. It's a fun afternoon hanging around with Zach and Kael. You can tell the two of them love each other dearly. They tease each other like brothers, and float around each other in a way that only comes about from spending lots of time together. It's nice to witness.

Adam comes home around five-thirty with Chinese food. Zach must have warned him Kael was here because he brings enough for three.

I notice Zach takes off his glasses to eat. Curious, I ask, "Zach, about the glasses. I thought hunters had super vision."

He smiles. "We do. I only use them to read, and when I'm looking at my laptop for a long while. They just help me focus. I actually needed them all the time before my hunter ceremony, so now I guess I'm just so used to wearing them when I look at a screen."

"Leave my sexy professor alone, Sarah," Adam scolds.

Zach blushes and looks over at Adam. "Sexy professor?"

"Yes, that's Sarah's and my name for you when you're not around," Adam informs him, not the least bit embarrassed by his confession.

Kael chuckles, reaching over and intertwining are fingers together.

"It's true," I admit. "I asked if you two play professor and doctor in the bedroom, but Adam won't admit to anything."

The whole room laughs, and they finish eating while we converse with light banter all around, but mostly from Adam and me. The hunter men tend to be more on the quieter side, happy just to listen.

My happiness from the day quickly fades, however, when it's time to head back to the Academy to have the meeting that was interrupted by my birth mother. That feels weird to say, even inwardly. I spent the day not thinking too hard on the fact that I even have a birth mother, but it's hitting me hard as night falls.

Zach gives Adam a quick kiss and promises to be back later tonight. Adam is not coming this time, since, technically, he's not even supposed to know about the Academy, let alone be invited to hunter meetings. I wish I wasn't invited, but I know they need my help with the knowledge I have on Mr. Leon. I have to be there. Which means I have to face my long-lost family.

# Chapter 37
# Sarah

W E WALK INTO THE Academy an hour later. Everyone else is already here, so the three of us quickly grab the remaining seats toward the back. I ignore Shyann's hard glare as Kael slips his hand in mine giving it a gentle squeeze.

As soon as we sit, Aquila starts the meeting. "Unfortunately, Sarah's information about the penthouse was a bust. Likely, Caesar moved locations since her time with him."

Kael told me that the team went to the penthouse address I gave them, but that when they got there, an abandoned factory building stood there instead. I never even thought to go anywhere near that building again, but still. How can a building just disappear in two years?

Is it possible I'm remembering it wrong? Whenever I think about the place, the haunting memories surface like I'm right back there again; it's visceral. No way I'm making this up. But then, where the hell did the building go?

"That leaves us with Leon Tower," Aquila continues. "We only have two weeks before the Christmas party at Leon Tower. I want to go over our plan once more so that we are all on the same page." He looks over at Liam.

Liam clears his throat and starts. "Kayda and Zach will be handling video feed and surveillance. Shy, Nick, and I will be on guard on the roof and floor below. Sarah and Kael will be at the party. Kael, your goal is to set up the cameras. Zach will go over exactly where he wants them placed after the meeting."

Kael nods to Zach as Liam continues. "The goal is to be in and out before Caesar shows up. Sarah said he usually makes his entrance around an hour after the party starts. We want to install the cameras once most guests have arrived. It'll be easier for Kael to move around through the crowd unnoticed. That gives us about thirty minutes."

"I can get it done in time," Kael assures him.

"And what if Caesar shows up?" Nick asks, rubbing his hands together as if he's already preparing for a fight.

He reminds me of a caged, hungry predator, always itching for a fight, pacing and ready to be set free on unsuspecting prey.

"*If* he shows up and *if* we can get Leon alone, we can take him out, but remember this is a recon mission first and foremost. If he does show up with members of his coven and we find ourselves outnumbered, we are to abort immediately." Liam narrows his eyes at Nick, willing him to agree and temper his energy.

"Patrick's squad is already aware that we may have the coven leader's identity. His team is willing to help. They will be hunting in Chinatown that night, so they won't be too far away if we need backup. Geralt's squad will also be out that night, at McLaren Park, so farther away, but they are on standby if we need."

Liam delves into details, reviewing the building's blueprint and various scenarios of possible outcomes. Frankly, it's a lot. A lot of words, and ifs, buts, and maybes, and I start to lose focus around the end of the second hour. I didn't realize so much went into their hunts and patrols. Everyone contributes to the meeting, throwing in their ideas and opinions. Liam finally concludes the three-hour meeting, asking everyone to dedicate at least five hours a day to training in the room for the next two weeks.

Kael suggests that I join the training, but I remind him that I'm a vampire and am not completely welcome in an Academy of vampire hunters.

He gives a sheepish grin. "Sorry, I keep forgetting. I would still like to show you a few fighting moves that might be useful to you," he says.

"We can go to the roof of my apartment building. It's a big, open area and no one really goes up there," I tell him.

"Sounds good," he says. "Let's go there."

We start to head out when Liam walks up to us. He didn't say anything to us when we walked in, and he barely looked at me all during the meeting.

"Sarah," he says softly, not at all in his leader voice he was using just moments ago. "May I have a word with you?"

He seems a bit nervous, which in itself is unsettling. I didn't think Liam could get nervous. Granted, I haven't known him for very long, but he seems to always walk around with this hard shell. Not the cold or dismissive kind. But the controlled and collected kind. This vulnerability helps lower my guard. He's just as confused and lost about this whole situation as I am.

"Of course," I say quickly.

Liam looks over at Kael. "We won't be long."

Kael nods. He brings our intertwined hands up to his lips, kissing the top of my hand before releasing me. "I'll be right outside if you need me."

"Thanks," I say, giving him a small smile.

Liam leads me back through the conference room, and into a smaller, more intimate meeting room with just a rectangular table in the center. He pulls out a chair and gestures for me to take a seat, while he takes the one across.

The silence between us stretches out for what feels like minutes when I know it's only been seconds. I can see him forming the words in his mind, taking care and thinking about what he wants to say, how he wants to sound. He leans forward, resting his elbows on the table. His eyes finally meeting mine.

"Sarah, I wanted to apologize for my behavior yesterday. I shouldn't have walked out like I did."

I shake my head. "Liam, you don't need to apologize. Your world got flipped upside down, too. I don't blame you for walking out."

"Still, I am sorry. I was and still am upset with my—our mom."

"I understand that, too," I say honestly.

Learning everything she kept from me is infuriating. It is clear that she didn't even keep tabs since she only just learned about my parents dying. Was it really all for my safety? To top it all off, I have a half-brother. Did she think we didn't have the right to know about each other?

"I know you have things you need to work out with her," he says, continuing on, oblivious to my inner turmoil. "I also know that it may take time for you to forgive her or want anything to do with her. But maybe you and I could spend some time together, separately from our mother."

He pauses briefly, and his eyes never leave mine. In them I see a man who's been mourning. Quietly. "I know it sounds crazy, but it feels like this secret wish of mine has come true. The wish of my sister being alive. Of having the chance to be a brother. And I'm not trying to put all of that on you. I don't want you to feel pressured. I just mean that—even though this whole thing is a mess..." Liam sighs and chuckles to himself, raking a hand through his hair, and looks back at me with kind, genuine eyes. "What I'm trying to say is that I'd like to get to know you, if that is something you would want to do."

Tears sting my eyes. I fight for them to stay inside as I nod my head. "I would like that very much," I say softly. "I've always wanted a sibling. I never thought I would get a Superman lookalike for a brother; it's pretty cool."

He laughs, and it's nice to see him smile. "Can I ask you something?" he asks, becoming serious once again.

"Sure, ask away."

"Why is your last name Summers if your adoptive parents are Greenwood?"

"Oh, that," I say, tucking a strand of hair behind my ear. "I changed it after becoming a vampire so that Mr. Leon wouldn't find me. Not that that matters anymore. He found me anyway."

A shudder runs through me at the shift back to reality.

"We're going to catch him and kill him, Sarah. I promise you. And Kael and I will keep you safe." He says it with such confidence, it's hard not to believe him.

If I had a properly working heart, it would be filled with warmth at his reassurance. I'd accepted that my life was going to be filled with a certain degree of loneliness. Of course, I have Adam, but I know that his future doesn't involve growing old beside me. We've never really spoken about this, but I wouldn't want that for him anyway. He deserves a life and a family of his own. And so, a part of me is always ready for the day when I'm truly alone.

But now, I find myself with something akin to hope. Kael has made me feel alive in ways I haven't since dying. And on top of that, I have a brother. One I don't know very well yet, but another person I can be my true self around, who wants to look out for me and protect me. I have a mother, too. Someone I never thought I'd have again. But I'm not ready to unpack that quite yet.

So, I just nod.

"Thanks," I say. After a moment I add, "I have a question for you. What will happen to the coven if Mr. Leon dies? Are their lives connected to his in a way that if he dies, they all die? Am I in danger of dying if he dies, since he made me?"

Liam shakes his head. "No, Sarah. You're not in danger of dying. Unfortunately, neither is the rest of the coven. It doesn't work that way. From what I know, the coven just finds a new leader, or maybe the next most powerful vampire amongst them is promoted to coven leader. A lot of this is still a mystery to us. It's why we don't particularly seek out the coven leader. Another one just takes its place."

"But you're seeking out Mr. Leon," I remind him.

His lips quirk up on one side. "Yes, to help save you."

When I give him a "really?" look, he just laughs.

That may be Kael's reason, but not everyone else's.

"And because Caesar is an ancient. He's too powerful to be left to run loose in the city," he adds.

I nod, accepting his second reason much easier than the first.

"Is it okay if I ask you a question about being a vampire?" he inquires after a beat.

"You hunters and your questions," I say in laughter. I'm sure his curiosity won't even compare to the mountain of questions Zach has already hurled at me. The man asked more questions in two hours than Kael asked in two weeks.

I wave my hand for him to proceed.

"The other night, Kael was covered in blood, but you didn't so much as flinch. You were just worried about getting him help."

"Because I care about him. I wouldn't do anything to hurt him," I say, not knowing if he believes me or not.

"I can see that," he says. "I just wanted to know if it was hard for you? Every time I've seen a vampire exposed to blood, they turn into a crazed animal. It's like they can't help themselves. I guess I just wanted to know what it feels like for you, being that you still have your soul intact. You don't have to answer if you would rather not." He adds the last statement as a speedy afterthought.

"I don't mind answering," I say, but then take a moment to gather my thoughts before speaking. No one has ever asked me what it feels like on my end before. I briefly consider how honest I want to be, but I don't want to build Liam's and my relationship on half-lies and tainted truths.

"It does hurt to be around blood," I admit. "It's like alarm bells go off in my body, telling me I'm starving, and the only thing that will satiate me and make this pain go away is to have blood. But then I know deep down that's a lie. I don't need blood every second of every day to survive, but when I see blood, all my sense of reason goes out the window, and I have to fight it." I glance at Liam. A flicker of doubt crosses my mind. Have I said too much? Is he disappointed at what he's hearing? But Liam's face remains curious and genuine, and so I continue.

"I can see why vampires with no soul would give in to that. It's the easier route to take. I, however, still have that moral compass that tells me what's right and what's wrong. I can look past the blood to the person. It also helps to never be too hungry. If I'm already hungry, then it's harder to hold back, but I still can," I add quickly.

He nods, but I can see the cogs in his brain turning, trying to understand and process what I'm saying.

I try again. "Imagine, you are in the desert with someone you care about. You've been there for days without any form of substance. Suddenly, you come across a stream of clear, cool water. Your mouth's dry, your stomach aches, and all you want to do is take a sip of the enticing water to relieve some of the physical pain you're feeling, but you know if you take a sip, the person with you will die.

"That's how it is to be around blood for me. I'm able to resist because the consequence is hurting another person, and that's simply not an option for me."

Liam seems to take a moment to let my words sink in. "Wow, when you put it like that, you are a superhero," he says after a moment.

"I'm the Supergirl to your Superman?" I tease. "They're cousins, not siblings, but close enough."

He smiles. "Exactly."

"You would do the same if our roles were reversed," I say confidently.

He shrugs. "I hope I would."

"I know you would," I say. "Besides, being around humans in general is not bad at all. As long as you aren't bleeding. It's just like being around your favorite food all the time. What is your favorite food?"

"Frosted Flakes," he answers.

I raise my eyebrow at him. "Frosted Flakes. You can pick anything in the world, and you're going with Frosted Flakes?"

"What?" he asks innocently. "I love Frosted Flakes."

I shake my head in disbelief. "I don't think we are related after all."

He barks out a laugh. "Is loving a good bowl of cereal really so terrible?"

I smile. "I guess you are allowed to love whatever you love," I say, and then continue on with my analogy. "Well, then imagine being around a big bowl of sugary cereal all the time. That's what it feels like to be around people in general. It doesn't hurt, just a little tempting."

"I definitely don't know if I would be able to be around cereal all the time and not want to take a bite."

I laugh, and the air between us becomes a little lighter. "I have a brother, and his favorite food is Frosted Flakes. Life is so crazy."

"Okay, Chef Sarah," Liam teases. "So what's your favorite food?"

I'm loving this. I can't help it. Sitting here, joking around with Liam is the best thing in the world. He's so funny and kind. It's easy to love him, even in this short amount of time.

"Pot roast," I say, thinking of my mom's pot roast. She made the best in the world. My father and I would insist she make it every Sunday. It became our tradition.

I wonder what they would think about everything that is going on now. Apparently, they knew about the supernatural world from the beginning. There is so much I want to ask them.

Why didn't they tell me the truth about everything? How long had they known, and how did they find out? I would give anything to speak with them again. I wonder how they would have reacted to me becoming a vampire.

"That is a good one," Liam says, taking me out of the depressing rabbit hole of emotions I was sinking into.

"Well, it's no Frosted Flakes," I tease.

Liam smirks. "Kael is probably going crazy outside waiting for us," he says, gesturing to the door.

"I guess I should go back out there, put him out of his misery," I joke.

"He's different, you know," he tells me. "I know you don't see it, but he's happier now than I have ever seen him. He's been angry for such a long time. It's like he didn't know any other way to be—until you. I love seeing him this way."

I feel giddy at his words. I don't think he realizes what that means to hear him say that.

"Thank you. He is pretty amazing. He's going to teach me some fighting moves," I say proudly.

"That's a good idea," he says. "Do you mind if I tag along?"

# Chapter 38
# Kael

L IAM, KAYDA, AND ZACH end up accompanying Sarah and me to the rooftop of her apartment building. As she predicted, it is deserted of people, just like the night I followed her back here on Halloween.

That night feels like a lifetime ago, when in reality, it was just a little over a month ago. So much has happened since then. Back then, I was still struggling with my feelings on whether or not I should kill Sarah. Now, I would die for her.

We bring our own light fixture since there are no lights on the roof. It's a dual-head work light normally used at construction sites.

I know from experience that Sarah is untrained. After a few rounds though, it's clear that she has at least taken a few self-defense classes, so she's not completely starting at square one. Plus, she's a quick learner and eager to get it right.

Adam joins us, becoming Zach and Sarah's cheerleader from the sidelines. He even brought up a lounge chair and a giant coffee from a popular cafe down the street.

Kayda can't seem to stop laughing at everything that comes out of Adam's mouth. I personally find it distracting. This isn't some fun activity; we're preparing for something serious.

"Watch Clark Kent behind you," Adam shouts to Sarah, putting both hands to his face like he can't watch, but also compelled to peek between his fingers.

Liam grabs hold of Sarah, tossing her over his shoulder in one fluid motion and pinning her to the ground. Liam explains what he did to pin her and how she should counterattack.

I wince, my feet wanting to propel me forward to her side, but I force myself to stay put. She needs to learn to fight.

"Let's try again," Liam says patiently, extending his hand to Sarah helping her up to her feet.

I'm glad Liam came. He really is the best coach.

Sarah relayed their conversation from earlier. Liam wants to get to know Sarah as his sister, and I'm happy for them both. Sarah seems so excited, and I know Liam always mourned the sister he thought died at birth.

"Zach, honey, you're looking a little sweaty. Why don't you go on ahead and take your shirt off?" Adam shouts, bringing me back to the here and now.

Kayda laughs and ends up on her ass because of it. I'm currently sparring with her and use the moment to move in for the kill. I bring my knee to her solar plexus, pinning her down, and my forearm presses down on her neck. She doesn't even seem to notice or care, just keeps laughing as she pushes me off her.

"Can we bring him to all our training sessions?" she asks as I help her to her feet.

"No," I say through gritted teeth.

"Aww, I'm sure he didn't mean it when he said you look like a boy band member on steroids trying to play wrestling."

I roll my eyes. "You just like him because he keeps calling you a queen."

"I like him because he really seems to make Zach happy. This is the first time I've ever seen Zach so—alive. He has always been nose-deep in a book or laptop. It's nice knowing that Zach is getting out into the world a little bit."

She's right. I know she's right. Adam is just a lot to take in. He has a big personality. He makes his presence known. It doesn't help knowing that I'm not Adam's favorite person, not by a long shot. Not that I care.

"Just the way that I like Sarah because of what she does to you," she continues, bumping my shoulder with hers. "You're so different around her, so much happier. It's a little weird to see you so committed to someone for the first time in your life, but it's a good weird."

I mock frown. "Are you saying I'm not the sexy, brooding guy you all have grown to love?"

She laughs. "I'm not sure about sexy, but you still do your fair share of brooding."

I smirk as we set up to go another round. We train for two more hours before calling it quits. Sarah had her turn sparing with everyone to give her a feel for fighting with different opponents.

I'll admit, I was the worst one. I didn't like aggressively tackling Sarah to the ground. It felt wrong. Liam quickly benched me and had me coaching from the sidelines instead.

We have plans to meet back here tomorrow for more practice. This time, with weapons. Sarah needs to be ready for anything.

I packed an overnight bag since I plan to stay at Sarah's tonight. With everything that's going on, I want to stay close to her.

I grab my bag and start to head down with everyone when Liam pulls me aside. "I'm headed over to the new apartment tomorrow for the first look through, if you want to come."

"Yeah, man," I say excitedly. "What time?"

"We need to be there for ten a.m."

"Sounds good. I'll meet you there."

"One more thing," he says a little uncomfortably. "Are you ever going to forgive Shy?"

I tense up. She's the only one who hasn't come around to the fact that I'm dating Sarah.

Even Nick has accepted it. He apologized to me and everything. I told him when Sarah forgives him, that's when I'll forgive him.

To be honest, I can kind of see Sarah starting to warm up to him, but if she wants to hold a grudge, she has every right to. The fucker did try to murder her.

Shyann is a different story.

"She doesn't deserve my forgiveness," I say a little too sharply. "If it was up to her, Sarah would be dead. She's your sister now. I'm surprised you don't feel the same. Shy tried to kill Sarah, don't you care?"

I see the slightest flinch from Liam. "I do care," he says calmly. "Shyann is sorry for what she did. She doesn't plan to try to kill Sarah again, and having you two at odds with each other doesn't help the squad dynamic. We have one of the biggest hunts of our lives coming up, and I need everyone to be on good terms with each other. If you don't want to do it for her, then do it for me—and Sarah. Sarah needs Leon killed more than any of us."

Frustrated, I let out a sigh. "Fine, I'll talk to her."

"Tomorrow?" he persists.

"Yes, tomorrow," I tell him just to get him off my back. I'll talk to her, but I sure as hell am not forgiving her.

Liam seems to be satisfied with my answer, and the two of us walk down together, joining the others.

# Chapter 39
# Kael

AFTER TAKING TURNS SHOWERING, Sarah, Zach, Adam, and I hang around for a few hours in their living room until we all finally call it a night.

I'm walking into Sarah's room, after brushing my teeth, to find her in bed typing away at her laptop. She looks sexy in her little pink, silky, matching shorts and shirt pajama set. Her eyes are focused in concentration; she has no idea I'm even in her room, so I take a moment to observe her. I like how she keeps her bottom lip tucked in between her teeth as she types. The way her fingers fly across the keyboard.

I shuffle closer, and she does a quick glance up when she hears me. "Sorry, I'm just trying to get a few hundred words in for my book. I've been slacking lately. My editor emailed me asking how the second book is coming along. I'm debating whether or not to fake an illness to buy me more time. I've been so distracted recently."

"Really? What has you so distracted?" I ask as I take off my shirt and toss it to the ground.

"Just with everything going on lately, I..." She looks up and stops mid-sentence. Her eyes grow wide as they trail from my arms, to my chest, to my stomach, and finally back up to meet my eyes. "Umm, just lots of stuff distracting me," she says dreamily.

Truthfully, I know she's been distracted, not that anyone can blame her. Finding out about her birth parents couldn't have been easy. I know she's not ready to talk about it, but I can be here for her in other ways.

I give a small, "Hmm," as I slip off my sweatpants so that I'm standing before her in just my boxer briefs. Her mouth parts, and those big brown eyes fill with desire as she slams her laptop closed and places it haphazardly on the bedside table.

"Is there something I can do to help?" I question playfully, sauntering over to the bed.

She rises to her knees. "*You* are my distraction now, but I'm not complaining."

I let out a soft chuckle as I ease onto the bed and move toward her. With both hands, Sarah glides her fingers down my chest, running them to my stomach. My body comes alive under her touch. My heart constricts, and my world narrows to only her.

"I love these," she tells me, her palms resting on my abs.

I lean in and whisper in her ear, "Do you now?" as I trial little open-mouth kisses from her neck to her cheek and finally, her lips.

This kiss is different from our others. The other times were rough, passionate, and desperate. But we're in no rush now. I'm taking my time to savor the softness of her lips, the way they mold against mine.

I pull back just enough so I can slide her shirt up over her head and toss it on the floor to join my discarded clothes. She isn't wearing a bra, and I take a moment to get my fill at the sight of her. I run both my thumbs over her breasts, feeling her peaks harden at my touch. I bend down, taking one in my mouth, sucking on her nipple, giving it a gentle bite.

Sarah whimpers, arching backwards as I do the same to the other side. Fuck, I love the sounds she makes. The energy between us changes. There's urgency now. Her fingers tangle in my hair, her body responding to my stimulation, silently begging for more.

My lips find hers again. It's a little rougher this time. I slide my tongue to caress with hers. Soon, we are all tongue and teeth, her body pressed to mine as if she wants to fuse with me.

Sarah pulls me down on top of her. I grab one of her thighs and raise it to my hip as I grind into her. Her nails track down my back, sending shivers through me, pulling me into a frenzy. I let go of her leg so I can slip my hand inside her tiny shorts.

"You're not wearing any underwear," I say. "Good girl."

I slip one finger inside her. Sarah's want has me hardening even further. "Always so wet for me," I whisper, slowly stroking.

"Yes," she cries out, her hips circling to match my rhythm. I want to take my time. I want to push her to the edge and keep her there. We have nowhere to be but in this moment, and I want it to last as long as possible.

"Please," she whispers between moans.

"I love it when you beg me, baby," I say. "Tell me what you want."

"I want... I want..."

*Fuck.* Sarah is a whimpering mess, and I'm loving every second of it.

"Tell me," I demand, stopping all movements.

Sarah groans. "Don't stop," she rasps.

"I'm waiting," I tease.

Sarah looks at me, licking her lips. "I want you to touch me. I want you inside me, bare," she whispers.

"Bare? Are you sure?" I brought condoms just in case, but the thought of fucking Sarah with nothing between us flips a primal switch in my brain.

"Yes," she says, grinding her hips so my finger moves inside her. I slip another in and curve my fingers, eliciting a cry from her. "I'm a vampire, I can't get pregnant, or catch anything, for that matter."

"I get tested regularly anyway. I don't have anything," I assure her.

"And I haven't had sex in—well, let's just say it's been a while, so I'm good too," she tells me.

I wonder vaguely if this is the first time she is having sex as a vampire. I can't help but wonder about her past relationships. I hate the thought of anyone touching her but me. No one ever will again.

Suddenly, I want nothing more than to brand her as mine in every way possible tonight. I kiss her softly before saying, "I plan to feel you come undone around my cock, Sarah, but first I want you to cum by my tongue," I demand as I slowly make my way down her body.

# Chapter 40
# Sarah

KAEL RUNS KISSES DOWN my neck and chest, stopping to play with both breasts before continuing to my stomach. He takes his time, and every kiss, every flick of his tongue, is driving me crazy. The anticipation builds quickly. He gets up on his knees and slides my pajama shorts down my legs, slow and sensual. He throws the shorts to the side, utterly forgotten.

"So smooth," he whispers, sliding his fingers over my skin, leaving heated tingles in his wake.

He lifts one of my legs up over his shoulder and plants little kisses starting at my ankle and working his way up the inner part of my thigh.

Thank goodness I decided on a full leg shave in the shower. I'm one of those girls who only does knee down most days.

He positions himself between my legs. I shiver as he takes in a breath and softly says, "I bet you taste as good as you smell." Then his mouth is on me. His warm tongue travels up my base all the way to my clit, where he softly begins to suck. Pleasure shoots through me immediately.

"Oh, my God, Kael," I cry out, my hands raking through his hair, grasping tightly.

Then he moves, his tongue burying inside me again and again before he makes his way back to my clit, working me over and over. My legs begin to tense and close around his head, my hips buck and grind, but his hands have a firm grip on my thighs, keeping me where he needs me, feasting on me. I fist his hair as a deep pressure builds in my core. I'm moaning, calling out his name.

"Yes, Kael, yes."

The sensation is overwhelming. I simultaneously feel like I can't take it anymore, but never want him to stop. He pays attention, sucking and licking at just the right spots. Just when I think I'm on the precipice, he slips a finger inside me to stroke in time with his tongue. It takes only seconds before my earth-shattering orgasm erupts, tingling spikes of pleasure coursing through my entire body. My back arches and toes curl as I cry out once more, my legs turning to jelly. I don't think I'll ever be able to use them again.

"You really are a Greek god," I breathe out.

He chuckles as he positions himself above me. "Baby, I'm not done with you yet, not even close." Kael kisses me hard, and I can taste the sweet saltiness of me on his tongue.

He moves to the side to slip off his boxer briefs, freeing his manhood, and it is glorious. I know this isn't the first time I've seen it, but I'm just as amazed with it now as I was the first time. I suddenly can't wait to get him inside me. I want to feel him.

Kael moves to reposition himself on top of me, claiming my lips before placing himself between my legs. I'm so wet that it would only take one thrust to be fully inside me, but Kael is controlled. He starts off slow, with just the tip, adding in a little more each time. He slowly, deliberately pulls out and pushes back in.

I let out a moan. "Please," I beg, wanting him to fill me.

A ghost of a smile appears on Kael's face. "Desperate for me, Sarah?"

"Yes," I utter instantly. "Kael, please."

I don't have to beg a third time, as Kael slams into me. I cry out, but the scream catches in my throat, suffocated by pleasure as he hits that sweet spot inside me that's been begging for attention.

He gets on his knees, throwing my legs over either side of his shoulders so that he can get deeper, thrust for thrust, in a perfect rhythm. With his thumb, he starts circling the ball of my clit, and I feel the pressure building inside me once more.

"Fuck, Sarah, you feel so good," he tells me breathlessly, letting my legs fall to his hips as he leans in to kiss me. Hearing him tell me how I feel, hearing him grunt and moan while he moves inside me, takes me to the edge once more. I could shatter at a whisper. "Cum with me, baby," he urges, never taking his lips off mine.

At his words, I explode once more. It takes several more strokes before Kael finds his own release, collapsing on top of me.

We stay like this for several moments before peeling ourselves apart, taking turns cleaning up in the bathroom.

When we are both back in bed, I snuggle up to him, lying my head on his chest as he holds me close.

We sit in silence, just basking in bliss. He gives me a kiss on the top of the head as I absentmindedly rub his chest. He doesn't have much chest hair, just a light patch of brown curls. My fingers comb through it, before slowly tracing a long, pink scar going vertically down the right side of his chest. It's at least five inches long, the center cutting right through the nipple.

"How did you get this?" I ask. "I thought hunters healed almost completely every time." Even his recent injuries are just faded red marks now, and will probably disappear altogether in a few days.

"It happened before I became a hunter. I snuck out one night when I was around thirteen. Followed my brother's squad to where they were hunting. I thought I was badass. I wanted to prove I could do what my brother was doing. But then I got in a fight with a vampire." Kael's eyes seem far away, like he is back there. Suddenly, he shakes his head, as if shaking away the memory, and then turns to me with a soft smile, his fingers absentmindedly running through my hair.

"Thankfully, my older brother, Bartlett, wasn't too far away and heard me cry out. He killed the thing before it killed me, but not before it left a permanent reminder of why it's important to wait until after the hunter's ceremony to start with all of this."

He has a brother? "Tell me about your family," I encourage after a moment, snuggling closer to him.

I want to know everything there is to know about Kael Hart.

But, I feel him stiffen at my statement. His fingers stop running through my hair, and I sit up so I can gauge his face better. By the looks of it, I've hit a sore subject even though he was the one who mentioned his brother. I'm not sure if I should apologize for pushing for more information.

I'm about to tell him he doesn't have to talk about it when he says, "It's just me and my mom now. My dad and Bartlett both died on hunting patrols."

My breath catches in my throat. Whatever I thought he was going to say, that wasn't it. I mean, sure, I assumed his family were hunters. Kael has mentioned that vampire hunting is a family business, but I didn't realize that he's lost half of his family that way.

"Kael, I'm so sorry," I say, but it doesn't feel like it's enough.

"It was years ago, but my mother was never the same. She quit being a hunter and begged me to do the same, but I didn't listen. I was angry. I wanted revenge. And for a long time, I put all of that into hunting, let it consume me. Let it fuel me."

A slight shudder passes through me at his last comment, although he doesn't seem to notice. I guess meeting his mother for Christmas is out of the question.

"My mother was angry with me for staying. She didn't speak with me for a whole month after that, but she couldn't stay mad at me forever. One day, she came over to my dorm room at the Academy with a batch of her homemade chocolate chip cookies. She makes the best chocolate chip cookies," he says with fondness.

"Anyway, she made me promise not to get killed on patrol, or I wouldn't get a single cookie. I told her I didn't want to make promises I wasn't sure I could keep, so she threw up a hand in surrender and shoved the cookies at me." Kael smiles at the memory.

"She sounds fun," I say. "Do you see her often now?"

He looks at me and shrugs. "Occasionally, but now that she's walked away from being a hunter, she doesn't come around much. I think the Academy reminds her too much of what she's lost. So, she travels instead. The last postcard I got was from Athens. She got remarried to this retired, wealthy investment banker named Robert, and they live in Colorado."

"And do you like this banker of hers?" I ask.

Kael shrugs again. "Yeah, he's fine. She's happy. And I'm happy for her."

I smile. "You're very sweet."

He rolls his eyes, but a grin creeps across his lips. "Oh yeah, I'll show you sweet," he says, right before he starts tickling me.

I giggle and try to kick away. He jumps on top of me and starts kissing me again. Playfully, at first. Little nips in between tickles. But when I realize he's too strong to shove off, I capture his lips with mine and lock my hands behind his neck to keep his mouth there. Our lips slide over each other, and quickly, desire encases us in a bubble.

His kisses turn hungry, his hands caressing my waist, and my legs hook around his hips. It looks like recovery time is over.

# Chapter 41
# Sarah

I WAKE UP, TURNING to reach out for Kael, but finding rumpled sheets instead. He is already gone. One day I'll wake up and Kael will still be sleeping in my bed—one day.

I do find a note next to my phone. It's in perfect cursive because, of course, Kael would have impeccable penmanship.

*I'm meeting Liam to do the first look-through of our new apartment. I'll be back around six for training.*

Alrighty then. I force myself up and make my bed before gathering my things to take a shower.

No one is here. I know Adam is at work, and I guess Zach finally decided to go back to his own dorm room at the Academy. Most likely to prepare for training tonight.

I take the day to work on my book, and I email my editor what I'm able to complete before it's time to stop and get dressed. Luckily, my new two-piece athletic wear outfit was delivered today.

I have to admit, the black and pink leggings make my ass look great, and I love the sheer zig zags starting from my hip and going down my thighs.

I'm just zipping up the matching sports jacket when I hear a knock at the door. I look at the time, four forty-five p.m. It's earlier than Kael said he would be, but maybe he wrapped things up sooner than expected.

I head to the front door, making sure to look through the peephole first before answering. I'll forever be wary about who lurks on the other side of the door now.

To my surprise, it's Liam's father, Client Bell.

*What in the wizarding world is he doing here?* I take a second to compose myself, smoothing down my already smooth jacket, before unhooking the deadbolt and opening the door.

"Mr. Bell?" I state it as a question, because really, what is he doing here?

Client gives a slight bow of his head in greeting. "Ms. Summers. May I come in? I have something I would like to share with you."

I purse my lips, not quite sure if I want to hear whatever it is that he has to share. In the end, my curiosity overpowers any other reason I may have for keeping him out.

I step to the side, opening the door wider and gesture for him to come in. He smiles warmly at me before entering.

He takes a moment to observe my apartment. I see his lips curve slightly upward as he looks at pictures of Adam and me that we have displayed around the room.

He smells of Old Spice and cinnamon, which makes me pause, because it immediately reminds me of my dad. He used to chew on cinnamon sticks. I don't know why he loved them so much. I wonder if Mr. Client does the same thing.

I doubt it.

"Would you like something to drink?" I offer, remembering my manners. "Water, or I can make a pot of coffee if you like?"

He seems shocked by my offerings, as if vampires knowing how to be cordial to a house guest is unheard of, but he manages to get over it quickly. "Water would be great, thank you," Client replies.

I usher him to the small kitchen table, where he takes a seat. I hand him a bottle of water and take a seat opposite him.

"How do you know where I live?" I ask.

With a guilty frown he says, "I got your address from Liam. I hope that's okay."

*Is it okay?*

"I guess it depends on why you're here," I say truthfully.

I wonder if he is here on his wife's behalf, which doesn't make sense. This man should hate me. I'm the product of his wife's infidelity. I would completely understand if he never wanted to see me again.

Could it be that maybe he is here to try to convince me to talk to Danielle? Well, if that's the reason, it's a wasted trip. I'm not ready to talk to her.

He stares at me for a long moment without saying anything. I fidget a little in my seat, because I'm starting to feel quite uncomfortable.

"Nice weather we're having," I say, just to fill the silence.

He shakes his head and coughs. "Sorry, I just... I'm not used to being so close to a vampire. However, you feel different."

*Oh,* he's not trying to persuade me to talk to Danielle. It might be just the opposite. He probably doesn't like the fact that I'm friends with his son and dating that son's best friend.

"Yes, some of the hunters might have mentioned that once or twice before."

He smiles. "You're a rarity. Only banned history books speak of your kind. If your mother and I had known what we could potentially cause, we would have found a mage to perform the birthing rituals on you, but we didn't know. It was Zach who showed us the book that mentions the *Validus*."

I nod slowly. "Why didn't you do the birthing rituals?"

Client gives a slight shrug of his shoulders. "We thought the fewer people who knew that you were alive, the better. We didn't really know a mage we could trust with such an important secret."

"If you had done the birthing rituals, then I wouldn't be here. Not causing stress for your wife," I point out.

"Forgive me, that's not what I meant," he says quickly. "Danielle doesn't care that you are a vampire. She's saddened by it, of course, but you are still her daughter. She wouldn't want any harm to come to you."

I want to argue that she is not my mother, but think better of it. His intentions still aren't clear, and I don't want to distract him. I keep silent, letting him get whatever it is that he needs off his chest.

He uncaps the water and takes a small sip. "Right, well, I guess I'd better get on as to why I'm here."

"Yes, please."

"Right," he says again, tapping his middle finger on the kitchen table. "I would like to tell you a bit about your father, if that is okay with you?"

*Tap. Tap. Tap.*

"You knew my father—like really knew him?" I ask, completely and utterly shocked. He suddenly has my attention, and I lean forward in my seat a little.

"Yes, I knew your father. Hector and I met on our first day at the Academy," he begins, leaning back in his chair. "Our dorm rooms were side by side. I remember it like it was yesterday. We were both so happy to finally be at the Hunter's Academy. My family had just moved from Pittsburgh. At the time, the San Francisco clan was short on hunters. Lots of families were relocating for the good of the cause.

"Another reason why Dani didn't want to perform the birthing ritual on you," he adds. "We were still short hunters at the time, and if the mages found out about you, they would have never let a future hunter be raised human."

I nod in understanding. It makes sense, I guess.

"Anyway," he continues, "the year Hector and I started was the year with the most transfers on record. His family transferred all the way from Spain. We instantly became best friends." He pauses there for a moment and sighs, as if the memory of his early years still weighs heavily on his mind.

He and my father were best friends? That's shocking to hear. Client didn't say anything when Danielle was telling me the story. Clearly, whatever happened between the three of them was much more complicated than initially presented.

"Hector and I were inseparable for the first three years at the Academy. We didn't meet Dani until our fourth year there. Sure, we knew who she was. Everyone knew who she was. Danielle was top of the class, and way out of our league—or so I thought. But, my God, did she steal my heart immediately. I personally would have never had the courage to talk to her, let alone ask her out. Hector, on the other hand, was fearless."

My father, fearless. I wonder what he would have thought about me. Would he have kept me and raised me all by himself if Danielle would have let him?

Client continues with the story, breaking my imaginings. "He just walked up to Dani one day and asked her out. She said yes, of course. Hector was very handsome and talked with an accent that melted all the girls' hearts. He was my best friend, but boy, was I envious of him.

"In the four years since we started, Hector aged like fine wine. I did not. My arms and legs were too long for my body. I was gangly and didn't know how to walk between two desks without bumping into them," he says as he gives a self-deprecating laugh.

I look at him, really look at him. It's hard to picture the man he is describing. The Client in front of me is muscular, with broad shoulders, like he's worked on a farm his whole life. Just how I would picture the father of Superman to look.

*Wait, did I hear him right?* My dad asked Danielle out first?

He must see me come to the realization because he starts to nod.

"Yes, Hector dated Dani first. I was out of this world jealous of the two of them, and over the years, the more the three of us hung out, the angrier I became. I told myself that Hector could have anyone. Why did he have to pick the one girl that I was in love with? I didn't see that Dani was also the one girl he was in love with, too."

He pauses, taking a sip of his water. I know the story is about to take a turn for the worse, and I want to brace myself for the fall, but not sure how.

"Dani knew that I had feelings for her. I think Hector did as well, although he never mentioned it aloud. I don't think I hid it very well, either. And we let that tension between us fester and bubble. He and I started arguing more, over the smallest, most insignificant things.

"In the end, I'm not sure what exactly caused them to break up. I never asked. Maybe it was the fact that Hector had to suddenly fly back to Spain with his parents for a few weeks because of a family emergency.

"I'm ashamed to say, I did not wait long after he left to make my move. When Hector came back, everything was different," Client averts his eyes, no longer able to meet mine. "Danielle got pregnant. The night she told me was the night I asked her to marry me. We were married within a month.

"The friendship I valued so much with Hector was over. We became enemies. He could not forgive me for taking Dani away from him. I couldn't forgive him for ever loving her in the first place. To me, Danielle was my soulmate, not his. I was both right and wrong."

I want to ask what he means by that, but he continues on, so I don't get a chance.

"Dani tried to be happy with me in our marriage, but I could see that there was a part of her that was still with Hector, that a part of her would always be with Hector, even now."

Client swallows hard, his throat bobbing with the movement. His voice coming out a bit rougher when he says, "When Danielle got pregnant a second time, I knew it wasn't mine. She and I were going through a bit of a rough patch.

"Hector always wanted a child. He loved children, and he was so good with them, too. He was always volunteering to help train the first and second-year tyros. He would have made a wonderful father." Client meets my eyes once more. "Hector fought for you. He wanted you more than you could ever know."

Client gets up and grabs the box of tissues from the kitchen island directly behind me. He comes and sits right back down in his chair, sliding the tissues toward me.

It's then that I realize I'm crying. I grab a tissue to dry my eyes and wipe my nose. I hate crying. It's so messy. Why couldn't crying be one of the things that vampires can no longer do?

When I muster up the will to talk again, I ask, "Mr. Bell, why did you tell me all this?"

He sighs. "I guess I wanted you to know that Hector wasn't just someone that your mom slept with to sow wild oats, or however you put it. She really did love your dad and was devastated when he died. We both were.

"I thought—I thought that I had time to make amends. I truly thought that maybe one day I was going to get my best friend back, but he died with us hating each other. I wanted you to know that if anyone is to blame for your father dying, it was me. I stole the love of his life because she was also the love of my life," he says, almost pleadingly.

Does he want my absolution or just my understanding? Can I give him either? A part of me knows that I can, but more importantly, that I want to.

"Most of all," he continues, "I wanted you to know that you were wanted. Not just by your father, but by your mother, too. I know she said she considered not having you, but I don't think she would have ever gone through with it. I also think she wanted to keep you, but was scared it would end our marriage if she did. To be honest, I don't know if it would have. Our marriage was a bit fragile at the time."

"Looking at you now, I wish we had kept you, even though I know you loved the parents that raised you. The Greenwoods were lovely people.

"I can see Hector in you. I know he would have loved to see how beautiful you grew up to be, and by the way my son talks about you, how wonderful a person you turned out to be."

The last part he says with a slight inflection in his voice. The way some men talk when trying not to get too emotional.

I'm speechless and still crying. I grab for another tissue, trying to blow my nose as politely as possible, if there is such a thing. I'm not sure whether to hate him or like him after what he just told me. I know deep down that I don't hate him. Their love triangle was messy and heart-shattering. It sounds like it was a no-win situation.

"I don't think I'm mentally capable of hearing any more tonight, but if it's alright with you, I would like to hear more about my father soon. Sounds like maybe you have some good memories along with the bad," I say.

He smiles a little. "Yes, I have lots and lots of good memories with your father. I would love to share them with you whenever you're ready."

He stands up, arching his back a little to stretch.

"Well, I should go. Dani will be wondering where I am."

I get up and walk him to the door.

He stops just at the threshold, turning to face me. "Try not to hate her too much. It wasn't easy for her to give you up. She has never forgiven herself for doing it."

I give a slight nod. I can't seem to find my voice to say actual words, but it's okay because he doesn't wait for any as he turns back and walks out the door.

# Chapter 42
# Kael

SARAH IS STILL SLEEPING when it's time for me to meet up with Liam. I quickly write her a note, letting her know where I'm going and what time I should be back, before heading out the door.

I meet Liam at the apartment that will be ours in a few weeks. It's nice. Not a luxury apartment by any means, but still comfortable. It's a two-bedroom and, of course, Liam takes the master with the ensuite. The other room is located at the end of the hall, right across from the main bathroom.

I walk into the room, noticing that it's a perfect square, unlike my rectangle-shaped dorm room. It's bigger than my current room, too, so that's a plus.

"What do you think?" Liam asks as I walk out of my future bedroom into the living room. It's an open floor plan, so the kitchen and living room connect together into one large area. It reminds me of Sarah and Adam's apartment.

"It's great," I tell him. "When can we start bringing our things over?"

"We start the lease on the Monday after New Year's," he informs me as we make our way outside.

The landlord, Sid, is waiting for us outside the door. Liam thanks him and hands him the key.

New Year's isn't for another four weeks, which means I have plenty of time to pack all my belongings in boxes, not that it will take that long anyway. I keep my possessions to a minimum.

The Christmas party at the Leon building is less than two weeks away. I can't wait to get this whole Leon business over with. He needs to die so that Sarah can feel safe.

Thinking of Sarah, I never got a chance to talk to Liam since finding out that Sarah is his half-sister.

"Hey man, how have you been since finding out everything?" I ask as we make our way back to his truck. I don't need to explain further; he already knows what I'm talking about.

"It's a lot to take in," he admits. "Knowing that my mom cheated on my dad with Sarah's dad. Sarah being alive when my parents let me believe she was dead this whole time. I talked to my dad about it last night. I asked him why he stayed with my mom after what she did, but he just said that when you love someone, you have to love all of them, even their faults.

"He tried to say something about it being his fault, too. That he isn't innocent in all this, but I didn't let him finish. I guess I wasn't in the mood to hear him defend my mom. I also asked if he was the real reason they didn't keep Sarah. He just said it was complicated," Liam says the last line with a sneer as he hops into the driver's side. We pause the conversation briefly while he starts the truck and I fiddle with my seatbelt.

"I think he is just trying to make more excuses for her," Liam continues, putting the truck into drive. "He tried to tell me that it was the hardest decision my mom ever made, but I think she just didn't want a living reminder of what she did. It was Sarah who had to grow up with the consequences of her decisions."

"If it helps, Sarah said she loved her adoptive parents," I tell him. "She was their miracle child." Liam looks over at me and smiles, somewhat returning to his usual self. "That does help, and Sarah's amazing. I can't wait to get to know her more. It's a little weird, knowing that you are dating my sister. I'm debating whether to give you the big brother speech about treating her right."

I roll my eyes and grin. "Seeing as I would die before letting anything happen to Sarah, you have nothing to worry about."

He nods. "I know."

Liam is silent for a moment, tapping his hands on the steering wheel a few times. I can tell he wants to say something more.

"Is there something else?" I ask.

"We still have plenty of time before the sun sets. I figure this would be a good time for you to talk to Shyann."

I sigh. "Do I even have a choice?"

"Not if you want our team at a hundred percent for when we hunt Caesar Leon."

"Fine," I say defeatedly.

There is no point in arguing with Liam when he has made up his mind about something pertaining to the good of the team.

***

I decide to only try Shyann's room.

If she's not here, then at least I can tell Liam that I tried but couldn't find her. I knock and a second later I hear her shout, "Come in."

*Damn*, just my luck.

I open the door and pop my head in. She is lying on her bed, texting away on her phone. She looks like a teenage girl, on her belly with her feet crossed in the air.

She doesn't even look up when I open the door. I can hear music blasting from an earbud. She's only wearing one, so I know she can still hear her surroundings.

"Hey, Shy, can I talk to you for a second?"

Shyann jumps at the sound of my voice, throwing the earbud out of her ear and sitting up. "Kael," she says with a squeak. "I—yes, please come in."

I step into the room and get a big whiff of perfume. *What does she do, use it as air freshener?* I take a quick glance at the abomination of this room. It looks like it was run through by a tornado. Clothes are everywhere, and when I say everywhere, I mean I can't take another step without landing on a piece of clothing.

She even has clothes piled up on her dresser. I would bet money that there are more clothes on the ground and on top of that dresser than there are *in* the dresser.

It's not just clothes. She has jewelry, makeup, and magazines splayed out all around the room as well.

She notices me looking and gives a guilty smile. "Sorry about the mess," she says sheepishly. "I, uh... haven't had time to clean up lately."

I nod, even though I know she's lying. She literally could have been cleaning now.

I stay standing, leaning against the door. There isn't a place for me to sit except for the bed with her, and that's not happening.

"Listen, I came here to clear the air," I tell her. "We're part of a team, and we need to be working together. If things are off between us, it'll affect everyone else, and that's not fair."

Shy frowns a little. "We're also friends, or so I thought." She says the last bit softly, more to herself than to me.

"I don't know, Shyann, are we friends?" I ask incredulously.

"Yes," she says quickly. "I'm sorry about what I did, but she's a vampire. I did nothing wrong."

"Doesn't sound like you're sorry," I shout. I guess trying to tamp down my emotions is out the window.

"I'm not sorry about wanting to kill her, but I am sorry that you are upset with me," she amends.

Is she serious right now? She is unbelievable. I don't need, nor do I want, to make amends with Shyann anyway, but then I think about Sarah and how much she needs us to be at one hundred percent to defeat Caesar.

"I love her, Shyann. And she's not just any vampire. She's a *Validus*. That changes things. I won't let you or anyone else in this building hurt her," I say, not able to keep the anger from seeping into my words.

It's not lost on me that I've professed my love for Sarah to Shyann before telling Sarah, which only adds fuel to my rage.

"Is this because of your feelings for me? If it is, you need to get over it," I say with a growl. "I'm never going to care for you in that way, so you need to stop pining over me. It's pathetic."

Silence fills the room. *Fuck.* I went too far. I knew it the moment the words were out of my mouth. I wish I could rewind the last few seconds and take them all back. The look she's giving me is heartbreaking.

"Shit, Shy, I'm sorry," I say quickly. I walk over, trying my best to navigate her floor so that I'm not stepping on too many clothes, and go to sit next to her on her bed. "I didn't mean any of that. I spoke out of anger."

She is staring down at her hands in her lap, but I can see tears starting to fall down her face, which makes me feel even worse. She doesn't say anything, or even try to wipe the tears away.

"Shy, look at me," I say. "Please."

She slowly raises her head, her eyes glossy from fresh tears.

"I'm sorry," I repeat. "I have a bad habit of saying awful, hurtful things when I'm upset, as you may already know. It's something I need to work on. I didn't mean it. Forgive me."

She wipes her face with the back of her sleeve, but manages to give me a faint smile and nod of her head. "I promise I'll leave Sarah alone."

I know that's the best I'm going to get from her. "Thanks," I say.

I take a look around the room again. "I guess I'll take off so that you can have time to clean your room," I tease, using finger quotes. I'm trying my best to end our conversation on a lighter note.

"Jerk," she says with a laugh as she grabs a nearby pillow to hurl at me. "It's an organized clutter. I know exactly where everything is."

I smirk. "If you say so."

# Chapter 43
# Sarah

T HE SUN IS DOWN by the time Kael returns to my apartment. He looks at me and his eyes darken.

"I can't wait to rip that outfit off you later," he tells me as he pulls me to him, his lips grazing my neck.

I grin. The sexy athletic wear outfit is provoking the exact reaction I was hoping for.

I feel my phone vibrate and take a step back to look down at a message from an unknown number.

Unknown number: Hey, this is Nick Carmack. I want to join your rooftop training, but Liam says I have to get permission from u first. Just a heads up, I'm already in the car with the rest of the squad. We're pulling into your apartment building now. So if u say no, I'll have to walk back to the Academy all alone.

I sigh. I really hate that I like Nick. I save his number before replying.

Me: What a way to force my hand. Fine, you can join us.

Nick: Awesome we're well on our way to becoming BFs. One more thing. I kinda told Liam and the rest

that I asked u an hour ago and u said yes, so that
they would let me in the van. If they ask, just say
that we had this convo an hour ago. Gotta go, about
to knock on your door.

Less than ten seconds later, I hear a *knock, knock, knock.*

"That should be Liam and all," Kael says as he goes to open the door but
then blocks the doorway as soon as he does. "What the fuck are you doing here,
Carmack?"

Nick looks pleadingly at me, and I narrow my eyes.

I exhale. "I said it was okay for him to come," I tell Kael.

Nick smiles, pushing past Kael and giving me a wink as they all file in, clad in
all black. I dramatically scowl at him. Unfortunately, it quickly turns into a smile,
so I feel like it loses some of its meaning.

Kael catches the exchange and arches a brow at me.

"I'll explain later," I whisper to him as we all head up to the roof, Adam
included.

Only Shyann is missing now.

It is an unusually cold and windy night. I can smell the salty ocean breeze.

Liam has us starting the same way we did last night, stretches, drills, and then
sparring. In the second half of training, they bring out the weapons. I try my hand
at throwing knives and axes, swords, and daggers. But the one I do best with is the
short bow, which is what Liam specializes in. Must run in the family.

I watch him hit his target every single time. He looks like he belongs with the
Justice League.

I try to get the hang of the longbow, which Liam is quite talented at, too. I'm
thinking if he's got a penchant for it, so must I, but I give up after half an hour,
preferring the agility of the short bow instead. Liam is a great teacher, reminding
me that I'll get better with more practice. And I see evidence of that in the weeks
that follow. With every training session, my aim is improving, the arrows sliding
from my fingers with precision and ease.

Liam and I do not mention his mom to each other again. Every time we talk, we skate around the topic. I just can't bring myself to call her *my* mom yet.

For now, we stay focused on the task ahead. I enjoy training with the hunters more than I thought I would. I always feel more empowered and stronger afterwards.

I hope Liam continues to train me with Kael, even after Caesar Leon is dead. I learn a little more with him around. He's a little more aggressive than Kael, who seems to think I'm breakable, even though I'm physically stronger than everyone on this roof.

By the end of the final night before the Christmas party, I officially decide to forgive Nick. He's really fun to train with, and it's taking too much effort to continue hating him. He is definitely the carefree one of their group, kidnapping and torturing aside.

We train late into the last night, stopping only when it starts raining. Adam went downstairs hours ago, complaining about the cold.

After we load up all the lights, weapons, and the target practice stand, everyone slowly disperses. We all plan to meet at a designated spot tomorrow night at six o'clock.

Though none of them say it, I can tell they are nervous about tomorrow's patrol. Although it's just a recon mission, they have never dealt with the city coven leader before, and from what they've told me about ancient vampires, the fact that Caesar could be both ancient and a coven leader makes him almost invincible.

Apparently, vampires get stronger with age, so Caesar is already one of the strongest vampires currently around. The coven leader mark, as far as the hunters are aware, gives extra abilities like increased strength and increased persuasion. Add the fact that with it, the leader can control their whole coven...

Yeah, I think a little dose of fear is understandable in this case.

Kael spends another night with me in my apartment. I'm quickly getting way too used to falling asleep beside him.

I'm in the shower, rinsing off my hair, when I hear the door open. A moment later, the shower door opens, and a naked Kael steps in.

"Mind if I join you?" he asks, stepping against my back and wrapping his arms around my waist. "Fuck, that's hot," he hisses, jerking back a bit so that he's no longer in the spray zone.

I laugh and reach over to turn the water temp down just a bit.

"Men. Can't handle a little hot water," I tease, turning so that I'm facing him.

He playfully rolls his eyes. "Women like to test whether or not they can handle hellfire temperatures. No wonder your skin is so soft. You burn off a layer every time you shower."

I laugh again. I love Kael's playful side and wonder how many others get to see it.

He reaches for me once more, and I step into his arms, lifting my head and running my hands over his sculpted arms and shoulders, which are tense from the earlier training session. He leans in and presses his lips to mine, and I melt into him.

His hard erection presses into my lower belly, but Kael pulls back and I groan in protest. He smirks down at me before reaching for the bottle of soap.

He pumps some onto his palm and rubs his hands together. "May I wash you?"

"I actually already did that," I tell him, pointing to my dripping loofah hanging from the shower rack.

"Hmm," he hums, bringing his hands to my shoulders. "I think you missed a spot," he whispers, turning me around so that I'm facing away from him again.

He starts to rub soft circles on my neck, slowly moving down to my chest, cupping my breasts, and I relax into him, letting him play with me.

The water is spraying directly on my body, so the soap cascades off me, but that doesn't deter Kael. He massages my breasts, rubbing my hard nipples between his fingers.

He presses me to him, running his tongue down my neck, one arm wrapping under my chest, the other traveling down between my legs. My knees go weak, but he holds me up, nudging my legs apart slightly with his. He spreads me with two fingers, and just as he slides them into me, he bites down on my neck, causing me to cry out in pleasure.

I shamelessly grind against his fingers, one of my hands reaching up to grasp his hair, calling out his name over and over again.

"That's right, baby," he coos, his thumb moving up to rub against my clit. "I love the way you cry out my name, Sarah. All your needy little sounds are making me as hard as a fucking rock."

To prove his point, he tilts his hips forward, pressing his erection against my ass, my body surging and filling with desire until I can't take it anymore and cry out through my release.

Kael doesn't waste another second as he turns me around and presses me against the shower wall, his mouth descending on mine.

I whimper, still lost in the aftershocks of my orgasm. He grabs my hips and lifts me up. I instinctively wrap my legs around his waist, my arms circling around his neck.

He reaches a hand between our bodies, grabbing his shaft and guiding it toward my entrance. In one hard thrust, he buries himself inside me.

I cry out at his roughness, wanting more, wanting him to take me however he deems fit.

"Fuck," he shouts, his hands squeezing my hips. "Sarah, you feel so good around my cock. You're so fucking tight."

He pumps in and out of me with slow, agonizing strokes, his strong hands on my hips helping me move with him.

The tension in my lower belly hums to life once more as his thrusts become harder and faster. I cum again, only seconds before he does.

Afterwards, we clean ourselves off quickly before drying and moving to the bed, not bothering with clothes. Hours later, I'm not sure who wakes up whom, but he ends up inside me once more.

He's more loving and tender this time around, peppering me with long, soft kisses like he knows something about tomorrow that I don't. Maybe it's just the fact that we are going up against an all-powerful vampire that has him cradling my face, whispering sweet, loving things as he cums inside me.

All the while, I'm wishing we could freeze this moment and live in it forever, hoping tomorrow never comes.

But it does.

***

The next night, Kael leaves a few hours before the scheduled meetup time to get dressed. I told him it's a black-tie event, so he has to find himself a tux.

I'm doing a few finishing touches in the bathroom; some of my curls didn't curl the way I wanted, so I'm trying to fix them.

Adam knocks on the door frame of the open bathroom. "Knock, knock," he says. He's dressed in his teal scrubs, about to head for work. "I just wanted to come tell you to break a leg tonight, preferably not your own."

I smile. "I'll try my best."

He hesitates by the door. I can see he wants to say more. It's not like him to hold back.

"What's wrong?" I ask as I wrap a small wad of hair around my curling wand. I decided to arrange my hair in a side do, adding in the tight curls to my normally wavy hair.

"I just want to remind you that you are not a hunter."

My eyebrows draw together, and I give a sad puppy face. "I was Van Helsing. The greatest vampire hunter in the world. How dare you try to take that away from me," I say teasingly.

"You're not a hunter," he continues in a serious tone, as though I didn't say a thing. "And although you are a good fighter, I've watched you all train and can say with confidence that the hunters are better, even though you're stronger."

"Well, aren't you a ray of compliments."

Adam sighs. "Please don't go and get yourself killed. Let the hunters fight the invincible Julius Caesar."

"Caesar Leon," I correct.

"I also ask that if a life-or-death situation occurs, you run like hell and don't try to be the hero that I secretly know you want to be. Just for tonight, be like Mark

Antony and flee from battle. Maybe take Zach with you. He'll be upset, but he'll get over it."

I grin and set down my curling wand to face him. "No one is running away and no one will die," I say with a confidence that I don't totally feel. The truth is that I'm terrified about tonight. I have no idea what to expect. But that's a burden I need to bear, not Adam. Adam needs to go to work, and do his job, and not worry that he's going to come home to his roommate and boyfriend hurt or dead.

"We're all going to be fine. It's just a recon mission, remember? This isn't the actual hunt for Mr. Leon. Everything will be fine." I walk over to give him a hug.

He holds on a little longer and tighter than normal before letting out a small sniff. He pulls back and points a finger at me. "Good, because Mrs. May and Mr. George want us to have dinner with them Tuesday night, and I don't want to have to tell them you died and can't make it. Also, since you refuse to tell me whether Cassie ends up with Basille or Caspian, you have to stay alive long enough to finish your book."

"Exactly, I have too much to do. I simply don't have time to die—again, like real death."

"Please, you are the most alive person I know, and you better keep it that way."

He pulls me into another hug, and I return it without hesitation. We stay this way for a long moment before a knock on the door interrupts us.

Adam pulls back. "That would be our guys here to sweep you away to the ball. You look absolutely stunning, not sure if I told you that yet." He gestures to my ensemble.

I decided to go with a cocktail dress instead of a gown tonight. I figure I'll be more agile in a short dress. It's a purple, one-shoulder, sequin dress with a small side split. I pick the shortest heels I own to wear with it, little open-toe silver strappies

I smile. "You did not. Thank you," I say as I give a little curtsy.

I turn off my curling wand and follow Adam to the living room. He goes to let Kael and Zach in.

Zach is wearing his standard black hunting leathers, while Kael is dressed in a black tuxedo. Something about Kael wearing a bow tie has me thinking all sorts of devious thoughts.

Kael's green eyes darken when he sees me. He walks over to me and caresses my cheek with the back of his hand ever so gently, but I feel it everywhere. I lean into his touch.

"You look beautiful," he whispers in my ear.

"Thanks," I say. "You don't look too bad yourself."

A smile tugs at his lips. "I can't wait to get you alone tonight."

Only this man can give me pleasure tingles using just his words.

"What do you plan to do with me once you get me alone?" I ask softly.

Kael's eyes narrow as he grabs my face using both his hands, lifting my head up so he can lay claim to my lips. His tongue envelopes my mouth as I sink into him.

He kisses me for I don't know how long before I hear Zach clear his throat at the same time Adam says, "You two do realize you are not alone in the room?"

Kael releases me; there's a hint of humor, and something darker, in his eyes that leaves me with goose bumps.

I look over at Adam and Zach and give a small, apologetic smile. I actually did forget they were in the room. When Kael has his attention on me, it's like everything else falls away, and it's just the two of us.

"I never pegged you to be such a prude, Adam," Kael says in a teasing tone.

"Oh, he can be very reserved," I say. "He does not like public displays of affection."

Adam frowns. "Forgive me for having class, and I don't mind some PDA. You just need to know your limits. This isn't your bedroom or a sex club. Time and place, boo-boo."

Zach reaches for Adam and gives him a small but passionate kiss. "I'll come back tonight," he says, resting his forehead against Adam's and holding both his hands tightly between them.

"You better," Adam whispers, giving Zach a tight hug. "Be careful." He steps back and looks over at me. "FYI, this—" gesturing to Zach and himself "—was an appropriate exchange between lovers when in the presence of other people. Not that gross make-out session you two just did."

Zach laughs, and I stick my tongue out at Adam playfully before turning to leave.

# Chapter 44
# Kael

WE ARRIVE AT THE Leon Tower around six-thirty. The Christmas party started at six, but we agreed it would be best if the party was in full swing when we arrived. It will help us blend in more, although that gives us little room for error.

Everyone is in their position. Nick and Shy are on the floor below the party. Liam is on the roof, and Zach and Kayda are in the van parked on the curb. They have the videos set up from the cameras hidden on Sarah and me, hers on a necklace and mine on a hawk pin fastened to my suit jacket. I set up my comms earpiece and do some final testing and checks before Sarah and I leave to go to the party on the top floor.

We hit our first snag of the night when the bouncer checks us in. Apparently, Sarah's old coworker and friend made good on her promise to put Sarah on the list, but since Sarah doesn't have a plus one, I won't be allowed in. Fortunately, it's an easy fix with Sarah's vampire persuasion.

"Look again," Sarah coaxes the big, hulky guy, giving a slight wave of her hand in a weird way. "I do have a plus one after all."

I can tell she is using the vampire ability because the man's eyes glaze over as he looks down. "You do have a plus one after all," he repeats in a stupor.

Sarah smiles. "Thank you. You're doing a wonderful job." She does the hand thing again. "Keep up the good work."

"Thank you," he says dreamily.

We walk past him and into the elevator. Once the doors close, I turn to her. "What was with you waving your hand in front of you like that?" I ask, curiously.

She looks at me in disbelief. "I was using my Jedi mind trick, so I had to do the Jedi hand motion. You know... 'These aren't the droids you're looking for—or—credits will do fine.'" She does the hand thing yet again. "Have you never seen Star Wars?"

I give her an exasperated look. "I think you already know the answer to that question."

She laughs. "Yeah, I guess I do," she says playfully. "Well, you are missing out."

"I've tried to tell him that, but he refuses to watch them with me," Nick says over comms.

"No one's talking to you, Carmack," I say.

Sarah's shoulders shake with silent laughter. Then she asks, "The vamp mind tricks don't work on you, right?"

I fail to suppress a smile. "Try it and find out."

She beams and rubs her hands together as she faces me. Doing the small wave of her hand thing toward me, she says, "You want to kiss me."

I cup her face with both hands and give her a hard kiss before pulling back and saying, "Now try and make me do something that I don't already crave every minute of every day."

Sarah flushes, taking a second to compose herself after my sudden kiss. I must admit, I enjoy watching her body respond to me. I never want to stop making Sarah get flustered. I never want her to stop wanting me the way that I want her.

I hear Shyann give a disgusted grunt over the comms, but I ignore it.

"Okay, umm, how about this?" She looks me in the eye, does her hand thing and says, "You want to give me a high five." She lifts her hand in the air, waiting for me to comply.

I smirk, feeling something graze over my thoughts. Like a pressure wanting to take hold, but I easily push it away. "Nope, no sudden urge to high five you."

At that moment, the elevator doors open to an extravagant lobby decorated like a winter wonderland. Silver garland adorns the walls while giant snowflakes hang from the ceiling. A humongous, flocked Christmas tree with silver and gold ornaments is placed at the center of the dance floor.

The room is fancy as shit with its marbled floor and high ceiling. The glass walls make up ninety percent of the outer frame, giving us a spectacular view of the Golden Gate Bridge on the horizon, and Christmas music plays softly in the background.

There are hundreds of people here. Some are in suits and dresses, others are in black and white uniforms walking around holding various trays of food and champagne glasses. The one thing they don't have here is vampires.

I turn to Sarah, "I don't sense any vampires."

She's still looking around the room. When she's satisfied that she doesn't see Caesar Leon, her body relaxes.

I hate that she's so nervous to be here. Scared to run into the man who stole her life away. I want to get this asshole. He needs to die so she can feel safe.

"Stay vigilant. We need to be ready. Kael, keep us updated on your progress," Liam orders.

A girl around our age squeals and runs up to Sarah. She is wearing a bright pink dress that resembles something a teenage girl would wear to a prom rather than what an adult woman would wear to a company Christmas party.

"Oh my God, oh my God, oh my God. Sarah," she shouts, jumping up and down. "I haven't seen you in like, forever. How have you been, girl? I heard you went MIA only like a month after getting promoted to Mr. Leon's personal assistant," she says as she adjusts her round-framed glasses that are too big for her face.

"I'm still around. The job just wasn't for me. I ended up writing and publishing a book instead," Sarah tells her sweetly.

The girl squeals again. "Yes, I read your book. The *Out of this World* series, book one. I can't wait for book two to come out. I'm definitely Team Basille. He's so sweet to Cassie. I don't know if you saw, but I started an *Out of this World* fan page on pretty much every social media outlet there is."

Sarah smiles. "Thank you, that's so sweet of you. You don't know how much it means to me that you liked my book so much. I'm working on the second one right now."

"Of course," the girl says. "You were always so nice to me here. I miss you so much."

"I miss you too," Sarah tells her. She turns and puts a gentle hand on my shoulder. "Abby, this is Kael, my boyfriend."

My body jolts at the sound of Sarah referring to me as her boyfriend in public for the first time. I love it.

"It's nice to meet you, Abby." I extend my hand to shake hers.

Abby looks at me with wide eyes as if she is just noticing me standing here. The round-framed glasses make her eyes look even bigger. She reminds me of a fly with her big, bug eyes.

"H—Hi," she stammers. She turns to Sarah and fake whispers, "That's your boyfriend? He looks like a movie star."

"I tend to refer to him as a Greek god," Sarah says playfully.

Abby nods in approval. "I mean, not that I'm surprised, you are so beautiful. I figured you would end up with someone that looks like him, but wow." Abby stares at me and starts fanning herself.

I give a polite smile and then ask Sarah, "Why don't I go find us some drinks and give you two ladies a chance to catch up a bit more?"

Sarah smiles and nods, knowing what I'm saying. It's time for me to get to work. "Sounds good. Thank you."

I give her a quick kiss on the cheek before starting toward the back of the room. As I walk away, I hear Abby squeal again. How Sarah didn't go deaf working with that girl, I'll never know.

I grab a glass of champagne from the tray of a passing server and chug it, setting the empty glass back on the tray before the server has a chance to walk away. The burning feeling as the liquid goes down feels good. I walk to the end of the room, scanning everyone as I do.

"Start in the CEO's office. Even if Caesar doesn't frequently go there, we have to assume his proxy knows something," Zach reminds me.

I nod even though I know he can't see me. I make my way down the hall, passing a few people talking amongst themselves. There are two people fucking on a desk in the meeting room three doors down from CEO's office. But clearly, they're too busy to notice me. Thankfully, I have night vision, so I don't need to turn on any lights and can avoid drawing attention to myself.

I slip into the office, pulling out the mini camera. I look around, trying to find a good place to put it.

It's a huge office with a massive desk and three monitors set up in a semi-circle facing a black leather chair. Behind the desk, a bookshelf takes up the wall. There are a few leather-bound books, framed certificates, trophies, and a picture frame of a middle-aged, balding white guy holding a fishing line and a large, striped bass standing on a luxury cruiser.

I decide to place the camera in the eye of a mini-sphinx statue located on the bookshelf. It fits so perfectly that unless you examine thoroughly, someone looking at it would assume it's just the eye.

I quickly slip into another office and plant a camera there too. I have to wait for the two people whispering drunkenly to themselves to leave in order to plant a camera near the reception desk.

"How's it looking on the rooftop?" Nick asks, after I successfully plant one in the hallway intersection.

"All clear up here, for now," Liam replies. "How about there? Any sign of Leon?"

"Nah, Shy and I are the only ones on this floor."

"Kayda? Zach? How about you two?" Liam asks.

Kayda answers. "All good here. We are getting no sense of vampires on the ground."

I wonder if we would even recognize him if he did show up. I've only ever seen a pencil-drawn photo of him in the seventeenth century from our history books. He probably looks nothing like that photo now.

Although I don't sense vampires nearby, I suddenly don't want to be away from Sarah a second longer, knowing he could appear at any moment. I turn to make my way back.

I lock eyes with Sarah the second I rejoin the party, like our bodies and souls know just where to find each other.

She excuses herself from an eager, glassy-eyed man around my age, who is looking at Sarah with a little too much interest.

"How did everything go?" she asks as she walks up to me, slipping her hands around my neck.

"Fine. It's done. How's everything going over here?" I ask, nodding my head toward the eager beaver. "The little blond pretty boy you were talking to is staring at us."

Sarah stifles a laugh. "His name is T.J. We started working here at the same time. He just came by to see how I've been doing."

I arch my brow at her. "Is that all, because he looks like a kicked puppy now that you left him."

Sarah giggles a little at my comment. "He did ask me out a few weeks into us working together, but I was dating Jared at the time."

I stiffen, my hands automatically going around her waist. I don't know why I hate Jared so much after our five-second meet and greet.

Sarah cocks her head a little and smiles. "Kael Hart, are you jealous?"

I grin down at her and decide to go with the truth. "When it comes to you? Always, Sarah."

Sarah hums. "Is it disturbing that I find your jealousy hot?"

I suppress a grin. "It bodes well for me that you do," I say, taking her hand and leading her to the dance floor.

I pull her in close and sway back and forth to the music for about five seconds before Kayda says over comms, "Guys, we can't see anything through the cameras when you are facing each other. Plus, you need to be making your escape."

Sarah laughs. "I forgot about the cameras," she says as she takes a step back.

I don't let go of one of her hands and instead spin her into a twirl. "One dance and then we'll go," I tell Kayda.

But we don't get to finish the dance because the elevator doors open, and the hairs on the back of my neck prickle in warning. Vampires have joined the party.

# Chapter 45
# Sarah

KAEL STIFFENS, AND IT doesn't take long for me to figure out why. The elevator doors open, and in walks Caesar Leon and his top bodyguard, Taylor, one step behind him.

My heart lurches at the sight of him. A twinge of fear courses through me, but I try my best to suppress it. This man took my life away. He kidnapped and killed me. I mean, sure, I came back to life, but still.

We should have left as soon as Kael was finished. What was I thinking, trying to enjoy one dance?

Mr. Leon's eyes lock onto mine the second he steps out of the elevator. It's like he knew I was going to be here and where to look. He gives me a slight grin that tells me my suspicions are correct.

Kael tenses even more at the sight of Mr. Leon staring at me. He reaches for my hand and gives it a reassuring squeeze. At least I thought it was going to be a reassuring squeeze, but he never loosens his hold, which tells me he is anything but reassured.

"It's going to be okay," I whisper to him.

Over Kael's comms, I can hear fighting going on and Kayda shouting that she and Zach are headed to the rooftop to help. It doesn't sound good.

Mr. Leon was ready for us. I hope Liam has time to call in those reinforcements he was talking about at the meeting.

"Sarah, darling," Mr. Leon greets warmly as he approaches, like this is just another engagement. The sounds of the party dim with the heat of his stare.

"Mr. Leon," I greet back, trying to sound indifferent. I look over at his bodyguard. "Taylor, I see you are not lurking around parks tonight."

Taylor's only response is a slight grimace. I know he remembers our two little encounters. I bet Mr. Leon didn't take kindly to the fact that I got away from his best soldier twice.

"You look magnificent, as always," Mr. Leon says to me, ignoring my comment to Taylor. "I was hoping our next rendezvous would be you submitting to me." His eyes flit briefly to Kael. "I assume that is not the case."

"She isn't going anywhere with you," Kael spits. He tries to push me protectively behind him, but I hold my ground. I will not cower.

Mr. Leon ignores Kael like he isn't even here.

"I'm never going to change my mind," I say coolly, though my nerves are at an all-time high and every muscle in my body is on alert.

"Never is a long time, my young darling. You'll come around," he says with an air of confidence, like getting what he wants is inevitable, and what he wants is me.

"You don't have the luxury of waiting until she comes around, because you'll be dead by morning," Kael promises in a low, menacing tone.

I look around, hoping that no one heard the threat Kael just aimed at Mr. Leon, but thankfully, no one is rushing to come to Mr. Leon's rescue, so I think we are in the clear.

Mr. Leon finally turns his head to Kael. "Do you hear your friends being detained on the rooftop in your earpiece? *That*, little hunter, is the sound of you being defeated. Did you honestly think you were a match for me? I am a thousand years old. Your tiny brain can't even comprehend what I am."

*A thousand years old*. He's right about one thing. *My* brain definitely can't comprehend that. He must have been one of the first vampires created after the banishment of the fae.

I stare at Mr. Leon. He has a timeless face, all lean muscle and sharp edges. He's wearing an expensive, tailored suit, probably Brioni or Tom Ford; his usual attire. I don't think I ever saw him in anything else, no casual wear to speak of. I remember picking up his dry cleaning once. Just one of his suits could have paid my rent for an entire year.

"Fuck you," Kael says coldly, bringing me back to the present. "I don't care how old you are. Touch Sarah, and I will end you."

"Hmm," Mr. Leon hums. "Perhaps we should take this conversation to the rooftop. It seems visual aids might help you grasp your situation better."

Normally, I would rather eat dirt than agree with Mr. Leon, but people are starting to stare at us. Abby looks like she wants to come over but is too scared to. I hope she stays away. I hope everyone stays away. Even though I doubt they can hear our conversation, it's obvious that tensions are running high.

Kael seems to think the exact same thing. Either that, or he is eager to get to the squad. Probably a little bit of both.

We all make our way past the crowded room and into the elevator, no one talking until the elevator doors open at the rooftop where a scene straight out of nightmares has unfolded.

# Chapter 46
# Kael

I T TAKES ONLY A second to realize how absolutely fucked we all are. At least three dozen vampires are spread out along the rooftop. Liam and the rest of the team are on their knees at the vampires' feet. Zach lies unconscious next to Kayda.

All vampire eyes are fixed hungrily on Zach's bloody body, ready to feast, waiting for their coven leader to give the order.

Sarah's gasp mirrors my internal one. "Zach," she screams, and before anyone can stop her, she is at his side.

A flicker of shock ghosts Caesar's face, followed by what I can only describe as awe. Did he not know what Sarah is, or what she can do? I thought that's why he wants her so badly, because she is so much stronger and faster than any other vampire, except for maybe him. But his gaze fills with a certain wonder at watching her be what he created; he might as well be drooling.

Perhaps knowing about it is one thing, but seeing it in action is a whole other thing entirely. I remember seeing Sarah's speed for the first time. It still takes my breath away—she takes my breath away.

But is she faster than him? The coven mark heightens the bearer's abilities, but by how much? I'm not sure. If Sarah had more time training, could she take on Caesar? Not that I would want her to be the one to fight him. Of course, there is always a chance that he isn't skilled in hand-to-hand combat, but given his age, I doubt it. He must have some battle experience. You don't become a coven leader by sitting around.

Sarah examines Zach for a moment and then looks over to me. "He's alive."

I exhale in relief. Zach's alive, but for how long? His chest and neck look swollen, and he's bleeding a lot from his head. Sarah must see it too because she is up and behind the closest vampire to her in a flash. She snaps his neck and rips off half his shirt before he hits the ground.

She's back at Zach's side, wrapping his head with the scrap of shirt she stole from the vampire. All this took less than a second.

It's only now that I take in the several dead vampire bodies on the ground. Looks like the team was able to take down nine or ten before the vampires got the best of them.

Two vampires are holding down Shyann. One on each side of her, holding her arms behind her back and stepping on her legs so she can't move. The same for Kayda, but it takes three vampires to hold Liam and Nick each. There is a deep gash on Liam's left eye, congealed blood slowly leaking from the wound.

Tears are rolling down Kayda's cheeks as she stares fixedly at Zach.

Sarah stands to face Caesar, looking for the first time like a real vampire.

"Let them go," she demands, her voice so full of rage anyone listening would be a fool not to take her seriously.

"My darling Sarah," Caesar says in dismay. "Why would I want to let vampire hunters go? These humans have made it their life's mission to hunt and kill us. You should want them dead just as much as I do, as any vampire would."

"Let them go," Sarah repeats in response.

"Perhaps, we can make a deal. You come with me now, and I will allow one of your hunters to live," he offers.

"All of them," she counters.

*What is she doing?* This won't end well. I know that Sarah will try and bargain for all our lives, but what about her life?

Caesar shakes his head. "Oh no, I'm afraid I can't allow so many hunters to go free in exchange for you coming willingly with me this one time. You would have to offer much more than that."

"What do you have in mind?" she questions.

Caesar smiles as though the conversation is going exactly as planned. "Pledge your loyalty to me and the coven."

*Fuck that.* There is no way Sarah can pledge herself to Caesar. He would get to use her anytime he wanted. For anything. I know he wants her to be with him. Jealousy courses through me like lava cascading down a volcano, hot and all-consuming.

Being the only one not bound, I lurch toward Caesar. If he's dead, then Sarah won't have to pledge her allegiance to anyone. Before I can get close to him, however, his bodyguard, Taylor, intercepts.

He rams his shoulder into me, and I go flying several feet in the air before landing on my back, sliding several more feet along the hard concrete. I quickly jump up and pull one of the wooden daggers hidden on me from its sheath. If Leon wants a fight, he's going to get one, even if I have to go through every one of his vampires.

Taylor and I start to circle each other. I can see other vampires coming to aid him, descending on me like a wave.

"Kill him," Caesar says with a flick of his hand, like he's bored and just wants this over and done with.

"No," Sarah screams and runs to stand in front of me.

"Sarah," I yell, hating that she's put herself between me and the vampires. I try to move around her, but she's too fast and just mirrors my movements.

"I'll do it," she says to Caesar, never taking her eyes off me. "I'll go with you tonight, and I'll promise my loyalty to you, just let them go."

Caesar holds up his hand to stop the approaching vampires.

"No, Sarah," I shout, gripping her by the shoulders. "Don't do this—please."

Her eyes start to water before she blinks the tears away. "I have to," she says in a tone that leaves no room for argument. "You are outnumbered, and this is the only way to save all of you."

"Sarah," Liam huffs. "Sometimes, the best thing to do is nothing at all. Don't give in to his demands. We knew what we signed up for when we became hunters."

The vampire standing directly behind Liam, holding his head up, sneers and claws at Liam's neck. Blood seeps through each cut formed. To Liam's credit, he doesn't flinch or cry out in pain, only grits his teeth.

"Stop that," Sarah yells.

"Darling, Sarah," Caesar says evenly, like everything in the last ten seconds didn't happen. "It's time to pledge your loyalty."

Sarah turns to face Caesar. "How do I know you won't kill them after I pledge my loyalty? Let us leave now together, and once we are safely away from them, then I will surrender to you fully."

"And how do I know you won't go back on your word?"

She shrugs. "I'm the good guy, remember? You'll just have to trust me."

Caesar grins. "I trust no one."

Sarah lets out an exasperated sigh. "Do you want me to go with you or not? I'm not pledging anything until I know they are safe." She gestures to me and then to the rest of the team.

"Sarah," I say through gritted teeth. "I'm not going to let you just leave without a fight."

She turns to me once more. "Zach needs to get to your med bay now. We don't know how much time he has left. He's losing a lot of blood. I can smell it." She says the next part in a whisper, perhaps not wanting to get too emotional in front of the other vampires. "I can hear his heart beating. It has gotten weaker since we've been up here."

That paralyzes me. I'm not sure what to do. If everything she says about Zach is right, he needs help now, but how can I just let Sarah go?

"I'll come get you," I promise. "I don't care how long it takes. I will find you and come get you."

Sarah puts her hand on my face. I feel a slight tug in my ear, so quick I must have imagined it. "Do you trust me?" she asks.

"Yes," I say instantly. I don't even have to think about it. I trust Sarah with my life.

She pulls me in for a hug and then is by Caesar's side in a flash. She allows Caesar to wrap his arm around her waist, securing her to his side. I can't wait to rip that arm right off him.

"We are done here," is all Caesar has to say, before all thirty-plus vampires disappear from the roof—including Sarah.

# Chapter 47
# Kael

W E MAKE IT BACK to the Academy in record time. I call for Orla on the way, letting her know that it's an extreme emergency.

Zach is slipping in and out of consciousness in the van.

"Where's Sarah?" he asks me the first time he wakes up, but he passes out again before I can answer.

Liam carries him to one of the med bay rooms, where Orla, Dana, and Cynthia are all waiting.

Dana's bottom lip trembles in terror at the sight of Zach. The three of them start moving at once. Orla gives orders to Cynthia, who listens and reacts with precision. Dana turns and ushers us all out of the room quickly.

"Let us work, we will update you afterwards," she says and slams the door in our faces before we can respond.

Liam turns to me. "You should probably call Adam to let him know what's going on."

"He's at the hospital tonight. I don't even know if he keeps his phone on him, but I'll text him and tell him to call me when he has a moment." I say, taking out my phone to type out the quick message.

We head to the end of the hallway to wait. Kayda starts pacing back and forth, biting the tip of her fingernail. Shyann slumps on the floor, looking defeated.

Nick is bouncing on his heels. "What the hell happened out there?"

"We were outnumbered," Shyann says. "It's like they knew we were coming. Caesar brought half his damn coven tonight."

"We shouldn't have tried to go at this alone. We should have had the other squads at the Academy come with us," Kayda says, shaking her head.

I don't say anything, because Kayda's right. We shouldn't have tried to go at this alone, even if it was supposed to be just a recon mission. If we had the rest of the squads at the Academy join us, Zach wouldn't be in that room fighting for his life, and I would still have Sarah.

Liam sighs. "Kayda's right," he says through an exhale, mirroring my thoughts. "We were arrogant to try and take on the San Francisco clan leader without backup on sight. Tonight is on me."

"You can't blame yourself," Shyann tells him. "This seemed more like a setup. How did he even know?" She looks over at me. "Are we sure this wasn't all Sarah's big master plan? She went with them pretty easily tonight."

"To save us," Kayda says, defending Sarah.

"Or so she says," Shyann argues.

Immediately, blood is firing through my veins, and I march toward her. "You don't know what you're talking about," I snarl. "Without Sarah, we would all be dead. She risked her life and freedom to save ours."

"I gotta agree with Kael on this one," Nick says, shocking the hell out of me. "Sarah saved our asses out there. And what fucking sense would it make to leave us all alive if this was just all a big scheme."

"Then how did they know we would be there tonight?" Shyann asks, raising her voice.

"I don't know, but it wasn't Sarah," I shout back, letting my anger get the better of me.

Liam pulls me back by my shoulders and steps between us, obscuring my line of vision to Shyann. "Enough, Shy. There is no point arguing about this at the moment." He turns to face me. "Let's stay focused on what we need to do now, which is firstly, to make sure Zach will be okay. Then, we have to find a way to get Sarah back."

I hear Shyann huff, but she doesn't say another word, which is good because I don't know how much more of her I can take. Forget trying to make amends for the sake of the team. Look where that got us tonight. Zach is fighting for his life, Sarah was taken right in front of my eyes, and I was fucking powerless to stop any of it.

It's comforting to hear that Liam plans to help get Sarah back. I would have done it on my own if I had to, but it's reassuring to know Liam will have my back. Nick nods in agreement, which, surprisingly, makes me feel relieved as well.

Nick can be annoying as fuck, but he's a great asset to the team and will greatly help our chances of getting Sarah back quickly, not that I would ever tell him that. His head is big enough as it is.

Cynthia walks out of the med bay, followed by Dana.

"Zach will be alright," she tells us. "He did suffer a concussion, lots of broken bones and contusions. To be honest, if it wasn't for his fast healing, we might be having a different conversation right now, but he's going to make a full recovery."

"Can we see him?" Kayda asks.

"He's sleeping," Cynthia says calmly.

"I don't care," Kayda persists. "I still would like to go in there."

Dana must sense Kayda's anxiousness to see her best friend because she gives a little nod.

"Okay, but only you. Orla is checking his vitals one last time, but I know she will want to wait until he has a good night's sleep before having the whole squad crowding his bed."

Kayda nods her head and mumbles a quick, "Thank you." She rushes past Liam and me to slip into Zach's room.

Once Kayda is out of sight, Dana turns to the rest of us. "What happened tonight?" she asks.

I turn to Liam, wanting to hear the story myself. I got the gist of it through the comms but still would like to hear the whole story from someone who was up on that rooftop the entire time.

"We were ambushed," Liam says. "One minute I'm on the rooftop alone and the next, twenty vampires surround me. Nick and Shyann got to the roof pretty fast, but we were just outnumbered. We took down maybe eight or nine of them when they brought Kayda and Zach up." Liam shakes his head as if trying to dispel a bad memory.

"I know Kayda and Zach were already on their way up to help us, but the vampires must've found them first. From what I gathered, they were scaling the fire escape and several vampires started fighting them, and then Zach was pushed off the building about a fifth of the way up."

We all wince at that last sentence. That's about six, maybe seven stories. He is lucky to be alive. Zach falling off a building is not something I ever want to see. I'm going crazy just thinking about it. Poor Kayda. Zach is the kindest and purest of us all. The world would be a darker place without him in it.

"Another ten or so vampires appeared from the side of the building. The one carrying Zach threw his unconscious body at my feet and told me that if I didn't order my squad to stop, they would tear his head from his body right in front of us. I gave the order immediately, that's when we all surrendered," Liam says a little shamefully.

"You did the right thing," I say truthfully. "You couldn't just let Zach get killed." I turn to Dana for backup, but she is just staring at Liam.

"How did you know that they would let you go?" Cynthia asks. "They aren't known for keeping their word."

"They were under orders from their coven leader, Caesar Leon, not to kill us, I think," Liam tells her. "He was using us as a bargaining chip to get Sarah, and it worked. She agreed to pledge loyalty to him for our freedom."

"Sarah did what?" Dana asks in shocked horror. "She can't. Does he know what she is? Someone like Sarah is a powerful weapon in the coven leader's hands. I don't think she even grasps all of what she can do, but I'll bet Caesar won't hesitate to find out."

"Which is why we have to save her," I say. "We need to go now."

"Go where?" Nick asks, walking up to us from where he was leaning against the hallway wall. "We don't even know where they are. We have never been able to find their hive location."

"Hey, is this thing working?"

I hear the voice faintly, coming from both Nick's and Liam's comms.

It's Sarah.

# Chapter 48
# Sarah

"SARAH?" I CAN HEAR Liam's confusion, and then I hear the voice I'm most anxious to hear again.

"Sarah, Sarah baby, are you okay?" Kael asks, his voice a little lighter than Liam's, probably because he is talking to me through Liam's comms piece.

"Yes," I assure him. "I don't have much time. I'm in the bathroom right now. They have guards stationed inside my room this time. Is Zach alright?"

"Yes," Liam assures me. "He will make a full recovery."

*Thank goodness*. It's been a few hours since we first left the rooftop, and I've been worried sick that Zach didn't make it, but he did.

*Zach will make a full recovery*, I repeat to myself over and over, until it really sinks in. Tears sting my eyes, but I blink them away rapidly. This is not the time.

"Where are you, Sarah?" Kael asks quickly. "I'm coming to get you."

"They blindfolded me. I have no idea where I am." I remember taking a look around the room when I first walked in, and it is definitely not the same room Mr. Leon imprisoned me in two years ago. Whether or not it's the same house, I can't be sure.

The room I was in last time was a blend of Victorian and modern styles. This room, however, is modern chic all the way. The walls are ivory white with sand-colored moldings, and the hardwood floor are complemented by a huge area rug. On top of the rug is a king-sized bed with more natural-colored pillows and blankets. There are nightstands on either side of the bed, both holding big, vase-shaped lamps. This whole room looks like something you would find on a Pottery Barn magazine cover, except for maybe the painting displayed on the wall above the bed.

It's an impressionist piece of a lake, and on the banks is an ebony-skinned woman wearing a colorful dashiki dress in yellow, orange, teal and red. She is on her knees, eyes closed, mouth slightly parted. She's leaning back and covering the modest parts of a naked, dark-skinned man, who has his arms around her, one hand reaching inside her dress, cupping her breast. It's quite a spicy piece of art. I wonder if I'll be able to steal it when I escape here... If I escape.

*Nope. All good vibes until further notice, Sarah. I will escape*, I tell myself.

I hear Nick curse loudly, dampening my "all good vibes" moment just a little. I guess Nick is there too. I'm a little surprised at how happy I am to hear his voice. It's now been a little more than a month since he kidnapped me. Now he's working with Kael to save me from another kidnapping situation.

*Oh, how the tide tables have turned... or something like that.*

"Why don't you just use the comms to track her location?" Dana, another person I was unaware was in on the conversation, says like that should have been the most obvious solution. "It's Kael's earpiece she has, right? I'm assuming you have it registered on a laptop somewhere. You should be able to track its location."

That's what I was hoping for when I stole it from Kael on the rooftop.

"Do you know how to track it?" Liam asks, and then adds more somberly, "Anything we have on it would be on Zach's laptop. He's always the one who does this sort of thing."

I wonder just how bad Zach's injuries are that Liam doesn't want to disturb him, not that I would want Liam to anyway. I saw enough on the rooftop to know that Zach's injuries were severe. Still, I hope that with his speedy healing, he will be good as new in a few days. I also hope Kael thought to keep Adam updated. The first thing Mr. Leon took from me was my phone. It's probably smashed into pieces by now.

I know he plans to come back soon and complete the loyalty pledge. I keep racking my brain to try and come up with reasons to stall, but I'm all out of ideas. What will it feel like when he gives me an order once I pledge? I'm not looking forward to finding out.

Someone bangs on the bathroom door three times in quick succession. "Time's up, princess."

I roll my eyes and yell, "It's rude to rush a girl out of the bathroom, you know." I quickly take the earpiece out without saying goodbye or waiting to hear what Dana's answer is.

I look around for a place to hide it and end up shoving it between a clean stack of towels. I can't take it with me because I don't want any of the vampires' super hearing to pick up on any of the hunters talking.

I turn off the faucet I had running and flush the toilet for good measure. Then, I take one final, deep breath before walking back out.

There are five guards in the room. The male vamp that was banging on the door is standing right by the door frame, blocking my way. He gives me a hard look before stepping aside so I can pass.

"Took you long enough," he says curtly.

"I'm sorry," I say in fake innocence. "Were you waiting to use the restroom?"

"Quiet, bitch, unless spoken to," he barks.

I narrow my eyes at him. Someone needs an attitude adjustment.

"If Mr. Leon makes me queen like I think he plans to, the first thing I'm going to do is cut out your tongue," I say with as much authority as I can muster. I'm totally bluffing, of course, but he doesn't need to know that.

His body goes rigid in fear, like he is just remembering the fact that very soon I might have power over him. I kind of wish I could forget it, too. Just the thought makes me nauseous. But right now, I can use it to my advantage. He shifts uncomfortably and mutters a quick apology.

The only other male guard in the room takes a step toward me and says, "Are you hungry? We can have someone delivered here for you."

I turn to look at him and internally shudder at the thought of them bringing someone in here for me to feed on, knowing that they will kill the person as soon as I'm done.

"No, thank you. I drank earlier."

He gives a quick nod and then looks over at one of the female guards, giving her a nod as well before both men step out of the room.

I'm left with three guards, all women. Two of them take their place in front of the door while the third stays standing by the barred-up window.

It's quiet in the room for a long while. I go to sit at the edge of the king-sized bed, mostly because I feel silly just standing awkwardly in the center of the room.

Finally, because I can't stand the silence, and also because I'm curious, I ask, "How did Mr. Leon know that I was going to be at the Christmas party tonight?"

All three girls look at one another. They must decide that there is no harm in telling me because the tall girl by the window answers, "Master had the whole office under his persuasion. He has ever since your escape. If any of them were to be contacted by you, they were to tell him immediately and then forget that they did."

So that's how he knew. Abby told him, but wait... "How is that possible? The persuasion doesn't last forever."

"Master's one does," the tall girl states.

*What? Mr. Leon's persuasion doesn't wear off?* That's something I didn't know. I doubt the hunters do either.

I decide to ask another question since they answered my first so easily. "How does it feel to pledge your allegiance to Mr. Leon?"

"We pledge to the coven," another one of them corrects. She's of average height and stands as if she grew up in the military, her legs slightly spread and her arms clasped behind her back.

"I thought they were one in the same."

"It is," says the tall one by the window.

"So, how does it feel?" I ask again.

They all seem to look at each other for a moment before the tall girl says, "It feels good to have the security and protection that the coven and our master give us."

"Right," I say slowly. "But like, does it feel different? For instance, did any of you ladies not like Mr. Leon before pledging your loyalty, and then boom, you suddenly love and praise him?"

"No," the military girl says. "We were happy to give our loyalty."

I decide to give up on getting anywhere with these ladies, so I just nod. "How long have you all been vampires?" I inquire.

Military girl speaks first. "I turned about thirty years ago, and Lilah here has been one for about nine."

I vaguely wonder why the third girl, Lilah, hasn't uttered a word tonight. Maybe she is shy. Can vampires who don't have souls even be shy? Before the tall girl can answer, Taylor walks into the room, interrupting our sharing circle.

# Chapter 49
# Sarah

Taylor looks me up and down. "The boss will see you now," he says with a self-satisfying grin.

I know there is no point in fighting, and I can't talk my way out of this. Fear truly creeps in for the first time since I got here. I don't want to lose myself or my freewill.

A little shakily, I push off the bed and follow Taylor out the room. As we walk, I notice that we are indeed in the same mansion where I was held captive two years ago. It's just redecorated, and as I pass a window, I don't see the woods that I ran to when I escaped. I don't think much of it. It could be that I'm just in a different wing.

Taylor takes me to a self-made throne room that resembles a former ballroom. It's a large, mostly empty space with an extravagant crystal chandelier in the center of the high ceiling. To the back is a dais, and on it sit two chairs, or should I say thrones. One is slightly bigger than the other and more centered. The smaller one sits just to it's left.

Mr. Leon, of course, is sitting in the big one and is in deep conversation with a woman with pale skin and auburn hair, who stands to his right with an iPad. She is tapping and nodding her head as Mr. Leon talks.

She's definitely a vampire, and a very beautiful one at that. She looks like a teenager, but with vampires looks can be deceiving.

He looks up when we walk in and gives a big smile.

"Sarah, my darling, I'm so glad you've joined me," he says delightfully, like I had a choice in the matter.

"Yes, well, I did cancel a few meetings to be here, so I'm hoping it's important," I say sarcastically, masking my fear the only way I know how.

Maybe, if I fight it hard enough, whatever magical powers that cleave me to him won't work even after I pledge my loyalty. I mean, seriously, can it even still work if it's only words with no genuine feeling behind them?

Mr. Leon laughs lightheartedly, showing off his pristine white teeth, both cheeks creasing with dimples. He's actually quite handsome; if only he weren't so evil.

His broad shoulders and dark hair, naturally highlighted with silver, deemed him a silver fox back when I worked at Leon Tower with Abby and the rest of my coworkers. Although, I can't be sure what age he was when he was turned. I always just assumed it was mid-thirties. But it's his cold, dead eyes that give away his true, sinister nature.

"Look at you, Sarah, darling. You seem to have grown into a strong, confident woman with quite the sharp tongue on you," Mr. Leon says.

I clamp my mouth shut. I don't want to give him any credit for my "sharp tongue" as he called it, but my vice of using humor as a way to hide my fear came after becoming a vampire.

He turns to the young woman. "That will be all for now, Natalie," he tells her, his tone letting her know she is dismissed.

The young-looking vampire takes one quizzical look at me before walking out the room. The clickety-clack of her heels is the only sound until she is out the door.

"Can I ask you a question?" I say before he has a chance to speak again, partially because I'm stalling for time, but mostly, it's something I've been dying to know.

"Of course, dear," he says, giving me the floor.

"Why me?" I ask. "Why go through all this trouble to get me here?"

His eyes narrow. "That is a good question. You are very special, my dear. I had hoped that a mating bond would form between us. You're beautiful and are a perfect conduit for my plans. I'm still hoping that a bond will form between us. There is still time."

I arch a brow. "I can assure you it won't," I tell him. I don't feel a single thing toward this monster, unless disgust and disdain count.

"Perhaps when your free will is mine, you will feel differently."

"Is that really all it is? You want to be mated to me?" I ask, not believing his answer.

He smiles. "Always so intelligent. As I said, you are a very special vampire, and with some training, will become priceless to me. I've waited a long time to find someone like you. A *Validus.*"

"How did you know that's what I would become?" I ask, not all that surprised to learn that was the real reason he wanted me.

"I've met only one *Validus* in my years of immortality. His name was Augustus Amato. Such talent my young friend had," he says, his mind no doubt going back in time to well before I was born. "When he died, I searched the world looking for another *Validus*, though the mages made it impossible for one to come into existence. Until you, that is. You slipped through their cracks. From the moment you were born, you were mine. You were always going to be mine."

"You knew since I was born?" I ask, shocked.

"Yes, I've had eyes on you your whole life. That time you were alone in your backyard, and you fell in the swimming pool because you were going to teach yourself how to swim," he says with a laugh as if he's reminiscing about fond moments together.

I shake my head. "My neighbor saved me," I say in a doubtful whisper, not trusting my own memories.

"Ah, yes, my guard had to call me after saving you. As you know, vampires' persuasion fades over time. Only I can persuade someone and it lasts a lifetime. Your neighbor saved you, but now you know not to ever have life-threatening self-taught lessons alone again."

*Now I know not to ever have life-threatening self-taught lessons alone again.* I stagger back. That's exactly what I thought after being saved. Those exact words... because he planted them in my mind. My whole life. He's been there, watching me. A shudder runs through me, dark and cold.

"I almost turned you at eighteen when you landed yourself in the hospital because you recklessly got in the car with a drunk driver, and then he ended up crashing. Humans are so weak, feeble. One wreck into a telephone pole and you can die instantly. How my patience would have been wasted, but I needed you to be a little older. I've seen firsthand what turning someone so young could do. Yes, twenty-two was a much better age. More mature."

He relaxes back, crossing one leg over the other, happy to indulge me as I learn just how much control he had over my life.

"Imagine my surprise when I got a call saying that it wasn't in life, but in your turning, that I would lose you. That, in a quest for escape, you ran outside during the day, not remembering the sun is our greatest Achilles' heel," he gives a self-deprecating laugh.

"In anger, I had all the guards that day slaughtered. I didn't even stop to think that they were being deceitful. As you will soon see, I run a rather tight ship around here. My subjects aren't capable of lying to me. In my hubris, I didn't think my guards were cunning enough to find a loophole."

He shakes his head at his mistake. "They relayed the news to Taylor, who told me what he thought to be true. But, alas, all's well that ends well. Now," Mr. Leon says, clapping his hands together. "I think I have been more than generous in answering your questions. Are you ready, my dear?" He stands up and offers me his hand.

There is so much I need to mentally organize after everything he told me, but that will have to wait. I want to recoil at the thought of touching him, but I square my shoulders and walk up to him, placing my hands in his.

"If I say I need more time, will it be granted to me?" I ask, already knowing the answer.

He tsks, "I'm afraid not. I've given you more time than I anticipated. Almost two and a half years, to be exact. I want you in training as soon as possible. The time is now."

*What does he mean by training?*

He glances down at me, laying a gentle hand on my head.

*No, no, no. I don't want to do this.* But I made a deal. This is for Kael, Liam, Zach, and the rest of the squad. I refuse to show weakness now.

*Kael, please forgive me.*

I lift my chin to Mr. Leon. "Fine," I say with assurance I definitely don't feel. "What do I have to do?"

# Chapter 50
# Kael

"WHAT'S TAKING SO LONG?" I bark, pacing back and forth behind Cynthia as she tries to track my comms piece that Sarah stole.

"I'm doing the best I can," Cynthia says through gritted teeth. She's sitting in front of one of the computers in the Academy library. "I don't know why it's not loading. It should have found the signal by now."

Dana walks up to me. "Kael, give it time," she says gently, like she is talking to an unhinged person about to go off at any second.

"We don't have time," I say, trying harder to calm my voice. I know Cynthia is trying her best, but Sarah could be hurt, or worse.

I shake my head and remind myself that Caesar wants her alive. Not knowing the extent of his reason for wanting her has my blood boiling. All I know is that he better keep his fucking hands to himself.

"Maybe I can be of some help," Zach says, his voice weak and throaty.

We all turn to see him being led into the room by Adam, who, if possible, hates me more now than he did yesterday.

"What do you mean Sarah was taken? This isn't a Liam Neeson movie." Adam had shouted to me over the phone when he finally called me back hours after I texted him.

I don't even know who Liam Neeson is.

"I'm saying it was a trap and the bastard, Caesar, took her," I shouted back, not wanting to explain my failure to keep Sarah safe over and over again.

"And Zach is over there fighting for his life?" he asked, repeating again what I already told him. The sound of him unlocking his car and getting in echoed in the background.

"No, I said he was fighting for his life, but our mage was able to patch him up in time, and he will pull through."

I could practically feel the annoyance emanating from him through the phone. "I'm on my way there. Apparently, you can't be trusted to keep the ones we care about safe." And with that, he ended the call.

Not that I can blame him for being angry with me. It's nothing compared to the anger I feel at myself. I can't believe I let her go. If something happens to her, I will never forgive myself.

"Zach, you are supposed to be resting," Dana says, bringing me back to the present.

"That's what I told him," Adam says sternly, giving Zach a hard look. Kayda is right behind them, also glaring at Zach.

Zach smiles warmly at Adam. "This is important. I care for Sarah too. I want to help get her back." He walks over to Cynthia. "May I help?"

Cynthia stands up and moves out of his way. "It's all yours," she says, clearly relieved to give the responsibility to more capable hands.

Zach slowly sits with the help of Adam, who made sure to stop and scowl at me as they passed. The second Zach sits down, his fingers start moving a mile a minute. After a few seconds, his eyes narrow in confusion.

"That's odd," he says, more to himself than to anyone else.

"What is?" I say anxiously.

"The tracker keeps bouncing around like Sarah, or at least your comms piece, is everywhere all at the same time." He looks over at Dana and Cynthia. "Is it possible that a mage could have spelled the vampire lair so it would be untraceable?"

"I mean, yeah, technically. We do that with the Magisterium. It's untraceable to vampires and humans. That's why you can only get to it by the open portal here at the Academy," Cynthia informs him.

Something tells me Zach already knew this information, which is why he knew to ask.

"But a mage would never do that," Dana says defensively.

"Dean," Cynthia whispers, turning to Dana. "When he was exiled, he said that the vampires would win in the end."

"Who's Dean?" Kayda asks.

Dana shakes her head. "He was a mage who became a bit of a problem. He got it in his head that we should work with the vampires instead of against them. We could rule the world that way. He was banished from the mage community."

"So, let's say, for the sake of argument, that the vampires did have a mage working with them," Zach says. "Is there a way to bypass his spell so we can find the lair?"

"Maybe." Dana says, deep in thought. She turns to look at Zach. "We use magic to move the Magisterium throughout the city. We create pockets of space and insert the building there. You all enter through the portal we created between the Academy and the Magisterium, but if you were ever to look out one of the windows, you would see that we are never in the same place twice. If that's what's happening to the vampire lair, then Cynthia and I may be able to get its location, but only for a few moments. We would lose it again once the building moves."

"How often does the building move?" Zach asks.

Dana shrugs. "Depends on how often the mage wants it to move. The Magisterium moves once every half hour."

"Sounds dizzying," Adam says.

Cynthia smirks. "It's magic. We don't actually feel the building moving."

"A half hour doesn't give us much time," Zach says with a frown.

"We'll make it work," I tell him. "We have to."

He nods in agreement. "Let's get the others."

"Oh no, you are not going anywhere," Adam scolds. "You're going to stay right here where I can keep an eye on your injuries."

"I'm fine," Zach tells Adam.

"You fell off a building," Adam reminds him. I note the slight crack in his voice.

As much as I want every bit of help to get Sarah back, Adam is right. Zach isn't ready to get back out there. He needs a few days' rest to let his speed healing do its job. I'm sure Orla ordered bed rest for him just as she did for me when I was injured.

Still, I'm surprised Adam is saying it. I would think that he would want to get Sarah back at all costs, but the way he is looking at Zach makes me think he wouldn't sacrifice more than necessary.

I've been so caught up in Sarah's and my relationship that I missed how serious Zach and Adam have become. The love they have for each other is evident in their eyes. It reverberates throughout the room.

"Kael will bring her back," Adam says, turning to me. "Right?"

I'm shocked by his confidence in me, or maybe it's just desperation. Either way, I manage to recover my surprise quickly. "Right, I'm not leaving the place without her. In fact..." I say, a plan starting to form. "Maybe going in guns blazing isn't the best way to go about this."

"I have a feeling I'm not going to like this," Liam says, walking in with a bow and arrow already strapped to his back.

***

It takes a lot of arguing and time, more time than I wish, to convince everyone of my plan. As much as I would like to storm the vampire lair and finally kill off the whole San Francisco coven for good, I think a stealth mission will have a higher rate of success. There's too much that can go wrong if we try to take on the entire coven.

We would need more time and a lot more hunters to do that. Even if we get all the Academy squads together, we still wouldn't meet the coven numbers. Although we have the skills to fight them, it's the time that we lack. It would take strategizing and deep planning to pull off a mission of that size, and to be honest, right now, all I want is Sarah back.

If I have to choose between killing off the entirety of the city's vampires or saving Sarah, then I choose Sarah. I will always choose Sarah.

Liam refuses to let me go alone, so he and I will be going to the lair together. I need a mage for the second part of my plan, and although Cynthia is going to stay in the car the whole time, Dana refuses to let her go alone, so both of them will be joining the mission as well.

Zach tries to argue that he wants to come too, but in the end, he is outvoted by everyone in the room.

Liam and I are dressed in our fighting leathers and have stacked ourselves to the brim with various wooden weapons. Liam, of course, also has his bow and quiver secured to his back.

As sunrise approaches, Cynthia and Dana start chanting around the computer that Zach has opened to the tracking site. The little pin that is supposed to be my comms piece is bouncing around frantically on the map of San Francisco pulled up on the monitor.

At first, I think it's not going to work.

"Do you think it could be expanded to more than just the city?" I ask after several minutes.

"No, it would take more than just one mage to expand any further. If this is what's happening to the vampire lair, then it's a very powerful mage they have working for them," Cynthia says quickly, before continuing to chant in those mage words that I swear sometimes sound made up.

After another minute, the pin stops, and so does the chanting.

"We got it," Dana says triumphantly, her face lighting up with confidence before it turns to one of shock and horror when realization dawns.

It "working" means that a mage did in fact put a spell on the lair. I guess this Dean guy is working for the vampires after all. I'll let the mages handle Dean. I'm only worried about Sarah.

Still sitting, Zach puts the address in Liam's phone and hands it back to him. Cynthia, Dana, Liam, and I run out the door without another word.

"It's twenty minutes away," Liam says as he pulls onto the highway. "The sun will be completely up by then, most of the vampires should be sleeping."

At least, that's the hope. I wish Sarah would try and contact us again, but we haven't heard a word from her since last night.

*Please be alright. Please be alright.* I force myself not to lean into the panic, to focus on the task, on the mission.

We pull onto a dirt road that is hidden amongst trees right outside the city center. I pray that the mansion will still be here. I've never been here before, not even sure if it existed until an hour ago.

The street leads to massive, locked iron gate.

Liam stops just outside the gate, pushing the car onto the grass. Dana and Cynthia insist that they can cloak the car so no one can see it while Liam and I scale and hop over the gate. I can see the top of the mansion from here; it's just a short run around a bend in the road.

We make our way silently toward the house. Liam, of course, is taking the lead. It's in his nature. He gestures with his hand for us to go around back, where we find another entrance and a window. I peek inside but see no one.

Liam tries the knob. It is, of course, locked. I stand guard as he reaches into his pocket and pulls out a silver lock pick. He makes quick work of the door, and I let him go first, waiting for him to give the okay to follow.

All my senses are on high alert, especially the one that allows me to feel when a vampire is near. It's so strong, I can barely stand it. It surrounds me, letting me know just how many vampires are nearby. By the deep furrow in Liam's brow, I can tell he's experiencing the same.

I concentrate and try to feel Sarah, searching the mansion, pushing past every dark aura, straining to tune into to her unique pulse. Even just a hint of it would be enough. I've spent enough nights inhaling her scent. Enough hours buried and covered in her essence. I know I can find her.

Something in me pings. My senses have found that hint of familiarity. That hint of Sarah. I make eye contact with Liam and signal toward the left wing. He nods and lets me take the lead.

This has always been what makes us such a great team. We can communicate without saying a word. I don't know if he can feel her, too, or if he just trusts that I can, but either way, he knows it's time for me to spearhead this hunt.

I try to stay locked in on Sarah's aura, but I'm uncertain as we walk down a deserted hallway. We were right to come during the day when the vampires should be sleeping. This place feels both alive and dead at the same time.

Alive because I can sense the presence of many vampires. Dead because they are nowhere to be found, hiding in darkened rooms. Still, I don't let my guard down. There is no way Caesar would leave the mansion unguarded.

"Something seems off," Liam whispers. "We should have come across someone by now."

I nod in agreement. This could very well be a trap, but one that I'm willing to walk into if it means getting to Sarah.

Still, Liam and I both know to stay vigilant.

Sure enough, as we round the corner, two male vampires are guarding a door. Is she in there? The darkness of the two vampires' auras would mask Sarah's lighter one, making me second-guess whether she's actually in there or not. Still, they must be guarding the door for a reason.

Liam shoots an arrow straight through one of the vampires' hearts before they even see us. The other one turns and starts to say something, but I throw a knife at his neck, shutting him up. I charge quickly, staking him in the heart just as his hand reaches for the knife.

A second of unease hits me. This all feels a little too easy.

I knock the thought away, open the unlocked door and run in, desperate to see Sarah, but she isn't in here. The only sign of her is the dress from the party lying on a bed.

Instead, two huge vampires stand at the center of the room, their arms crossed over their chests as if they've been waiting for us.

I recognize one as Taylor, the bodyguard.

In my peripheral vision, I see Liam reach for a dagger.

"I wouldn't if I were you," Taylor says to Liam. "After all, I'm here to take you to Sarah."

He looks behind us, and before I know it, my body stiffens as painful jolts of electricity trigger my muscles, forcing them to contract. Someone from behind forces me to my knees, grabbing and cuffing my hands behind my back.

I look over and see Liam being tased and brought to his knees beside me. He gives me a quick shake of his head. We both could get out of cuffs if we want to, but since Taylor plans to bring us to Sarah, Liam wants us to play along... for now.

# Chapter 51
# Sarah

I LAND FLAT ON my ass for the fifth time in five minutes. This is not at all what I pictured I would be doing once I submitted to Mr.—I mean Master.

I was naive to think that pledging loyalty wouldn't work on me if I just believed that it wouldn't. The second I said the words, I felt a chain and lock wrap around my willpower, and only Master has the key.

Of course, my feelings are still my own, so I can hate what he makes me do; I'm just powerless to stop myself from doing it anyway, like making me address him as Master and nothing else.

*Ugh, men.* I guess the so-called mating bond didn't register with me after all.

"Again," Master says from his seat up on a dais.

Once I submitted, I was forced to change into some spandex and a sports bra, then brought into a gym. In the center is a fighting ring, similar to the ones boxers use.

My training apparently consists of getting my ass handed to me by not one, but two vampires, over and over again. I don't get it. Is this really why he wanted me so badly?

He has an army of vampires at his disposal. I might be stronger and faster than all other vampires, but I'm nowhere near as good of a fighter. Even if I were to become great, he still has an army. He doesn't need me.

The two vampires wait for me to stand up before converging on me again. I kick out as one of the men reaches for me. He flies back, rebounding against the ring ropes, but as I'm focused on him, the other comes up from behind and slams his whole body against me. I fall to the ground and he jumps on top of me, landing a few punches to my face before I block him with my forearm.

313

This vampire did not pull his punches. Aching pain immediately reverberates through my cheek and jaw. The taste of blood slowly fills my mouth.

I buck under his weight, trying to throw him off me. I manage, but my victory is short-lived as the second vampire is back and grabs me by the hair, yanking me up and lifting me over his head with both arms. He slams me down, lifting his leg so that my back snaps across his knee before I tumble to the ground.

I am unable to hold back my cry of pain as I move to get my hands under me, forcing myself into a sitting position. Master holds out a hand, silently ordering the two men to stop.

"Sarah," Master says disappointedly. "You are untrained, but how can that be? I know the hunters were training you. Did you not learn anything from them?"

*How does he know that?* It's infuriating.

"I didn't train long with them," I admit, as I'm sure he already knows.

"I really need you to master control of the body before we can move to mastering the mind," he tells me.

Taylor walks in and gives a slight nod to Master who nods back in understanding.

"It's cute that you two can communicate with just a nod, like an old married couple," I say, not sure why I'm trying to get a rise out of him. It feels like my only way left to defy him. To let him know I'm not all his. Not that he ever shows anything other than complete control. It's probably why I'm trying so hard.

Master smiles. "So cheeky. We are done for today. Cameron will show you to your room. You are to wear what's been laid out for you to dinner. Tonight's entertainment should be most illuminating."

Dinner? I picture Master sitting at the head of a grand dining room table, casually drinking from a human where a plate of food would normally be. What does he mean by tonight's entertainment?

I do as I'm told and allow Cameron to escort me back to my room. The scent of fresh blood lingers in the halls. I guess the coven really is preparing for dinner.

I freeze when I pick up a hint of Kael, but Cameron tugs me along so I don't have time to dwell on it. Is my brain playing tricks on me?

I walk out of my bathroom an hour later, showered and dressed. I look at myself in the full-length mirror in the corner of the room and wince at my outfit. I'm wearing an all-black, cut-out satin jumpsuit that crisscrosses at my breast and leaves my whole torso exposed. It's a bit risqué for my taste, but whatever. I can already see that I won't have much control over my wardrobe from now on.

***

Cameron and another vampire, who's name I don't know, escort me to the throne room. I guess dinner isn't served at a dining table like I had pictured.

It's quiet down this hall. The only sounds are my stilettos clicking hard on the marble floor and the soft footsteps of my two bodyguards on either side of me, although I can hear faint voices echoing from other places in the mansion.

I fight the urge to cover myself with my arms as I walk into the throne room. To no one's surprise, Master is up on the dais, sitting on his throne, looking pristine as always in his custom-tailored Italian suit.

Natalie, the petite woman from last night, is tapping away on her iPad. Taylor stands behind the throne, and there are two guards at the open door, but other than that, the room is empty—no dining table.

My two personal guards stopped just outside, positioning themselves on either side of the door.

Master looks up at the sound of my heels. Natalie quietly steps back into the shadows.

He takes a moment to examine me, his eyes roaming over every inch, darkening as he takes me in, making goosebumps prickle my arms. What if he forces me to sleep with him? My body goes rigid and bile rises in my throat. I want to run away. Not that I can. I've been ordered never to leave the mansion unless told otherwise by Master.

"Sarah, darling, you look stunning as always," he finally says, beckoning me forward. "Come, sit with me. The entertainment I mentioned before is ready for us." He looks to one of the guards. "Bring them in."

My heart lurches as I approach Master. "What's going on?" I ask. The look on his face makes me scared to hear the answer.

He smiles, grabbing my hips and turning me around so I'm no longer facing him, but out toward the doors. My heart plummets as Kael and Liam are escorted in, both handcuffed behind their backs.

*No, no, no. What are they doing here? They can't be here.*

It's my fault. I stole Kael's earpiece so that they had a way to find me, but I thought it would take time to plan out an attack. Surely, they wouldn't come just the two of them.

The look in Kael's eyes tells me I'm wrong. Of course he'd want to rush in and save me as soon as possible. Liam probably agreed because he knew Kael would have come regardless.

Master's hands are still on my hips, and he pulls me back onto his lap. I can't take my eyes off Kael's as his grows wide at my acceptance of Master's touch.

"Sarah?" Kael speaks with so much hurt and betrayal in his voice. It makes me want to scream.

"She pledged her loyalty," Liam says beside him, quickly putting the pieces together.

"Fuck," Kael swears.

Master's hand slides into the open fabric of my jumpsuit and up over my breast. I want to scream and tear his arm from his body, but I can't. I can't do anything but sit on his lap until he says otherwise.

Right after I vowed to submit to the coven, he gave me a list of demands. One of them is that I'm never allowed to speak out against him or his advances toward me. I am only to welcome him.

"Get your fucking hands off her," Kael shouts in a dangerous rage. In an instant, he breaks the cuffs binding his hands. He extracts a wooden dagger no one bothered to seize from his belt and charges.

"Kill him," Master says, giving a flick of his hand to Taylor.

"My pleasure," Taylor says eagerly as he jumps to block Kael from coming any closer toward us.

*Kael!* I want to scream. I want to fight. *Come on, come on, please don't die, Kael.*

Liam curses and breaks his restraints, too. He starts to advance as well, but the two guards at the door rush him. They are trained warriors and put up a good fight, but Liam is able to fight both at once.

"Natalie, send for more guards. The leader also needs to be taken out," Master commands.

She nods once and then runs out of the room.

I watch in fear as both fights happen right before me. Kael and Taylor are equally matched in skill and strength. Taylor swings a few punches that Kael quickly dodges.

Kael is a beauty to watch, even when fighting. He's fast and agile, never letting Taylor get close enough to strike.

Master runs a hand over my exposed stomach, his fingers tracing small circles. I whimper softly at the unwanted touch, but Kael must have heard it. He looks my way for only a moment, but that's all Taylor needs.

He manages to make contact with Kael, punching him in the stomach. Kael bends forward, coughing out a struggling breath. Taylor goes to punch Kael again, but Kael grabs his fist and twists it at an odd angle. Using his free hand, he throws a punch, hitting Taylor square in the nose.

Taylor pushes free, wiping the blood gushing down his face with the back of his sleeve before charging at Kael. He starts swinging frantically, letting his anger get the best of him. His last punch is thrown with so much force that Taylor slightly stumbles when Kael dodges it at the last second. Kael loops around and stabs Taylor in the back with the wooden dagger he grabbed from one of the many sheaths on his person.

The stab won't kill him, only a stake to the heart will, but I hear Taylor huff out a groan. Kael unsheathes another hidden dagger, leaving the first one lodged in Taylor's back to weaken him. Then Kael goes for the kill, stabbing Taylor in the heart.

"Hmm," is all Master says in an almost bored but disappointed way when Taylor drops dead at Kael's feet.

I get only a second's reprieve, knowing that Kael won when fear engulfs me again as I turn my attention to Liam.

By now, three other guards have come in. They are all fighting Liam, who has managed to kill the first two guards. Liam is incredibly skilled, but he can only keep up with the constant attacks he is getting from three different angles for so long on his own.

I notice Kael turn and glare at Master, but before he can even take a step, Master gives the one order I prayed he would never give to me.

"Sarah, kill your hunter."

# Chapter 52
# Kael

TEARS WELL UP IN Sarah's eyes as her fangs appear.

*Shit. Shit. Shit. This cannot be happening.*

"Sarah, fight it," I say as she walks toward me.

Her face does a jerking movement. I can see she is struggling to say something, but he must have ordered her not to speak. She reaches me, and at first I think she's able to fight it, but then she grabs me and throws me against the wall. My back takes the brunt of it before velocity has my head whipping back. It hits the wall with a loud crack.

Pain shoots through the back of my head and spine as I fall to the ground.

*Well, fuck.*

I reach to rub the part of my head that hit the wall, and my hand comes back bloody.

What am I going to do now? I can't fight her. Even in her current state, I can't bring myself to hurt her.

Sarah is by my side in a second. She pulls me up by my neck, her nails digging into my skin, her eyes filled with fear and pain.

"Sarah," I cough out. The pressure of her grip is grating on my throat, making it hard to breathe. "Please, baby, fight it. You are stronger than he is."

She throws me again. This time, I skid across the floor, the push making me bite my tongue. The taste of blood fills my mouth. I spit blood on the floor as she stalks toward me, actual tears falling down her cheeks now. She looks over at Liam for a moment. I follow her gaze.

Liam is starting to have a hard time keeping up with the number of vampires he's fighting. It seems that for every one he kills, another takes their place. He's covered in blood, his or theirs, I'm not sure. Bodies are splayed out around him.

He'll start to lose at some point. He needs help. I want to go to him, but I know that I can't leave Sarah. This has to end soon. None of us can last much longer.

"Sarah, I love you," I tell her for the first time. Her head whips back to focus on me once more.

I don't know why I didn't say it sooner, but I don't want to die without her knowing.

"It's not your fault if you kill me," I tell her, because I don't see a way out of it. I can't kill her, and she can't stop until she kills me.

Her head is jerking uncontrollably now. "Kael," she forces out. "Kill me, please."

"Sarah," Caesar says, a little on edge now. He points and shouts, "Kill him, that's an order. Do it now. Rip his heart out."

I stand up and face her. "Keep fighting it, Sarah. You can do it."

She reaches for me, her hand on my chest. She's applying pressure, but not enough.

I place my hand over hers and squeeze. "I love you," I say again. "I love you so much."

Sarah shuts her eyes tight for a moment. The pressure on my chest increases, and I ready myself for the end. This is it. I brace myself. Then suddenly, Sarah jumps back like someone pushed her, landing on her knees, her hands splayed out before her.

Finally, she looks at me and gives a slight grin. "I love you too."

*She broke it!*

Whatever power he had over her is gone. I can see it in the way she stands, sure and steady. She's no longer fighting her own actions. I knew Sarah could do it.

Caesar jumps out of his seat. "What is going on here? Sarah?" he shouts, taking a step toward us.

Sarah turns to Caesar. "Yes, asshole?"

His eyes widen. "How is this possible?"

"You said it yourself, I'm very special," she replies right before she runs up the dais and pounces on him.

He's so shocked that at first, he lets her tackle him to the ground. Sarah starts savagely beating on him, swinging at him over and over again.

"You evil bastard," she shouts in between hits. "You evil, violating bastard."

Caesar grabs her hands and pushes her off him with ease. She lands on her feet and charges at him again. In a flash, he meets her halfway and locks her neck between the crook of his elbow in a chokehold. Then, with a whisper of something that I can't hear, he slams his free elbow down on her back. The sound of her spine cracking reverberates through the room like the snapping of a branch. Sarah's limp body falls to the ground.

Somewhere in my brain, I know Sarah isn't dead, but my brain and heart aren't coordinating with each other at the moment, and panic drowns me like a tsunami. I'm flying up the steps to the thrones in a flash, desperate to kill him.

One, for putting his hands on her. Two, for turning her into a vampire two years ago. And three, just because I don't like this motherfucker, but I don't say any of that. Instead, I lift my wooden dagger and drive it down toward his heart.

Caesar, however, is faster, rolls away, and jumps to his feet. My stake hits the floor. He kicks me hard in the stomach. The sound of my ribs breaking echoes through my body as pain envelopes me and I flip several times down the steps of the dais.

I groan as I stumble to my feet, trying desperately to push the discomfort to the back of my mind. I've had lots of practice ignoring pain during intense fighting times. A hunter is trained to, but my vision is a little hazy at the moment.

Caesar descends the steps casually, adjusting his cuffed sleeves as he walks.

"You, boy, were nothing but a distraction for Sarah," he says as he cocks his fist back and punches me in the face, busting my lip. I spit blood at his feet, but he ignores it.

"She is to be my queen." He throws another punch, this one to the abdomen. I bow forward in a cough of blood and saliva.

He grabs hold of me, leaning in so his lips graze my ear to whisper, "After I kill you, I will take her to bed tonight, and I will fuck her so hard she will forget all about you by morning."

His words knock me out of my painful haze. I take hold of his head and force it down while simultaneously jerking my knee up until they meet with a force that has him crying out in a howl that's like music to my ears. Then I push him back and land a few punches of my own.

"You will never touch her against her will again," I say, landing another punch to his face, breaking his nose in the process. I reach for a dagger on my belt, ready to end this now, but I find that I have none left.

Taking a quick scan around the room, I see that I've lost the ones I still had. They are a few feet away, lying by the dais. I run to grab one, but the second I turn my back, Caesar tackles me to the ground.

"Did you really think you can defeat me?" he asks, flipping me onto my back and putting his weight down on me as he squeezes my neck, choking me. The blood dripping from his nose trickles onto my face.

"I'm the most powerful vampire in the city. You are nothing compared to me. I will take great pleasure in ripping out your heart." He lifts his hand back, ready to plunge it into my chest, when suddenly he jolts forward and a small, strained grunt escapes him. His eyes go wide before he collapses on top of me.

I push his lifeless body off, letting it fall to the side, and there is Sarah, standing over us, his heart in her hands.

"We need to stab the heart," I tell her, knowing it's not enough just to remove it. We need to stab it with wood.

I can vaguely hear several vampires cry out, but I only see Sarah, wild-eyed and unsure. I get up and run to secure a stake. I hand it to her, and she quickly stabs it through Caesar's bloody heart, ensuring his death.

Sarah drops the heart and stake, closes her eyes, tilts her head up, arms out as if she is waiting for the sky to open up and take her. Nothing dramatic appears to be happening from what I can see. When Sarah opens her eyes again, she touches her forearm, where what looks like a new tattoo has appeared.

The coven leader mark.

# Chapter 53
# Sarah

"Sarah," Kael shouts as he reaches for me, but then we hear Liam bellow in agony.

I turn to see that he is getting beaten to the ground by three vampires, with about half a dozen vampires dead around him.

Kael goes to help him, but I shout, "Stop!"

Kael turns to me until he realizes I wasn't talking to him.

I look over his shoulder at the vampires that were attacking Liam, and they all stop at once.

I'm not sure what possessed me to say—to command that of them. I just knew if I told them to stop they would.

There is so much power surging through my veins right now. It's overwhelming. Somewhere in the deepest parts of my mind, I know what's happened. I'm the new coven leader. A fact that is so hard to grasp, I can't quite wrap my head around it at the moment, so I don't. I have more pressing matters to deal with anyway, like getting the hell out of here.

"Your orders, my queen?" one of the vampires ask.

My mouth gapes open. *What am I supposed to do or say?*

"Leave us," I say softly and watch in shock as all the vampires in the room file out.

Thankfully, Kael is busy at Liam's side and didn't see the exchange. It takes a minute for him to call Dana and Cynthia so that they can open a portal straight to the Academy.

Kael, Liam, and I all head to the medical bay as soon as we walk through the portal. Dana and Cynthia are staying behind to drive the car back.

Apparently, the two mages were waiting outside by the gate until they were needed for the portal. It was a smart plan to come and rescue me during the day, knowing that none of the vampires would be able to chase or follow us until sunset.

The portal also keeps me out of the sun, which I'm thankful for. Although I wish we transported my apartment, not the Academy.

I still don't like being here. I don't think I'll ever like it if I'm being honest with myself.

Orla, the Academy mage healer, is already waiting in the room, along with another male mage I've never seen, and with a sigh of relief, I spot Adam and Zach.

I didn't realize how anxious I was to see Zach again until just now, but he looks good. He has a bandage around his head, but he's here sitting in a wheelchair, which is a good sign. Adam wouldn't let him leave his room if he didn't think Zach was healed enough to do so.

The two mages surround Liam and Kael, ignoring me altogether, which surprises me. Someone must have warned them I would be coming. Kael looks at me for a moment, bringing our entwined hands up to his lips, kissing my hand softly before letting go and doing as the mage healer says.

We haven't said a word to each other since I ordered the vampires to stop attacking Liam, but Kael has not let go of my hand since we stepped into the portal together. Zach rolls himself out of the way, but close enough to watch Liam's progress.

He alone must have killed six or seven vampires. I'm surprised he was able to survive. The sheer number of vampires he was fighting at one time was astounding.

"Oh my God, Sarah," Adam shouts as he runs to me.

"I'm fine," I say, although I feel anything but fine.

Adam shakes his head. "I'll be the judge of that. Go sit over there," he orders, pointing to the last empty medical bed in the corner.

He's in his teal scrubs, meaning he must have come straight here after a shift. He also has his emergency medical bag with him, which he sets down at the edge of the bed. He opens it up and pulls out his stethoscope.

I arch an eyebrow at him. He must realize what he did and rolls his eyes. "It's a habit," he says, shoving it back in his bag.

"Does it hurt anywhere?" he asks after looking into his bag again and giving up on using anything. I don't really have vitals like a normal human.

I give a slight shake of my head. "No," I tell him honestly. "I'll be fine as soon as I drink."

"Right!" he shouts, running to the small fridge they have set up in the corner. He opens it up and pulls out a blood bag. As he closes it, I notice herbs and what appears to be vials of potions or medicines, all stacked neatly inside. "I forgot I brought this for you. I figured you would need it."

I smile for the first time today. "You are a lifesaver," I say as I rip open the bag and start to drink, not caring who may be watching.

My body immediately reacts to the effects of the blood. Euphoria fills me from the inside out. When I finish, I wipe my mouth. My mind is rapidly clearing as my body rejuvenates.

I look over at Kael and Liam, both being treated for their injuries. Orla and the other mage are in the middle of chanting while waving their hands over the hunter's bodies.

"I'm really okay now," I tell Adam, my feet dangling over the side of the bed. My tippy toes are just reaching the floor. I point to Liam and Kael and say, "Go see if they can use your hel—"

"What is that monstrosity?" Adam asks, cutting me off and pointing to my arm.

The coven leader mark, now branded on my forearm, hums as if coming to life. I cover it with my other hand reflexively.

"Did you get a tattoo while in Vampireland?" he asks.

"It's the coven leader mark," I say in a whisper, but of course, all the hunters look my way.

Zach's eyes shoot to me in horror.

"I'll explain later," I tell Adam, who nods, but looks stricken.

"Alright, Liam, you're all patched up. You'll be right as rain in a few days. How's Kael lookin'?" Orla asks as she makes her way to Kael.

"Just about done as well, ma'am," the other mage says, finishing wrapping a bandage around Kael's arm.

She nods approvingly and says, "Well, we'd better get goin'. Our work here is done." She walks out without another word. The guy gives me a weird look, although not necessarily in disgust, just curiosity, before following Orla out.

As soon as they leave, all eyes land on me.

"Sarah," Kael says, jumping off his bed to come sit next to me. He pulls me in for a hug. "God, I was so fucking worried about you."

"I'm okay, really," I say as he looks me over. "What about you?" I ask. He has a busted lip that looks pretty bad.

He presses a kiss to my forehead. "I'm good now that you're here with me."

I smile and lean into him, resting my head on his shoulder. I'll never get enough of Kael saying sweet things like that. I want to savor every word he utters to me in a tiny box in my mind and keep it forever, like my mini treasure box.

There is a knock on the door and Kayda, Nick, and Shyann enter.

"Knock, knock," Kayda says, announcing herself and the others. "Orla said it was okay for us to come in now."

I can't help but notice Shyann's eyes land straight on Kael. Hate and anger bubble to the surface, but I manage to tamp it down before I do or say something I'll regret.

"Yes, we're all patched up," Liam tells them.

"Oh my God, Liam," Kayda says in horror as she goes over to inspect him.

I look over at Liam, who is now sitting up on his bed. He looks worse for wear. One of his eyes is swollen shut and a big bruise is forming on his right cheek. He isn't wearing a shirt, so I can see bruises peeking out from where the bandages end.

"Liam, are you okay?" I ask, concerned.

He nods and gives a slight grin. "Yes, nothing too bad."

I give him an incredulous look. "You were a total ninja-warrior-assassin back there," I tell him. "Seriously, you should have seen him," I say to the room, and then look at Adam. "He was like Green Arrow, but with superhuman strength."

Adam shakes his head and looks at Liam, placing a hand on his chest. "Looks and acts like Superman, but fights like Stephen Amell. My, my, Liam, are you sure you're real?"

Liam shakes his head, grinning. "Sarah is making it out to be more than it was," he says.

Kael chips in, "Nah, man, you were badass. I'm glad you didn't let me talk you into staying behind. I definitely wouldn't have been able to take on what you took on today."

"Yes, you could have, and I was just doing my job," he says humbly. "Enough about me." He looks over to me. "Sarah, you're the coven leader now."

Shock emanates around the room for the second time in less than an hour.

"What the fuck?" Nick says in disbelief. "Are you serious?"

I sigh, extending my forearm to show everyone the mark. "Yes, I guess since I, being a vampire, was the one who killed Caesar, the mark got transported to me."

I glance down at my own arm, getting a good look at what they are seeing. It's a black long-tailed cross with curved T's in the shape of fangs, just like Caesar's tattoo.

"You commanded the vampires back there, and they listened," Liam says, like I don't already know this.

"They technically pledge their loyalty to the coven. Since the mark controls who the leader of the coven is, whoever wears the mark has control over the coven," I inform the group, even though I know they already know this.

"It's fascinating," Zach says to no one in particular.

"Ew, does that mean we are going to have a bunch of vampires hanging around the apartment?" Adam asks. "Because I don't know how I feel about that. Especially, if they are going to be making noise all hours of the night when I'm trying to sleep. You know I need to immerse myself in deep REM cycles to wake up the best possible me."

I laugh. "Don't worry, I don't plan to invite the vamps over to watch Netflix."

"Why doesn't Sarah just command all the vampires to run out into the sun? Problem solved," Nick says. "Or," he continues, rubbing his hands together, clearly starting to get excited, "she can get them all to stand in a straight line, and we just stab them in the heart one by one."

I shudder at the thought. "What are you, a fucking psycho?" I ask sharply.

Adam's eyes widen as he looks at me with a concerned look on his face, but I ignore it.

"Damn, Sarah," Nick says, raising his hands in surrender. "I was just trying to help."

I shake my head as if to clear it. "Sorry," I say, a little surprised at myself. "I'm not sure what came over me. I guess I'm just tired. It's been a long twenty-four hours."

Kael squeezes my hand. "Hey, we don't have to decide anything right now," he tells me, tucking a strand of hair behind my ear with his free hand. "We can always find a way to get rid of it, if that's what you want."

I nod. "Yeah, I think that's what I want."

He brings our joined hands to his lips and gives my hand another kiss. He does this a lot, and I love it. His way of being affectionate. I hope he always kisses my hand like this.

"We'll figure it out," he says softly. "There has to be a way to get the mark off you."

Getting the mark off me has to be the best option. I can't live with it on me. I don't want this burden. I can almost feel its darkness and power. The temptation is strong and hard to resist, but I'll resist as long as I have to. I won't let a mark control me.

I also won't let Nick go through with any of his plans either. *Line them up and let the hunters kill them off one by one...* Over my dead body. They aren't going anywhere near my coven.

# Epilogue
## One Week Later

"THE BUTTERCREAM FROSTING IS thick and creamy with a sweet, rich taste. The cake has a smooth, velvety texture. Overall, very decadent and delicious," Adam describes, as he takes another bite of a cupcake that was given to him by a nurse at the hospital. It's her birthday today, so she made cupcakes for everyone on her floor.

Since I've become a vampire, I sometimes ask Adam to describe the foods he eats to me so I can enjoy them vicariously through him.

We're sitting on our couch playing catch-up with our lives. I don't, however, tell him about the added inner commentary that started only hours after I received my new coven leader tattoo.

*"As it should be. It's a mistake to be here. We should be ruling over the vampire coven, not playing around with food. Humans are for eating not for toying around with."*

I groan loudly. So, I'm a "we" now.

*No. I'm the only one in my head,* I remind myself. The mark is not its own entity. *Get it together, Sarah.*

Adam furrows his brow at me. "Did I not describe it to your liking?"

I look at him in confusion. "What?"

"You groaned," he tells me in exasperation. "Did I not describe the cupcake right?"

"Oh, no," I tell him. "It's not you."

He frowns again as he looks around at the empty apartment, aside from the two of us. "Can you suddenly start seeing ghosts, and you forgot to mention it?"

329

I shake my head. "Just forget it. It's nothing. I'm tired. I think I'll go lie down in my room for a while."

I don't wait for him to respond, and I ignore the edge of concern on his face. I just get up and head straight for my room, closing the door behind me.

I take a deep breath and brace myself against the dresser. I'm losing my mind. That has to be it. The mark is slowly driving me insane.

*"Just let me take over, and everything will be as it should be."*

*No. This is my body, my mind, my life.*

*"This is something bigger than you."*

"God, shut up!"

My dresser cracks beneath my hands. I let the pieces of wood fall to the carpet.

I hear a soft knock on the door. "Sarah, sweetie, are you okay? Who are you yelling at?"

*Damn it.* I didn't realize I said that last comment out loud.

"I'm fine, Adam," I shout. "Just leave me alone."

I can hear him lingering, but he doesn't say another word. Finally, I see his feet shuffle away from under the gap in my door.

I have never in my life yelled at Adam that way. I'll have to apologize to him later.

*"Like hell you will. He is beneath you. A weak little human. Let's snack on him now and be done with it."*

*I swear to Zordon if you don't stop talking, I will binge-watch every episode of the Power Rangers, and I'm not just talking about the Mighty Morphin Power Rangers.*

My phone starts ringing, and I walk over to my bedside table where I have it charging.

It's Kael.

"Hello?"

"Sarah, it's me, baby. How are you? Adam just texted and said something was wrong?"

*Damn you, Adam.*

"I'm fine, just tired, so I guess I was being a bit cranky," I tell him. "I'll apologize to Adam in a minute. You know how sensitive he can get."

Kael laughs, and my heart warms. It's so good to hear his voice. I think about telling him the truth about what's been going on with me, but I don't want to burden him. If I'm being honest with myself, I'm a little afraid of how he'll react.

"I'm sorry I have to patrol tonight, but I'll be over there tomorrow."

"Can't wait. Be careful out there," I tell him.

"I will. I promise. See you tomorrow. I love you."

"I love you, too," I say, loving how easily we say it to each other now. I hang up and throw myself onto the bed.

I should have told him about what's going on with me. I need to tell him; maybe he can help.

*"He can't help. No one can."*

"Argh, stop being annoying," I tell whatever this thing in my head is.

I need to get some air. I look at the clock.

Yes, the sun is down. I'm in desperate need to get out of this apartment before I really do go find Adam to snack on.

Thankfully, he's in his room when I peek out and quickly slip out the apartment. I start at a leisurely walk down the street, the winter breeze swaying my hair. It's a nice night out; the sky is clear with a slight dip in temperature. It's the perfect weather.

I don't really have a destination in mind; I just really need to get out. This past week has been crazy. This voice inside my head is slowly driving me insane.

At first, it happened slowly, only hearing it once or twice a day, but now, it's like it won't stop. I wish this thing had a fucking mute button. It won't leave me alone. I hear it all the time. It invades my every conversation, my every thought.

*"It's because I'm getting stronger."*

"No, you're not. I'm going to figure out a way to get rid of you, and then, you won't be anything."

I continue at a brisk walk now. Twenty minutes later, I'm standing by a gate. I'm not sure how I ended up here; maybe the mark led me. In fact, I know the mark led me here. I just don't know how.

*"As I said before, I'm getting stronger, and soon you will realize there is nothing you can do to stop me."*

I ignore the intrusive thought as I stare up at the gate. I know from the short time I've been here that the coven mansion moves around. It's not always in the same spot twice, so how did I find it?

*"We will always be able to find our home."*

I nod, somehow knowing that to be true. I walk through the gate, taking my time.

Once at the door, I hesitate. *What am I doing here? I should leave.*

The vampires probably don't even want me here. Not after killing their previous leader and forcing them to stop fighting the hunters, so that we could all escape.

Before I have too much time to think about it, the door opens. A tall, golden-brown skinned man, who looks to be in his forties, stands at the door.

He gives me a big smile and says, "Ms. Sarah, come on in. We've been expecting you."